Rise of Magir

The Archer Chronicles

Shantel Norton

KDP

This book is dedicated to my daughters, Payton and Kimber. May you always shine from your independence and what makes you each unique but find immense strength in each other. Together, you are unstoppable, and know that the love you two share will one day change the world!

Editors:
Tamara Negrete
& Donna May

Contents

Chapter 1

Evelyn

It felt like I was in a trance of some kind. Griffin carefully ushered me to sit on the edge of his bed before releasing my shoulders to close the door behind us. What had just happened? I found myself thinking that same question over and over again in my mind.

My father's dead...that couldn't have been my father... could it...no...my father is dead...isn't he?

The minute that man had entered the room, something in my stomach told me I knew him. Maybe not so much my stomach, but my heart. Which, even though I knew my heart wasn't responsible for the rush of emotion that came upon me after seeing this man, didn't seem to stop the tightening of my chest. Just looking at him made my pulse start to race and my palms begin to sweat. Instantly, it felt like I was going to be sick. Now, even having left the dining room, my chest was starting to heave up and down as I replayed his dramatic entrance over again in my mind.

One of the more confusing parts of his return was him claiming to know what was wrong with Violet — what had been keeping her locked in the comatose state she was in.

Hearing him say that didn't even allow me to question the fact that he had secretly been alive my entire life. Not that it would have mattered if I had pressed the matter because as soon as his name left my lips, King Barin launched into a fury that was like nothing I had ever seen from him. He was screaming for the guards and demanding to know why Lucas Archer, *the traitor*, had returned.

I stood there frozen while King Barin shouted, and the queen tried fruitlessly to settle him. I couldn't even comprehend everything that the king was shouting because my mind was consumed by the man standing mere feet away from me. His warm eyes pierced through me. It was like he had waited for this moment his entire life. Yet, despite his welcoming eyes, I didn't move. I could hardly breathe in that moment, nonetheless, get my feet to take steps closer toward him.

When the guards finally made their entrance, they each grabbed onto one of Lucas's arms and it was that contact that finally managed to finally break my daze. I shouted for them to stop, but was surprisingly cut off by Hale's voice suddenly demanding that Griffin take me away from there.

Before I could protest, Griffin was practically dragging me through corridors of the Magirian castle — unexpectedly heeding Hale's advice to get me away from the chaos that was occurring in the dining room. I wasn't even sure where we were going and despite my mind trying to focus...I just didn't care. Was that really my father? Did he really have the answers on how to wake Vi? *What in the hell had just happened!*

"Are you alright?"

Griffin's voice pulled me back to reality, but all I could do was stare blankly at him. Was I alright? The answer was simple...no. No part of me was alright. My aunt was probably undergoing another surgery, as we speak, and it was due to the spinal injury I caused her while in one of my Fear episodes. Then there was my best friend in the entire world, who was lying in a hospital bed, potentially dying for all we really knew.

A fate she had only been forced to suffer because of me. Not to mention the fact that, despite the vast amount of testing I had gone through, nobody knew what was wrong with me. I could feel that something was off. Something was different about me, and I felt sick because of it. My father...my supposedly *dead* father, just showing up was simply one more thing to add to my growing list of reasons for not being alright.

Watching as Griffin stared back at me, his soft eyes begging me for a response, my resolve began to melt. Tears erupted from eyes, and he quickly pulled me up from his bed, holding me tightly in his arms.

Bawling against his chest was just one more way to back up my theory that something was wrong with me. I had never been the type of person to cry like this. I always kept my emotions in check. When I let emotion get the best of me, I usually caused a tsunami or something equally devastating. Even before I knew about magic...my emotions always seemed to cause situations to worsen around me. I didn't just stand, crying while someone helped me like this. And as amazing as it felt to feel the warmth of his body against mine, our magic beginning to dance at our direct contact, the sensation of magic just reinforced everything my mind was screaming at me.

He pulled away from me and brushed the hair away from my face. Unable to meet his eyes, I kept my eyes low, dreading that he was about to start asking me if I was okay again — not that I had any more of an answer now than I did a couple minutes ago.

His thumb ran across my jaw line and settled on my chin. Just as I found the courage to look up at him, he swiveled and opened the door, revealing Sean on the other side with his fist up as if he was about to knock.

"Sorry to interrupt," Sean said stiffly. "Your mother has asked for you to return, Griffin. For all of us Knights to return."

"I'm not leaving E right now."

"I'll stay with her," Johanna's voice rang from behind

3

Sean. "We will be fine for a few minutes. We both know when your ruler beckons, you should listen. Especially when said ruler is also your mother."

Sean looked past Griffin at me, and I could see the worry in his eyes. Johanna appeared from behind him, placing her hand gently on his shoulder. I watched as Sean instantly relaxed a little and shot her a brief smile before shifting his gaze to Griffin.

We all just stood there a moment and then Griffin groaned loudly before turning back to me.

"I'll be back as soon as I can," he promised.

Before I could answer he gently grabbed my face in his hands and gave me the fastest, yet most passionate, kiss I had ever felt. My hard expression faded as his magic moved into my veins and I swooned as he pulled away, leaving the room without another word. Sean followed closely behind him with a whispered goodbye to Johanna.

"It's weird how much they affect you, isn't it?" Johanna asked, as she watched the main door close tightly behind the Knights. "I'm beginning to think it is a Knight thing and not just a bonding thing. Their magic is still quite mysterious. Despite recent revelations."

"Griffin and I aren't bonded like that," I absentmindedly reminded her.

My voice was scratchy, and it made her finally turn to look at me. Her expression took me by surprise as it wasn't the same look of worry that I got from both Griffin and Sean. It was almost as if I was a puzzle she was trying to figure out. Like she had some pieces but couldn't figure out where they fit or which one to try next.

As close as we were becoming, Johanna didn't know me as well as the others. Not that I really knew much about her either. There was the possibility she knew more about me then she let on...being connected to Sean and all. But there were still moments like this, where I was convinced that she was studying me. Almost as if I was some sort of challenge to her.

4

"Well," she finally huffed. "I think if we are going to be stuck in this room until they return, we might as well enjoy it."

She spun on her heels and headed out of the room. Enjoy it? Was she crazy? There was nothing to enjoy right now. My mind still couldn't even wrap around the events of this evening, nonetheless, enjoy the coming ones.

Still, out of curiosity, or maybe a strange urge to not be alone right now, I followed her into the Knights' kitchen. Almost as if she was in her own kitchen at home, she began pulling things from the fridge and placing them on the counter.

"What are you doing?"

"Making you something to drink," she answered plainly.

"I don't drink."

"Please. We all do," she rolled her eyes. "And it's not that kind of drink. Magicals don't drink like you're used to. It's not like you have to be twenty-one like you do back in the non-magical realm."

She continued to make the drinks and then pushed one across the counter to me as I sat onto one of the bar stools.

"Sugar impacts us differently. But it has to be a special sugar. Not the kind non-magicals use."

"Why can't Magirians just be normally and take a shot of whiskey or something?"

"We can," she chuckled. "But it's kinda pointless. We would have to drink the equivalent of at least three experienced drinkers to even get a good buzz from that stuff. Now sugar...it leaves us feeling a little bit more dizzy. I'm sure you've noticed how easy it is to get that *sugar high* non-magicals refer to, haven't you? Sometimes it makes you even feel a little sick if you have too much?"

I thought about it for a second and I could recall a handful of times when eating a second cupcake or indulging in an extra scoop of ice cream made me feel a little sick later. But that happened to non-magicals too...right?

"But *this* sugar is a Magirian treat," she added, inching

the drink closer to me, and not giving me time to actually answer her questions. "Just give it a try."

"It feels like you are asking me to do drugs or something."

"First off, this body," she began, as she moved her arms down both sides of her body to emphasize her words, "is a temple. I would never poison it. Not like non-magicals do with their drugs. Look, it's hard to explain. But trust me. I'm not getting you drunk, and you aren't taking drugs. The sugar has a healing effect. It is just going to help you relax. Be yourself for once."

"And how do you know I'm not? Being myself, I mean."

"I'm a Mind," she said, taking a hefty sip of her drink. "And while you may have some seriously strong magic, I know there is something different about you now. Just haven't figured out what it is just yet."

I stared down at the drink. She wasn't wrong. I knew something wasn't right with me. The drink fizzed a little bit and I began to remember when Sean took me to Draíocht, and I spent the next few days miserable. Sure, felt like getting drunk — not that I had much experience in that department.

"Last time I drank this *sugar* it left me feeling very hungover," I explained. "Draíocht and I didn't quite get along."

"You must have had way too much. It's seriously just supposed to be a treat. If you have too much, it will definitely make you sick. Look, I'm not saying you aren't going to feel a little buzz, but you need to unwind. This will help to heal your troubled mind. And when I say *you* need to unwind...I mean we both do."

Again, she wasn't wrong. Not that drinking was even remotely something I enjoyed, but Johanna was right. I did need to relax a little. With everything going on around me, maybe a night of relaxing with a girl friend was just what I needed. Not to mention, healing my troubled mind sounded like a great place to start.

I grabbed my drink and followed her over to the couch

and chairs beside the Knights' fireplace. We sat in silence for a few minutes, just sipping our drinks. It was as delicious as the Shirley I had in Draíocht, and I remembered quickly how it was so easy for me to indulge in several glasses.

"So, Sean took you to Draíocht?" Johanna suddenly asked.

"Yep," I answered. "He wanted me to unwind after putting me through the ringer in mentor lessons. You know what? I'm starting to think you guys are like the same person."

"You're hilarious," she laughed. "Great minds just think alike I guess."

"I'm glad the two of you can be so open now. Sean is a great guy. A really great guy. He deserves to be happy."

I don't know what made me say that. Maybe it was the look on her face as she compared herself to him in her mind. But as she looked over at me, I saw Johanna for one of the first times as the young woman she was. She was only a year or so older than me after all. Yet there was always this strength that she carried around. This intense level of confidence. She was always so hard to read. But now, as I watched her grip her glass with both hands, pulling her knees to her chest, I saw her for the lovesick woman she was.

"He is," she said, smiling at the fire. "He's by far the best man I've ever known. I find myself lucky every day that I managed to snag him up a few years ago. It's nice being able to finally be one with him again. Even if all the logistics aren't worked out. It's like...I can finally see the light at the end of the tunnel...you know?"

She turned to me as if she was genuinely asking me a question and I offered her a half smile in response.

"You know who else is a great man?" she asked. "Griffin."

She answered her own question before I even had a chance. And now it was my turn to be taking hefty sips of my drink.

"I know you've got a lot going on," she continued. "But I think it's time you cut the shit and just admit to the poor guy how you really feel."

"I'm sorry?"

It still amazed me how she talked sometimes. Before we had started to get to know each other, I was under the impression Johanna was a fancy, upper class daughter of a councilman. Practically a princess in this realm. But no. Johanna was an entirely new breed of upper class. One that — despite seeing how different Griffin was from others in the court — I had yet to experience.

"You heard me!" she exclaimed, as she threw her feet from the chair, leaning toward me. "It's time to cut the shit and just admit it!"

"We've had a lot going on. We haven't really had time to talk about it."

"Talk about what? There is nothing to talk about. You're in love with him and literally everyone knows it except for you. Lord knows he's in love with you. He's just way too much of a gentleman to push you into saying how you feel."

"I've never been good with...with expressing my feelings," I defended.

"No shit."

I couldn't help but smile at her. But there was this pinch in my gut and I looked instinctively back down at my drink. It felt wrong to be sitting here having a girl talk with Johanna while Violet was across the castle lying in a hospital bed still.

"Don't you dare sulk over me!"

I could practically hear Violet's voice in my head as I swirled the drink in my hand and thought of her helplessly laying in that hospital bed.

"That's because I am in your head, Evey! Listen to me!"

But that wasn't possible. I couldn't be hearing her voice in my head. My magic didn't work that way. So, I shook away her voice as it echoed in my mind again. *Magic couldn't just bring somebody back.* That much I knew. While I had to force myself to believe Vi would be okay, the fact was, in that moment, she wasn't. And despite all the questions I had running through my mind, I was certain of one thing...Violet was not here. She was not in my head. She was suffering from my own inability to control my Fear magic. Suffering because of my wicked Fear magic.

As I turned my focus back to Johanna, who was still rattling on about how wonderful Griffin is, I took another gulp of my drink. I could have sworn I almost heard Violet groaning in frustration as I continued to push her voice out of my mind. It was time to let this magical drink do its job. Time to heal my troubled mind.

Chapter 2

Violet

"Ugh!"

I threw my arms up in pointless frustration as Evelyn continued to ignore me. I couldn't see more than a couple of feet around me, as the darkness of this realm quickly enveloped me, so I found myself...yet again...walking through the endless number of trees, with seemingly no way out.

When I left my grammy and the light around us began to fade, I thought for sure I would wake up tightly wrapped in Callen's warm arms. I mean, that's what always happened in the movies! But no. Instead, I found myself in this dreadful place. Not that I even knew where this horrendous excuse for a forest even was.

All I knew for sure was that I was trapped in some sort of Fear induced coma. At first, when I landed in this rotten place, I had no idea what was going on. I was walking around for hours before I heard their voices. I knew immediately that I was trapped in my own mind because I could hear or feel Evey and Callen when they came to visit my lifeless body.

This, however, was the first time I had been able to actually communicate with one of them. Yet Evey — in all her bullheaded stubbornness — just absolutely refused to accept that hearing my voice in her head was real. But of course, that would be the case. Why would anything the Fears do be that easy to overcome? How could I possibly get that lucky?

So rather than celebrating that I had finally found a way out of this hellhole, I continued to pace through the woods, with only my thoughts for company.

I had become very familiar with these woods. Whatever Fear trick this was, it wasn't very well thought out. Instead of putting me in an endless section of the forest, it was like they had trapped me in a box. It was deceptive though. At first glance, the woods would go on forever...but, as I quickly found out, there were invisible walls all around me.

It wasn't a small box by any means. But I could walk the whole thing in what seemed like only half a day. And since sleep wasn't a thing here, I wasn't even sure how many times I paced around the entire space. So maybe...just maybe...it was a better thought out trap than I gave them credit for...I hated small spaces like this. But I wasn't about to give them credit for this. I was frustrated and tired of this place, but I was not about to give them an ounce of satisfaction.

I knew from listening to Evey and Callen that it had been several days since our battle with the Fears. Probably pushing a week or more at this point. The more I tried to troubleshoot my timeline, the more I knew that I had to get out of here. I was no help to them sittin' in here mopin' to myself. And after what I saw from Evey before I ended up here...they needed my help. Now more than ever.

I plopped down onto the grass and closed my eyes, trying hard to focus my mind on Evey. How had I managed to get to her a few minutes ago? Was it minutes ago? It felt like it...but I couldn't even say that for sure.

Taking deep breaths, I urged myself to push some sort of vision to Evey. Or to Callen. Anyone who would be out there to listen. But no matter how hard I tried, nothing happened. Since I had discovered my magic all I had heard was how I was some amazing magical...the strongest Vision they had seen in centuries. A lot of good that was doing me now.

Pounding my fists into the ground, I felt an instant earthquake forming as the dirt beneath me began to shake. As my eyes adjusted to the darkness, I could see the trees begin to sway in front of me, and my head swiveled as I took in the scene around me.

I rushed behind a nearby oak to take in the storm that was developing out of thin air. This had to be another part of this trap. I didn't make storms with my firsts. This was Evey's magic...not mine. And she surely wasn't here. It didn't make any sense to me. How could this even be possible?

As the winds died down and the ground slowly settled, I emerged from behind my tree and began to walk the perimeter again. Everything had returned to normal. It was as if none of what I just saw even happened. Had I imagined it?

"You didn't imagine anything?"

The sound of another person's voice made me jump higher than a pro basketball player goin' for a dunk.

"Don't be frightened."

I tried to follow the sound of the man's voice, but as I turned around again, I still could not see anyone. It had finally happened. I had been here long enough that I was going mad. Hearing voices, and surely going mad as that damn Hatter.

"I'm not trying to hide," the voice said. "It's harder to get into your mind than it was before."

"Before?"

I hadn't meant to ask the question out loud, but at this point I was so startled by the sudden visitor that I was finding myself grateful that, like sleeping, bathrooms weren't a need here.

When he emerged and even in the darkness, I recognized him, a gasp escaping my lips. Of course! Now it made sense why he had said it was harder for him to get into my mind this time. He really had done it before.

Lucas slowly moved closer to me, and I took a few steps

closer to him. I knew it was a projection, but I had to admit, it was nice seein' another person finally. Not to mention actually being heard by someone.

"How did you know I'd be here?" I asked.

"Because I know what you did to get here."

"I suspect you do," I agreed, crossing my arms. "I learned the damn spell from a vision of you."

"Yes, but your magic is different from mine. And significantly stronger."

"Well, do you know how to get me the hell out of here?"

"I think so," he surmised.

"Care to share?"

I watched as Lucas studied me. I could see the resemblance between him and Evey. It almost made it hard to be so stern with him. But as I continued to stare at him, I saw more and more of my father. Even though I would always love my father, I loathed the man that he had chosen to become. So unfortunately for Lucas, his genetics made it impossible for me to be nice right now.

"Are you harnessing your new magic right now?" Lucas suddenly asked.

"Harnessing my what?"

"You do know how much Fear magic you took in, don't you?"

I didn't. I had only intended on taking Evey's Fear. And it was supposed to go into the necklace. It wasn't supposed to go into me.

"I didn't take in anything," I argued. "I copied how you got rid of your magic. I put it into the necklace."

"No, Violet. You didn't," he sighed, as he shook his head.

Lucas suddenly lurched forward, and I watched his projection phase in front of me.

"Wait!"

"I'll get you out of here," he groaned, as his projection phased again. "I promise, Violet."

And just like that I was alone again. Alone...but with

an answer I desperately needed. The spell had worked. I had saved Evey from her Fear magic. But at the cost of myself. *I had taken in her magic...not the necklace. Which meant, Fear magic wasn't keeping me in here. I was.*

I slunk down onto the ground and put my face in my hands. How was I supposed to get myself out if I was the one keeping myself here? And how was Evey going to stand a chance if she had no Fear magic to help her fight?

When I made the choice to do the spell, I thought it would trap her Fear magic into the necklace, and I could just release it when she needed it back. When she was calm enough to handle it, and far away from the Dark Woods. I never intended to take in her magic. Not to permanently strip it away from her.

As I sat there on the ground, I felt the tears forming in my eyes just as a warm sensation filled my body. Lifting my head toward the rising sun, I knew what that feeling meant. Callen had grabbed hold of my hand in the real world. I closed my eyes to soak up the feelin' of his skin on mine and tried like hell to push my thoughts to him.

"I'm here, Cal," I said softly. "I love you."

I knew he wouldn't hear me. But it felt good to have the words leave my lips. As much as I was dying to see Evey, my heart felt like it was legit broken from being away from him this long. Just as I let a long, defeated sigh escape my lips, I heard his smooth voice echo in the woods around me.

"I love you more, Violet."

But just as I was about to allow myself to get excited that he heard me, there was a wrestling sound in the trees and another shadow began to emerge.

Chapter 3

Evelyn

When I woke up the next morning, the first thing to run through my mind was how much I hated Johanna. She had one thousand percent lied to me. This magical sugar, or whatever she called it, was definitely worse than non-magical alcohol. I don't care how nicely she put it.

I rolled over, groaning, while still avoiding opening my eyes. I was grateful, as I rolled against the pillows, that I had somehow made it back to my bed. Sleeping in the chair I had been in would not have made my back very happy when I woke up. Stretching my arm, I suddenly felt warm skin beneath me, and my eyes shot open. Then, taking in the sight before me, I found myself hating Johanna a little less.

Turns out, I hadn't made it back to my room last night. And as I stared at Griffin, lying shirtless in the bed beside me, I vaguely remember him returning to the Knight suite and lifting my sleeping body out of the chair. A brief memory of me throwing myself at him as he laid me down in his bed also flashed in my mind. I moaned, a little quieter than before, at my own embarrassment. Magical sugar wasn't like alcohol, my ass.

"Good morning."

Griffin's groggy, morning voice was almost enough to make my knees buckle. If I hadn't been laying down already, I would have likely wavered on my feet...if not actually fallen over. And with the little stubble of a beard, I could see beginning to form on his face, I couldn't help but just stare back at him.

"You feeling okay?" he asked, as he raised an eyebrow at me.

"Me...I'm...I'm sorry, what did you say?"

Jesus. He was just a man. A man I had clearly not slept with, since despite his shirtless state, I was fully dressed. But definitely a man, I knew my body wanted. And a man I would gladly let take me as his. As various dirty thoughts raced through my mind, I didn't even recognize myself. Since when did I so openly admit what I was feeling? Even if it was just to myself! I buried my face into the blankets, praying he had not seen me blushing so much.

"Clearly you and Johanna are never being left alone together again," he laughed. "How many dolce ragus drinks did you have last night?"

"How many what?" I asked, turning back to look at him.

"Dolce ragus," he repeated. "It's that Magirian sugar Johanna put in your drink."

"Oh...I didn't know that awful stuff had a name."

"Awful?" He rolled onto his side and up on his elbow to look at me. "Dolce ragus is actually a healing drink in Magir."

"Then why do I feel so hungover every time I drink it?" I groaned.

"Well, one can only be healed so much," he chuckled. "I'm guessing it couldn't figure out what to do with you and just kept giving you a sugar high. Johanna did explain what sugar does to a magical right?"

"You make me sound like a five-year-old."

"Well, I will have to tell Johanna no sugar for you before

16

bed."

I playfully swatted his chest but found myself leaving my hand there. Feeling his chest under my fingertips, I just stared at my fingers for a moment before moving to his eyes. There was a lust there that seemed to get stronger every time we found ourselves in this position. But as I continued to run my fingers across his chest, I began to vividly remember throwing my sugar-drunk self at him and quickly pulled my hand back as I buried my head back into the sheets.

"I'm so sorry about last night," I groaned.

"Why?"

I peeked out just a bit and saw he was genuinely confused by my apology.

"Uh...for after you brought me in here. Which was exceedingly kind of you, by the way!"

"Oh," he chuckled, and I felt my heart race at the sight of his sleepy smile. "I had almost forgotten about that. I won't hold it against you."

He playfully winked at me, and I sunk back into the bed. This was a whole new side of embarrassment...and it had to be with the one person I actually wanted...ugh...I needed Violet right now.

"Really, it was nothing," he chuckled again, as he wrapped an arm around me and pulled me to his side.

"I am literally so embarrassed." I felt my cheeks getting hotter as I laid on his chest and began making little circles across his muscles with my fingers. "I've never done anything like this before. Never just openly told someone how badly I wanted them."

"At least you just tried to get me into bed," he said, as he ran his fingers casually through my hair. "Johanna full blown proposed to Sean."

"She what?"

I practically launched from the bed, and despite my dizzy state, I went bursting through his door. I didn't think the drinks affected Johanna like they did me. If she proposed to

17

him, maybe she actually meant it.

"E, wait up."

I heard Griffin behind me but couldn't stop myself. I found the door that had *O'Connor* inscribed on it and pushed it open without even attempting to knock.

Johanna and Sean were tightly wrapped together, and still sound asleep. Though from what I could see neither of them looked clothed. So, before I became the crazy friend, I loudly cleared my throat.

I had to clear my throat a second time before Johanna opened her eyes and hastily grabbed the blankets to hold them close to her chest. She smacked Sean twice, he too, finally woke up.

"What the hell, Jo?" Sean groaned. "I really thought for once you'd sleep in after being up all ni...Red?"

He finally saw me standing in the doorway and I crossed my arms over my chest just as Griffin appeared behind me. Thankfully with a shirt on...I needed my mind to focus on my friends right now...not his perfect body.

"Sorry, I couldn't stop her," Griffin apologized.

"Did you need something, Red?" Sean asked.

"Do I need something?" I asked back sarcastically. "Are you being serious?"

"Very," Sean quipped, as he scooted up in bed and rested against his headboard.

"What did you say to her?" I asked.

"Say to who?"

"Johanna!"

"Wait, what?" Johanna asked. "What are you talking about Evelyn?"

"Did you, or did you not, legit propose to Sean last night?" I asked bluntly.

Johanna's face went bright red, and she tucked her dark hair behind her ear. She had definitely asked him. Her reaction was confirmation of that. Now to find out if it was real or not.

"Well," I pushed. "Did you mean it?"

"Red, why is it so important to you right now?" Sean asked. "Don't you have a million other things to think about?"

"Of course, I do," I sighed, losing some of my tough girl resolve like I always did with Sean. "But you two are my friends. So, damn it, I want to know!"

"Well, I asked him," Johanna softly smiled before turning to Sean.

"And you said?" I questioned Sean.

"That she was already engaged," Sean joked.

Johanna laughed beside him, but part of me knew it wasn't real. I looked between the two of them and I knew what had happened now.

"Is that really all you needed, Red?" Sean asked. "Because if so, I'm going to get a few more hours of sleep before our awkward reunion breakfast."

"Our what?" I asked.

"Get some sleep," Griffin instructed, as he closed the door and placed his hand on the small of my back.

I let him lead me back to his room without question. I hadn't even realized how early it was. And it was *very* early. Sun not even up yet, early. I'm sure Griffin wanted to get back to sleep too. The second we made it back to his room, he closed the door and then removed the shirt he had thrown on, before climbing back into bed. I settled into the other side and stared at the ceiling.

"What was he talking about?"

"With breakfast, you mean?"

"Yes, Griffin. What is this *reunion breakfast* that he's talking about?"

Griffin sighed and rolled onto his side to face me. I turned just enough to be able to see him, and his silver eyes looked worried again.

"My mother, the Knights, and I, convinced my father to hear Lucas out," he explained. "He will be joining us all for breakfast to discuss what he knows about Violet. And also, what he knows about the Fears."

19

"Oh…" I sighed, looking back at the ceiling. "So, it's *my* awkward reunion."

"Yes. And my mother's. And the king's. They both have history with him too."

"I suppose so."

Since waking up beside him, Griffin, and our friends' potential wedding, was all I had allowed myself to think about. The memory of my father that now flooded through me, made my heart begin to pound in my chest again. Was I ready to see him again? Did I really want to?

Before more questions filled my mind, Griffin pulled me toward him, and I rolled onto my side allowing my back to mold itself against his chest.

"I will be there the entire time," Griffin said softly in my ear. "Hopefully he can help us wake Violet."

I nodded slightly and I felt his lips kiss the back of my head, sending a magical surge throughout my body.

"She meant it, you know," I suddenly said.

"Who?"

"Johanna."

"About proposing to Sean?"

"Yeah," I replied. "He thinks it was a spur of the moment question from too much of that drink, but she meant it."

"How do you know that?"

"Because the drink is meant to heal you right?"

"Yes."

"It did that for me. I may have been a little bit over the top, but I was able to finally admit what I wanted. It did the same thing for her."

I felt his heart start beating faster against my back and the room was suddenly becoming incredibly warm. He let out a soft sigh and kissed my head again before he whispered goodnight and we both drifted off to sleep.

****

When I woke up a few hours later, I could hear Griffin in the shower, and I used it as a chance to sneak back over to my suite. I'd hoped to get out unseen, but Nicholas was sitting quietly at a kitchen stool as I made my way to their door. We gave each other a nod of understanding, but there was no denying, with the Knights link, Griffin would know that I had left. I just needed a few minutes to myself before what was coming next. I had to wrap my head around everything before this breakfast happened. After all, it wasn't every day that a woman gets to meet her dead father.

Thankfully, nobody was in the girls' suite, and I swiftly made my way to my room. I closed the door behind me and undressed to take a hot shower. I had hoped the warm water would help me relax a little more, but the silence only gave me more time to think.

What would I say to him? Should I say anything, or just let him talk? Could I just sit by him and pretend to be happy he was here, when just a day ago, I thought he was dead? How could he possibly know what was wrong with Vi? How did he even know there *was* something wrong?

As the questions and scenarios raced through my mind, I realized I didn't have answers to any of them. I had no clue what I was going to say to him when I saw him. I didn't know if I should slap him for leaving me or hug him for being alive. I wasn't sure if he just magically — no pun intended — had all of the answers to Vi's illness or if I should call him a fraud and forbid him from going near her. These weren't decisions I normally made alone. Normally Vi was here to explain my own feelings to me. To talk me through the tough parts of my crazy life. Which lately seemed to be all of my life.

"I'm always here for you, sugar."

Violet's voice rang through my head again and I couldn't help but smile. Even though I knew deep down her being hurt was my fault, it was incredible to feel how strong our friendship was. I could still hear her advice for Pete's sake. I could hear it as if she was standing right beside me.

"*Not standing beside you! Just talking to you from my Fear comma.*"

I turned off the water and poked my head around the curtain. Violet's voice was definitely in my head, but it sounded like she was actually in the bathroom with me. And how could she really be in my head if she wasn't even conscious?

I looked around as I stepped out, but only to find that I was still alone in the room. Judging by the lack of noise from outside my door, probably still alone in the entire suite.

I shrugged off the voice in my head and quickly got myself dressed. As I blow dried my hair, I thought back to my father and Auntie Saraya. I wondered if anyone had even told her that he was alive yet. I'm sure Ariana had. Even though the Healing magicals had been adamant that I wasn't to visit my aunt, Ariana was the queen. They couldn't deny her the way they did me.

I knew how much she longed for my father to be alive. I think that was why I secretly caught her talking to him so many times. Talking to him when he wasn't really there. She had been clinging to this hope that her brother was still alive. That someday I would actually get to meet my own father. Yet when that day did shockingly arrive, she was undergoing surgery. She wasn't even there to see the magnificent failure that it was. Which was, again, my fault.

"*Pity party it up later!*" Violet's voice sang in my head. "*I need you to listen to me!*"

I looked up from my hairbrush and peaked out from the bathroom again. When I saw nothing, or rather nobody, inside I shrugged and went back to pulling my hair into a high ponytail.

"*Girl! I need you to listen to me! It's really me! I'm in your head!*"

"Okay, now this is just getting weird!" I exclaimed out loud, as I dropped the brush back onto the counter.

"What's weird?"

Griffin's voice startled me, and I uncontrollably jerked backward, before he caught hold of both my shoulders to steady me.

"Whoa! Didn't mean to scare you."

"Griffin," I sighed. "It wasn't you...it..."

"What is it? Did Hale project in here again?" Griffin asked, looking worried and furious at the same time. "I swear, I won't give him mercy this—"

"Griffin!" I interrupted. "It wasn't Hale."

"Oh. Well, are you alright? You look spooked, and you were gone before I even knew you were up."

"I just...I just thought I heard something, is all. I'm sure it was nothing. And I wasn't trying to sneak out. I just needed a few minutes to compose myself before breakfast."

I thought I could cover one lie with the truth. Maybe if I told him the truth about leaving this morning, he wouldn't question the sound I thought I was hearing. Yet, the look in his eye told me he wasn't buying my lie for a second. But with everything going on, how was I supposed to tell him that now I was hearing Violet's voice in my head.

"It's easy to tell him! Believe me, I'm here! Stop trying to convince yourself I'm not real and listen to me!"

I ignored Vi's instructions and interlaced my fingers with Griffin's.

"Ready to go?" I asked. "I'm assuming it's time."

"If you are," he responded, not changing his expression.

"I'm never going to be ready for this." I half smiled at him, and his eyes went from worried to warm. "But if he knows something about Vi, it will be worth it."

"It will be worth it," Griffin said, bringing my hand to his lips. "I have a feeling in more ways than one."

"Then let's go."

"Ugh!"

Violet's groans echoed in my mind as we made our way out of the suite. Magic had shown me that crazy things like this were possible…but as much as I wanted it to be, I couldn't wrap my head around it. My stomach was turning at the thought of this family reunion so I couldn't let my worries for Violet intensify that. Maybe I could even use the meal as a chance to ask Lucas — who seemed to know more about Violet than we did — if I could be hearing her somehow. It would be best to find more pieces of this puzzle before I put it together. Lord, now I was even sounding like Vi.

Chapter 4

Evelyn

Walking beside Griffin to the dining room this time around was different. In the past he would walk very close to my side or with our arms linked, while this time he was tightly gripping my hand. Not the hand in hand that friends sometimes did, either. No, this was the fingers interlaced while he held me as close to him as he could, hand in hand. And it wasn't just us.

In front of us Sean and Johanna walked so tightly together you would have thought their hands were glued together. Then in front of them Nicholas had his arm wrapped into Nixie, who was pulled against his side. And even Daniel had Katerie's arm in his — though that seemed more of a polite formality.

We were even walking in reverse order. No matter where we went, Griffin always walked first. Usually with me right beside him, if not just off his shoulder. But today we were in the back, while Daniel led the charge. It was like overnight, I had entered a parallel universe. Which wasn't too strange a thing to think about when considering it hadn't been long since I had actually stepped through a portal into a magical realm.

The entire thing was just...odd. It was like suddenly everyone was okay with openly expressing their feelings with each other. There were no secrets. It was like between the Fear battle and the return of Lucas, everyone realized there were bigger problems in the realm. Who we loved, and who knew about it, was the least of our worries.

"What's going through that brain of yours?" Griffin asked, squeezing my hand. "Nervous about seeing Lucas again?"

"No...yes," I stammered. "But should we be openly...you know."

"Yes," he defended, without needing a second to think. "I'm done pretending. I want every realm to know who you are to me. And I certainly don't care what the people having breakfast with us think. With the exception of maybe my mother, because...well she's, my mom."

"Such a momma's boy," I laughed. "But seriously, who's all coming? All of you Knights? Lucas? Hale?"

"Unfortunately."

I felt his body tense up beside me as Hale's name left my lips.

"Are you ever going to tell me what happened between you two?"

"Yes." Griffin stopped walking and nodded to the others to continue. "Tonight."

"What?"

"I want to take you on an actual date."

"A date?"

"Like an actual date," he grinned. "I'm talking, dinner, flowers, and whatever else I can do to spoil you. Then we will talk. I'll tell you whatever you want to know."

"Griffin—"

"And," he interrupted, "before you start worrying about everything going on, just let me do this one thing. After that —"

"Griffin!" I excitedly interjected. "I'd love that."

"You would?" His voice half asking and half leaping for joy.

"Yes," I said, stepping toward him. "I would really...really love that."

I didn't even recognize myself as I pushed onto my toes and kissed his cheek. Between this and last night, I wasn't even sure I knew who was allowing these words to pass through my lips. It sure as hell couldn't have been me. Normally I'd be questioning everything. Giving myself every reason why we shouldn't be spending our valuable time on a date. But now... there wasn't a doubt in my mind. No nagging voice in the back of my head. No chest pains, making me nervous to be alone with him. Just certainty that I wanted it.

"Well, then," Griffin began, as he squeezed my hand again and began to guide us down the hall further. "I wasn't quite expecting that to be so easy."

"Why do you say that?" I asked. "You didn't think I'd want to?"

"No, it isn't that," he grinned. "I just thought you'd put up a little bit more of a fight."

He winked at me, and I used my free hand to playfully swat his arm, just as we reached the door to the dining room. Seeing the door, I felt my hands instantly start sweating and instinctively tried to pull away from Griffin.

"Not a chance."

He squeezed my hand tighter and winked at me again. Whatever held back my emotions a few days ago, I was definitely missing it now. This man was turning my insides to jelly just by looking at me. The Fears didn't make me anywhere near as nervous as this feeling did.

But if I thought his admiration made me nervous, the group beyond the door made me feel like crawling back to the Dark Woods and begging for death. Each of their eyes pierced into me as Griffin continued to hold my hand and escorted me all the way to my seat. Ariana's eyes were warm, Hale looked oddly irritated, and King Barin looked like he may burst at the seams. I could only have imagined his reaction when Sean and Johanna had entered. If it was anything like this, I'm shocked Johanna even sat down.

"Good morning you two," Ariana smiled at us.

"Good morning," Griffin replied as he returned her smile.

"Mo...morning," I choked out.

Hale's eyes narrowed as they studied me across the table. Maybe he knew something was wrong with me too. Either that or maybe Violet was right. Maybe he was actually jealous of Griffin. Was it possible that Hale had some form of feelings for me?

"I demand to know what is going on here!" King Barin suddenly bellowed.

"We are having breakfast," Ariana answered softly and without looking at him. "As you demanded."

"I mean this!" He growled, as he pointed between Griffin and I. "First it was at Woodburn Rose, then at our holiday events, and now he is just galivanting around with her in front of our people!"

"Sir, if I may," Johanna tried to intervene.

"You may not!" King Barin shouted at her. "Don't even get me started on you!"

I watched as Johanna's head sank and she looked at Sean with a worried expression.

"How dare you show up here hand and hand with this...this commoner," King Barin spat at Johanna.

"Barin!" Ariana gasped.

"No, I have had enough of this!" he continued. "These children parade around my kingdom pretending to be worthy of it and then make a mockery of our laws. Johanna, how dare you disgrace your father in such a manner!"

"Your Majesty," Hale interjected, "EvelynRose is a much better candidate for a Queen. Perhaps it is for the best."

The king did not scold Hale the way he did Johanna or

even his own wife. Instead, he turned to me with hateful eyes and glared.

"Don't you dare," Griffin seethed, as he rose slowly from his chair.

The way they both looked at each other, I thought they were going to fight to the death. I knew it would blow up in our faces to be so open about our feelings. And no matter how I felt about Griffin, his position as a prince — as a prince with King Barin as his father — would never allow me to be with him.

I couldn't help but glance across the table at Hale. I had felt his eyes on me from the moment the king dismissed his comments about me making the better wife. But the look in his eyes wasn't that of curiosity or his usual smirk, it was almost... apologetic.

The king opened his mouth to speak again — or likely shout — when the doors to the dining room swung open and two guards came flowing through like they were escorting someone important. Following behind them were two more guards, and Lucas sandwiched in the middle. So not someone important, someone they thought was guilty of treason.

"I see royal family meals haven't changed much," Lucas joked from the doorway. "Arguing before you eat still? Seems a bit melodramatic, don't you think, Barin?"

Glancing from Lucas and back to the king, I watched as King Barin's anger shifted off of his son and onto my father. This man genuinely despised my father. The veins in his neck were growing larger with every breath he took while gazing upon his prisoner.

Griffin returned to his seat beside me and visibly reached over to grab hold of my hands, which were tightly clenched together on my lap. I could hear King Barin growl in disgust, as I watched the guards escort Lucas to his seat at the end of the table. Whether his growls of disapproval were at Lucas approaching or at Griffin holding my hand was unclear.

"You better have something good to provide," King Barin hissed. "Or I will have you executed for your treachery."

"Executed?" I questioned.

"I have had enough questioning for today!" He turned to me. "Speak again and you will join him in the line."

Griffin's grip tightened against my hands, and I felt a sudden rush of rage move through my body. Before he could stand up to his father though, mine loudly cleared his throat.

"Now, now," Lucas calmly intervened. "I thought we were here to eat peacefully and discuss my return. If you plan to continue threatening my daughter, I can promise you that peaceful is far from what I'll be."

As he spoke, I watched him closely. Nothing in his face changed. He went from speaking in a smooth, calm manner to threatening a king without even a wrinkle of his brows. Not to mention how incredibly easy the words, *my daughter*, slipped from his lips. It gave me goosebumps to hear someone calling me that. Especially when three months ago I had no parents.

King Barin said nothing as he sank back into his chair and continued his optical assault on Lucas. As I looked between the two of them, my eyes stopped for a moment on Hale. His eyes were still glued on me as a small twitch occurred in the corner of his mouth. *Did he just smile at me?* He finally broke away just as food was brought to the table.

"Where shall we begin?" Ariana asked.

Clearly, she wanted out just as badly as I did. As I'm sure *all* of us did.

"Why did you betray your people?" King Barin asked. "Why betray the crown when you had everything you could have ever wanted?"

"I didn't have everything," Lucas answered solemnly. "I didn't believe then, and I don't believe now, that all Magirian Fears are without a heart. I never felt that Rana should have been banished just because the Fear stone chose her. She was someone we all trusted before, I couldn't just let that trust dissipate."

"Your belief in their hearts almost cost you your life," Ariana softly reminded him.

"A sacrifice I would willingly make a million times over if it brought me to this same point," Lucas said, as his eyes flickered from Ariana to me. "Rana may have lost herself to the darkness of Fear magic, but that is not the case with all of them. I have met some of them. In the non-magical realm. Not all of them let their hate control their magic the way Rana does."

"Morana."

Hale's voice made everyone's head turn from Lucas. But Hale wasn't looking at Lucas. No, he was staring right at me. Griffin gave my hand a squeeze, and I knew he was comforting me while also fighting back his own opinion of Hale's involvement with the Fears. It was no secret after all how Hale felt about the Fears or their magic.

"Yes," Lucas agreed. "I guess it's time I call her by the name she so proudly wears. But it's hard, even now, to believe that the woman I loved isn't there anymore."

"Well, she isn't," Hale confirmed. His expression still blank as he stared at me, rather than Lucas. "Morana has no heart for anything. She only wants power."

"I couldn't agree more," Lucas replied. "I know that now more than ever. I've been left with a few scars from her Fear magic as well. I'm assuming that mark across your face was not given to you in a sparring match?"

Hale's face twitched and I couldn't help but study at the length of the scar running through his, once flawless, face. Not that the scar deterred that much. He was still very nice to look at. The scar just served as another reminder that he wasn't someone we could put our trust in. Even if he had come through for me in the woods, there was a side to him that left me uneasy.

"Hale does as he is told," King Barin informed Lucas. "He accepts that the tasks he is given may not always leave him unscathed. But he accepts them all the same."

"I would imagine he does," Lucas said. "Becoming a marked one, isn't something the Fears take lightly."

Now Hale had been pushed. His gaze darkened and he shifted his eyes to Lucas, just for a moment before returning to me. I quickly looked back down at my plate. There was something deeper going on here. And what the hell was a *marked one*?

"Saraya told me why it was you ran," Ariana offered kindly, as she smiled from me to Lucas. "But how did you avoid my spell? After Saraya left to find you and did not return, I tracked you myself. How did you block my magic?"

"I knew eventually someone would ask you to track me," Lucas replied in a guilty tone. "And I knew Ra...Morana, would either find a way to do the same, or tap into yours. So, I had to make my magical imprint vanish."

"But that can't be done," Nicholas surmised.

"Not without an absorbing emerald," Lucas corrected.

"A what?" Katerie asked.

"An absorbing emerald," Lucas repeated. "It's a magical object. Most of them are documented, but still thought to be a myth because no living Magirian has ever been able to find. The absorbing emerald is a gem that can absorb magic when the right spell is used."

"So, you stripped away your magic?" Ariana gasped. "But then how are you here? How did you make it through the veil without magic?"

"A single gem can only hold onto so much," Lucas explained. "When my gem was used again to absorb additional magic, it released mine to make room for the rest."

The table was silent for a minute as Lucas's explanation sunk in. I had no idea such objects even existed. But I bet Violet did. She was always in the library back at Woodburn Rose and it didn't change when we got Magir. That's when it hit me.

"My necklace."

The words left my lips almost like a whisper, but everyone at the table dropped whatever food they had grabbed and stared at me. Slowly I moved my gaze from my plate to Lucas, who was looking at me with proud eyes.

"Yes, EvelynRose," Lucas responded. "The necklace Sar gave to you is the only absorbing emerald known in existence."

A guard came through the door suddenly and advised King Barin that he had an urgent matter to attend to. King Barin stood, making sure to puff out his chest to seem more important, and informed us all that our meeting would continue, but with Hale as his stand in.

As King Barin made his announcement and left the room, I heard Griffin chuckle lightly beside me. But it was an irritated laugh...not a happy one.

Looking over at Hale, I couldn't read him. He nodded to King Barin as he passed by and then suddenly moved his eyes from me to his plate. I would think that he would want to be paying even more attention to the people at the table now rather than staring at the food. But the longer I stared at him, the more it appeared as if he drifted off to sleep.

"Hang on a second," Nixie suddenly said. "From what I've read about the emerald, only a descendant of the line in which it was originally passed down can activate its magic. If EvelynRose didn't do that, and Saraya was either locked up or mind controlled, then who was it?"

Lucas stared at me, as he waited for me to piece everything together. I had a theory before Nixie offered her information. And now that theory was shot. I remembered what had happened in the Dark Woods. I know who grabbed the necklace. But if the necklace was from my family...it couldn't have been from hers too.

"Violet," Griffin surmised beside me. "E, you said Violet grabbed your necklace in the Dark Woods before you passed out. She muttered something but you couldn't remember."

"But that's impossible," I shook my head. "If only family members can harness the emerald's magic, then Violet couldn't have done it. She's like a sister to me, but not literally family."

"Actually," Lucas said, clearing his throat. "That's not entirely true."

Chapter 5

Violet

I was practically screaming at Callen in my mind, but he still wasn't hearing me. Since he returned my I love you, I hadn't gotten him to notice me at all. He was probably thinkin' just like Evey. That I was just some voice in his head. But damn it, I wasn't! And I knew I needed his help if I was ever going to get out of this god forsaken forest in a box.

Exhausted from screaming and pacing around, I sunk down to the forest floor. Crossing my legs like a kindergartener at story time, I placed my chin on top of my fists, and tried to think of a solution.

I knew that Callen was still here with me. I could feel his magic coursing through my veins and feel the warmth he always brought to me. But I wasn't getting through to him in the way that I had been getting through to Evey.

It didn't make sense either. I was bonded to Callen. Evey was my best friend, but we weren't bonded in any way. Well best friend and long lost, didn't know she existed, cousin… but that was beside the point. Or was that the point? Could us being related be bond enough to let me through?

Callen moved his hand from my arm, and cupped my

hand in his, sending another surge of magic through me.

I cringed at the thought of never really getting to truly feel him again. Never getting to have him kiss me to the point of making me dizzy. Or of what would happen to him if I really didn't come out of this nightmare. Of him never knowing that I was really here, telling him I loved him, every single day.

Just as the thought crossed my mind, I felt his warmth leave me and his magic was gone too. I knew that meant he had been asked to leave by a doctor. I'm sure they were coming in to try some other test or some new medicine to try to wake me up. Little did they know it was a complete waste of their time.

Yeah, this was my own personal hell. Being able to talk to people without being heard. It was a literal nightmare. Being stuck in the middle of the woods, with no way out. This was my own purgatory. And only I was going to pull myself from it.

If only Lucas had given me some real instructions! I'd have taken anything he had to give me. At this point I would eat bugs from the ground if it meant gettin' myself out of here and back to Magir with the people I loved.

But no. In true Lucas fashion, he gave me a tiny piece of information and just vanished. Now that I really thought about it, he had done that to me a couple times now. In the vision I had of the necklace, I had only seen the spell, not what it did. When he projected to me in the library, he just told me to trust my instincts. And now...now he was telling me that he could get me out and then, poof...gone without a trace. For being my so-called, long-lost uncle, he sure wasn't going to be winnin' any *family member of the year* award from me.

There was another rustle in the trees and a dark figure began to emerge. I rose quickly from my spot on the forest floor and stared in the direction of the creature. This one seemed to be alone, but it wasn't like I had anything to fight it with.

"That creature is dangerous, Violet. Run."

The voice rang through my head, and I immediately knew it wasn't Lucas. This person was younger. There was something familiar, but something new that I couldn't put my finger on. Yet, as I stared at the dark, scaly creature inching closer in my direction, I also knew the voice had a point.

I wasn't sure it had actually seen me, but then it charged forward, and I instantly began climbing the tree behind me. I moved up the tree as fast as I could, but the demon leapt off the ground just high enough to sink its claws into my left deltoid.

Letting out a scream from the pain as its claws ran down my arm, I forced myself up the tree until there was nowhere else, I could go. No more places that I could try to hide. Perched on a branch, cradling my bleeding arm, I looked back down at the demon just as it jumped again. My heart leapt as it narrowly missed my foot and then landed hard, but stable, on the ground.

Certain it would jump again, and downright terrified it wouldn't miss again, I closed my eyes as it prepared to jump again. As I squeezed my eyes tighter, I felt rays of sunshine touch my cheeks and opened them again to look back at the demon.

Before my eyes, the demon was convulsing on the ground and disappearing in a haze of smoke. I watched in horror as the creature died before my eyes and when it was gone, I found myself still staring at the spot, not entirely convinced it wouldn't reappear the moment I jumped down.

"*It's gone. You are safe to come down.*"

"And how exactly do I know I can trust you?" I shouted.

I looked at my arm and saw the bleeding only getting more severe.

"*I'm not your enemy,*" the voice assured me. "*Are there no Fears here with you? Just the creatures?*"

"*Just* the creatures?" I repeated. "I am trapped in a freaking forest in my own mind with magical demons trying to kill me and you are concerned with why only these creatures are attacking and not Fears? You have got to be freakin' kiddin' me!"

"*This really isn't her. Morana didn't do this.*"

The voice trailed off as if whoever it was had deduced something that I had not been able to.

"Look, I don't really give a damn who you are but please..."

A burst of pain suddenly pulled my attention back to my arm, which was still bleeding severely. I groaned in pain and tried to move so I could rest against the tree trunk to evaluate my arm.

"Please just get me out of here."

"*Violet that injury may be real. You need to stay safe until I return.*"

"Return? No, I need out of here now!"

"*It is not that simple, but we will free you. Whatever you do, keep yourself safe. Do not think of the darkness. Think only of the daylight. Think only of the sun and happy memories.*"

"What the hell are you talkin' about?"

No answer came. I waited for what felt like hours for the voice to return, but I heard no sounds other than a light breeze rustling through the branches.

I was alone again, in this nightmare of mine. But what was it the voice had said to me? *That injury may be real?* The more I thought about it, the more I realized what he was referring to. But that couldn't be possible. Could it?

My head started to hurt as I thought about the possibility of dying here in this nightmare. Dying without kissing Cal or hugging Evey again. I reached down with my one good arm and ripped off the bottom of my shirt. I'd seen it done in movies plenty of times, but it was surprisingly more challenging than I had anticipated.

I wrapped up my arm the best I could and clumsily made my way down the tree. What else had the man's voice in my head said? *Do not think of the darkness. Think only of the daylight. Think only of the sun and happy memories.*

Now that was going to be a chore in this horrid place. Darkness was all I could think of! I was trapped in a Fear coma. Darkness. I was being hunted and attacked by creepy demon creatures. Darkness. Now it turned out that I could potentially die here because of said demons. Darkness.

Darkness. Darkness. Darkness.

The thoughts continued to race through my mind as I made it to the bottom of the tree and my feet sank into the soft grass. The shadows around me moved slowly up the tree and I spun in a panic.

"How is the sun setting?" I asked out loud. "It just rose!"

What if the voice had been speaking in literals when he said think of the sun. When I let my thoughts think only of darkness, the sun literally began to set. I was going to be wrapped in physical darkness again.

Grabbing leaves to add to my makeshift bandage, I thought only of happy things. Callen being the star in most of those thoughts for the time being. As I glanced back up at the sky, it was like I had turned back the clock. The sun was rising again.

I smiled — in spite of my current situation — and continued to wrap up my arm. Magic was weird, and impossible to fully understand, but it wasn't getting the best of me here.

This Fear nightmare could kiss my southern ass. I wasn't going to die here without one hell of a fight.

Chapter 6

Evelyn

Griffin squeezed my hand again, as I tried to take in all the information Lucas was offering from the end of the table.

"I'm sorry we didn't tell you, EvelynRose," Lucas said. "I didn't have all of the information myself. I knew that I had a brother. But I didn't know anything about him. My father spoke of him as if he and my true mother were already dead."

"So, Vi isn't just my friend," I said softly. "She's my cousin?"

"Yes," Lucas nodded. "My twin brother's daughter."

I finally looked up from my plate and noticed across from me, Hale was still staring down with his eyes closed. Ariana on the other hand was in awe. She sat completely still, eyes fixated on my father with her mouth hanging slightly open. Clearly, I wasn't the only one completely stunned by this information.

"You never mentioned you had," Ariana began, "a brother."

"Ari, I apologize," Lucas said solemnly. "I never meant to keep it from you. Saraya doesn't even know. My father only told me just before I left Magir. I knew that Willa wasn't my birth mother from the time I was very young. But everything about her was a secret. I never imagined that secret included my having another sibling. A twin."

"But she's my family?" I asked again. "Then us meeting wasn't a coincidence?"

"It was fate," Griffin said beside me.

I shifted my gaze away from Lucas and found Griffin softly smiling at me. The memory of him promising to teach me about fate on my first night at WRA flashed through my mind. Though never in a million years would I have thought that this was how he would do it.

Just as I was about to ask Lucas more about Violet and her father, Callen came bursting through the doors. He was panting and clearly out of breath from running to us.

"Callen?" Griffin questioned as he stood from his chair.

"I couldn't reach you," Callen said.

"What's going on?" Sean asked.

"It's Violet," Hale practically shouted, as he stood from the chair.

"How do you..." Callen stammered.

"We don't have time for explanations," Hale declared, as he interrupted Callen. "We need to get the medical wing at once."

"Why?" I questioned.

"I'm going to need you to trust me."

Hale began to move swiftly towards the door as Callen and Griffin stared at each other. Trusting Hale was not something they were going to do willingly, but something was clearly wrong. And even though I knew that none of the Knights would admit it, they all knew that Hale was a strong magical. Maybe he had figured out what was wrong with her.

Not listening to him, just wasn't a risk I was willing to take. Violet was my best friend. No, she was apparently my own blood. I had to at least hear what Hale had to say. Without a second thought, I stood from my chair and grabbed Griffin's hand back before pulling him toward the door.

To my surprise, he didn't fight me. I did notice that as we passed the end of the table he nodded to Lucas. I wondered in the back of my mind if it was his princely manners that demanded that of him, or if it was because he was holding my hand.

Either way, I didn't mention noticing it and instead followed Hale swiftly and silently down the hall. With Griffin on my right and Callen to my left, I knew that if Hale tried to pull something, I was safe. Though in the back of my head, I knew better. Hale may have been a mystery to me and almost everyone else, but I knew he wouldn't do anything to harm me. Despite the testing in his classroom even...there was this voice in the back of my head telling me he wasn't a physical threat to me. Maybe not a threat at all.

When we entered the hall that led to Violet's room inside the palace's medical wing, medical staff filled the hall, and just past them I could see another large group of them around where I knew Violet's bed was placed. While I couldn't see her from where they stood, I could feel that something was very wrong. She was in pain. I had visited her countless times and I had never come down the hall with this feeling. I couldn't help but wonder if this is what Violet always felt like. Was this empathy magic?

Hale sternly dismissed all the staff and Griffin nodded as they looked past Hale to him for confirmation. To no surprise, Hale shot a cynical smile over his shoulder at Griffin, who glared sternly back. Their childish antics made it impossible not to roll my eyes as we walked further into Violet's room. But the irritated look on my face quickly faded to worry as we entered the room and I saw Violet lying in the Magirian version of a hospital bed. My chest tightened, and I dropped Griffin's hand as I rushed to her bedside.

She didn't look how I remembered from just yesterday. She was paler, which said a lot considering how pale she already was, and as I grabbed her hand, I realized she was freezing. More than her outward appearance, the most alarming thing was that her body was shaking. Not violently, but like she was in a constant shiver. And when I thought it couldn't possibly get any worse, I saw the pool of blood growing under her now bandaged left arm.

"What's happening to her?" I asked.

"I don't know," Callen replied, grabbing Violet's other hand. "She just started shaking out of nowhere. I rushed to find you as soon as Lucian confirmed he didn't know what was happening."

"How long has she been bleeding?"

"Bleeding?"

Callen leaned over and took in the pool of blood growing underneath Violet's arm.

"She...she wasn't bleeding when I left. Where did that bandage come from?"

He kept her hand in his, but took a small step back from her body.

"Let me look," Hale demanded.

He quickly moved closer, and it almost seemed as if he was going to shove me out of the way to get to her.

"Evelyn, you are going to have to trust me on this," he pleaded. "I need to examine her injury."

My narrowed eyes softened at the tone in his voice. He was worried. Genuinely worried about what was happening to Violet.

I nodded, dropping Violet's hand and moving to stand beside Griffin. He wrapped his arm around my shoulders and pulled me tightly to his side.

Hale studied Violet's body for only a moment before gently lifting her arm, carefully removing her bandages and revealing the source of the blood. Four long, deep gashes went down the entirety of her deltoid.

"How the hell did she get those?" Griffin demanded.

"I have hardly left her side," Callen defended. "What could have done this?"

"Fiends," Hale asserted.

"The Fear devils?" I questioned.

All three men turned to me. Griffin and Callen both looked surprised that I knew what that term even meant, while Hale looked mildly impressed.

"Yes," Hale grinned. "They are attacking her from within."

"I'm sorry, what?" Callen questioned. "How in the fuck are those things inside Violet?"

I could see the mixture of emotions overcoming Callen. He was usually so composed in situations such as this. It made him the perfect person to be Griffin's right hand. But now he looked like he may burst out of his skin in anger or drop to his knees in tears at any moment. Watching him closely, the shift in his eyes made me wonder if there was actually something inside him trying to fight its way out.

"This isn't the time for those explanations," Hale said, turning her arm as another large amount of blood gushed onto the bed sheets.

"He's right."

I pulled away from Griffin and stood directly beside Hale at Violet's head.

"This injury is deep enough that it may have nicked her brachial artery," I explained.

"You mean she could bleed out?" Callen asked, knowing the answer and starting to look sick.

"That's exactly what I mean," I nodded. "Hale, I need you to tell me what I need to do."

"You need to —"

Before he could finish Callen staggered backward and collapsed to his knees. Griffin rushed to his side, starting to look pale himself. Even I had to admit that I was starting to feel a little nauseous standing over my best friend's body as she bled to death.

"Damn bonds. We must hurry," Hale commanded. "Evelyn, you need to focus on both your connection to Violet and your Healing magic."

"But my magic isn't —"

"I am aware of your condition, but you have to try," Hale interrupted.

"How…"

"Now, Evelyn. She's dying."

He was right. As much as I wanted to know how he knew about the issues with my magic, Violet had to be my focus right now.

Grabbing hold of her hand and placing my other hand gently over her wound, I closed my eyes to channel my Healing magic. I could feel her warm blood pouring onto my fingers and I instinctively gripped her arm a little tighter.

"Healing won't be enough, Evelyn," Hale explained softly beside me. "You need to channel your relationship with Violet. Your bond to her."

I focused on the memory of Violet comforting me after our battle in Rosebud Park. How she managed to make me feel sane after the worst moment of life — at least to that date. I recalled how it felt to hug her close and how even my magic reacted to her embrace — not that we knew at the time that feeling was magic.

"It's working, Evelyn."

Griffin's voice across the room interrupted my thoughts before I could even begin to interpret them.

Opening my eyes, I saw Violet's skin pulling back together and the bleeding had almost completely stopped. Sighing, I stopped channeling my magic and took a wobbly step back from the bed.

Hale's arm wrapped around me in an attempt to steady me and fire pulsed through my veins at his touch.

"That's new. You've saved my life, sugar."

Violet's voice was in my head again, as clear as it had been in my bathroom just hours ago. And she was right, that was new. I had saved her life, and I'd never felt anything like the surge I had just gotten from Hale. Somehow, I knew that feeling wasn't a good thing.

"I think you should sit for a moment," Hale suggested, as he removed his arm from me.

I walked slowly to a chair beside the one where Callen now sat. I had been so focused on Vi, I hadn't even noticed Griffin had managed to lift him from the floor.

Once I was seated, I instinctively went to put my face in my hands, but instead found myself staring at their blood covered state.

"It's okay, sug. You saved me."

Her blood was everywhere. Dripping from my hands, down my arms and splattered across my clothes. For the first time since we walked into this hospital my chest was tightening to a point where it felt hard to breathe. My best friend had almost died. Almost died...in my hands.

Callen's hand suddenly wrapped around both of mine. He didn't care that they were bloody as he squeezed them tighter and forced my chair to turn and face him.

"You saved her life," he assured me once I was face to face with him. "You saved all of our lives."

"He's right." Griffin agreed.

"They are," Hale explained. "Now if you will excuse me, I have some research to do."

"Wait!"

Hale stopped in the doorway and turned to face us. I caught Griffin's expression and he seemed confused at my stopping Hale.

"Can you wake her?" I asked.

"Possibly."

At that Griffin and Callen both perked up a bit behind me. I didn't have to see it, but I heard Callen's chair shift as he perked up a little, and I felt a sudden change in Griffin.

"Hale, please," I begged. "No matter what everyone thinks, I know there is good in you. Please help her."

He stared at me, his face unchanged. I couldn't put my finger on Hale or his motives. The scar on his face was a reminder of the side he had chosen, but then why would he have helped me heal Violet?

"You have plans this evening," he finally said. "I need to confirm a few things prior to any attempts to wake her anyway. Meet me back here in the morning. Let's say nine o'clock."

"Thank you."

Hale nodded at me and left the room. Griffin and Callen both stared at me with concerned expressions.

"Lucas said he could wake Violet," Griffin reminded me.

"He did," I agreed. "And while he may truly know what is going on with her, I think Hale can physically pull her out of it."

"I don't trust him," Callen said, rising from his chair.

"Neither do I. At least not entirely. But this is Fear magic. And since mine seems to be problematic at the moment, Hale may be our best chance at getting Violet back."

"She may be right," Griffin surprisingly agreed. "If this is Fear magic, then Hale would be the expert. We may not trust him, but let's at least figure out what he knows."

Callen nodded and walked back to Violet's side.

"Whatever it takes then," he said, tucking Violet's hair behind her ear. "Whatever I have to do to get her back."

Chapter 7

Violet

I unwrapped my arm and ran my finger down the forming scars. The voice had been correct. My injuries in this nightmare actually happened to my physical body too. When I collapsed onto the grass from the bleeding, I thought I was going to die here. But then my girl had come though! And surprisingly, Hale.

Making my way back to the small clearing where I had first seen Lucas's projection and heard the mystery voice, I hoped that one of them would present themselves again. Coming so close to death brought out some scary thoughts in my head, and as a result the sun had not just set...no matter how much I tried to think of rainbows and sunshine, the sun wouldn't rise again.

I'd already outrun one dark devil. Granted, I had thrown a large rock at it, possibly bashing its head in...but I was running for my life. It wasn't like I could watch to see if I had gotten him or not.

With the darkness quickly setting in, I had a feeling that more of those creatures would be coming after me. And I had zero weapons here. I could throw a rock like a baseball pitcher, but rocks would only go so far when there was an army of these things.

"Hello!" I shouted in the empty abyss, as I walked into the clearing. "Whoever you are, can you please for the love of God, tell me how to get out of here?"

Nothing. Just silence. How could I reach that voice again? Had I somehow called it to me the first time?

"Lucas? I could use a little help here!"

"Pumpkin, who are you shouting at?"

This was neither Lucas, nor the voice in my head. This voice made all of the hairs on the back of my neck stand up. There was no way he was really here. He wasn't a magical. But as I spun around...there he was.

A tall, slightly rounded man with light brown hair and green eyes stood just at the edge of the trees staring at me. He wore a well pressed black suit with a dark gray tie and his favorite black Oxfords.

"Dad?"

"Violet Aurora Rae, where the devil are we?"

"How are you..."

"And why have you not been returning any of my emails? My assistant has been calling you for weeks with no response. Your mother is worried sick."

"Momma..."

"Well, you better start giving me answers, young lady."

I couldn't form any more words. How was he here? He sure looked like my father. Sounded just like him. Of course, he wouldn't have taken the time to call me himself. Him having his assistant call me for him definitely seemed like something he would do. But it didn't make sense. I couldn't wrap my brain around how this was possible. Even with magic.

"You're right to question him."

The voice rang through my head, but I didn't see my father flinch. The voice must have been solely in my head, where he couldn't hear it.

"Fiends can transform, Violet. They feed off of your worst

fears and memories. Trust your gut. This creature is not your father."

"How do you know?" I mentally asked the voice.

"Ask it about something your father shouldn't know."

I pondered the voice for a moment. The more it spoke the more familiar it became.

"Hale, is that you?"

"Ask him, Violet."

His proposition made sense. If this creature was portraying my father and trying to feed off of memories I supposedly had of him, introducing a fake one may just trip the creepy thing up.

"Do you remember that time when you came to Woodburn Rose for Parent's Day?" I asked my father. "Where you first meet Callen?"

My *father's* face scrunched up in a way I had only seen during times of true frustration.

"Woodburn Rose? I've never heard of such a place. And who in God's name is Callen?"

Well, that backfired. Maybe the voice was wrong, and this really was my father. Was it possible the Fears had gone after him and trapped him here too? Could it be just another way to torture me?

"No, Violet. Trust me. He is not what he seems."

"How can I trust you? You won't even tell me who you are."

The voice didn't respond but the trees around me began to shift in the breeze. Still my *father* didn't flinch. It was as if he couldn't see anything except me.

A haze began to form in front of me and I took a small step back. The blur of it began to pull together into the shape of a man, and Hale emerged.

"It was you!"

"Yes."

"Why didn't you just say so?!"

"I thought for sure if you knew who I was you wouldn't

listen to me. I needed you to trust me."

"Well, you are certainly right about that."

Behind Hale, my father stood still silently staring at me.

"He can't see me," Hale expounded. "I'm tied to your mind, not the magic."

"How is that possible?"

"I'm a Mind magical, Violet. Connecting a mind, even as challenging as your situation may be, is child's play for me."

"Why are you helping me?"

"Why does it matter?"

"It matters, Hale. If this is some pathetic trick to get Evey to love, you it will fail."

Hale's face shifted. Even in his current state I could tell I had touched a nerve.

"I have zero intentions of competing with Griffin."

"And if there was no competition?"

"I care for Evelyn," Hale said sternly. "But I know better than to question or intervene between fates."

He seemed genuine, but I still wasn't sure.

"Then why?"

"I am not the enemy you all think I am."

In the distraction of our banter, I had not noticed my father moving from his place at the edge of the woods. He had moved closer to the brush that was just in front of me and stood with his arms out.

"Pumpkin, come with me. We can talk through all of this," he said sweetly.

Hale's apparition faded into the wind and his voice echoed again in my head.

"It's not him, Violet. I promise you."

Just as I was about to question my father again, another person emerged from the trees and my chest tightened as I saw him.

"Vi, thank God," Callen breathed. "I thought I was never going to see you again."

"Callen!"

"*Violet, wait!*"

Hale's voice in my head stopped me after just a few steps.

"*Think this through. Logically. How can Callen be in your head with you and holding your hand back in Magir? Trust the magic you have. Feel for him.*"

I had to admit that Hale had a point. It did seem rather strange that after what felt like a lifetime of trying to reach Callen, he just appeared here in the same moment my father mysteriously had. The convenience of the timing...the number of coincidences that would involve...it logically — as Hale so clearly pointed out — just wasn't possible.

Closing my eyes, I tried to focus on my bond to Callen.

"Violet, trust me. I can get you out of here. Just come with me."

I slightly opened one of my eyes and saw dream Callen standing before me with his hand out. His charming smile was drawing me in.

"*And here I was beginning to think you were Callen's stronger half.*"

I may have actually groaned out loud in response, or maybe it was just in my head...at this point it was hard to tell. But I did clearly hear the chuckle from Hale that followed.

Focus on Callen. I tried to remember what his touch felt like. What it felt like when our magic would dance together. His lips on mine. And then, it was like he was there with me. I could hear him talking to me, or more accurately, the shell of me back in Magir. His thumb moved across my hand, and I couldn't help but touch my hand. And if I could feel him there, he wasn't really *here*.

"*Told you. Now you have to beat these fiends.*"

"And how do you propose I do that? I don't exactly have weapons coming out my ears here."

"*This is your mind, Violet. You can bring whatever you want into it. Fear magic can't control you. You're far too good hearted for that.*"

With Hale's word of encouragement, my eyes shot open. That hadn't even crossed my mind, and yet, it made perfect sense. This was my nightmare. It was my imagination. I had control of this world.

"Not total control," Hale corrected. *"You cannot will yourself awake. Or wish the fiends away. But if you wanted a weapon, or perhaps some armor. Now that could be arranged."*

"Pumpkin, come with us. This strange boy does have a point. Let us get you to safety."

These fiends definitely weren't as sly as they thought. My dad hadn't called me *Pumpkin* since I was a child. I should have remembered that from the moment the creature had spoken. And the longer I stared at Callen, his eyes were missing something. They didn't have the same desire in them that he normally did when he looked at me.

Remembering what Callen had told me about guns not functioning in Magir, I remembered the knives that my father had given me after I successfully hunted and killed my first white-tail deer. Before long, I felt the cool metal in each of my hands and what I am sure looked like a devilish grin crossed my lips.

"Well, well, well," my fiend-father spat. "Aren't you just a clever little magical?"

"Considering you're here because of me, you shouldn't be so surprised," I taunted.

My fiend-father and the fiend-Callen both showed nothing but disgust as they launched at me. I did my best to channel my magic as I evaded their attack and swung my knives around. Rolling to evade a hit from fiend-Callen, I found myself face-to-face with my father.

"Do you really think you could kill him?" the fiend hissed, as it grabbed me by the arm. "And if you can, what does that say about you?"

It also had a point. I could do a lot of things, but could I really stab him? Despite being a devil straight from hell, it did look exactly like my father. I may have despised him in a lot of ways, but at the end of the day, he was still my dad. I couldn't just look past that...could I?

"It's pathetic how weak you are."

My fiend-father lifted me from the ground like I was an empty potato sack. Before I could grasp what was going on, he slammed me back to the ground, and pain radiated through my entire body. It felt like I couldn't breathe. I wondered how many ribs I had just cracked, if not completely broken.

For my entire life, I had been a strong, do-it-myself, kind of person. But I had prided myself on knowing it was okay to ask for help. Especially knowing when I needed to ask for it. The shit part about this awful place was there was nobody here to ask. I really was all on my own.

"*Violet, get over yourself!*" Hale's voice shouted at me. "*You have friends here and we will get you out of here. But you have to get through this battle first.*"

"*I don't think I can...*" I thought, unable to find actual words. "*I can't kill them when they look like this.*"

"*Then call upon something that can.*"

My mind instantly flashed to the beasts the Knights could become. How they had ripped apart Fears as if they were children breaking twigs. That's what I needed to get out of this.

Opening up my mind as much as I could before my fiend-father could push his now forming claws into my chest, I thought of Callen's beast. How beautiful it was in color. How fierce it was on the battlefield. How sharp it's teeth...

And then it was there, ripping the fiend portraying my father off of me and tossing it through the air. My eyes followed the nasty creature, and I watched in horror as it hit the ground and my father's facade began to melt away. And melt was the correct word for it. Its skin began to drip off until all that was left was a dark, shaded creature that soon vanished into the air.

I had hoped to have a moment to revel in my small victory, but behind where that fiend had died, more black creatures began emerging from the trees. There had to have been at least ten of them coming ominously slow out from their hiding spots in the woods.

Twisting my knives in my hands, I launched across the field. It was like I was acting on instinct...an instinct I didn't have...but instinct, nonetheless.

"It's his instinct, not yours," Hale informed me. "Now act on it and stay alive. I'll return."

I could hold back the groan that passed my lips as Hale dismissed himself from the fight, leaving me to battle the endless number of Fear demons that were in this freakin' nightmare.

Slicing through another one of the fiends that resembled my father, I heard a cackle from the tree line that made all the baby hairs on the back of neck stand up. The Callen fiend was laughing as the mentally called upon Beast Callen ripped through another fiend.

My chest began to tighten, my hands began to ball into fists, and anger was filling my body so quickly that I could feel the heat in my cheeks. As the Callen fiend turned to look at me, the anger I felt turned to rage and I felt a surge of magic inside of me.

The magic was nearly boiling over inside of me, and that damn fiend was still just laughing. It wasn't just laughing at the situation either...it was staring right at me. That abomination was laughing at me. It had the nerve to laugh right in my face!

The scream that pierced my ears next was so blood curdling that if I hadn't felt the magic leave my body or my mouth hanging open, I would have never believed the sound had come from me. But it most definitely was from me, and it was causing magic to pulse out of me like a damn concert speaker.

I felt lighter as I pulled the scream back and noticed the destruction, I had caused around me. Trees had been uprooted and fiends were literally exploding before me. Yet, moving closer to me...still laughing...was the fiend Callen. And the

Fear inside me just couldn't handle it. I tossed the knife I had in my hand and as it spun in the air, I willed for it to shift into a spear.

Watching almost in awe as my mind took the small blade and transformed into a long, ancient warrior spear, the world around me suddenly went into slow motion. The spear hit the fiend Callen but unlike the other fiends, it didn't disintegrate. Instead, it collapsed onto its knee, holding the spear in its hands.

"Vi..."

The voice that came from the fiend wasn't the scary voice it had been before...it was Callen's voice. My Callen. And I watched in horror as his eyes pleaded with mine and blood slowly began to drip from his mouth.

What had I done?

Chapter 8

Evelyn

I sat on the couch in my suite unsure of what to do. After leaving Vi, we attempted to return to breakfast, but had only found an empty dining room. Guards quickly informed Griffin that the Queen had ended the meal shortly after our departure.

So instead, we walked back to the suite in silence but with Griffin holding tightly onto my hand. I felt the looks we got from passersby, and I honestly wasn't sure if it was because I was holding their betrothed prince's hand or if it was because there was visible blood on my hands and clothes. Yet, unlike our walk earlier, I couldn't bring myself to care what they were thinking, nonetheless why they were thinking it.

When we had made it back to the getting-slightly-less-creepy hall that led to the suites, Griffin suggested I go wait in the guest suite while he spoke with the Knights. So, that left me alone...still confused as all hell about what was going on. I mindlessly walked to the couch and stared at the ceiling as I plopped myself onto the cushion.

"Rough start to the day?"

I turned my head, still in a daze, to find that Katerie and Nixie had sat on either side of me. Lowering the pillow, I had unknowingly been clutching to my chest, I let out a heavy breath.

"Well, that is most certainly a yes," Nixie smiled. "Granted, you've had a lot thrown at you this morning, so it's acceptable. Isn't it just great to reunite with family?"

"Did you have any idea that you were actually related to Violet?" Katerie asked me.

I shook my head no and then glanced between the two of them.

"What is it?" Nixie asked. "Something is wrong."

"I'm not really sure that's all there is between Vi and I," I began. "Something Hale said in Vi's room has my brain spinning."

"What do you mean?" Katerie asked.

They were both watching me with wide eyes. I wanted to talk to them about this. They had more than proved themselves to be trustworthy in my eyes. Even though Katerie had been an unwilling spy for Hale, I trusted her now. But even knowing that, I wasn't sure what to tell them. Hale had to focus on my bond to Vi. But we weren't bonded. Were we?

"Never mind," I said, faking a smile. "It's nothing."

"EvelynRose," Nixie began, as she placed her hand on my knee. "You can't lie to me. My tinker magic can see right through it."

"Tinker?" I questioned.

"Remember when I told you my magic manifests in a way that allows me to fix broken things?"

"Yes."

"All magical gifts that present outside of the five families of magic are given a unique name," she continued. "Johanna has transference. You have obstruction, assuming Professor Hyperion stuck with that name. And me, I have tinker. I fix things."

"I swear," Katerie sighed. "Everyone in this group has cool magic but me."

"Really?" I questioned, looking back at her. "You're a

vital part of our group."

"Why? Because I'm new enough to magic that I couldn't even keep a Mind out of my head. Or because I have so little skill that I had to get a boost to help you save Nixie in the first place. I'm not exactly ranking in the top asset category of this group. Especially not with all of you to compete with. I'm the liability on this team. The weak link. I know that."

Was she being serious right now? She really saw herself as something that was holding us back. Like she wasn't worth us making her a part of this. Sure, she was young, but she was only a year younger than me. And yeah, only one family had chosen her, but I was just as new to magic as she was. I couldn't help but wonder if this was how Vi felt when I was constantly harking on myself.

"Girl, you need to believe in yourself a little more than that," I smiled.

"I concur!" said a voice from the door.

Johanna came waltzing in at that moment carrying a large garment bag and a small handbag.

"And, might I add," she continued, "that had it not been for you, Nixie would be dead. Transference only allows a boost to the magic that already exists within the magical it is used on. I can't give you magic that you didn't already have within you."

"You're saying I could do that magic without you?" Katerie clarified.

"I'm saying the magic is there. Magic can take years of practice," Joahnna said, as she walked into my room and placed the bags on my bed. "But yes. With hard work and practice, you can do that and probably a lot more."

Katerie was almost blushing now and Nixie let out a sigh of relief like she had been waiting for Katerie to accept her magic for a long time. As happy as I was for Katerie to finally have some faith in herself, I was more concerned right now with what Johanna was doing putting bags in my room.

"What are you up to?" I asked her.

"Me? Whatever do you mean?" she joked.

"Johanna...I know you are up to something. What's in the bag?"

"Well, that's our cue to go!" Nixie sang, hopping up. "Katerie, let's go snatch up Danny boy and Nicky for some lunch. We will finish this chat with EvelynRose later."

As they left the room, Katerie chuckled while shaking her head and I exchanged skeptical looks with Johanna.

"Danny boy?" I questioned through a laugh.

"I don't think I'll be able to look at *Nicky* ever again," Johanna giggled.

"Alright," I said, laughing it off. "Back to the real issue. What's in the bag?"

"Right, that," she said, turning back toward my door.

I got up and followed her into my room. She unzipped the garment bag she had thrown onto my bed and pulled out a couple pairs of tight looking pants, a few different polo shirts and two pairs of knee-high boots.

"What is all this for?"

"We are going on a double date," she explained, laying out the clothes.

"I'm sorry?" I questioned, shaking my head. "You're gonna have to run that by me again. Did you say double date?"

"I sure did," she confirmed. "Now, I think you should go with the red polo and black pants. I mean I have a green one, but you always wear green. I say, mix it up with the red."

"Johanna, I'm not going on a date right now," I protested. "My dead dad just showed up, I just had to save my best friend from bleeding out while in a coma, and...let's just say I have a family reunion that really needs to happen."

"This invitation is not optional," she corrected me. "We are going on this date whether you want to or not. And don't lie to me. I know you want to."

"I do," I agreed. "I told Griffin just this morning that I do. But when he said tonight, I had thought that was an exaggeration. Johanna, I want to, but..."

"Then don't waste time trying to get out of it. Griffin wants to take you somewhere special, and he wants extra protection to do it. So, we opted for a double date. The rest of the Knights, including Callen, will stay behind to keep everyone here safe."

I continued to watch her move around the clothes. I still wasn't sold on this idea, and I got the feeling she clearly knew that.

"Everyone here will be fine. And you — and I for that matter — deserve this. It's just one evening, Evelyn. One evening. We will be back before you know it."

She was right about that. Well, right about a few things. We did both deserve a night off. And I could think of a million things that would be worse than spending an entire evening with the man I was realizing I was in love with and two of my best friends. Not to mention that I really did want to. I hadn't lied to Griffin about that earlier this morning. I wanted to go on a date with him. I wanted our relationship to just be normal for five minutes…or an hour, if we got the chance.

"Before you let out that defeated breath I know you are holding in," Johanna began, "I need to know which pants you want. Because I'm thinking I'd like to wear the tan with the light blue top."

"I think the black and red is a great idea for me," I smiled, as I lifted the red shirt. "Maybe it is time to mix it up a bit."

She smiled so wide that I couldn't help but chuckle a little. She scooped up her outfit and escaped into her own room across the suite. I quickly walked into my bathroom and began to wash Vi's blood off my hands. It was dry now and stubborn to get off, but the more I scrubbed, the more it began to fade.

I still couldn't fathom that I had my best friend's blood on my hands, and I was washing it off to go on a date…what the hell was going on with me?

Johanna started shouting from across the suite about how I should do my hair and I realized I didn't have time to question my priorities right now. Yet, as I slipped into the clothes Johanna had brought for me, Hale's parting words echoed in my mind.

"You need to channel your relationship with Violet. Your bond to her."

The tone of his voice was what stood out more than the words themselves. He wasn't just talking about my friendship with her...he had been quite precise in his use of the word *bond*.

As I slipped on the jeans, thoughts raced through my mind, my fingers brushed along the light patch of skin I had at the top of my left hip. And then, like a damn freight train, it hit me.

Bursting out of my room, I practically ran over Johanna.

"Whoa girl! Where's the fire?"

"I'm so sorry, but I have to go."

"Go? Go where? Eveyln, what's going on?"

"I have to get to the library and then talk to Hale."

"What about our date?"

"I just need a couple hours," I insisted, as I opened the suite door. "Please let Griffin know I only need a couple hours and then I think I will finally have an answer."

Before she could respond, I was out the door and racing to the library. I wondered if that was one of the reasons Vi had been in the library so often. Had she come to the same conclusion? The further down the halls I raced, I wondered if Lucas knew. If I was right, then he had to...right?

First, I needed proof. I needed something to tell me I wasn't crazy and then I needed Hale to tell me the truth about what he knew. A feeling deep in my gut told me that answer was in the library.

Chapter 9

Evelyn

As I burst through the door to the library, the various library staff working inside all looked at me like I had waltzed into a wedding shouting objections. A few of the older librarians scoffed at me, but I didn't have time to care about library etiquette.

"Excuse me," I said breathlessly. "Where are your books on Fear magic?"

The older woman's eyes narrowed and the irritation on her face told me everything I needed to know. When she turned away, not-so-quietly whispering about how awful it was for a Fear to be in the castle, I knew she was going to be no help and opted to just move on.

Three librarians later, I found myself growing agitated by their treatment of me and my inquiry. One of them had been kind enough to actually speak to me, but her answer had only been that *Magir would never allow such dangerous texts into its most sacred of libraries.* And of course not. I mean why would they want to be able to educate themselves against their biggest threat?

"Can't say I disagree with you."

I turned around and found a woman smiling at me as she restocked a bookshelf. She was younger than the others by several decades, but I still would have guessed was in her mid-forties. She had shoulder length auburn colored hair and blue eyes.

"Did I actually speak out loud?" I asked. "Because I had definitely meant for that to stay in my head."

"You didn't have to," she said, placing a book down on the cart beside her and smiling at me again. "I'm a mind magical and being in here seems to amplify my magic. I've heard your poor mind racing for the last ten minutes."

"Can you help me?" I asked, slightly deterred by wanting to ask about how a library enhanced her magic, but I remained focused. "Are there *any* books in here on Fear magic?"

"Unfortunately, no," she shook her head. "But there are a few history books near the top of the library that may help you."

"I'll take whatever you have to offer," I replied eagerly. "Thank you."

She walked me deep into the library, toward a stairwell I didn't even realize was there. Silently I followed her up several flights of stairs before she finally spoke.

"I do agree with your reasoning for needing texts on Fear magic here," she offered.

"I really had meant for that to be a private thought," I reiterated. "But I appreciate that you found merit in it."

"More than merit," she corrected. "Truth is, the angst a Magirian has toward all Fear magic is ingrained at a very young age. And while it may have been warranted long ago, times change. And to restrict an entire realm from certain knowledge…it's just preposterous."

"You don't think Fear magic should be banned from Magir?"

From the first moment I arrived in Magir, nearly every Magirian had the same outlook on Fear magicals. They didn't belong here. But there was something about how this woman spoke that maybe not everyone felt that way.

"In a sense," she explained. "If the stone choses you, then you have every right to practice and wield its magic. At that point, the stone has deemed you worthy of the power it comes with. But being a self-taught Fear magical, now that is an outrageous idea and that should be prohibited to all."

"I can understand…"

"What really gets to me though," she interrupted, "is that our current regime thinks they have the right to actually control what the Magirian people learn about. To restrict an entire people from even reading a historical text just because Fear magic is mentioned. It's absurd! Laughable even!"

We stopped after the seventh flight of stairs and she opened a door, standing aside for me to walk past her.

"The book you seek is on self 737, just down this row," she directed. "I should be getting back to my restocking. I do apologize if I have spoken out of turn. I know you have a… relationship with our prince. I don't wish to speak ill of him."

"I didn't think that at all," I assured her. "I appreciate your honesty and admire your passion for these books. I can relate to that."

"Not just books. Learning. Life is an ever expanding chance to learn new things. Whether that be through books such as these, through travel or other experiences. We are creatures that are constantly learning, and we can't let history dictate how we move forward, or we will never grow."

"What's your name?"

"I do apologize," she said with a sudden bow of her head. "Kimberly Joy. Mind magical and Royal Library Aid."

"Well, Kimberly, I know it may not be my place, but I think your knowledge and passions would make you an ideal teacher in the Magirian grade school or maybe even at Woodburn Rose."

The woman met my eyes and then she gave a long glance around the library.

"I appreciate your kindness," she said. "Perhaps someday. I will be downstairs should you need further assistance."

"Thank you."

She slipped out the door and I couldn't help but smile as I moved down the shelves in search of 737. Kimberly was a gem of a magical being. She was real. Said what she thought, even if she did apologize in fear of insulting the royal family. But she had passions, and strong beliefs. Ones that she wasn't afraid to share. Even when some of those were regarding magic she knew I possessed. It was refreshing and inspiring. At least I knew that some Magirians didn't completely despise me just because of my magic or lineage.

I froze when I made it to the shelf that should have been marked 737. The shelves went from a fully stocked 736 to fully stocked 738. In between them, where a shelf should have been, was a statue sunk into the wall. This couldn't have been where Kimberly had meant to send me. I looked over the railing and wasn't able to make out where she had gone.

Turning back to the statue, I found myself staring at the bust of a man who looked oddly familiar. Even in statue form, his eyes were so incredibly kind. There were deep lines on his face that told me he had a stern side too, but they didn't take away from the warmth seeing his face brought to me. Then it came to me.

"Thomas," I whispered.

I looked all around for a plate or tag that would identify the statue and saw nothing. But I was certain. The longer I looked at the statue, the more positive I was that it was him. Thomas was the sweet man that came to me outside of Woodburn Rose. He had appeared again to help Griffin when they were looking for me, and to Vi after I pushed them out of the park. At the time, I had no idea who he actually was, but I arrived in Magir, I learned that he was my grandfather.

But that didn't explain why his statue was here. Yes, he kept showing up whenever I needed direction. Whenever any of us did...but this...this didn't make sense. And how did Kimberly know to lead me here?

Reaching for the statue, I placed my hand against my grandfather's cheek. I wondered if he knew he had met both his granddaughters that day. And what it would have been like to have grown close to him. Having a grandparent to tell us our father's childhood stories...

Lost in thought, I hadn't noticed that my hand was growing hot against the mental. But when suddenly it felt like someone had lit my palm on fire, I was pulled from my wandering thoughts. I yanked back my hand and saw the statue's eyes glowing a warm orange. Then there was a soft clicking sound, and the glow began to fade.

Swiveling my head around, I looked for the source of the sound...a secret door or something...but I saw nothing. It wouldn't have surprised me if there had been a hidden room in this library. Most of Magir felt like a medieval Indiana Jones movie in that sense.

Wondering if the statue was still warm to the touch, I extended my hand. The second my fingertips touched the, now ice cold, statue, I felt my body being yanked forward and the entire room went dark.

I felt like I was going to be sick when the world around me became visible. My fingers were still pressed gently against my grandfather's statue, but as I slowly looked over my shoulder, I realized that I was in some sort of study.

"Remarkable, isn't it?"

Distracted by the side of the study I was looking at, I hadn't even noticed one of the armchairs by the small fireplace was occupied. But sure enough, Hale was now peering around the side of the chair at me.

"I should have known the room would let you in too," he said, turning back toward the fireplace.

"Where are we?" I asked. "Is this some sort of trick?"

"Always so suspicious of others' intentions. I really would have thought after I helped you save Nixie's life, you'd be a little less apprehensive towards me. Not to mention what I did for your own cousin."

There was no denying that. While I was still quite suspicious of Hale, he seemed to know things we didn't. Whether that was good or not, was yet to be determined. But for now, I had to at least give him the benefit of the doubt. And while I wanted to believe I was doing that out of selfish desire to access the information he had, there was something about Hale that I knew wasn't all that bad.

"You're right," I conceded, as I took the seat beside him.

He looked tired. More exhausted than he had been at breakfast or when we had helped Violet.

"Are you alright?"

"Are you concerned about me, Evelyn?"

There was a tone behind his comment that neared flirtation and I couldn't help but roll my eyes.

"I am fine," he said through a chuckle. "Investigating what is plaguing Violet has me using a lot of magic these days. As I had explained to you in class, our magic behaves more like a battery that needs to be recharged."

"And your batteries are running low?"

"Even the strongest of magicals need rest."

I rolled my eyes again and he laughed softly as he placed his book onto the table beside him. He grabbed a coffee cup and took a few sips as he watched the small flames dancing in the fire.

"So, what exactly is this place?"

"It's a private study."

"Hidden behind a statue of my grandfather?"

"Well, your grandfather, from what I've been able to discover, was an interesting man," Hale explained.

"What does that mean?"

"When your father vanished with Morana, your grandfather needed a place to study Fear magic."

"Why would he do that? He was a councilman. Seems risky with how Magirians feel about Fears."

"I won't get into it with you about what was wrong with the statement you just made," he shook his head. "Regardless of the *risk*, he was studying Fear magic. I found several texts in here when the room revealed itself to me. From the journal I discovered…"

"You found his journal?"

"If you would let me finish. From the side notes on this journal, which he may have been reading, he was definitely trying to understand the Fears."

"So, if this place was my grandfather's secret, then why did it let you in?"

"Because I don't think it was ever really his."

My look of confusion must have been enough because he shook his head a little and placed his coffee back down before turning to directly face me.

"This hidden room is filled with information on a magic that nobody in Magir is supposed to be practicing or even learning about. Yet here is it. It exists. I think this room presented itself to your grandfather when he came looking. It somehow deemed him worthy of the information. I never really spoke with him, but I saw the respect he commanded. It doesn't surprise me that the magic of this place saw him as an equal."

"So, you're saying this room is a secret room that only those interested in or chosen by Fear can access?"

"It's more than that," he assessed. "Just because the other families are frightened by the Fears, doesn't mean that they aren't interested. Many non-Fears have tried to study their magic, and few have even wished to practice it. Yet, this room never revealed itself to them."

"Not everyone has access to it either."

"While that is true, and it is somewhere that most wouldn't look, I think that is also part of the acceptance. If you really want to know Fear, and want to know it for the right reasons, the room will reveal itself to you. But you also have to have the drive to come looking for it."

"Makes sense," I agreed. "But why is there a statue of my grandfather outside? Why is that the key to get in? Did he create this place?"

"I don't think so. Some of the notes I found predate your grandfather by many years. And I had heard that the statue had actually been commissioned by one of the library aids. Fought like hell to get it in too."

"Kimberly," I whispered to myself.

"Kim Joy?" he questioned. "It definitely could have been her. I take it she brought you up here?"

Suddenly, I felt a twinge of pain in my chest and for a moment it felt like I couldn't bring in any air.

"Evey...I've killed him. I think I've actually killed him."

Violet's voice echoed in my mind, and I couldn't think straight. Hale's eyes were narrowing on me, and I wondered if his Mind allowed him to hear Violet too.

"You've got to get me out of here...please, Evey."

Once I was finally able to inhale a breath, I took in a huge gasp of air, followed by a series of pants. Hale had risen from his seat now and was leaning over my chair. There was curiosity in his eyes, but there was also worry. Like he was genuinely concerned for my wellbeing.

"Evelyn, are you alright?"

"I'm fine," I whispered through heavy breaths. "You said earlier to rely on my *bond* to Violet. What did you mean by that?"

His back straightened and he moved toward one of the small desks on the far side of the room.

"Hale, what aren't you telling me?" I asked, rising from my chair.

He didn't speak at first, just continued to flip through books, even tossing a few of them to the side. Right as I was about to push him again, he whipped around, turning the book in his hands so that I could see it.

"Can you read this?"

I kept my gaze on him for a few moments before I

shifted to focus on the book he was holding. For a moment, the language was foreign to me. Knowing how magical texts reveal themselves, I reached out and grabbed the book from Hale. My fingers brushed against his and he pulled his hands as he took a small step back.

Trying not to read into his brash movement, I continued to focus on the book. My eyes narrowed as I took a deep breath, channeling as much of my magic as I could. Once the words began to reveal themselves, my eyes widened.

Shadow Twins

"What the hell is this?" I asked.

"You can read it?" he asked, without answering me and with a surprisingly shocked tone.

"Yes, I can read it," I replied, slightly annoyed. "What is this?"

"It's a Fear book."

"A Fear book? Hale, I'm confused. What is a Shadow Twin and what does this have to do with Fear magic? And how does this help Violet?"

"That Fear book won't reveal its knowledge to just anyone," he explained. "I've taken this book to several, trusted Fears, and nobody could read it."

"If you're going to tell me my magic is special, you're going to have to get in line."

His sly grin formed on his lips, and he took the book out of my hands. Turning it towards me, I saw that the language had reverted back, and I was no longer able to read the intricate writing on the page.

"It is indeed special, but this isn't just yours." He closed the book and set it back on the table before turning about and leaning against it. "Do you have a birthmark?"

"How did you..."

"Does Violet have the same one?"

"No...sort of," I stammered. "We've always thought it

was funny, but where she has a birthmark, I have a pale patch on my skin. It doesn't burn or tan, it's always a fair white."

"Interesting," he mused. "I meant what I said before. That you and Violet are bonded to one another. But I need the knowledge that this book explains."

"Can it wake her up?"

"I believe it can, but it's going to require you to give me something. Something that I know is going to be hard for you to give up."

"What is that?"

"I need a couple drops of your blood."

The request didn't overtly shock me, but it made me feel uneasy. It had been emphasized to me from the moment my stone ceremony was complete, that my magic...my blood was special. Giving it to Hale, or to anyone, was risky. And I wasn't sure I could trust him, despite that tiny voice in the back of my head saying that I could...I just wasn't confident in that. And yet, in the few seconds it took me to question his intentions...I decided there was far more at stake here.

"You have to promise me you will save her."

An unrecognizable look of sympathy crossed his face for the briefest second before he nodded. Walking over to a bookshelf, I pulled down a small jar holding a tealight candle.

Dumping the candle onto the ground and blowing the dust out of the jar, I walked back over toward the fireplace. Squeezing the fire poker with one hand and yanking it down with the other, I sliced into my hand, letting the blood drip into the jar. After a couple tablespoons of blood had pooled, I focused my Healing magic and watched as my skin slowly began to reconnect.

With as much confidence as I could muster, I marched the jar over to where Hale had been standing silently.

"You can trust me," he said, accepting the jar.

"Just save her. Maybe then I'll trust you."

Before he could say anything else, I walked across the room and placed my hand on my grandfather's statue. It quickly pulled me out of the room, and I swiftly made my way out of the library.

I was right...Violet and I were connected. Even if I didn't know exactly what that meant, we were. While I had hoped to find out more by my little trip to the library...I had an answer. Something to go off of. Now it was in Hale's hands. And for some strange reason, after leaving the secret study, I had this sense he was going to stand by his word.

As I walked out of the library, I smiled at Kimberly, who returned my smile with a nod of understanding. Maybe I really wasn't in this alone...maybe I could defeat the Fears and have a life. A life that begins with a double date.

Chapter 10

Evelyn

When I came bursting back into our suite, Johanna practically launched off of the couch.

"What the hell is going on?" Johanna asked, walking towards me. "You just run out of here like a bat out of hell and then come barging back in like you've uncovered a hidden treasure vault."

Walking around the suite, I checked every room to ensure we were alone before I dove into what had happened in the library. Johanna sank back into her seat on the couch about halfway through my explanation, with an expression on her face that was unreadable.

"Well?" I questioned once I was finished.

"I mean...wow. So, you and Violet are...what did you call it? Shadow Twins?"

"Hale thinks so. But he's looking into it as we speak."

"And he needed your blood in order to do that, so you just gave him a jar of it?"

"Not really a jar," I corrected. "I mean it was in a jar, but it wasn't like it was full or anything."

"It's risky, Evelyn," she sighed. "I want to wake Violet

too but..."

"But nothing," I interrupted. "Johanna there is nothing I wouldn't risk to wake her up. Whatever she is going through is because of me. That's my Fear magic causing this. And it's killing her. I just barely saved her life earlier. I don't care if Hale takes my blood and uses it to kill me. As long as he can wake up Violet, it's a risk I'd take time-and-time again."

She pondered what I said for a moment and then slapped her hands against her thighs as she stood up.

"Well, can't argue with that," she smiled. "And I definitely can't say I'd have done it any differently."

"Thank you."

"But listen closely to this," she added, her expression going stern. "*You* are important to this realm, Evelyn. *You* are the only one who has been able to wield all five forms of magic in thousands of years, if not all of history. And *you* are my friend. I don't want to see you just giving up your life. The Knights don't trust Hale."

I tried to interject but she raised her hand and kept going.

"I realize that it may be for something that they don't fully understand, but that distrust is there. And I don't think it's going away anytime soon. You have Griffin's heart and if you are going to put your faith in Hale, you better have a damn good reason to do so because Griffin is the one who is going to suffer in that alliance. Assuming an alliance is all this is."

She stopped talking and gave her words a few minutes to sink in. From the look in her eyes, I could see that she was genuinely questioning whether or not there was something between Hale and I. And while I couldn't deny there was a connection between us, I knew it wasn't the connection I had with Griffin.

"I'm trusting him for Violet's sake," I assured her. "And I would never risk losing Griffin."

"Glad to hear it," she grinned. "Now let's finish getting you ready because Sean is getting antsy."

Johanna pulled me into her bathroom and began applying a light amount of makeup to my face. Once she was finished, she placed a headband around my head, tucking my hair inside, leaving a bun-like effect with only a few loose strands of hair left around my face.

Without even giving me a chance to approve of the design, she spritzed hair spray over my hair. She gave a few grunts of approval and then grabbed my arm, leading me out of the suite and through the palace halls.

"Oh wow," Nicholas exclaimed as we approached the front doors to the palace.

"What is it?" I questioned, suddenly second-guessing Johanna's hairstyle.

"It's nothing." He shook his head. "You ladies look great."

He smiled and kept walking down the hall as Johanna nodded to the guards who then opened the doors as commanded. It didn't make sense to me why people seemed to be so mesmerized by these outfits we wore. We weren't all dressed up or anything. This was simple horse-back riding gear. Form fitting, sure — but simple, nonetheless.

Yet, as we walked down the halls, many staff members had glanced in our direction with looks of awe on their faces. At first, I thought maybe it was just shock over the fact that we would choose a time like this to go riding. But when we passed a maid who smiled and said, "you look lovely, my ladies", I knew it wasn't that.

"Are you sure these outfits are okay?" I asked Johanna, as I adjusted where my polo shirt was tucked into my pants.

"What do you think?" She winked, as she nodded in the direction of Sean and Griffin.

They were standing beside their horses in clothes that made them look like equestrian models. Each in tight fitting pants and v-neck shirts. I wasn't sure if I was blushing from the hungry look in Griffin's eyes or the desire that was suddenly flooding my veins.

"Your fashion skills never disappoint, Jo," Sean smiled, as he kissed her cheek.

"And here I thought you loved me for my combat skills," she joked, as she let him help her onto his horse.

I chuckled to myself as I watched Sean's face go a little red and then turned my gaze back to Griffin. The closer I moved to him the more I felt the magical temperature between us rising. I shyly ran my right hand down my left arm and then turned to pet Fury.

"Long time no see, Fury," I said, running my hand from his forehead to his muzzle. "Did you miss me, boy?"

Fury let out a small neigh and shook his mane.

"I'll take that as a yes."

I smiled at Fury as Griffin mounted his horse and lowered his hand to help me up behind him. Once I was settled and had tightly wrapped my arms around Griffin's waist, Fury let out another neigh and took off for the gate with Sean's horse following closely behind us.

We rode in silence for the first twenty minutes or so. The breeze began to rush over my face, and I found myself laying my head against Griffin's back to block it out a little, and to feel the warmth radiating from him. I felt him let out a heavy breath beneath my head, and then his hand gently caressed mine before returning to Fury's bridle.

When we slowed a little, I lifted my head and took in the scene around me. Magir truly was a beautiful place. There was something about it that made even the trees even more mesmerizing than the non-magical realm. Everything from the trees to the way the sun shined behind the clouds, was absolutely breathtaking.

At this point I didn't know how long we had been riding. Griffin and I still hadn't said a word to each other. I just held onto him tightly and he occasionally ran his hand across my arm or gripped my hand for a second. But still no words. It was amazing to me how close I felt to him as we rode, despite our silence. The connection growing between us made me slightly exhilarated, yet nervous at the same time.

When Fury came to a stop we were beside a beautiful hillside. Sean and Johanna rode up beside us and Johanna was laughing so hard that her head was thrown back. I had a feeling they really did need this time away just as badly as Griffin and I did.

"We miss something good?" Griffin asked, as he dismounted Fury.

"Did you?" Sean asked with a confused look on his face, as he too dismounted and rounded his horse. "I guess Red's obstruction really is strong."

"I was blocking you?" I asked, as Griffin reached up and helped me off of Fury.

"I told you," he began, as he lowered me down to the ground and very close to his chest. "We use magic when our emotions are high. Usually without even noticing what we are actually doing."

"Well, with that I think Sean and I will head to the falls," Johanna declared. "We can all meet back here whenever you are done with your tour."

"Tour?" I questioned.

She winked at me and grabbed Sean's hand, leading him away. I looked back at Griffin who hadn't moved from his spot in front of me.

"Is that what this date is?" I asked. "A tour?"

"And a chance for us to be alone together," he replied with a heavy breath.

"If I remember right, we were alone in your room. What makes this different?"

"There aren't six Knights on the other side of my door," he laughed.

I loved the sparkle that gleamed his silver eyes when he let out his real laugh. His smile alone was enough to melt my insides, but that look in his eyes when he was truly happy made my mouth go dry.

"So, where are we?" I asked, turning away from him and

moving around Fury.

"This is the Eastern border of Magir," he said, returning to my side and interlacing our hands.

"Wait," I said, turning to him. "If this is the border of Magir, then what is across the river?"

He chuckled a little to himself and moved us closer to the hillside. Once we were at the top of the hill he stopped and dropped my hand.

"From here you can see all of Magir," he explained, as he turned me to face the palace that looked like a speck on a map. "You can see the woods, the western border, which is where we believe the entrance to the Dark Woods is, and if you look this way," — he spun me again — "you can see into the next realm."

"So, there is another realm within Magir?" I asked.

"Sort of," he smiled at me. "Magir and that realm have a veil between them. It's no different than the veil we used to get into Magir from the outside realm."

"What's it called?"

"Fantazi. I'll take you to visit there one day. It's almost as beautiful as Magir. And if you think the magic here is hard to believe, Fantazi will blow your mind."

"What do you mean?"

"There is more to magic than the five families that created our realm. There are creatures there that you only thought were part of your imagination."

"Wait! So, were those beasts in the woods that helped us...were they creatures from Fantazi?"

"No," he said with a strange smile. "Those...those are the only creature of their kind that exist in Magir."

"Where'd they come from then?" I asked. "How did they know to help us? How did you know we could trust them?"

"I trust them with my life," he explained, his face contorting a little.

There was something about this topic that made it seem like he was having a tough time being honest with me. Not

80

that I thought he was intentionally trying to lie to me, but it seemed like every time he started to speak, he was almost in pain. Just like Sean had been when we tried to talk in the palace garden.

"Is there a Knight rule that makes it so you can't share certain things with me? Are Knightly secrets truly only for Knights?" I bluntly asked.

"I had a feeling you'd figure that out eventually," he chuckled. "But yes. There are secrets that come with being a Knight. We are only allowed to share them with certain people. It's a sacrifice we all make to become a Knight. I've never intentionally shut you out, E. There's a lot of things I haven't been able to share with you. Not because I don't want, I just can't. There are rules in magic that have prevented me from sharing everything I want to."

"But you can kind of share them now?" I asked. "Why?"

"Let's ease into that," he grinned.

I raised an eyebrow at him skeptically. I wanted to know what he was talking about, but before I could argue, he grabbed my hand and led me in the opposite direction that Sean and Johanna had went.

We walked a little way down a hill where I saw a beautiful picnic blanket laid out on the grass. The closer we got I could see candles, flowers, bottles of amber liquid and a picnic basket.

"Wow," I sighed.

"Too much for a first date?"

I looked over at him and he looked genuinely nervous.

"Nobody has even done anything like this for me," I smiled. "It's amazing."

"I took you for more of a picnic girl versus the fancy dinner type," he said, lowering me on to the blanket and taking a seat opposite me.

"You'd be right about that," I laughed. "Fancy dinners are great on occasion, but I'd rather do this every night for the rest of my life."

I hadn't meant for that to come out with such finality, but it did. My God...I was putting my foot in my mouth again. You'd think I'd have learned by now how to not pressure a guy too soon...but yet here I was. I was hopeless when it came to dating.

"You think you'd be happy here in Magir?" Griffin asked, as he opened the basket, taking out some grapes, cheese and crackers. "Permanently?"

"I mean...I guess I'd have to be here for more days like this," I shrugged. "This makes me love it here. But most of the memories here so far aren't as great as this."

I instinctively looked down at my lap and fiddled with my fingers. The image of Auntie Saraya pinned to that tree flashed in my mind and I physically shook my head to block the image.

"We will take care of the Fears," Griffin assured me, as he grabbed my hands and brought me back to reality. "It may not seem like it now, but I think you will be happy here."

"Happy with you?"

I lifted my gaze and met his silver eyes. He flashed a smile and pulled his hand back.

"If that's what you wanted."

"Everyone seems very concerned with what I want," I sighed, opening my drink. "I wish someone would be honest with me about what it is they want for once."

I sipped my drink and saw his eyes follow the bottle to my lips and linger as I licked the leftover amber liquid from them.

"Mmm. You always know my favorite things," I smiled.

I had put pressure on him again and that wasn't what I wanted out of today. Sure, I wanted him to spit out his feelings, in the same way I knew I needed to. But I wanted this to be a date with us getting to know each other too. Really getting to know each other.

"I won't lie to you," I said, as I put down my drink and his gaze finally broke away from my lips. "I haven't been on many first dates that weren't more than a quick dinner. Several didn't even last through the meal."

"Really?" He asked, seeming genuinely surprised. "I mean, I know you told Sean you used to think of yourself as an outcast, but..."

"Wait," I interrupted. "Sean told you that?"

"He didn't physically tell me, E," he said, plopping another grape into his mouth. "But Knights don't really have secrets from one another, remember? As soon as he was away from you, I knew everything you talked about."

"Oh..."

I remembered that conversation. That was when I was convinced Griffin was avoiding me. The day that Sean had started to walk me home and tried to convince me that Griffin was a good person. But I wasn't having it. As the memory flooded back, Sean's reaction to Michael's name flashed in my mind.

"Did you know about Michael then?" I asked. "Is that why Sean acted weird when I said his name?"

"Yes," Griffin nodded. "Violet had told Callen and I about the call she had gotten from him. That he was a Fear. The plan was to keep it between us, but Sean got the message before I could even try to block it. He is very protective over you."

"He is like the brother I never had," I smiled.

"Yeah, he's a special guy. One of a kind. I owe him more than he knows."

"Why do you say that?"

Griffin leaned back and stared up at the sky. I watched as his muscles flexed to hold up the weight of his body. The broad span of his chest began to rise and fall as he let out one sigh after the next.

"Even though Sean grew up outside of Magir, his parents told him all about my family. He always knew his parents followed a different leadership. They didn't have a president, but rather a king and queen. He knew that. As a result, they showed him pictures of all of us. Sean knew of me far before I ever knew of him."

"Well, I'd imagine that comes with the territory of being a prince," I joked.

"Yes, but Sean was different," Griffin continued, still looking at the sky. "Even though he knew who I was from the moment we met, he never treated me any different. That wasn't something I was used to. We were easy friends. Then everything happened with Johanna, and he should have had every reason to hate me. But he didn't. Instead, he became my brother in ways I never could have imagined. He never held any of it against me or blamed me for threatening his bond with her."

"Because you didn't."

"But I could have." He shook his head. "I never intended to marry Johanna. I told her that from the minute she came to me about Sean. But the king isn't an easy person to say no to. Not with something like this. But it wasn't even just everything with Johanna and Sean. It was you."

"Me?"

"With Callen wrapped up with Violet, and already helping me with every random task I threw at him, I knew Sean was the one person I could trust with you."

"I'm not sure how your other Knights would feel about that."

"You know what I mean," he retorted, shooting me a quick playful look. "I knew I could trust him with you. Not because he was already bonded to someone, but because he knew what it was like to have a person be so important that you would do anything and everything to protect them. He understood what it felt like to have that one person you would give up your life for."

I didn't know what to say to him. He just continued to stare at the sky as I tried to find my words. Words that were not going to be coming any time soon. I looked down at my lap and fiddled with my hands. Even knowing how badly I wanted a relationship with him, I couldn't bring myself to return his heartfelt sentiment.

"It's weird, isn't it?" he began. "It's weird to feel so attached to someone you barely know. I mean, to anyone outside of us, the whole thing seems crazy. Falling in love after only knowing one another for a few months. To most that doesn't happen."

"In love," I repeated, as I looked up to find his eyes on me now. "But it's magic right? Or are you saying we are a modern Romeo and Juliet? Forever in love, but forever kept apart."

"I'd be naive to think our magic doesn't play a part. But I don't think that's all of it," he said, pushing himself onto his side and reaching for my hand. "Remember the first night I walked you to your cottage at WRA?"

"Of course," I answered softly. "You said you were going to teach me about fate."

"And you told me that you didn't believe in fate because you didn't want a cosmic plan controlling your life. Well, I hate to say it and you may not believe me, but I think you and I were meant to meet."

"Why do you think that?"

"I was dreaming of you long before I met you, EvelynRose. Not in the sense of dreaming of the woman you are. But actually you. I've been dreaming of you my entire life."

At that moment I remembered what Johanna had said to Violet and I. She said that Griffin had been having visions of his dream girl since they were kids. She had told me to talk to him about it, but I never had. Until now, I had actually completely forgotten about it.

"Johanna told me," I choked out. "She told me that you had been having visions of your dream girl since you were a child."

"I wouldn't say a child," he chuckled. "I was about fourteen when I first saw her face in my dreams. It was sporadic. I didn't dream of her every night. But whenever I was stressed, which admittedly was frequently, I dreamt of her."

"And this is the girl you've been in love with?" I asked.

"She had always been the one person who was consistently in my life. Even my mother was not in my life as much as this mystery girl. But it wasn't constant until a year ago."

"What changed?"

"I became a Knight."

"Wait! You've only been a Knight for a year?"

I watched as his brows quickly rise. He looked at me genuinely surprised by my blatant shock.

"Yes. When a Magirian becomes a Knight, it is only because the Knights before them have fallen or are incapable of performing the magic being a Knight requires."

"So, that is why you are all so young?"

"Unfortunately, our age does explain it. The Knights that came before us all fell together. It's rare, but it happens. Even as strong as our magic is, we have a vulnerability that is easy to take advantage of."

"What do you mean?"

"When you become a Knight," he sighed, "there are rules you are bound to. You can't share things about the magic a Knight possesses. You are bound to one another in ways we also can't share. And you follow your chosen leader."

"Like you."

"Exactly. Like me. As the leader of the Knights, I can control them in ways even the *great* King Barin himself can't."

I watched as his lips curled into a smile. It must have been nice to call his father out like that. But even as I found myself slightly mesmerized by the dazzling smile on his face, my mind was racing to put together the pieces of what he was saying.

"So, something happened to the leader of the last group of Knights?"

"Yes. He was attacked. Not physically, but mentally. He was tricked into being a pawn in a test to amuse the king. But the test was far more successful than anyone could have predicted. Though I for one never trusted it. Not that my opinion has ever held weight with my father."

"It was Hale," I surmised before I even thought it through.

Maybe I was right. Maybe I wasn't. Either way, I knew Hale was involved. Griffin may not have liked him prior, and I'm sure there was a reason for that, but this was the reason for the hatred.

It made perfect sense. They may have been enemies before, but Hale must have hurt his predecessor. And that was why the rest of the Knights hated him so much too. It wasn't just Griffin. Hale had hurt all of them.

"Yes," Griffin said, standing up from his position on the blanket. "Hale always had this incessant need to impress my father. He craved the approval of King Barin more than I ever have. He began learning Fear magic in secret just to prove to the king that he was a better magical than anyone in his court."

"So, your father put him to the test?"

"It is no secret," Griffin began, "not to a single person in Magir, that my father is a cruel man. When he discovered Hale was learning Fear magic, he was furious and elated all at once. When he announced Hale's test, he demanded I be present. I protested the entire situation, of course. Hale would have risked anything to prove himself. But I knew it wasn't safe."

Griffin had his back to me now. He stared out toward Fantazi with his hands tucked away in his pockets. I took his moment of silence as my chance, and moved from my spot on the blanket so I was standing beside him.

"Hale used his Mind and the Fear magic he had learned to poison the brain of the Knight's leader. His name was Cadel and he had been my mentor since I was child. He was more of a father to me than Barin ever was. Since Callen's father died when we were young, he even stepped in to take care of him too. He was the best man I had ever known."

"So, that is why you hate Hale so much?"

He let out a heavy sigh and finally looked away from the scenery and back at me.

"The truth of it is, I have despised Hale most of my life. He was constantly vying for my father's approval and knowing the cruelty of my father, I surmised that Hale was just as bad. When he poisoned Cadel, I found myself hating him. I hated him so much I wanted him dead. Then he hurt you, and it only got worse. But..."

"But?"

"But I don't know. Hating him is exhausting. And there is something about him and...you. Something that makes me want to hug and choke him all at once. I can't explain it."

"Thank you," I said softly, as I interlaced my arm into his and laid my head on his shoulder.

"For what?"

"For being open with me."

"Eveyln," he said, stepping in front of me and placing both of his hands on my shoulders. "I'm sorry if I ever made you think that I wouldn't be open with you. I tend to be slightly guarded. But I can promise you that I will always be open with you. You were the girl in my dreams."

"Me?"

I wasn't sure exactly how we had gone from talking about the wicked side of Hale and how Griffin thought Hale and I were connected, to this. To this beautiful moment that mere months ago I would have run from.

"Remember when I told you that I couldn't resist talking to you at the resort because you were both interesting and intriguing?"

I nodded as he wrapped his arms around me and pulled me tight against his chest.

"It wasn't just because you were a magical that I couldn't sense. It was your eyes."

"My eyes?"

All my life I had been told that my green eyes were distracting. Violet had told me it was a sign of my sheer beauty. Auntie Saraya had always looked at them with longing and I knew it was because I had inherited them from my father.

Either way, I always saw them as both my best and worst features.

"The eyes of the woman who had been invading my dreams for years. The woman who, especially in this last year, had brought me so much peace and comfort, without ever speaking a word. I knew I had to get to know you because you had her eyes."

The loving look he was giving me made my throat go uncomfortably dry and my lips slowly parted like I was going to speak. After waiting a few seconds though, we both knew those words were never coming. Not that I would have known what to say in the first place.

"I told you I would teach you about fate because I knew you were meant for me. *You* have always been my dream."

Before I could even react, his lips were pressed against mine and I was rushed with the warm sensation that I had come to know as our magic moving fluidly within each other's bodies. But there was something different about this. It was intoxicating—as it always was—but this time the heat wasn't making me dizzy. I didn't feel sick, or like I was going to lose control from the overload. I felt...at peace. I felt...loved.

When he pulled away from me, I knew that's what it was. I loved Auntie Saraya and Violet, so I always expected that the feeling of a romantic love would be similar, but more enhanced. It wasn't. As I looked back at him, it wasn't just that I cared for him deeply enough that I would have given anything for him, but I would give anything to *be* with him. I knew what it felt like to be apart, and I knew I never wanted that again. I wanted to grow with him. Not just in age, but as people. I wanted to grow in our own ways, but also together as one. Violet was right—like she normally was—Griffin was my person. He had always been my person.

"I love you."

The words left my lips before I could allow my brain to stop them.

"I'm sorry it took me so long to admit that," I added.

"I've always kept my heart a little over guarded."

"Evelyn," he smiled, as he tucked a loose hair behind my ear, "I don't care how long it takes us to get where we are going. As long as my journey includes you, it's the only adventure I want to be on."

And this time it was me that leaned in and kissed him.

I had never been the type to be romantic or mushy when it came to the idea of love. Feeling special was important, but I didn't need the constant gratification that came from being someone's *true love*. Yet this version of love I felt now...I never wanted it to end. I wanted him to always say sweet things to me, and to push my buttons. I wanted him to surprise me with picnics and laugh at my little quirks. I wanted us to be constantly learning new things about each other. *This* was what real love feels like. And I never wanted to let it go.

"Alright, love birds!" Johanna's voice broke through. "We should start heading back now!"

"Yeah!" Sean shouted. "Plus, beds are more comfortable than grass!"

I pulled away from Griffin and I laughed a little as Sean let out a groan that told me Johanna had just smacked him for his humorous quip.

"They're right," I agreed, as I interlaced our hands. "As much as I want to stay, we should be getting back."

"We have forever to be together," he grinned. "And forever can spare just a moment."

We walked silently, as we headed to where we had left Fury. Both of us were smiling like school kids and stealing looks at each other. As if we couldn't smile any bigger, our grins always seemed to grow when one of us caught the eye of the other. God, I was glad Violet wasn't here to give me her *I told you so* speech.

When we made it back to Fury, we found Sean and Johanna sitting impatiently on Sean's horse. Griffin and I mounted Fury and the two horses sped off through the fields of Magir, back towards the palace gates.

Chapter 11

Griffin

The sun had almost completely set by the time the palace was in view. As the horses approached the village grounds, I noticed that lanterns and sparkling garlands now decorated the village square. The Magirian people had flooded the streets and were dancing as a small band blared music throughout the square. With the excitement of the last several days, I had forgotten what time of year it was.

"What's going on?" Evelyn asked.

"It's the Festival of the Stars," Johanna explained.

"A Magirian version of a New Year's celebration," Sean added. "But this celebration lasts an entire week."

"A week? We only get one night."

"Would you like to join them?" I asked her.

"Are you sure?" she asked back. "It's already getting late."

Fury suddenly halted and so did Sean's horse. He let out a small whinny and Griffin chuckled as he dismounted.

"Looks like someone thinks we're staying," I said, helping her down.

"Either that or we're walking back to the palace," Sean

added.

Grabbing onto her hand, I led her towards the center of town where the people would normally congregate for the celebration. The music was vibrant and every Magirian there seemed to be thoroughly enjoying themselves. There were men and women dancing their hearts out, while others stood around tables of food laughing, and children ran all around playing what appeared to be various games of tag.

Before she even had a chance to take it all in, Johanna pulled her out of my grasp and into the sea of dancing Magirians. As Jo pulled her further in, I could hear Evelyn trying to explain she wasn't a great dancer, but Jo wasn't having it. She was holding E by the arm, spinning her around to the traditional Magirian Dance of the Stars. Around them people clapped or danced along, and I couldn't stop myself from smiling as I watched E laughing, smiling, and looking so incredibly ungraceful, it was nearing comical.

"She truly can't dance," Sean joked beside me.

"For the daughter of a councilman, Jo's not exactly winning any contests either, though," I mocked in return.

"Red does look happy though," Sean admitted. "It's nice to see her let her hair down."

The fun-filled music faded to a stop before shifting to soft sounding violins that began to play a graceful tune. Couples began to take the place of the group that had been dancing before and Sean cleared his throat beside me.

"I would go ask her to dance before someone else does," he advised.

Still slightly spellbound, I nodded and began to move toward where E and Jo had been dancing. Sean was just behind me as we approached them and heard a few other gentlemen asking them to dance.

"I'm sorry I..."

"Their dance cards are full," I instructed.

Evelyn and Johanna both turned around to face Sean and I. Part of me had expected them to be relieved to not have to turn down the other men, but Johanna just shook her head and Evelyn's eyebrows went up with an attitude I hadn't been on this side of.

"Smooth," Sean whispered, as he held out a hand to Johanna. "May I?"

She took his hand and they slowly danced away from where I stood with Evelyn.

"Would you like to dance?"

"I'm sorry it appears my dance card is full," she sassed.

"It is," I agreed. "Your dance card is forever filled up with only my name."

She rolled her eyes and accepted my hand. Pulling her close, we swayed to the music. I heard the whispers of the people around us, but I couldn't bring myself to care anymore. I had made it clear by now that I had zero intentions of following through with my father's betrothal. But it was time the Magirian's saw how certain I was about E.

"I hadn't meant to seem controlling with your other suitors," I finally said. "I am slightly selfish when it comes to you."

"Slightly?" she mocked. "I wanted to dance with you, Griffin. Just next time let me be the one to turn them away. Even though I am fairly certain they were asking Jo."

"You seriously don't know how amazing you are do you?" I asked, pulling her closer to me.

She let out a heavy breath and I spun her out as the music demanded, before pulling her tightly back to my chest.

"Griffin, I do have something I need to talk with you about."

The tone in her voice had shifted. She sounded both nervous and maybe even scared.

"You can talk to me about anything, E."

"When I asked that you give us an extra hour to get ready," she began. "I went in search of information on Violet, but I ended up running into Hale."

I couldn't stop my body's natural reaction to his name.

My muscles tensed and my jaw tightened instinctively upon hearing his name.

"It wasn't like I intentionally went to go find him," she defended.

"Was he helpful?" I inquired.

The tone in my voice was sterner than I had intended, and I found myself looking down at Evelyn, almost apologetic.

"I know you don't trust him, but he was helpful. Or...I think he was."

The music stopped and I sighed.

"Evelyn, wait," I pleaded.

Her face shifted to worry, and I grabbed her hand, leading us away from the crowd of people.

She said nothing as we walked, but I could feel her heart racing. I felt awful knowing my response was causing her distress, but this wasn't a conversation I wanted to have in front of my people.

I finally stopped, not far from the gates of the palace, and turned to face her.

"I'm sorry," she said before I could speak. "I swear I wasn't intentionally seeking him out. He just happened to be in the secret room and then he had this book and..."

"Evelyn," I interrupted. "I'm not upset with you."

"You aren't?" she questioned. "Then why did you just sweep me away from everyone?"

"I am a prince to those people back there," I explained. "I want to be a partner to you and speak freely, but I can't always do that when it is on subjects like Hale. They see me as a person, but not a person who openly discusses matters such as Hale Reign in public."

"Oh...I suppose that makes sense. Sorry I didn't..."

"E, please stop apologizing," I interjected again. "Tell me what happened."

"Well," she said and took a deep breath in. "I went to the library and met this super great woman named Kimberly, who led me to a part of the library that may have Fear related texts.

But when I got where she had instructed me to go, I found a statue of my grandfather. The statue was incredibly hot to the touch and then all of a sudden it pulled me inside and revealed a secret room. Inside the room I found books upon books of Fear magic, and also Hale. Then Hale showed me this book that talked about Shadow Twins and said he could use the book's knowledge to wake up Violet but that he needed my blood to understand it. So, I gave him some of my blood on the promise that he would wake Vi and I don't know why but I think he is genuinely on our side here and is going to be able to save her."

She rattled off the story so quickly, it almost felt like for a second, I was talking to Violet. But after she was finished, she stared at me in the same way she had when we healed her ribs after Rosebud. She was scared. Scared that somehow, I would see this as a flaw in her. And as much I doubted, I would ever trust Hale, I couldn't live with myself if she didn't realize that to me, she was infallible.

"EvelynRose Archer," I began, gently grabbing her by the shoulders. "I realize that in the past, you speaking your mind and doing what you thought was right, wasn't taken well by the men you let in. But I can promise you, I am not one of those men. And while I do think we need to discuss more about you giving Hale an actual sample of your blood, I trust your judgment.

"And as much as it pains me to say this," I continued. "There is part of me that agrees with you. I do think Hale is willing to help with Violet. Granted I think that is because of something he feels for you, and that makes my blood boil, but..."

"You think Hale has some sort of romantic feelings for me?" she blurted out.

"You don't?"

"No, I don't," she shook her head. "I think Hale feels something toward me, but I don't think it is romantic. He has told me several times that he knows you and I belong together."

96

"That's…surprising," I admitted. "But did you just say that you and I belong together?"

I moved closer to her, and she smiled at me as she said, "I said Hale did."

"But you aren't denying it?"

"I'm done denying it."

Her lips merged with mine and I felt a surge of magic. She was intoxicating to be around, but kissing her was exhilarating beyond anything I had experienced. I knew there was more that we needed to discuss about what she had just revealed, but all I could think about was her.

When she pulled back, there was a drunken feeling that filled my body, slightly blurring my vision as I opened up my eyes. I was thankful, in that moment, that Evelyn had a gift to block out my fellow Knights. I was turning into quite the romantic thanks to this woman.

"We should get back."

She interlaced our fingers on both hands and pushed up to kiss my cheek, before turning back toward the crowd. It was then that I realized part of what she had said.

"Did you say that Hale called you a Shadow Twin?"

Before she could answer though, Sean and Johanna came rushing towards us.

"Griffin, Callen has been trying to reach you," Sean quickly explained. "We need to get to Violet now. Cal says she can't wait until morning."

Chapter 12

Evelyn

As we raced back to the castle, I felt my heart thumping hard in my chest. This was my punishment for going out on a date while my best friend was lying in a hospital bed. I should have known this was going to happen. I let my focus shift. My priorities weren't where they should have been.

Once we approached the door to her room, Sean and Johanna pushed inside but Griffin stopped outside, blocking my path.

"What are you doing?" I asked. "I need to get in there."

"I know what is going through that head of yours, and this is not your fault," he assured me. "Whatever is going on beyond this door is not your doing. And we will fix it. I won't let you blame yourself."

I nodded at him, and though I knew he didn't believe for two seconds that I wasn't blaming myself, he gave a quick smile and moved aside, ushering me through the door.

Violet's bed was surrounded by people when we made our way in. There were several Healing magicals, Callen, Sean and Johanna. The lead Healing magical, Lucian, was leaning over her with his hand hovering above her chest. The look on his face was stern and a few of the other Healing magicals had flustered expressions. Clearly, nobody knew what was wrong with her.

"Cal, what's happened?" Griffin asked.

"They aren't sure," Callen explained, from Violet's side. "She started sweating and shaking again. Then a large wound opened in her side. Lucian has been healing it, but it just reopens."

"*It stabbed me.*" Violet's voice echoed in my head and from the sudden change in Callen's expression, his too. "*I love you both.*"

"Is she seriously trying to say goodbye?" I blurted out.

Lucian and the other Healing magicals turned to me, confused. Callen looked both terrified and furious at the same time. While Griffin, Sean and Johanna began to look a little somber.

Almost the same moment I took a step closer to her bed, the door to the room burst open and Hale came swiftly into the room.

"All Healing magicals are excused," Hale declared.

Lucian stopped his Healing magic and turned to speak but Griffin spoke first.

"As he instructed," Griffin agreed. "Leave us."

I was surprised by Griffin instantly going along with Hale's instructions, but didn't really have time to dig into it. Hale placed the briefcase he held in his hands on a nearby chair and pulled out the book I remembered from the secret Fear library.

"Evelyn, I need you over here," he instructed, as he flipped through the book.

"What is that?" Callen and Griffin asked in unison, while I moved beside Hale.

"It's a book on Fear magic," I explained.

"Fear magic?" Sean questioned.

"Are you saying Fear magic is the only way we can save her?" Johanna added.

"There has to be another way that doesn't involve using Fear," Callen surmised.

"And how do we even know we can trust him?" Sean asked, glaring at Hale.

"Enough."

Griffin spoke in a tone that I had never heard before, but Sean and Callen both straightened their shoulders, as if they'd been commanded to attention.

"Hale," Griffin began, "is this book going to help save Violet?"

"With Evelyn and Callen's help...yes," Hale answered.

"Then do what has to be done," Griffin commanded. "And don't make me regret trusting you with this."

Hale smirked a little, then turned his focus back to Violet.

"Callen, I need you to place a hand on her forehead and her chest," Hale instructed. "Evelyn, you need to place your hand over the wound on her side and hold onto this book as you read the inscription on this page."

Looking down at the page, I saw that it was an enchantment used to strengthen the bond between Shadow Twins.

"You're sure this will work?" I asked him.

"It has to," Callen answered in Hale's place.

"Start reading," Hale directed. "I don't think she has much time."

As I read, Hale was quietly explaining to Callen what to do. He was telling him things about connecting to his bond with Violet and his true feelings for her. That he needed to push past their magical connection and embrace their deeper emotional connection. So, as I read the passage for the second time, I tried to do the same.

I recalled when I had first met her and punched that bully in the nose. How she'd helped me clean up my bloodied hand in the bathroom before the principal called us both to his office. Then it flashed to us laughing while we made coffees for our favorite customer at our after school job. Her comforting me at the park after Michael left me bruised for the last time. Her hair blowing crazy in the car as she drove to WRA. Dancing together in the Cottonwood Resort club.

I closed my eyes, and I relished in our memories. When I suddenly felt Violet's body jerk beneath my hand, my eyes burst open just in time to see her's flutter open.

"Vi!"

The book in my hand slipped to the floor as I launched myself over the bed, holding my best friend. She groaned beneath me, and I quickly stepped back, apologizing.

Staring at her, she didn't look the same. There was something in her eyes that was different. Like she was trying to decipher if what she was seeing was real or not.

"It's okay, Violet," Hale offered. "You're awake. You're safe."

Her eyes were glued to him and then she let out a heavy breath as her eyes settled on Callen beside her.

"You're...alive," she stammered.

"Of course, I am," he said, pressing his forehead to hers. "It's you we were worried about."

"No, you don't understand," she said softly.

She shook her head and pushed Callen away gently, as she sat up in the bed. Tears began to roll down her face and I gripped her hand tightly.

"Vi, whatever happened, it wasn't real," I assured her. "You're safe. We are all safe."

The tears continued to slowly roll down her face and she clutched her side where her wound had been. I felt my own eyes beginning to well up with tears as I watched my happy-go-lucky best friend cry before me.

"I think we should give Violet and Callen a moment or two," Hale suggested. "The rest of us can return to check on you in the morning if that is alright."

Violet nodded and squeezed my hand.

"*Thank you.*"

Her voice was only in my head again, but I smiled at her. I wondered if this would be our new normal. Being able to speak through thoughts alone. I had thought it would stop when she woke up, but that didn't appear to be the case.

Sean and Johanna left the room first, followed by Griffin, Hale and I. Once we were in the hallway, Hale shut the door and loudly cleared his throat, causing Griffin and I to stop.

"This is yours."

He handed me the jar I had put my blood into. Most of it was still there, but you could tell a small amount had been used from the drops left on the rim.

"Thank you. For this, and for saving her."

"You did that," Hale corrected. "I just provided the information you needed."

"Don't be modest, Hale," Griffin argued. "It doesn't suit you."

If I hadn't witnessed their shared, albeit brief, grins, I wouldn't have believed the moment had happened.

"There is still much to be discovered," Hale finally said. "From what I was able to decipher, a pair of Shadow Twins has never been recorded. It was all a mystical prophecy until you. Though, it seems you have that effect on magic."

"Isn't that an understatement," Griffin added.

Now they were sharing witty comments...what sort of parallel universe had I entered.

"I'll see if I can uncover more," Hale said, dismissing himself. "I'll be in the study if you all require me again."

After he was out of sight, Griffin grabbed my hand and pulled it to his lips. Without speaking a word, he pulled me through the halls and back to the Knight's suite. I wasn't sure how either of us was going to get any sleep, but at least I could embrace the fact that Violet was safe.

Chapter 13

Violet

Callen sat with me in silence for what felt like hours after everyone else had left. Eventually he crawled in the bed beside me and pulled me against his chest.

I wasn't sure how to begin to tell him what I had gone through. The things I had to do to survive in that nightmare. Would he still feel the same way about me? Or was he going to hate me now that I held Fear magic?

"I could never hate you, Vi," he responded out loud, reading my thoughts.

He attempted to comfort me as he ran his hands through my hair, but I couldn't help but feel like a fraud. He didn't know what I went through in that nightmare. He didn't know what I had to do.

"Violet," he began, but I couldn't let him finish.

"But you don't know what..."

"I don't have to," he interjected. "Whatever happened, you made it through. Whatever you had to do to get through it, is irrelevant to me. I'm just glad you came back to me."

He gently lifted my chin so that I was face to face with him.

"Actually. glad is an understatement," he smiled. "I was going to die without you here beside me, Vi. And I don't care if that seems drastic to everyone else. A life without you, is not a life I want to live."

A twinge in my side made my face scrunch in pain and his eyes darted to my wound.

"Whenever you are ready to tell me about it," he began, placing a kiss on my forehead. "I am here for you."

"I killed you, Cal," I blurted out.

My gaze remained on him and to my surprise, the expression on his face didn't change at all.

"In the nightmare there were these Fear creatures," I explained. "When I finally was able to speak to Hale, he informed me they are called fiends. After I had been able to defeat a few of them…it was like they had learned from what I was doin'…like they had discovered my weaknesses."

"Fears do that, Vi," Callen offered.

"You don't get it!" I growled and forced myself to sit up beside him. "The fiends figured out what made me weak. They transformed into my father. There were thousands them and I…I killed them. I murdered creatures that looked exactly like my own father, over and over again."

"But that wasn't…"

"And then one of them changed into you," I interjected. "I was certain it was still a fiend even though it actually sounded just like you. So, I killed it. I killed the creature, and it didn't die like the others. It pleaded with me. In your voice, it begged for its life."

"Violet…"

"I held the dying version of you in my arms, Callen," I continued, tears now streaming down my face. "And when I couldn't take watching you die any longer…I…I took my own blade and stabbed myself."

"You what?"

Now his expression changed. Through the entire story he had remained calm, while being the good listener I knew him to be. But his compassion faded when he heard me admit to trying to take my own life.

"It was like somethin' had taken over my mind. I couldn't stop my hand if I'd wanted to. But I knew I couldn't live in a world that I had killed you in," I sobbed. "I...I couldn't live in a world without you."

He pulled me close to him and I cried more tears than I had in years. I wasn't this person. I was open and welcoming to my emotions, but I never imagined I'd be openly admitting to trying to end my own life.

"That's what the fiend wanted, Violet," Callen whispered to me softly. "They knew they couldn't beat you, so they forced you to harm yourself."

"They saw my weaknesses."

"No," he countered. "Don't you see what they were using against you? In this world you may not have made that same choice. Did you ever wonder why the fiends never turned into Evelyn?"

"I...I guess I never gave myself time to think about it."

"Violet, they took advantage of your caring heart," Callen surmised. "They knew you were getting through to Evelyn. And yes, she told Griffin she was hearing your voice. I had only been able to hear you a couple times, so they took advantage and used my supposed death to make you heartbroken enough to think of ending your life. Even though a part of you probably knew it was fake, they snatched the part of you that believed it and made it reality in your mind."

"How do you know this?"

"I know what Fear magic can do to a person's mind," he sighed. "You, my love, are not weak."

I sniffled against him and burrowed my head back into his chest.

"And I'm never going to leave you. Not in your dreams. Not in reality. Never. What is that saying, you're stuck to me until pigs fly."

"You're stuck to me like butter or glue," I chuckled. "Pigs

fly is somethin' entirely different."

"That's the smile I've been yearning to see," he said, kissing my forehead again. "Now, let's get some rest. I have a feeling tomorrow is going to be a big day."

*****

When I first woke up the next morning, Callen and I were curled up together, barely fitting in the small hospital bed. Lucian came rushing in, almost as if he had an alarm or a nanny cam of some kind to tell him I was awake, and insisted Callen leave while I was evaluated.

It took a bit of convincing but eventually Callen agreed to go grab me some coffee and breakfast, so that Lucian could run his tests. Tests which of course turned out to be repeatedly looking at my wounds, which had all magically healed, leaving behind small, almost invisible scars, and then taking my temperature over, and over, and over again.

By the time Callen returned, Lucian was cursing under his breath while a few of the aids snickered at the foot of my bed. After a few more expletive words, Lucian stormed out of the room, with the Healing aids tucked closely behind him.

"What did you do to him?" Callen asked, as he walked over kissing my forehead and handing me a plate with some scrambled eggs, toast and a small pastry. "I haven't seen him like that in...well...ever."

"I did nothing besides lay here fabulously as he examined me," I countered, grabbing the pastry and taking a quick bite. "This is delicious. How did I get lucky enough to find a man that brings a girl breakfast in bed?"

"Get comfortable because you have centuries of this chivalry left."

He leaned over and kissed me. Lord did it feel good to feel his lips on mine again. Add in our magic dancing and he was lucky I didn't yank him into the bed right there.

"Am I interrupting?"

Callen pulled away and turned around to reveal Lucas standing in the doorway, pushing Saraya in a wheelchair.

"I was just visiting with Sar, and she insisted I bring her to see you," he explained.

"Auntie, I'm so glad to see you!" I exclaimed. "How are you?"

"Apparently more fragile than a flower," she groaned. "They won't even let me see EvelynRose yet. Which is ridiculous!"

She yelled the last part and leaned toward the door.

"Sorry, that was for Lucian," she winked. "How are you? I'm glad to see you made it through the magical overload."

"I wouldn't quite say that I made it through. But I'm here."

"Maybe I should give you three a moment," Callen said softly in my ear. "I'll go check in with Griffin and Evelyn."

Callen left the room and Auntie Saraya instructed Lucas to push her wheelchair to the edge of my bed. I sat up a little bit farther and Lucas stood awkwardly at the foot of the bed. He seemed more uncomfortable than a mouse realizing it had been thrown into a snake pit.

"How are you hanging in there, my dear?" Auntie Saraya asked. "I hear you've been through quite the ordeal since rescuing me."

"You have?" I questioned in return. "And did you say I rescued you? That was Evelyn and the others. I passed out."

She leaned forward a bit — her face wincing but straightening back before Lucas or I could question it — and grabbed hold of my hand.

"You took the first step in saving me, Violet," she assured me. "If you hadn't pulled the Fear magic from Evey and the Fear magic Morana had trapped me with, I doubt I would have been able to pull away from Morana's hold. So, you may have passed out, but you rescued me just as much as everyone else."

"If ya say so," I said softly.

"I do," she demanded, as she sat back at bit in her chair. "Now, Lucas filled me in on the big family secret."

"You seriously didn't know?"

I don't know why that was so shocking to me...but it was. I mean, how did she not know she had another older brother. Granted, if she had known I was really her niece, I feel like she would have had a much harder time hiding it. Then again, she did hide magic from Evey her whole life.

"Of course, I didn't!" She leaned back as she spoke, seeming genuinely offended by my accusation. "I had my reasons for keeping things from EvelynRose, but if I had known who you were...well I would have found a way to tell you."

Knowing the secrets she had kept from Evey, it was hard for me to believe she was completely clueless on this. Had she not heard the rumors? I mean, for heaven's sake, Hale knew who I was. Yet my own aunt was trying to sit across from me and say she had no idea we were part of the same gene pool. I just wasn't sure I bought it.

"She truly didn't know," Lucas finally interjected, still looking rather uncomfortable. "My father ensured that it was never spoken about. Especially in the presence of my sister or our mother."

"Be realistic here," I argued. "You mean to tell me that you never even heard a whisper about it? How could he have stopped that?"

"When Thomas Archer told someone not to do something," Lucas began with a smile. "Well let's just say it was never done. Not even thought of."

"I've met him, and he seemed like a kind and gentle man."

"You've what?" they asked in unison.

"He came to Evey's aid while she was heading to Rosebud," I explained. "Then he came to my aid when we were searching for her hopelessly and again after she forced us out of the park."

"Violet, he's…"

"Dead," I openly interjected. "I know. He was reincarnated as a phoenix."

They exchanged looks and then both of their stares turned back to me. Something was wrong. It wasn't that they didn't necessarily believe me, but there was clearly something I was missing.

"I met him," I assured them. "I'm certain of it."

"We believe you," Auntie finally said softly. "It's just…"

"People don't just get reincarnated, Violet."

"Johanna said something like that," I recalled. "Something about Evey calling upon one of the most powerful creatures in the realm. I guess I assumed that meant there weren't many of them."

"None," Lucas corrected. "Phoenix's are supposed to be extinct. Nobody has seen one in millions of years. How did you even know what or who he was?"

"Stop!" Saraya forcefully interjected. "This is not a conversation to be had here."

"How do you…"

"Lucas, I know!" she snapped. "Trust me, we shouldn't."

Callen came quickly back into the room before Lucas or I could figure out what was going on. His worry flooded my veins with a force I hadn't been expecting before he even made it through the door frame.

"What's going on?" I questioned.

"I apologize for the intrusion," he said, nodding to Lucas. "King Barin has asked that we all meet in the throne room."

"Why are you summoning us at this hour?" Lucas said. "The Barin I remember could hardly hold a conversation before lunch."

Callen swallowed a chuckle, but I felt his sudden amusement.

"I'm unaware of the reasoning behind the sudden need for our conference," Callen responded, in a very Knightly tone.

110

"However, I was instructed to ensure that Violet and Ms. Saraya are present."

I felt worried again. Possibly something more intense, but I couldn't focus long enough to figure it out. Lucas responded with a strong nod before grabbing Auntie's wheelchair and rolling her towards the door.

Without even giving him a chance to speak, a young woman came into the room carrying a stack of clothes. She handed them to Callen, curtseyed to him and left.

"I've never seen them treat you like this. What's going on?"

"We are in Magir now," he smiled. "It's one of the perks and downfalls to being the magical twin of their prince. These are for you though. I doubted that you'd want to show up in your hospital gown to meet with your royals."

Smiling at him, I moved to get dressed. He carefully helped me dress and the magical heat between us was suffocating. Yet, I felt this growing frustration with him. Why was he telling me what I wanted to wear? Was I not pretty enough for him to present to his king in my hospital gown? As I caught his eye the frustration settled, and I swallowed the growing lump in my throat. This Fear magic was no joke.

Chapter 14

Evelyn

"I was hoping to let you sleep," Griffin said softly, as he brushed my hair from my face. "But the king is insistent that we all join him in the throne room."

"Before breakfast?" I groaned.

"I can promise you," he said through a chuckle. "That I will make sure we get something to eat immediately after."

"Do I at least get to shower first?"

"Only if I can join you."

My eyes shot open at his forward comment, and I finally took in the man leaning over me. He had no shirt on, his hair was messy from his restless sleeping, and the desire in his eyes had my entire body vibrating. My mouth was so dry just from looking at him, that I couldn't even form words. Luckily, before I made a fool out of myself trying to speak, he leaned over and kissed my forehead.

"Go get your shower," he said softly. "I'll have Jo grab you some clothes from your suite."

He got up to leave and I pushed myself up to my elbows.

"What if I wanted to take you up on that offer?" I asked, just as his hand grasped the doorknob.

"E, if I get in that shower with you," he said in heavy breaths. "Then we won't ever make it to this meeting."

"I think it may be worth it."

He turned to me, his hand gripping the doorknob with such force his knuckles were turning white.

"I'm not sure there is anything more worth it," he smiled. "But everyone has been summoned to the throne room. Include Violet and Saraya."

"Auntie is coming?" I asked, completely shifting my focus. "Why didn't you lead with that?"

I threw the blankets off and raced for the bathroom. I could hear him chuckling at the door as I quickly pulled his shirt over my head and turned on the water.

"You know, you're turning out to be a bit of a tease," he joked.

"Yeah, yeah. I'm sure Vi would be so proud," I grinned, sticking my head out the door. "Now be a sweet prince and go get my clothes."

"As you wish, my princess."

He gave a playful bow as he left the room and I hopped in the shower, feeling slightly uneasy at being called a princess. I wasn't naive. I knew what it meant to be with a prince. But I was no princess. And as the water poured down my body, I found myself questioning if I ever could be.

*****

The throne room had already begun to fill by the time we made our way inside. Griffin had been insistent, yet again, that his father's opinion of our relationship was irrelevant and tightly held onto my hand as we walked through the double doors. Johanna and Sean were also hand-in-hand behind us, while the rest of the Knights, Nixie, and Katerie brought up the rear.

The knot in my stomach began to loosen as we approached the front of the room and I saw Violet and Callen seated together. Beside them Lucas stood behind a wheelchair that held Auntie Saraya.

As if just looking at her willed her to know I was there, she looked over her shoulder and smiled at me. Unable to control myself, I dropped Griffin's hand and rushed towards her, bending down to wrap my arms around her.

There was no surprise at the emotion that hugging her brought out of me. Tears quickly welled in my eyes as I took in her sweet smell and embraced the warmth of her hug.

"I'm so sorry," I whispered. "I should have found you sooner. I should have insisted on coming to see you. I…"

"Now you stop that," Auntie Saraya said, pushing me away slightly and moving her hands to cup my face. "As I have already informed Vi, this is not your fault. I am a grown ass woman, and I made my own choices. And if it meant saving you, I'd make the same choice over and over again."

"Just so we're clear," Violet added, wrapping her arm around me. "The same goes for me, so I don't wanna hear another word about it. We clear?"

I chuckled at Vi's attempt at being tough with me. There was a light feeling in the air as I was finally reunited with two of the most important people in my life. But as usual, as soon as King Barin came barreling into the room, he sucked the life out of it and all smiles and laughter ceased.

Griffin moved quickly from his spot beside Callen to my side and Callen did the same to Violet. It was disturbing how defensive they became in the presence of their king. Even more so when you consider that the king was also Griffin's father.

Behind the king, Ariana glided across the floor, an uneasy expression on her face. It was more than enough to tell me that the reasoning behind this meeting was not going to make the Knights happy. Acting on nothing more than an impulse to comfort him, I grabbed onto Griffin's hand, interlacing our fingers. I saw him smirk at my action, but his eyes never left his father.

"I am pleased that none of you challenged my invitation this morning," King Barin said as he sat in his chair. "Do you see now, how much easier things can be handled if you just obey the orders you are given?"

Griffin grew tense beside me, and I saw Callen's jaw clench. They despised having to take orders from Barin. Even when the order was something as simple as, *attend a meeting*.

"Barin."

The queen's voice was far more timid than I had ever heard it. As the king's gaze flicked over to her, I even saw her face scrunch as if she was trying to hold back a flinch. Knowing my magic wasn't the same, I was surprised when the enraged feeling my Fear gave me began to simmer in veins as I continued to watch the king scowl at his wife.

"Why have you summoned all of us?" Lucas questioned, his tone struggling to hold back his own anger. "Saraya and Violet are still recovering."

"They appear to be well enough." Barin smirked. "Though admittedly one looks better than the other."

Griffin quickly clasped my arm holding me back as the appalling excuse for a king winked in Violet's direction. Callen was harder to hold back and managed to take a step toward the king before Violet pulled him back.

"Calm yourselves. I was only jesting," Barin chuckled. "Onto the serious matter for which I have summoned you. I plan to throw a large feast here in my castle to celebrate the final day of The Festival of Stars."

"You summoned us to let us know you are throwing another party?"

Hale's voice came from the back of the room and all of our heads turned in his direction.

"With all due respect, my king," Hale began, moving closer to the throne. "Do you think it wise to have all of the kingdom present for such an event? Won't that potentially draw unwanted attention from the Fears?"

"You should not concern yourself with the wellbeing of *my* people," the king scoffed. "The preparations are already underway. The feast will be tonight."

"Tonight?" Griffin asked. "The Festival of Stars ends tomorrow."

"Enough!"

The king shouted so loud, I was certain it was echoing throughout the entire castle. As he exhaled a breath, he slammed his hands against the arms of his throne and straightened himself as he stood.

"I am King of Magir," he informed us. "I shall decide when events take place. If I want to end the festival tonight, I shall do so. You may be a prince to these people, but you have far from earned the right to take this throne one day."

With his words, Ariana straightened a little bit more too. Her brows dipped together and her nose scrunched for a moment as she acknowledged how truly disgusting of a man her husband was. Her role as queen meant nothing in comparison to her role as a mother. Barin could insult her, but she wasn't about to let him demean her son.

"This is a formal event," instructed the king, changing the subject back to *his* event. "You will all be present. Punishment will be issued for those who are not. You are dismissed."

I caught Hale take a step forward and the king stepped off of his throne with a force.

"You are *all* dismissed."

Once he had exited the room with several guards, and Ariana in tow, everyone who remained released a collective sigh.

"That man is lucky he is the king because I could have gutted him right where he stood for making a comment like that toward Vi," Callen growled.

"And I thought he was bad when we were teenagers," Lucas chimed in.

"I can't believe Ari had to marry that ass," Auntie added. "No offense to you, Griffin."

"None taken," Griffin shrugged. "I'd only be offended if you thought I was like him."

"You wouldn't be standing right there if I thought you were," Lucas replied, his eyes drifting to me.

It was strange to feel the protection of a father. Even I couldn't deny that it felt good to have a father figure care for me in that way. Yet, there was this angry voice in the back of my head that was shouting at me for giving a damn about what a man who had walked out on me thought of my choice in a companion.

Violet staring at me brought me out of my head and back to the conversation that was occurring around me.

"Why would he think now is the appropriate time for a party?" Sean asked. "I feel like there is something else going on here."

"He just wants everyone to think he has control of the situation with the Fears," Griffin explained.

"Even though we all know he doesn't," Callen appended.

"If I may."

I had almost forgotten that Hale was even in the room since he had been so rudely dismissed by the king. It seemed that the Knights had also forgotten his presence as they all turned to face him.

"I agree with Sean's assessment," Hale surmised in a hushed tone.

"Do you know something?" Nicholas asked.

"I wish I did," Hale answered. "But this is sudden. You may think him naive, but Barin makes decisions with a clear intent. I can't seem to see what this one may be."

"Have you seen his Mind?" Lucas asked, tilting his head slightly as he studied Hale.

"I've seen many minds."

Hale's eyes flicked to me and then to Griffin. There was something different about him. He seemed...vulnerable. Like he was almost scared of whatever the king was hiding. And I had a sense that not much frightened Hale Reign.

"I have known the king's mind," Hale continued. "But this I cannot see. He is hiding something."

"Knowing the king, he is likely going to announce our wedding date or something just to anger you, Griffin," Johanna surmised.

"No," Hale quickly replied. "It's not that simple. He wouldn't hide something that juvenile from me."

"Then what is your guess?" Auntie Saraya asked him.

A guard came back into the throne room and stood firmly at his post guarding the door. We all looked briefly in his direction and as I turned my gaze back to Hale, he shifted his weight nervously.

"I don't know," he answered in a hushed tone. "But be careful. Something is happening and it's happening tonight."

Hale took his leave without another word. All of the rest of us remained in our places, utterly confused by what was transpiring. Could the king truly be up to something? Or was it really going to be an arrogant announcement about a wedding that I was assured would never happen? Either of them seemed to be viable options, but the unknown made my skin crawl.

"Well, despite the uneasiness this meeting has caused, I say we all head to the dining hall for some breakfast," Lucas suggested. "Perhaps we can think of some plausible reasons for this sudden feast."

With no objection to Lucas's suggestion, we all headed toward the dining hall to eat. The servers began catering to our every need from the moment we entered. It seemed as if we had hardly sat down before plates piled high with food began being placed on the table.

As we began to eat, it was strange to feel how different the atmosphere was in here versus how it had been in the throne room. Everyone was seated where they wished. There was no pressure to do or be anything other than ourselves. Griffin even continuously seemed to be touching me in some way. From holding my hand to wrapping an arm around my chair or resting a hand on my thigh. They were such tiny gestures, yet so intimate that I wouldn't have been able to hold back my smile if I'd tried.

Violet, who was across from me at the table, also seemed to be embracing the happier feeling of the room. I could only imagine the rush of emotions she was battling back in the throne room. The color had returned to her skin and a flush of pink appeared on her cheek when Callen pulled her hand to his lips.

Beside me Sean was mercilessly teasing Johanna about something relating to her pending wedding announcement while Auntie playfully swatted Lucas's arm to agree with whatever it was Sean had said.

Auntie had the biggest change of all of us. Seeing her sit beside her brother, laughing like no time had passed, made my heart swell. I couldn't honestly think of a time I had seen her so relaxed or so genuinely happy.

"I don't think I've ever heard her laugh like that," Violet's voice said in my mind. *"Or smile that big."*

"Me either," I thought back. *"Are these mental conversations going to be our new thing?"*

"Why not?" she joked. *"Sisterhood of Knights, remember?"*

I looked at her across the table and she shot me a wink that made me chuckle.

"Something you two want to share?" Griffin asked in a jesting tone.

"Well, I'd like to know how Red here is feeling about this pending wedding announcement," Sean interjected. "I say we both go along with it and announce our own wedding just to piss off the king."

"In your dreams," I rolled my eyes.

"You go by Red?"

Lucas's question hushed the entire room. Violet, likely sensing my discomfort, spoke up before I could.

"Actually, only Sean calls her that strange name," Violet replied with a wink at Sean. "But it is better than calling her by a name that wasn't really hers."

Lucas looked at Sean and I with a confused look.

"Sean is like my best friend," I began, before Violet

loudly cleared her throat. "*One* of my best friends. When we met, we jokingly teased each other about our Irish roots and last names. So, I called him O'Connor and he called me McCalister. But when we discovered that wasn't who I was and I didn't really feel like an Archer yet, he just started calling me Red. It was something nobody could take away from me."

"So, you two are friends *and* partnered with each half of the latest royal betrothal?" Lucas questioned.

"Partnered? Lucas, you age yourself every time you speak," Auntie joked. "Clearly the younger generation has rejected the ridiculousness of the outdated betrothal process."

"I'm not an old man, Sar," he said, nudging her. "I was merely curious."

"Could have fooled me."

Auntie Saraya shot me a wink and the entire table burst into laughter. The meal continued with a light, fun-loving atmosphere and it provided a sense of comfort I didn't even realize I was missing. Even despite everyone at the table sharing thoughts about the feast this evening, it wasn't a dreadful or heavy conversation. Just a group of people who respected and cared for each other enough to have a hard conversation.

"There is something important we need to take care of before tonight," Johanna suddenly interjected.

"What's that?" Sean asked.

"Us ladies need to get new dresses for the feast."

"That's a priority right now?" questioned Daniel.

"Oh, you men are hopeless," Violet rolled her eyes. "I, for one, will not show my face at a royal event wearin' the same dress I wore to the ball."

"Vi, are you sure you're—"

"Callen Ivanti, don't you dare try to tell me that I am not up for goin' dress shopping with the girls. I am just fine, and I will not attend this feast in the same gown. Is that clear?"

The Knights stared at Callen with wide eyes as they waited for his response. Only Griffin was grinning and shaking his head as he gripped tightly onto my thigh.

"Fine, but only if you allow us to tag along for safety," Callen said, kissing her hand. "And I do love it when you try to act tough with me."

"Good," she smiled at him. "Because I ain't about to change that."

"But none of you are coming with us," I chimed in.

"And why is that?" Griffin asked.

"Because we have very few things in this magical realm that we can surprise you with. How we look in our dresses is one of those things," I explained.

"Then Nick can escort you," Griffin instructed.

"Absolutely not," Johanna argued. "Once one of you knows something, you all do."

"It's true," I agreed. "I'm sorry but none of you are going with us."

"Well, you aren't going alone," Sean commanded. "And Red's gift may stop that connection."

"Absolutely not," Violet pushed.

"I'll escort them."

Lucas's voice, again, stunned us all into silence. Had he just said what I thought he did? Volunteered to take us dress shopping. Volunteered to take *me* dress shopping. It was every girl's dream to have her daddy take her shopping like this. But it made my stomach twist.

"I think that is a splendid idea," Violet gushed. "But prepare for Twenty Questions, uncle."

"You ask and I'll answer."

Lucas was grinning widely as he took another bit of his sausage. Auntie Saraya placed a gentle hand in his arm before turning to me and giving me a warm, knowing smile.

"Relax, sugar," Violet's calm voice echoed in my head. *"This is your opportunity to really talk with him. Give it a chance."*

Chapter 15

Violet

"I still don't think this is a good idea."

Callen stood over me as I sat on the foot of his bed slipping into a pair of ankle-high boots that I had thankfully brought with us from Woodburn Rose.

"And for the millionth time," I groaned. "We will be fine."

"Vi, you were—"

"In a comma just yesterday."

"And we—"

"Don't even know Lucas."

"We also—"

"Don't know what the king is up to."

He paused for a moment, clearly frustrated by me continuously cutting him off. But I couldn't hold back the sass. I wasn't some gentle flower that needed to remain safely potted for everyone to watch over. I was a damn tree, and my roots would stretch whenever I damn well willed them to.

"Are you done?" he finally asked.

"Are you?" I questioned, as I stood from the bed.

"Vi, I'm worried about you."

"And I love you for it," I assured him, reaching up to wrap my arms around his neck. "But I'm fine. In the words of Britney, I'm stronger than yesterday. I'm not playing the self-blaming game anymore. I finally feel like my old self again."

"But you're not your old self, Vi. That Fear magic inside of you isn't just going away," he began, as he wrapped his strong arms around my waist. "And who is Britney?"

"Oh lord, your childhood was tragic," I joked. "And I know that Evey's Fear is still inside me. I can feel it. But it's strange. It's like...even though I can feel the darkness, my body won't allow it to take over. Like, even when I'm flustered and feel it boiling up, my inner light is just too much. Does that make sense?"

"No," he chuckled. "But I've never felt Fear like you can. I can sense it inside of you, yet I can't actually get to it. It's weird to feel so connected to you and yet so disconnected, too."

"There are no disconnections here."

I pushed up on my tippy-toes and kissed him. Feeling the rush of magic that came from our lips entangling was an intoxicating surge I had truly missed while bein' trapped in that nightmare, so intoxicating that it almost made it impossible to pull myself away from him.

"But in all seriousness," I said softly, as I pulled away. "If you don't stop bein' worried about me goin' out with the girls, I may just strangle you. I've spent the last few weeks trapped in a living hell. Now that, I can accept that, I plan to use it to my full advantage. I have earned a day out with the girls. No, I *deserve* a day with my girls. Is that clear mister?"

"Crystal," he whispered, pulling me back to him. "I wasn't joking before. This bossy side of you really gets to me."

*****

"We were contemplating sending a search party," Johanna joked, as Callen and I made our way down the front steps of the castle's main entrance.

"She's joking," Nixie smiled. "We were informed you were delayed."

I rolled my eyes but made sure to end it with a wink in Evey's direction. She did manage a giggle, but her discomfort was impossible to miss.

When Lucas volunteered as our escort, I genuinely believed that I was doin' her a favor by quickly accepting his offer. She most certainly was not going to be going out of her way to build a relationship with him. Granted there was valid reason for that. But I just wasn't going to let her miss a chance to have something with her father. And deep down, if she didn't really want this, she would have been far too angry with me to giggle at my wink.

Our group consisted of myself, Evey, Johanna, Nixie and Katerie. While Callen and the other Knights insisted that Lucas would not be enough protection, we eventually managed to convince them all that we would be gone only a few hours and it wasn't worth the fuss. Not to mention that between the five of us, we were far more likely to kick the asses of whoever came at us than be the ones gettin' their asses kicked.

As we made our way through the streets of Magir's main village, Lucas anxiously looked around, but I found his eyes routinely drifting back to Evey. Johanna noticed too and rolled her eyes in Evey's direction. Being so close to her father, this must have been hard for Johanna to understand. But it wasn't for me.

"So, Lucas," Johanna suddenly began. "How has it been living in the non-magical realm with zero magic all these years?"

"The non-magical realm is a fine place," Lucas answered. "It certainly isn't Magir, but it has its perks."

"Such as?"

"Technology for one thing," he chuckled. "Magir may be advanced due to its magic, but the technology of the non-magical realm leaves something to be desired. We really haven't even started to touch the technological advances the non-magical realm has."

"Oh my God!" I shrieked, causing Lucas to whip his head in my direction. "I just realized I haven't checked my phone since we got here! My father is gonna be furious with me!"

"I bet he's sending a search party after you," Evey joked. "You remember when you went a month without responding to him?"

"Don't remind me," I groaned.

"What is he like?" Lucas asked.

In trying to get Evey to build a relationship with Lucas, I hadn't really thought about building my own. It just didn't seem as important. Well, it just outright wasn't as important. But I definitely hadn't considered that he would want to get to know my father. Though the more I thought about it, who wouldn't want to know or at least be curious about their long-lost sibling?

I was suddenly nervous about being the person to introduce Lucas to his twin brother. I loved my father. There was no doubt about that. But I'd be lyin' through my teeth if I stood here and told him stories of this great man that he could have only wished he had the chance to know sooner. Our relationship just wasn't...well right at the moment it just wasn't anything.

"Time for that later," Nixie piped in. "We have arrived."

Lucas held the door open and we all walked in. Johanna was already tightly wrapped in Callista's arms by the time Evey and I made it through the door. Callista quickly spotted us, and her smile widened, but her expression vanished, as her eyes trailed behind us.

"If I wasn't seeing you in person," she began in the softest voice I'd heard her use. "Well, I just wouldn't believe it."

"Awe, but Callista I thought nothing made it past your Vision?"

Lucas shot her a wink and Callista practically flew across the room, giggling like a schoolgirl, before she reached Lucas and wrapped him a tight hug.

"Oh, it is good to see you back home," she said, patting him on the back. "I wish your parents were here to witness your triumphant return."

"I don't know if I would use the word triumphant," Lucas grinned. "But I have no intention of leaving again."

"Glad to hear it!" Callista gave Lucas a quick pat on the shoulder and then turned to us. "Now, let's see what we can work up for all of you ladies to attend this mysterious Festival of Stars Feast."

Callista must have known Katerie needed a shoppin' day because she pulled her behind the curtain and was throwin' dresses at her like a tornado. Nixie stood close to the curtain, assisting Katerie, leaving Evey, Johanna and I on the couches with Lucas hovering beside us.

"If you meant what you said about staying," Johanna said, bringing an end to our uncomfortable silence. "Then you should contact my father about retaking your place on the council."

"I thought you looked familiar," Lucas smiled. "You must be an Everton."

"Yes, sir," Johanna smiled proudly. "Did you know my father well?"

"Well as you know, Magir may be a large realm, but when your family is part of the council, you know pretty much everyone," Lucas replied. "Your father and I weren't close friends, but I certainly knew him."

"Yes, the realm does seem a little smaller when you're part of the council," Johanna agreed. "You really should talk to him about retaking your family position."

"Has the position not been filled?" he questioned. "I assumed after my father passed, they would give up the seat."

"The king removed your chair."

He looked at me with his eyes wide. I hadn't meant to interject but I blurted it out before I had a chance to think it through.

"Didn't mean to interrupt," I apologized. "But Barin

removed your seat from the council after your father passed. He said he didn't want anyone...didn't want anyone to succumb to the demons the rest of the family did."

Lucas stared at me with a quizzical expression. I hadn't meant to offend him. And in all actuality insulting his family was insulting mine just the same. So, it wasn't like I had intended to be malicious.

Just as I was about to defend my overshare, Lucas shocked all three of us by laughing. And not a chuckle...I'm talking fully belly laughing.

"Barin would believe that," Lucas laughed.

When he finally stopped laughing, I exchanged looks with Evey and even she was confused.

"As soon as his father started to groom him to take the crown, he became insufferable," Lucas explained. "I'd hoped marrying a woman like Ari that he would change for the better, but clearly that was me having false hope."

"You and Ariana really must have been close then."

Evey interjecting shocked me. I anticipated that she would give Lucas the cold shoulder for at least another day or so. There was no doubt she would eventually give in and talk to him. I just figured that she would use the events happening around us as a buffer for as long as possible.

"We were," Lucas smiled at her. "There was a time when all of Magir thought I would probably marry her."

"Good thing you didn't," Johanna chuckled and winked at Evey.

"True," Lucas joked in return. "But no matter how strong our feelings were, I fell in love with your mother and Ari believed in the laws of Magir. We couldn't have been together even if deep down we had wanted to."

Callista interrupted, pulling Evelyn and Johanna in next. As Evey walked away from me, I suddenly felt a sense of exhaustion. Like magic had somehow been pulled from my body just by her moving away from me.

"Are you feeling alright?" Lucas asked, placing a hand

on my shoulder. "Violet, you look a little pale."

"I'm fine," I assured him. "Just a little woozy still."

"I heard about your bond to EvelynRose. It's possible you two are drawing on each other's magic now."

"Like somehow just knowing allows us more access than we had before."

"Precisely."

As I made the assumption, something came to me. Understanding magic did allow you a certain level of extra access to its power. It was no different than the concept of learning something and being able to access your knowledge to accomplish something.

The more I contemplated, the closer I came to the realization of what this knowledge could mean for other forms of magic. Other forms of my magic.

"That's it!"

I launched from my seat, just as Evey and Johanna emerged in a couple of dresses. Smiling and also agreeing with them that those were certainly their best choices, I came to a conclusion all my own. And as I made my way behind the curtain with Callista for my own fitting, I knew I just had to figure out how to confirm my theory.

Chapter 16

Evelyn

We'd picked out our dresses and were heading back to the palace when Lucas suddenly stopped. He insisted on taking us all to a pastry shop and buying some sort of Danish style baked goods before returning.

Everyone except for myself and Violet seemed overjoyed by the idea. I wasn't sure why Vi seemed put out by the delay, but I knew it was an attempt at bonding. And when he emerged from the store, offering me a pastry as we began to walk, I knew my assumption was correct.

"So, tell me about your time at WRA," he said after a bite. "I've heard it's been spectacular since Ari took over."

"I'm sorry?" I questioned.

Was he really going to start questioning me about current events like a father who had actually been part of their child's life for more than five minutes?

"WRA," he repeated. "Did you enjoy it?"

"I didn't exactly get a chance to really immerse myself in the school," I answered.

"I suppose that is true."

"You suppose that is true?" I sneered back.

Without even realizing it, I stopped walking. Lucas stopped too and then nodded at Johanna to continue with the others.

"Are you seriously going to just pick up with questions about my current life?" I shouted. "Do you even care about, I don't know, the first 20 years of my life? Or are you just interested now that I'm some powerful magical?"

"Evelyn, I..."

"Don't!" I interrupted. "You show up here after abandoning me for my entire life and just expect me to welcome you with open arms? I don't think so. Auntie Saraya is all I've ever needed, and you don't get to walk back into our lives like no time has passed."

"Eveyln, I understand..."

"You don't!" I cried. "You don't understand, and I don't want you to. Let's just get through this dinner and then we can go back to our own lives."

The expression on Lucas's face showed how defeated and hurt he was by my outburst, but I couldn't bite my tongue any longer. I couldn't just pretend that I was overjoyed by his sudden return. And with everything going on, I hadn't even had time to process how I really felt about it.

Briskly, I walked away before I either started shouting again or burst into tears. Either way, it was going to be some form of emotional breakdown and I don't do that. I don't show emotion in that way. And I certainly wasn't going to do it in front of other people.

Walking back through the gates, all of the Knights waited anxiously on the stairs for us. Normally I would have questioned how they knew we were going to be back already, but instead I grabbed Griffin's hand, practically dragging him through the halls to the Knight's suite.

Callista had said our dresses would be delivered within the hour, so I took that as having a few minutes to decompress without Violet and Johanna to press me about my altercation with Lucas.

"Want to tell me where the fire is?"

Griffin closed the door to his room, and I spun around to face him. Just looking in his eyes, I felt my own beginning to well up with tears.

"E, what happened?"

"How can he just come back into my life after more than two decades and expect some happy family reunion?"

"E, he doesn't expect that," he assured me, placing his hands on my shoulders. "I'm sure he just wants to get to know you."

"Who says I want to know him," I cried.

He pulled me to his chest and slowly turned us, before sitting us both down on the end of his bed.

"I know this has to be a lot, E."

He held me close to his side, running a hand through my hair. It was incredibly comforting, but despite feeling his magic coursing through mine, I couldn't shake the overwhelming emotions.

"Griffin, I went from having no parents, to having both. One of which is a crazy, psycho killer and the other who voluntarily walked out of my life."

"Lucas was trying to protect you, E."

"You don't think I'd have been safer with him to protect me?" I questioned, sitting up and turning to look at him. "I could have grown up with my aunt and my dad. I could have known all about magic and this realm. If he hadn't left my life could have been so much different."

"E, sometimes we make rash decisions with the information we have because we think it is our best chance. You made a similar choice when you went to that park alone," he reminded me. "You knew we would have been stronger together. Whether that is you and I or you and Violet, you knew deep down that with someone by your side you would have had a better chance at beating him. But that wasn't a risk you were willing to take."

"So, you think I should just forgive him?"

There was a slight pulse of magic that went through my body as those words passed through my lips. It felt foreign and familiar all at the same time. And even as briefly as it passed, I noticed Griffin's expression shift for a moment before softening again.

"I didn't say that," he sighed, pulling me to him again. "But take it from someone whose father wouldn't save him from a rouge horse, having someone care for you enough to risk missing out on your life isn't something you want to just throw away."

Nestling back into his chest, Griffin pulled us backwards so that we were laying on his bed. I listened to the sound of his heart beating as I let his words sink in. There was no denying I was angry at Lucas. But what Griffin had said really got me thinking. Was I truly angry at him for leaving or was it that I was angry at him for not being a part of my life? And did I owe it to myself to get to know him before I just shut him out?

Far too soon after we laid down, there was a light knock on the door causing Griffin and I both to slowly rise. Callen pushed the door open a bit and squished his large body into the small opening he'd created.

"Couldn't reach you again," he began. "Violet asked me to come get you, so you had enough time, to quote unquote, 'be pampered'. And to also let you know that your attire for this evening has been delivered."

"Thanks, I'll head right over."

I gave Callen the most reassuring smile I could muster, and he left his spot in the door without fully closing it.

"Evelyn."

Griffin grabbed onto my arm and pulled me back onto the bed with him before I had a chance to completely stand up. His lips were on mine in seconds, and I felt like I couldn't breathe, but in the good kind of way.

"I am beside you," Griffin said breathless, as he pulled his lips from mine. "No matter what you decide. I'm here."

"I know."

I leaned over and kissed him again. My lips parted to welcome him, and he quickly shifted us off of the bed, pulling away from me again.

"If you don't leave now," he heaved. "You'll never be ready on time. And as much as I'd rather spend this night with you, if we don't arrive on time, my father may call for our heads."

"And if he doesn't, Vi will," I joked. "See you soon."

Every nerve in body was tingling as I leaned forward, placed a kiss on his cheek and quickly headed back to my own room. Magical connections managed to make you feel so strong and yet impossibly weak all in the same moment. Yet as I walked into the guest suite, I couldn't hide the smile on my face or the heavy panting of my breathing.

"And now we see why she was really late," Johanna mocked the moment I entered the room.

"I don't know what you're talking about."

Violet rolled her eyes across the room and Nixie chuckled from the couch.

"As much as I'd love to dig into the reasoning behind your breathless smile," Violet began. "We need to get your hair started. Lord knows those tangles will need at least thirty minutes of brushin'."

*****

We met the Knights just outside the door leading to the suites. Sean let out a whistle at Johanna in her deep purple, form hugging dress. Callen gushed over Violet in her pink, short flapper style dress. And I couldn't control my blush as Griffin's eyes moved over my body, examining my own dress.

"I swear I'm giving Callista a key to the jewel room after this," he joked, as he pulled me closer to him, while placing a kiss on my hand.

My dress hit just above my knees, with a sweetheart neckline and off the shoulder sleeves. It was a bold red with a black lace over the bodice and sparkling black tool down the skirt. It was one of my more daring choices, but it was a unanimous *must have* according to everyone at Callista's, including my father.

"You better stay close to me tonight," Griffin softly said in my ear, as we made our way to the ballroom.

"You certain he will try something in front of everyone?" I questioned.

"Without a doubt," Griffin replied, with a soft chuckle. "But I was more referring to the attention you are going to command in that dress. Nobody, especially the men, are giving you so much as a handshake tonight."

I rolled my eyes as he gave me a playful wink and we approached the door to the ballroom.

As I expected, we were stopped at the door and each of us were formally announced. One couple at a time, we entered the ball room. I could hear the commotion beyond the doors and knew that meant the king's *mandatory attendance* had been taken rather seriously throughout the entire realm.

Griffin and I were announced, and he held me as close to him as possible as we walked through the doors. Some people stared at us with quizzical expressions. There was a handful that leaned over to whisper to the person beside them. And, thankfully, some people smiled. I felt a twinge in my chest as I noticed the smiles and felt like I may be starting to earn their approval as a partner to their prince.

"Awe! There you are my son!"

Just like that, any happiness I had started to feel evaporated into thin air. King Barin crossed the room with a large, phony smile on his face. Making absolutely sure that he made a spectacle of gushing over his son. Ariana followed beside him with a genuine smile on her face. Though I could see in her eyes that she was just as surprised by Barin's reaction to his son as Griffin and I were.

"Evelyn Archer," King Barin bellowed as he approached us.

Once he was directly in front of us, he placed a hand on my shoulder, pulling me slightly forward before placing a kiss on my cheek. My entire body stiffened, and I felt my magic negatively reacting to his skin touching mine. It was a painful burn I hadn't encountered since I'd learned about my magic and that left me feeling even more uneasy than I already was.

"You look radiant," said the king as he pulled away and arrogantly glared at his son.

"Your majesty, what…"

"Augustus!" King Barin roared with a smile, as an older man walked by. "Griffin, come greet Augustus with me."

The king didn't even wait for a response and immediately turned, walking away. Griffin looked stunned and remained frozen in his place as he looked from his retreating father to his mother.

"I don't know," Arianna finally said. "He's been like this all day. You should follow him. Keep an eye on things."

Griffin nodded, interlacing our fingers and taking a step before his mother stopped him.

"Evelyn, may I actually have a word?"

"Of course."

With a nod and a kiss on the cheek his father had not touched, Griffin followed through the crowd, leaving me on the edge of the ball room with Arianna.

"Barin was right," Arianna said, accepting two champagne flutes from a passing server. "You do look radiant."

"Thank you, and I can't drink that."

"Sure, you can. It's cider. Griffin insisted."

"Of course, he did," I smiled, accepting the drink. "You also look incredible, your highness."

"We've talked about this," she began, shaking her head. "You may call me Arianna. Or mom-in-law if you prefer."

The sip of my drink I was taking didn't stand a chance as his words shocked me. She laughed the most regal, polite laugh I had ever heard as I choked on my cider, while trying to regain my composure.

"There is no doubt in my mind that my son will marry you one day, EvelynRose," she informed me, placing a soft hand on my shoulder. "It may not be tomorrow or even next year, but I see the way he looks at you. And the way you look at him."

My eyes instantly moved from Arianna to her son across the room. As soon as my gaze landed on him, he met my eyes and smiled. I couldn't hide the blush that I felt forming on my cheeks and I felt my magic tingling in my veins.

"Many responsibilities come with being future Queen of Magir," Ariana continued, pulling my focus back to her. "You will have many who support you, but you will also have many who question you."

"Because I'm part Fear?"

"That," she nodded. "And because your father was long believed to be a traitor to our realm. And also, because you are interfering with a long-standing tradition in our realm."

"Griffin's betrothal to Johanna you mean."

"It's archaic, but it's tradition," she explained.

My chest tightened as I feared what she would say next. She was the Queen of Magir, and I was stomping on her traditions. A tradition that she had proudly accepted at one point in her life. She may have been kind to me, but there had to be a part of her that despised me.

"Though, if being queen has taught me anything," she continued. "It's that traditions are ever changing. They morph with new generations. And I think you are paving a much better path for the future generations of Magir."

I released a breath, I didn't realize I had been holding, as Ariana grabbed my hand in hers.

"Griffin will be a marvelous king, but he will need a strong queen by his side. I have no doubt that you are going to make an amazing queen, EvelynRose. Magir will be a far better realm with you and Griffin guiding her."

"Thank you," I stammered.

"Take good care of my son," she smiled and hugged me

137

tightly.

She released the hug just as Griffin reappeared beside us. Without a word, Arianna gave her son a light pat on the shoulder and began to glide through the room.

"Dance with me?"

I smiled and took his hand, allowing him to lead me into the middle of the sea of dancing Magirians.

"Are you going to tell me what my mother wanted to talk with you about?" he asked, as he pulled me close to him and we began to sway with the music.

"We were discussing our wedding."

Maintaining the most sincere tone and serious face as I watched the expression on his face change. There was a clear sense of surprise as his eyebrows shot up, but there was also a glint of excitement in his eyes that I wasn't expecting. And after only a moment of him gaping at me he lightly cleared his throat, before continuing to sway with me.

"Anything I should know about our pending nuptials?" he asked.

There was a soft crack in his voice, and I instantly slowed our dancing while pulling my head back, so he was looking directly into my eyes.

"She thinks you and I will lead Magir into a new era," I smiled. "She just wanted to give her approval and ask that I take care of you."

The music stopped and Griffin stepped back, grabbing my hand and pressing his lips to it.

"You will make a great queen."

My magic raced through my body then froze as someone tapped on my shoulder. Turning around, I found Lucas standing behind me looking rather dapper in his well-tailored suit. He had shaved his stubble of a beard and actually looked like the councilman that I had pictured when other Magirians spoke of him or my grandfather.

"I wonder if I may have a dance with my daughter?" he asked.

Griffin nodded to him but looked to me to answer. He would never truly know how much I appreciated him not pushing my relationship with Lucas. The support he was giving by not speaking for me...it was a power not many had bestowed upon me.

"Sure."

Griffin whispered that he would go check in with Callen and Sean before walking away and leaving me with my father.

Lucas had a wide smile on his face, as he took my hands, and we began to dance to the music. It was weird to feel my magic interact with his touch. It was similar to the reaction I had with Violet in some ways and in others it made me feel uneasy.

"Griffin is a good man," Lucas suddenly said.

"He is."

"You two are lucky to have found each other," he continued. "Not everyone gets to meet their fated match. And not that I was eavesdropping, but I agree with Ari. You two will be exactly what Magir needs."

"Are you saying you approve of my potentially marrying Griffin one day?"

The idea that my absentee father was giving me the stamp of approval on my relationship made my blood boil and I think he knew it.

"Not that you need my approval," he responded. "But yes."

"You suddenly think that because you have known me for a whopping two days, that you know who the best match for me is?" I asked him, trying to be as quiet in my outburst as I could, so as not to cause a scene. "You are correct. I don't need any approval from you."

The music continued and Lucas kept us spinning on pace. I had expected him to argue back but he remained silent as a few moments passed.

"Do you really think I don't know you, EvelynRose?" he finally asked.

"You missed 90 percent of my life thus far," I assured him.

"Says who?"

"Um…maybe my Aunt who has been raising me since I was one."

"EvelynRose, I never truly left you."

The sincerity in his voice forced me to look at him, though I was genuinely confused at how he could possibly believe he had been there for me at any time in my life.

"EvelynRose, I have always been there for you. Sometimes it was as a substitute in one of your classes. Other times, I was a bystander in the park. Occasionally, I was a customer at the coffee stand you worked at with Violet. But *I* was always there. Sometimes there were larger gaps between when I was able to see you, but I was there. I was always there."

Before I could decipher what it was my father was saying, Griffin rushed up to us, a flustered look on his face.

"Something is wrong," he began. "My father is gone."

As the words left his mouth, King Barin appeared on the stage at the end of the ballroom. The smug look on his face, made my stomach turn and I felt both Griffin and Lucas stiffen beside me.

A trumpet blared and the music came to a halt. Griffin grabbed tightly onto my hand, and we began to move through the crowd toward his father. Off to the side of the room, I felt Violet staring at me, the worry on her face more than apparent.

"Thank you all for coming to this historic night," the king began. "As your king, I am proud of the realm I have built and wondrous events I allow you all to attend."

"Arrogance at a new level," Lucas whispered behind Griffin and I.

"And as your king, I have called upon all of you to bear witness to a historic occasion here in Magir," the king continued, his self-approving smile never leaving his lips. "As you all know, my son has returned from a trip to Woodburn

Rose, where he fell in love with one of the most powerful magicals our realm has ever seen."

Griffin inched closer to me and tightened his grip on my hand. People turned to look at us, but his expression remained stoic.

"My son, however, was already betrothed," the king announced. "Thinking only of the future of our realm it is my great honor to henceforth recall my previous betrothal and dissolve Johanna's obligation to marry Prince Griffin."

My gaze sought out Johanna and she looked like she was going to cry with excitement or be sick with embarrassment.

"This is not a tarnish on Miss Everton's reputation, and I wish her the best in her future endeavors."

The king continued in his speech and the crowd seemed split on whether or not they were buying this *good guy* facade he was portraying.

"And it is with that recall, that I am pleased to announce that Prince Griffin will now marry Miss EvelynRose Archer, granddaughter of the honorable Thomas Archer and descendent of The Five."

Applause filled the room, but Griffin hadn't moved. His gaze was fixated on his father. When I looked over to where Violet had been, she was pushing her way through the crowd to get to me. Something was wrong. The crowd may not have known it yet...but something was definitely wrong.

"And if she declines your offer?"

Lucas's outburst hushed the crowd almost instantaneously. I watched as Barin scrunched his nose and his smile went from arrogant to wicked.

"I forgot to mention," he announced to the crowd, rather than answering my father. "As this is already a change to our normal tradition, it only seems fair that the parent of the woman being offered such an honor be the one to accept on her behalf."

Lucas opened his mouth to speak but before he could, the king spoke again.

"And seeing as her father has yet to be fully pardoned from his treason sentence, it only seems right that," he paused and scanned the room with his smile only growing. "Her mother will be the one to accept the honor."

The crowd gasped in horror as a beautiful woman emerged from the shadows behind King Barin. She was unnaturally pale, with long, bright red hair and pitch-black eyes.

She was here. Standing before me. My mother. The Queen of the Fears.

Chapter 17

Violet

I felt the room get suffocatingly tense when the surprise guest was revealed. King Barin stood in front of his throne on the slightly raised stage as the woman beside him grinned wickedly. She stood disgustingly confident in the place where his wife should have been. Her hair bright red and blacked out eyes reminded me of when Evey's Fear took over, but there was something so much more evil about seeing no other color in a person's eyes.

I felt a strange surge of magic begin to tingle inside of me and I narrowed my eyes as I watched her grin even wider at Evey. I knew who the woman was. And as frightening as she was to look at, she was beautiful. Not in the same way Evey was. Evey was breathtaking — even though she'd never admit it. The woman before us now — even as beautiful as she was — she embodied the evil I could only equate to a siren.

"Tell Sean to get everyone out of here."

Hale appeared next to me, and Callen quickly nodded, closing his eyes.

"This won't end well," Hale whispered to me. "Keep yourself and Evelyn safe. No matter the cost."

Hale began to move forward to where Evelyn, Griffin and Lucas stood toward the bottom of the stage. And as I watched him quickly making his way through the crowd, I saw the crowd parting as the queen made her way to her husband. The fury on her face was evident, even from across the room.

"What's going on here?" Lucas asked.

"I would also love an answer to that," Griffin growled.

"I don't have to answer any of your questions," King Barin snapped at Griffin. "And I most certainly don't have to answer the questions of a traitor."

"Traitor?" Ariana questioned, as she approached the stage. "You cannot stand beside *her* and call Lucas a traitor. Barin, have you lost your mind? You can't honestly think this woman is your ally?"

"You do not question my judgment!" King Barin was shouting. "I will align myself with whomever I wish! No prophecy will ever guide what I do! This is my kingdom!"

"You've been working together this entire time?" Queen Ariana questioned. "And again...you have the nerve to call Lucas a traitor. You are a disgrace to your people."

"You are supposed to be silent! A queen in the eyes of the people, but you were to do as *I* say. Now, I have grown tired of your insistent need to protect Lucas over me. For that, I can promise that you won't live through this war."

As soon as the threat left the king's lips, I felt the tension in the room change. Callen and I had made it to Griffin and Evelyn, with Sean and Johanna appearing on the other side too. I grabbed hold of Evey's hand, and her chaotic mixture of emotions hit me like a burst of magic.

All three of our Knights were on edge. It was more than their usual protective nature. There was something different about them. It was like those beasts that lived inside of them were fighting to break out.

I tightened my grip on Evey's hand and felt another strange surge that made me blink at an alarming rate, making me slightly dizzy. As my vision cleared, Evey yanked her hand away and I could see that she too must have felt the same surge go through her.

King Barin finally noticed that the remaining Knights were slowly escorting people from the ball room and slammed his foot into the ground. I knew he was a Strength magical but hadn't anticipated the earthquake like shake his tantrum would cause.

Ariana stood so close to where the shaking began that she was knocked backwards. Lucas quickly moved to her aid, lifting her from the ground and I caught Morana's chest move in a subtle wicked laugh as she scoffed at his kindness.

"Mother is right," Griffin finally interjected. "You have lost your damn mind."

"You will never be capable of being the king of this realm," King Barin bellowed at his son. "What you lack is the ingenuity to create a plan such as mine. That, and your incessant need to coddle those who are beneath you."

"So, you have been planning this," Lucas surmised. "How do you expect this to end?"

"With me being all powerful!" — King Barin's fists shook in the air as his yell echoed throughout the room. — "With the right allies you can be known as a great leader, or you can be known as the conqueror of the world. I prefer the latter."

"We'd have been happy with a great king," Ariana said with far too much kindness.

"You'd have settled for him!" King Barin shouted at his wife, as he waved his hand toward Lucas. "Don't think for a second, I was blind to your feelings for him. Had I known he was alive, I would have killed him long ago."

"Oh, but then this reunion would have been far less entertaining," Morana finally said beside him.

Her voice came out with a luscious, almost intoxicating sound. It sent goosebumps up my arms and made me realize she really was a siren. Luring us all in with her tempting tones, but all the while knowing she could kill us all faster than a falcon swooping up a mouse.

"EvelynRose," Morana said, turning her gaze to Evey. "You seem...different."

"You don't know me," Evey snapped.

Something was missing in her tone. It lacked that surge of anger she always had inside of her. It was then that I realized that Morana was right. I had taken Evey's Fear magic. Without it, she was struggling. She couldn't be strong in the same way she could a week ago. Her Fear magic was both a poison and an asset to her.

"I know enough about you to know you are different than you were just a few days ago," Morana argued with her eyes narrowing. "But even my magic isn't sensing what it is."

"Maybe you're not as strong as you think," I snapped, as I moved closer to Evey.

Her chuckle was deafening, and I could barely fight the rage growing inside of me.

"She is."

Hale's voice surprised us, but as I watched Morana's smile falter for a moment, I knew she was even more surprised than we were. I thought I even felt a hint of irritation coming from her as he moved to stand near Lucas.

A strange smoke suddenly filled the room, and I instantly began looking around. People began to scream, and chaos took over the ballroom. The smoke shifted from a dark black to a gray and I turned back to the throne stage just in time to watch Michael materialize from within a plume of smoke.

"Hello there, Rosey." Michael winked at Evey. "Miss me?"

"Like a dog misses fleas," Evey snapped back.

I grinned at her a little — how could I not be proud of that come back — and inched a little closer to her.

"So, this was the plan all along?" Griffin growled. "You have been working with the Fears this entire time? You've betrayed your own people!"

"I have betrayed no one! You insolent boy! You will never have what it takes to be a king! You would never have the strength to make an ally of your worst enemy! The Fears will make me not only the King of Magir, but of *all* the magical realms. We will conquer this realm and then the next. I'll be the greatest king this universe has ever seen!"

"Griffin will be a greater king than you ever could have been," Ariana snapped.

"I have had enough of you, wife!"

"Actually, it is I that has had enough of you!" Ariana snapped back, standing taller than I have ever seen her. "You want to betray your people, fine. You want to hurt me, I can take your cruelty. But there will be no more berating my son. He will be the best king Magir has ever known. And with Evelyn by his side, they will rule with a kindness and equality that will prove you have been nothing but a tyrant."

"You think so?" King Barin scowled. "He won't get the chance."

Before we even realized what was happening King Barin launched sparks from his hands at Griffin. It was magic like nothing I had ever seen. Lucas shoved Griffin out of the way in the same moment that Ariana dove in front of him. All of the Knights quickly moved toward Griffin and his mother, ready to pounce on the king, but needing the order from Griffin to do so. After all he was their king — even if he didn't deserve it — and these Knights lived by a strict code. They couldn't mount an attack without Griffin's permission. Especially when that attack was on their own king. It was the same magic that I had seen Griffin use to wake Sean when Eveyln had knocked him out.

"What have you done?" Griffin shouted from the floor.

Queen Ariana was lying on the floor beside him. I could just make out her chest rising and falling...but barely. The feeling of dread rushed me just as the fear in the room began to mix with pure rage and a deep sadness.

"Your mother was a fool," King Barin said. "You are either part of my alliance or you will be a casualty of my conquest."

"You will never be the King of the Realms," Lucas shouted.

Lucas flew across the room at King Barin and the Knights moved quickly to surround Morana and Michael. But before they could all move that way, smoke filled the room again and more Fears began appearing out of thin air.

Somehow, the chaos in the room got even worse. Men, women, and children all screamed as they tried to escape the Fears that were attacking as quickly as they appeared.

I yanked Evey away from the crowd and Hale ushered us toward one of the walls. He moved in front of us, and unlike how the Knights took a fighting stance most of the time, he stood straight, waiting to be attacked. Callen and Griffin were both already caught up in their own battles, and despite having Evey's Fear magic inside of me, I was nervous about what that meant for Evey and I.

As a Fear woman moved toward us, Evey stepped out from behind Hale and threw her across the room hard with her Mind and Strength. The look on Hale's face showed me that even he was impressed. Even without her Fear magic, she was clearly one of the stronger magicals in Magir.

Morana stood beside the king's throne watching the battle as if she was at a sporting match. A look of sheer joy painted on her face. If you could call it joy...I wasn't even sure if a pure Fear could feel joy.

Only when a large group of Fears launched through the air did I see her grin falter. I turned to see where the Fears had come from and saw the same black smoke, they had arrived in surrounding a woman who was now fighting them. She had stunning, dark brown skin and what my Texas stylist called an updated bob, which was curled on the top of her head. As if she couldn't get any more gorgeous, when she finally turned toward me, I noticed that her eyes were gold. Like, actually gold.

Yet, there was something odd about her. I watched as she moved with the smoke. It was like she was one of them.

She had to have Fear magic in order to be able to move like that. I'd never seen any other magical harness that form of magic. She had to be a Fear. Yet she was fighting against them. And she was doing a damn good job! Who was this woman?

Michael appeared before us, pulling my gaze away from the mysterious woman.

"Look at you two cowering in the corner like scared little children," he mocked. "And instead of hiding behind the men who claim to love you, you have chosen to hide behind this pathetic waste of flesh?

"You should know better than to call me out, Michael," Hale threatened in an unusually calm tone.

"Tsk, tsk," Michael groaned. "Hale, you always think you have all the cards. But not this time. This time, we play with *my* deck."

Michael launched at Evey, as Hale — rather casually — threw himself between them. Watching them go blow for blow was nothing short of astonishing. They used the occasional force of magic, but unlike other magical battles I'd seen, this was more like a backyard brawl. Landing punches and kicks, it was almost like having front row tickets to a UFC title match.

I grabbed Evey's shoulder and tried to pull her towards the door, but even with her Fear magic inside of me, I couldn't move an inch. Evey's Strength must have been free flowing through her body because she was like a Goddamn statue standing there along the edges of the polished floor.

A couple more Fears appeared by Michael, and it started to seem like Hale was beginning to struggle. Though part of me wasn't sold on the fact that he was actually fighting with everything he had.

Evey moved to help him before I even had a chance of stopping her. I knew without her Fear magic, I couldn't let her fight on her own. She would need me close by. So, I quickly moved with her and felt the Fear begin to boil inside of me.

When the first Fear came to Evey and I, she moved him toward me with her Mind and then I raised my hands lifting him from the ground. Throwing my hands back to my side, he came crashing down to the floor so hard that the room shook again.

Evey looked at me in disbelief. Even I didn't really know what this Fear magic could do. But my God was she right. It felt good to have this magic flowing throughout your veins...I felt...completely invincible.

Just as we finished off our fourth Fear and they went disintegrating into the ground, two more came at us. I knew neither of us were experienced enough to redirect our magic that fast. I was just about to close my eyes and prepare for the hit, when a Hale stepped in front of us — tossing them to the side and into the wall with such ease I was now certain he had been holding back against Michael.

He turned to us — just for a second — to make sure we were okay, before I watched him glance in the direction of Callen and Griffin. Not one of them said a word but the stare down was fierce. In an unspoken thank you, Griffin and Callen both nodded slightly to Hale, then returned their focus to the battle.

I was fairly certain those three would never be friends, but if helping to save me from my deathbed hadn't been enough to call a truce, saving both of our lives from the people he was said to be allied with, certainly was.

As the battle continued, I noticed that many other Magirians had stayed behind and were helping in the fight. Across the room, I vaguely made out Callista and an older man who looked similar to Johanna. Looking around there were several older men fighting. I couldn't help but wonder if they were all council members. There was more than a small part of me that was hoping they were. Then there would be witnesses that held a vote there to see any other crazy stunt the king tried to pull.

A screeching sound suddenly filled the room, and we watched in helpless horror as Queen Ariana's limp body began to rise into the air. Everyone in the room immediately froze. No matter which magical family they were from, or which side they were fighting for, all eyes were on the queen. All, but mine. My focus remained on Morana and King Barin as they stood smugly at the front of the room.

"That is quite enough of that," Morana began, "Don't you think this is a waste? Surely, we can all be civilized about this. There are, after all, some of Magir's most talented magicals in this room. What a waste of magic it would be to just kill each other."

"Put her down," Griffin snarled.

"Griffin," Ariana whispered softly. "You'll make a great king. And Evelyn, a phenomenal queen."

"I mean it," Griffin warned again. "Put her down."

"You really aren't ready to be king, are you?" Morana chuckled. "I'm not going to be the one to kill your mother."

"I am."

We watched as King Barin twisted his wrist and Queen Ariana's head spun to the side.

"No!" Lucas and Griffin both shouted in unison.

Ariana's lifeless body collapsed to the floor, and I felt the Fear magic begin to surge within me.

"This war is at its end!" Morana declared. "In two days, when the moons are full, at the edge of Magir, we will end this worthless battle and you will all join us. Or you will die."

I couldn't hold the surge back anymore. I grabbed hold of Evey's hand and just looked at her. She closed her eyes, quickly filling the room with a fierce wind that forced a few of the Fears to vanish in their smoke. Fearless magicals, my ass.

Rain began to pour from the ceiling and thunder echoed in the room.

"I'll take care of this one," I heard Michael's voice declare.

The same sparks that flew through the air at Griffin came flying toward Evey. But before I could move to block it someone else did.

"No!"

I heard the voice shouting but couldn't tell where it came from. Evey's eyes shot open, and we both looked in disbelief at the floor in front of us.

The winds stopped and Evey fell to her knees.

"You'll need to learn to control that a little bit better," Morana derided. "Or you won't stand a chance against us."

The room filled quickly with black smoke, and as it cleared all of the Fears, along with King Barin, were gone.

"What were you thinking?" I heard Evey question Katerie.

I knelt down beside the two women as Nicholas, Daniel and Nixie appeared at our sides.

"I told you," Katerie choked. "I told you I would make up for letting them use me as a spy. It's you that is destined to win this war, Evelyn. Not me."

"Katerie, no." Evey cried as she shook her head. "You didn't owe us anything. And you are the bravest of all of us."

A small smile crept across Katerie's lips and then faded as her head fell to the side.

Across the room Griffin was on the ground beside Lucas and the body of his mother. Callen stood over him but was watching me with a somber expression. In an instant, I felt the room change. With the Fears gone and the two fallen women before us, we were broken. All of us, just completely heartbroken.

With a quick glance around the room, I tried to count the other fallen Magirians. There weren't many, and that was comforting...but was death in any number, really a statistic I wanted to give credence too?

Queen Ariana had been a true leader, in every sense, and a fierce mother. Katerie was a kindhearted fighter, who died to protect a friend. They died for us. They had all died for us. But more than that, they had died for Magir. To give it the best chance at a future. A future that didn't include King Barin or Morana.

Even as I tried to find purpose in their sacrifices, I knew

I couldn't just accept that they were gone. The truth of it was...death sucked. Death sucked bad. Even if I hadn't known them long, they were family. Family to the Knights. To Evey. And to me. We were a family, and two of our own had fallen. And even as the sadness consumed the room, the Fear magic inside me was telling me that Morana had bitten off more than she could chew this time. This was a battle Morana did not want to face me in.

A life for a life. It would never be enough. But as I felt Callen's grief pouring over me and I held my best friend's hand as I watched her cry over the dead body of another friend...I knew it was a good place to start.

Chapter 18

Evelyn

A burial ceremony in Magir honored the dead in ways a traditional funeral ceremony in the non-magical realm never could.

The garden was filled with the Magirian council members, Magirians who had stayed behind to pay respects to their queen, and then all of our group. We all somberly looked on, while Griffin, the Knights, and Lucas placed rocks over the bodies of Queen Ariana and Katerie. Both women had been wrapped in such beautiful drapes, it almost seemed a shame to cover them up. Then again, some non-magical people were buried in million-dollar coffins, so I guess this was a similar practice.

The biggest difference between a magical and non-magical ceremony was that with each rock that was placed over the body of the decedent, a small spark shot into the sky. Once it was high enough, the spark silently exploded, releasing a sprinkle of tiny stars. It reminded me of watching fireworks. Each rock was placed slowly to allow the spark to be completed. And with each burst of beautiful light, I found it more and more difficult to hold back the tears I had been fighting.

When Nicholas placed what appeared to be the final rock on Katerie, he waved me over to join him. I dropped Violet's hand and felt her magic slowly leave me as I made my way over to him.

"Would you like to help me send her to Estella?"

"Where?"

"Who," Nicholas corrected. "Estella was said to be the first Magirian to pass on from this life. When we lose someone, we perform this ceremony, and their magical soul is lifted into the night sky to become a star and live forever with Estella — the magical who watches over our fallen."

"That's beautiful," I said softly. "What do I need to do?"

"You'll tell Estella what to honor about Katerie and then you'll repeat a phrase with me. I'll go first."

He took a deep breath and placed his hand over the stones where Katerie's head would indefinitely rest. It was strange to see Nicholas, who had always seemed so stern, so utterly defeated.

"Her perseverance and her smile. Srats eht ni reverof."

He looked over at me and nodded toward the rocks, so I placed my hand close to his.

"Her kind heart and selfless soul. Srats eht ni reverof," I said.

"Now together," he whispered.

"Srats eht ni reverof."

Against my skin, the rocks began to feel warm, and Nicholas pulled my hand away from the pile as I watched the rocks begin to glow a warm red.

The rocks quickly melted into one another and entombed Katerie's body. Once they had molded into one large mass, they began to shine like polished metal and a bright green spark flew from the tomb, into the sky. Bursting bright enough to light up the entire garden as the green sparks slowly rained down on us.

"Srats eht ni reverof."

Everyone in the garden echoed the words around us as Katerie's tomb began to slowly settle into the ground.

Nicholas then placed his hand on my forearm and led me back toward where Violet and the other Knights were standing. As we reunited with our group, Nicholas instantly went to Nixie. She was a shell of her normal perky self. And the look in Violet's eyes told me she too was drowning in the heartbreak of everyone around us. I couldn't imagine having their gifts right now. Nixie with her need to fix everything and Violet feeling everyone's pain...a ceremony such as this had to be torture for both of them.

Beside the place where Katerie had just been laid to rest, Griffin and Lucas continued to slowly place rocks over Queen Ariana. I didn't know how to comfort Griffin about this. I grew up without parents. And while I felt pain similar to when I almost lost Auntie Saraya, I knew it wasn't the same. And then there was the fact that one of my long-lost parents had been the instigator, causing one of his parents to kill the other. Despite finally declaring how we truly felt about one another only a day ago, I didn't feel like I was the right person to be comforting him in this moment.

Just as the thought crossed my mind, Callen leaned over from the other side of Violet and shot me a forced, but still warm, smile.

"He'd like you to join him."

I wasn't sure if I was ready for that. To be his rock on the day he lost his mother. On the day his own father had killed her. But the closer I moved to him, the more I knew I had to be ready. I needed him to know that I would always be there for him. That no matter what we were going through, I would always be by his side.

As I stepped into the place beside him, he instantly interlaced our hands and gave me the most defeated smile I had ever seen from him. Beside us, Lucas placed another rock and another white firework shot high into the sky.

"Thank you for being up here with us," Lucas said as he

attempted a welcoming smile. "She would have wanted you to be part of this."

Griffin moved to place the final rock when a small group of men and women collectively moved to the front of the crowd. They all looked just as somber as the rest of us but there were other emotions in their eyes. There was a palpable level of anxiety behind their expressions.

"The Magirian council has come forward to honor their queen," Griffin whispered to me. "They've also called for an emergency session following the ceremony. So, I'll be joining you in the suite later."

"Of course," I responded. "Whatever you need."

He feebly smiled at me again before placing the final rock, resting his hand on it for a few moments before pulling it back and placing it into his pants pocket.

"Would you like me to officiate?" Lucas offered.

Griffin didn't respond, but instead simply nodded in his direction, his eyes never leaving where his mother now laid. It was one thing to officiate the burial ceremony of someone you care about, but to do that for your own mother...I wasn't sure how a person would ever be able to recover from that.

I could feel the pain my father was fighting himself. That ache in my heart had me feeling truly grateful for his presence in this moment and for his offer to take on that excruciating task in order to save Griffin from enduring it.

Lucas waved his arms for everyone else to come closer. The crowd moved toward us with their heads hung in grief. I could see a few more people still entering the garden, but it was hard to make out their faces as the others closed in on us.

Griffin gripped my hand tightly, as I shifted my gaze to him. His jaw was tightly clenched as he stared down at where his mother's head laid beneath the rocks.

I needed to find a way to comfort him. Comforting people was always Violet's thing though...not mine. But I had to do something. So, I grabbed onto his arm, pulling myself closer to him and somehow managed to pull his eyes to mine.

"Thank you for being here."

His words echoed in my head the same Violet's did when I was convinced that she was in my bathroom.

"I'll always stand beside you."

I thought the words and watched as Griffin's eyes lit up a little bit. Though it quickly faded as Lucas began the eulogy by thanking everyone for being there.

"I had the pleasure of growing up with Ariana, and being a mentor to her as we grew older," Lucas began. "She was always the type of person, that when she walked in a room, everyone was instantly smiling. But it wasn't just that she was beautiful...and she was beautiful. No, it was just her. She was so happy and full of life, that you couldn't help but be happy too."

I felt Griffin tighten beside me as I scanned the faces in the garden, before returning my gaze to Lucas. He was grieving too, that much was obvious. Yet, he had a slight smile forming on his lips that made my chest tighten, and I instinctively gripped Griffin a little tighter. I recognized that smile. It was the same smile I'd tried to hide from Griffin whenever he made me blush.

"But if you really knew Ari, you knew behind that contagious smile and beautiful face was the most passionate and fierce woman you would ever meet in your life," he boasted. "I mean the woman could argue for hours. And take it from me, by the end of those hours, you had been put in your place so many times that your great-great-great grandmother was feeling it."

The crowd chuckled a little through their sobs and Griffin's face contorted slightly as he fought back his own tears.

"No part of me was shocked when she was chosen to be the Queen of Magir," Lucas continued. "She was incredibly strong, both in magic and in heart. Her heart belonged to Magir. It was her home. She was proud to be Queen. And even though I hadn't been a part of her life in many years, I know that never changed.

"One thing did change though," he said, turning toward Griffin and I. "She became a mom. I only got a glimpse of Ari as a mother, but I could see the love she had for her son the minute I returned. She just had that look in her eye. I could even see it when she looked at my own daughter."

Eyes widened as they accepted that Lucas had *returned from the dead*, and I, the mysterious descendant of the Archer line, was standing mere feet from him.

"And she died because someone she trusted betrayed her and exploited that love," he declared with a cringe. "Barin betrayed Ari's loving nature and he tried to turn her into something that was not who she was and..."

Lucas paused and took a really long, deep breath.

"I apologize. This isn't about him...and I won't give him the satisfaction of being spoken about here. No, we are all here for her," he said, as he gestured toward where Ariana's body laid. "We are here to honor her. To say goodbye to her as our Queen...a friend...a mother. To send her to Estella, with nothing but happy thoughts and cherished memories."

With that he took a few steps toward Ariana and placed his hand over the rocks near where her head was. His eyes slowly closed, and he took another long, deep breath.

"Her warm, forgiving heart," he said, just loud enough for us to hear. "Srats eht ni reverof."

A bright purple spark shot into the sky and exploded into beautiful falling stars. When I looked away from the fireworks, I saw that Violet and Callen had stepped forward and placed their hands over the stones.

"Her fierceness," Violet began.

"Her welcoming, mothering nature," Callen added.

"Srats eht ni reverof," they said together.

Another bright purple spark erupted into the sky, as more people began to move forward and proclaim their favorite things about their queen. She truly had been a remarkable woman. That was clearer now, in that moment, than it had ever been.

When it looked like everyone who wanted to speak had done so, Griffin and I moved closer. He paused as we stood silently overlooking the stones. As he lifted his hand, it was shaking fiercely. I heard him swallow and grabbed hold of his hand before anyone else could notice his tremors.

I couldn't bear to look at him, knowing how sad he was. So, I moved his hand down to the pile and left mine over his.

"Her graceful regality, endless loyalty and her nurturing heart," I exclaimed softly.

"Her..." Griffin choked out. "Her amazing made up castle games. Her epic storytelling. And...and her unconditional love."

"Srats eht ni reverof," we said together.

Griffin's hand slowly relaxed beneath mine and I interlaced our fingers once again.

"Together," Lucas instructed the crowd.

"Srats eht ni reverof," the group echoed.

Unlike how Katerie had one large burst into the sky, Ariana had several. It was how I always imagined the Time Square New Years Eve Party would look like in person. A million beautiful lights shining in the sky together. Yet even though the lights sparked that thought, I knew this was even more special.

It was a celebration of even more magnitude. This was simply to honor the amazing women that Magir had lost. There was no need for theatrics. Just a nighttime glow to show our love for a Magirian we would mourn for the rest of our lives. Somehow just knowing that made it even more beautiful to witness.

We removed our hands as the stones melded together and formed a beautiful crystal over Ariana. As she sank into the ground, the crowd slowly began to disperse from the garden and back into the castle.

Griffin, Lucas and I did not move from our spots. We watched diligently as Queen Ariana was absorbed into the ground and just before her crystallized coffin was completely immersed, it stopped.

A small section of shining rock, which would have been near her head, remained above the ground and small purple flowers began to form around it. I looked at Griffin confused, but his eyes didn't leave his mother.

"Think of it like a headstone of sorts," Lucas explained. "Most Magirians are absorbed completely on their journey to Estella. But royals are forever part of Magir. So, their final resting place is marked."

"So where are all the others?" I asked, half expecting to find a large graveyard full of Griffin's ancestors.

"In their favorite places. Upon their appointment to the crown, all royals give instructions outlining where they want to be laid to rest," Griffin explained. "This was my mother's favorite place in all of Magir."

I nodded and returned to look at the flowers that continued to bloom around her. As beautiful as it was, there was still something about them that felt incomplete. If this was her final resting place, then she deserved something even more special.

Pulling on Griffin's hand I knelt next to the stone with him beside me. Placing my free hand on the stem of one of the flowers, I took a deep breath and channeled my healing magic.

I watched as the flower stems began to twirl around each other, forming a circular wreath. Large purple flowers began to take form, followed by small white ones. Just as I pulled my hand back, the leaves at the bottom twisted themselves into an intricate bow.

"Thank you," Griffin whispered softly. "She would have loved that."

I smiled up at him, although he still wasn't looking at me, and we stood slowly.

"Prince Griffin," a soldier suddenly said from the entryway to the garden. "The council is ready for you now."

"Thank you," Griffin nodded. "Lucas, will you join us?"

"If that is your wish," Lucas responded.

"It is," Griffin replied in a very official tone. "E, do you think you can find your way back to the suite?"

"I actually want to stay here for a bit," I said. "I'll find my way back soon."

"E, I don't want you out here alone," Griffin said softly to me. "After what the Fears just did, I wouldn't put anything past them."

"I'll stay with her, your highness."

I didn't recognize the voice, but immediately recognized the face as that of the mysterious woman who had appeared during the battle and fought alongside us.

"I can assure you EvelynRose, will be incredibly safe with her, my prince" Lucas assured him.

"Griffin," he corrected, "I am placing a great amount of trust in you. If anything happens to her..."

"Don't let the thought burden you," the woman interrupted. "I can assure you that no Fear can get the better of me."

"Very well then," Griffin nodded before turning back to me. "I shouldn't be long. I'll see you back in the Knights' suite. There is no need for you to retire to your suite tonight."

"I'll be there."

He leaned forward and softly kissed my cheek before turning to the door. Lucas followed behind him with a slight smile forming on the corner of his lips. In my head, I wasn't sure if it was because he was happy for me, or if he was just happy to be back in the good graces of the royal family.

"I can assure you, it's you." the woman said suddenly.

"What's me?"

"Your father's smile," she nodded toward where Griffin and Lucas had just disappeared. "He is smiling because he is happy for you. Happy that you have managed to find a love like this at your young age."

"How..."

"I have a magical gift too," she interrupted. "Nothing

like the magic you have...but a gift. I can read others' thoughts."

"You can?" I questioned, suddenly frightened of what might go through my head.

"It's alright," she laughed. "It's not like I can read everyone's thoughts all the time. I have to focus my energy on one person at a time in order to get the magic to work. It's easier now that it's just you and I."

"And who exactly are you?"

"Oh, damn. I forgot that we haven't actually met. It's just that your father has told me so much about you for so long, it feels like I have known you for your entire life. Armonee Emem," she said, holding out her hand. "I've been helping your father survive all these years."

I shook her hand and nodded at her.

"I think we should go for a walk."

I squinted at her a little. My intention was to stay a few more minutes with Ariana and Katerie. Not go for a walk around the garden with some woman I didn't even know.

"Come one," she winked. "I don't bite. Well, only sometimes."

I couldn't help but laugh as she made her joke before turning to walk further into the garden. As much as I knew better than to trust someone I didn't know, I somehow knew I was safe with her. That I could follow her, and I would be alright.

As I approached the gazebo where she had stopped, she turned to look at me over her shoulder. It was then that I really got a good look at her. Her curly black hair sat beautifully on the top of her head and her eyes shined a brilliant gold color that I couldn't imagine was real. Coupled with her flawless dark brown skin...she was breathtaking.

"They're real," she said suddenly. "My eyes. I don't know how. Not like gold is exactly a common eye color. But this is how I was born. Or so my grandmother used to say. Certainly, made blending into the non-magical realm difficult at times."

"Um....did you just?"

"Read your mind again? Yeah. You get used to it after a while. You know for a Mind magical, you sure are easy to read."

"It's my...my weakest form of magic," I said, studying her as she made her way to the bench and casually sat down. "What did you want to talk with me about?"

"Whatever you want to talk about," she shrugged. "Seems like you need an outsider's ear."

"Um..."

"Look," she began, as she leaned forward with hands on her knees. "I've watched over you for a long time and I have never seen you so...so happy."

"Happy?" I choked. "I just watched two strong women and a bunch of innocent Magirians die, yet you think that I'm happy? And what do you mean by, *you've watched me for a long time*?"

"Did you really think your father just left you alone?" she asked, leaning back against the rail.

I had never laid eyes on Lucas Archer even once in my entire life before he returned to Magir after our battle near the Dark Woods. But then I remembered his words as we had danced. But he couldn't have been telling the truth. I would have remembered him.

"Girl, you can't be that naive," she shook her head. "Your father and I have been following you around the best we could for years. Even if it meant living one town over in hopes to see you on a walk. Or only seeing you for a second while you were at work with Violet. Or even that time he was substituting at your school, even though he was a horrible science teacher. He never really left you. Actually, it was rather difficult to keep him from getting to close to you."

I stared at her. I wasn't even sure what to think. If what she was saying was true...how had I never noticed him? How did Auntie Saraya never notice him? I mean at least I had the excuse of never having met him. He was her brother! How could he have hidden from her?

"Listen," she sighed, as she stood up and moved towards me. "Just understand that Lucas really cares about you. And he is a good man. Just allow him the chance to prove that to you."

She walked past me and for a second, I stood there frozen as my brain was processing.

"And why should I trust your word?" I yelled after her. "Clearly you are his friend. Of course, you would say he is a good man."

"Because," she began with a shrug, "he saw past what I was and trusted me enough to help me become a better person. I'm a Fear, EvelynRose. I'm a Fear, yet he put his life in my hands. He's a good man. Give him a chance to prove it."

Without another word she turned and made her way across the garden.

I knew Griffin didn't want me out here alone, but if I thought I had been frozen in place before...I was a statue now. A Fear? Openly in Magir? A Fear, other than me, in the castle? How was that even possible? I mean, did Lucas really know she was a Fear? It would have made sense that after the fiasco with my mother he wouldn't take a chance on another Fear...but she had said Fear. Clear as day, she said, *I'm a Fear*.

"Excuse me, Lady Archer."

The voice had my head spinning, but I turned I saw a guard standing off to the side of the path back into the castle.

"Just Evelyn," I insisted. "And I should be inside in just a few."

"His royal highness has asked that you meet him in his quarters."

"I'll head back to the suite in a few."

"I'm sorry," he apologized. "Not the suite, Lady Archer. His royal highness would like to meet you in his personal quarters. On the other end of the castle."

Chapter 19

Evelyn

It made perfect sense that Griffin had another space in the castle. He had lived in this castle here long before he became a Knight. But in the time, I had been here, he had never once shown me his part of the castle. Not that we'd had a ton of time for a full-blown tour, but part of me was a little surprised he had never even mentioned it.

I had to get myself to stop thinking like that. The truth was that every good relationship was supposed to involve constantly learning about the other person. Having common things that brought you together while still having pieces of each other to discover. If there was one bit of relationship advice I had discovered after suffering with Michael, it was that being with another person meant that you were always learning new things about them. The difference was that once you found *your* person, no matter what you learned, you loved them just the same.

When we turned the corner down a hall I had yet to be in, the guard stopped suddenly and pushed open a large door.

"His royal highness will meet you here soon," the guard explained.

He held out his arm to escort me into the room and I walked in with a brief nod in his direction.

"If you need anything, I will be outside until his royal highness arrives."

He moved to close the door and I spun around to face him.

"You know," I began. "I've never heard anyone refer to Griffin as *his royal highness*."

He just stared at me, his face completely unchanged.

"His royal highness may prefer a less formal title, but things have changed," he informed me. "I shall be right outside, Lady Archer."

Without saying another word, he nodded to me and closed the door. He hadn't really answered the question I had posed, but he was right. Things had changed. With the Queen of Magir dead, and the King of Magir having murdered her, I knew that was going to put an enormous amount of responsibility and pressure on both Griffin and the council.

I turned back around to look at the room and realized immediately that I had been correct in my guess as to where we were heading. This was definitely Griffin's room before he became a Knight. This had been the space where he grew up. Where Griffin grew from a boy to a man.

Walking around, I admired a corner where a barrel of swords was tucked away. I could see the beat-up wooden ones that must have been for practice when he was a child. On a wall beside a tall hutch filled with artifacts, I saw many pictures of him and his mother. I could see how much Ariana and Griffin loved each other. The bond between a mother and son...it made my chest tighten.

I moved through his room admiring the history it held and noticed two archways. One led to a large bedroom that had a bed bigger than I thought was possible. But it was the other archway that really piqued my interest.

Stepping through that archway, I found myself in

Griffin's personal study. Bookshelves lined an entire wall, and in front of a small window in the back was an intricate desk that was covered in papers. I could see smaller desks and a couple of easels, all of which were covered in charts that looked similar to the ones for Fated and Magical Twin bonds.

As I moved closer to the largest desk, I could see that there were books, as well as drawings, covering its surface. Thinking of Griffin sitting in here creating these works of art made me smile a little. Mr. Big and Strong, always obeying his magical rules...I had never imagined him as having an artistic side.

Though once I picked up one of the drawings, it was clear that he was good...like, really good! But he'd drawn picture after picture, of the same face though. All from different angles, but it was clearly the same woman. Shuffling through them, I made my way to one that was a lightly sketched headshot of the woman looking straight at me. The love in her eyes was impossible to miss. But it was the shape of her eyes and the curls of her fluffy hair that made me grip the picture even tighter in my hands.

It was me...every picture he drew...they were all...me.

Griffin had told me all about the girl in his dreams. Johanna had known about her too. But this not a normal fantasy...or everyday dreaming. He really had seen me. That was my crazy hair. Those were my round cheekbones. And those eyes...those distracting eyes...were mine.

"I told you," Griffin's voice said behind me. "I told you... it was always you."

I didn't know what I could possibly say in that moment. Instead, I did something I normally wouldn't. Without overthinking it, I dropped the picture, rushed to him, quickly took his face in my hands and pressed my lips against his.

His body instantly relaxed as his arms wound around me, pulling me in closer. I don't know what had come over me, but I didn't want him to let me go. More so, I didn't want to let him go. There was something about the defeated and conflicted look on his face before I had kissed him. He needed this moment just as much as I did.

Moving my arms around his neck, I pressed my body into his as he lowered his hands down my back. Before I knew what was happening, he had lifted me from the ground and my legs wrapped around his waist as he cradled my backside in his hands. I shrieked a little at how easily he lifted me, and he chuckled beneath me, before I took his lips again.

He carried me across the room, but I was so engrossed in the kiss we were sharing, I hadn't considered where he was taking me until he laid me on the bed. As he released me, I scooted up, resting my head against the pillows, but even as my body moved, my eyes remained locked on his.

Moving himself up the bed, he held himself above me, not crushing me with his weight, but allowing me to feel all of him.

I kissed him again, knowing exactly where I wanted this moment to go, but he pulled away before I could successfully deepen the kiss or make my intentions known. Words escaped me for a moment, as I felt a rush of pain resulting from his magic attempting to pull away from me while mine fought to hold on to him.

"What's wrong?"

"E," he sighed. "I can't have you like this. You don't know what it means."

"I'm not naive, Griffin. I do know what it means."

"No," he corrected, as he shook his head. "You don't understand. They want me to be king."

"Um...you're a prince, Griffin. I figured that would be part of the deal eventually."

"Now," he said shortly. "They want to make me King of Magir, now."

"Oh..."

"So, this isn't just you and me anymore. Us being together means not only giving yourself to me in this way, but also dedicating your life to serving Magir. Dedicating yourself to all the responsibilities of being a queen. I can't ask you to give up the life you're building. Not while you're still learning who you are. I can't ask you to do that for me. I..."

"Griffin," I gently interrupted. "I meant what I said before. I love you. I love you as a Prince, as a King, or even as a Knight. Hell, I'd love you if you were simply the mysterious art loving, politician I'd met at the Cottonwood Resort. I want to be the woman that is forever by your side. And if that means I have to become the most magically unaware queen that Magir has ever seen...then so be it. As long as I am with you, everything else is irrelevant. All I need in this life is you. And if you can promise me your love in return, it doesn't matter if I wake up a queen tomorrow. I am ready for whatever comes out way."

He stared at me for a moment and my eyes widened a bit as a sudden rush of anxiety took over. I had just put my heart on a platter for the first time in my life. As he laid there, silently staring at me, I began to consider that he may not feel the same. Despite the mystical heat that I knew meant we were connected, my heart was tightening in my chest from the anxiety of wondering if I was alone in these feelings.

"Look, I know that was a lot..." I began.

"E."

"And I know this is definitely not the day to be professing my feelings."

"E!"

"But I meant it."

"So, you'll marry me?"

"What?"

I basically choked on the word as it burst from my mouth. Confessing my love was one thing. And obviously, I knew that the moment we moved forward, it meant a lifetime for a magical. But for some reason hearing the words *marry me* had me both schoolgirl-giddy and nauseous at the same time.

"You'd marry me?" he asked again. "If I was to ask you, right this second, would you marry me?"

Now it was my turn to stare. I studied the expression in his eyes for a moment. They were focused yet loving all at once. I may have only been in my early 20's, but damn...my entire being knew the answer already. I think I'd known it since I had fallen asleep on his chest back at Cottonwood. He was, as Violet would say, my person.

"Yes."

"Wait, what?"

"I'd marry you, right now," I pledged, as I wrapped my arms around his neck and pulled him down closer to me. "Well maybe not *right now*...I mean we do have a war to fight in a few days. But I'd marry you the moment we make it out alive."

His lips were on mine in a fraction of a second. The entire world began to fall away as he made me forever his. Forever his love. Forever his queen. In that moment, I realized that happiness was something I not only deserved...it was something I had found.

Chapter 20

Violet

"Where the hell are they?" Johanna cursed. "Council meeting or not, they have been gone for hours!"

She was right. We had been sittin' in this suite for at least two hours waiting to hear what in the world was goin' on. Granted, I could only imagine what all the council members wanted to discuss or what it was like to be in Griffin's shoes. There was likely a lot to discuss when your king teams up with your mortal enemy and then blatantly murders your queen in a room full of people.

But damn...the wait was exhausting. Not to mention I kept getting these strange hot flashes. Normally those only hit me when I was around Callen. And granted, he was right next to me, even my body wasn't dumb enough to think this was the place for that.

"The council has concluded their meeting," Callen confirmed. "But I stopped sensing Griffin a while ago, so I'm assuming he's with Evelyn now."

"Well, my God! What could possibly be taking them so long?" Johanna complained.

"Does it really matter?" Nicholas asked sharply. "The

point is that we need a plan. That witch may have said we had two days to prepare, but I have a feeling that the Fears won't hold their word and wait."

"You think they'll actually have the guts to attack the castle again?" I asked. "I mean that would be dumber than a bull rider gettin' back on the bull that just dumped her on her ass."

"All I'm saying is that even though they spilled first blood, that won't appease them for long," Nicholas continued. "They are addicted to inflicting pain on others. They know we are broken now. If they had even an ounce of war tactic, they'd know that now was the time to attack us, while we are distracted...and weak. Emotionally weak that is."

"On the contrary, not always wise to go after someone when they're down," Nixie surmised. "Sometimes one finds their true strength when life has them knocked on their knees."

Johanna stopped pacing and we both stared at the chair where Nixie was sitting. Her perky smile was gone, and her hair had turned a shade darker than black...if that was possible. Even Nicholas, who I was pretty sure was secretly in love with her, couldn't look at her and still be angry.

"You're both right," I concluded, knowing someone needed to speak. "Look, I know we need to make a plan, Nick, but I also think Nixie is right. I actually believe that despite their bloodlust, they know it wouldn't be smart to come back here tonight. I think we need to get some things straight in our heads and rest. Tomorrow morning, we can make a solid plan with clearer heads."

I could see the veins pulsing in Nicholas's neck, and his growing anger was enough to suffocate me. But it was the agonizing sadness, which he was trying to mask, that forced him to nod and retreat to his room without another word. Daniel quietly grabbed Nixie's hand and escorted her to Griffin's empty room, while explaining that she would be staying here under their protection. He then retreated to his room leaving Callen, Sean, Johanna and I alone by the fire.

"We all know he's right," Sean said, after Daniel's door closed. "The likelihood of them waiting two days is slim at best."

"I agree," Callen conferred, as he moved to sit on the arm of my chair and placed his hand on my back. "But he isn't thinking straight. Nicholas is far more emotionally driven than he lets on. Losing someone he was bonded to is going to wreak havoc on him. And we need him at his best for all of this. He has to be thinking clearly."

"Better keep Nixie safe then," Johanna whispered.

"Besides that," Sean began, as he playfully nudged Johanna, "I think he will need a very specific task to keep him focused for the next few days. Maybe assigning him to guard Nixie?"

"I think she may distract him too much," Callen argued. "I'd rather put him, Victor, Charles and Nixie together, and have them all be in charge of creating a battle strategy. Looking at area maps. Finding vantage points. All of those critical battle preparations. It's something that Nicholas would normally enjoy but will still challenge him enough to keep his mind from giving in to his anger."

"And for tonight?" Sean asked.

"Vi and I will go make sure everything with the council went okay and we will also check the training equipment," Callen explained. "Are you and Johanna good to keep watch here for a little while? Shouldn't need to be for long, but I'd like to make sure Nick doesn't come back out of that room tonight."

"You're assigning us to babysit?"

"He meant to say," Johanna began, as she elbowed Sean, "that sounds great."

"Yeah, I'm sure he did." Callen shook his head, as he began to move toward the door, and I stood to follow him. "You don't need to *babysit* for long. You both need to get some rest too. The coming days will be pretty grueling and once this battle begins...well, who knows how long it will be before we return. Enjoy the comfort of your bed as long as you can."

Sean nodded and Johanna grasped his hand, giving it a tight squeeze in a silent gesture of unity and support. I smiled at them both, trying to convey as much hope and warmth as possible...but I knew it was a lost cause. Even with them loving each other the way that they did, today's events had left a scar on all of us. Coupled with our looming future...hope and warmth was just not something any of us were feelin'.

Yet, as I interlaced my fingers with Callen's and let him lead me from the suite, I knew that closing the door with those two on the other side to watch over our brokenhearted friends, was the best choice. As much as I tried to not like her at first, Johanna was a force to be reckoned with. She had proven herself to be the type of person that could handle any situation. More than that though, her heart always seemed to be in the right place. Especially now that her heart was complete with Sean by her side.

As Callen led me down a couple hallways, I actually found myself smiling. Smiling because I knew, that somehow, this was going to work out. And even though I was terrified, anxious, angry, sad, and battling a million other emotions my empathy was too overstimulated to identify, I knew that everything, at least back in that suite, was going to be okay.

We entered a room that looked sort of like an outdated gymnasium and Callen dropped my hand as he crossed the room. Looking around, I surmised this was where the Knights's did their training. There were various swords, axes, and other medieval style weapons lining one of the walls. While more basic training equipment including weights and ropes covered the other wall. Large shelves also lined the back of the room, though it was too dark for me to see exactly what was on them.

"So, this is where the magic happens?" I joked. "This is where you learn to become a Knight?"

"Not exactly," Callen laughed. "This is where we come to train after we've been selected. This is a training facility designed for us Knights."

"Wait, so nobody else has access to this room? That seems a little silly. It is just a gym."

"There are a select group of people who can enter," he corrected, as he grabbed what appeared to be a duffel bag and began filling it.

"And how, may I ask, do you make this *sacred list*?"

"You get permission from the king."

Callen stood straight and even in the dark I could see his jaw clench as the voice rang through the room. I spun around to see who had provided the answer...though I recognized that voice immediately. And sure enough, I was right. Hale Reignn was now standing behind us.

I hadn't seen him since the battle in the ballroom. If he had attended Queen Ariana and Katerie's funeral he must have been hidin' in the back, because I never saw him. Not that I would have blamed him for not attending. Clearly, he had put his faith in the wrong side. Of course, when all the chips were actually on the table, he did choose right and fought alongside us...but I felt bad for the inner turmoil he was suffering through. As he locked eyes with Callen, who was fighting his own urges to punch or hug him, Hale's twisted tangle of anger and regret hit me with such a force that I felt like I had been pinned to the ground.

"I'm sorry," Hale said, breaking his eye contract with Callen and looking at me. "I didn't realize any of you would be in here."

Hale turned to leave, and I turned back to Callen who just stood there, imprisoned by years of hating the man before us. Despite him helping to save my life and then fighting by our side, there was still a part of Cal that didn't trust him.

"Hale, wait!" I shouted.

He stopped and turned back to face me. I hadn't really spoken to him since he woke me up. During the fight, I hadn't gotten the chance to really look at him either. Now, as I stared at him, even in the dark I could see that he had aged. And not just the normal aging of the few months since I'd met him. He looked like he was years older. And the scar that ran across his face wasn't helping his case.

"I…I never really got a chance to thank you," I stammered. "*We* never got a chance to thank you."

I made a gesture toward Callen and saw his hardened expression soften.

"No thanks necessary. I owe you the apology. I should have been more aware of the situation. I should have been on your side from the beginning. But I wasn't. I will leave you to your preparations."

"No wait!" I said, stepping toward him. "How did you know?"

"Know what, exactly?" he asked, squinting at me.

"How did you know about Evey and I being magically bonded? How did you know before either of us?"

"Actually," Callen said, suddenly appearing at my side. "I've been wanting to know that as well."

"I had my suspicions from the moment you had such a strong shining," Hale answered.

"So, you knew I was only strong because of Evey?"

"That's not how it works. It isn't one sided like that. One of you is not *stronger* than the other. No, you are that strong *because* of each other," he corrected. "It was my job to get EvelynRose to return to Sephtis with me. I knew who she was the moment she stepped foot on Woodburn Rose soil. But you…you were a pleasant surprise."

"What the hell does that mean?" Callen snapped.

"Cal!" I groaned, rolling my eyes at him. "But seriously…what do you mean by that?"

"I don't claim to be an expert," Hale began, while Callen let out a little chuckle as I glared at him. "But I was certain that you had to be connected to her by more than friendship. You both ooze power. And a strong power at that. The fact that Michael couldn't see it just proves he is even more inadequate than I'd thought."

"Evey probably was blocking him without him knowing. She does that."

"Hansel consulted with me before I left the school. I know of her Obstruction. It's fascinating magic."

"So, you put together that we were bonded somehow," I said, redirecting the discussion back to what I wanted to know. "But how did you break into my nightmare and know about the Fear magic I'd absorbed?"

"You took in her Fear magic? Do you still have it?"

I nodded and Callen's eyes widened. This was definitely not how I had imagined letting the cat out of the bag.

"That's why you feel so different. Why our connection feels slightly foreign."

"And it will," Hale confirmed. "The magic inside you isn't yours. You can use it, but your body knows it doesn't belong to you. Though I can confirm for you both, that this does not impact your own bond. Once the magic leaves your body, your bond will return to normal. Not that it isn't there now. It's just harder to feel and harness the power it gives you. But with how the four of you are all connected..."

Hale trailed off like he was calculating a hypothesis of some kind. But I didn't have time for that.

"Hale, please," I begged. "How did you get into my head like that? I had been trying to get through to both Evey and Callen for what felt like weeks. Why were you able to break through, when I couldn't even pull in the people I was bonded to?"

"I hate to disappoint, but I'm not entirely sure how I got in either. I could feel something was going on with the king, and before you go getting all upset with me Callen, I feel bad enough without a lecture from you."

"No lecture, Hale," Callen conceded.

"When I realized that something was going to happen — though I never imagined it would be what was — I knew that the best chance for EvelynRose to return to her strength was with you by her side. So, I dove into magical books on

Healing to search for an answer but found nothing. Absolutely nothing. It wasn't until I saw EvelynRose being almost shy, that I realized her Fear was gone. I knew then what had happened to you. Having suffered at the hand of Fears, and their magic, I knew it would trap you in something horrible.

Being a Mind, I knew my best chance at getting through to you was by entering your thoughts. So, I decided to try a form of magic I am not very good at. Projection. After talking with Lucian, I had to lie down for hours, keeping my mind completely clear, just to get through to you. Only after failing, did I realize I needed to be close EvelynRose in order to truly reach you. As the pieces came together, I knew that I was right about the two of you. And I knew it would take both her and Callen to pull you away from so much Fear magic."

A guard knocked loudly on the door and we all immediately turned our attention to him.

"I'm sorry, to disturb you Mr. Ivanti, but there are guests here that need addressing and his royal highness is indisposed."

"Who is it?" Callen asked in an authoritative tone.

"Her royal majesty of Fantazi."

"Tatiana is here?" Callen said, straightening his stance. "Place her in the royal guest suite and any of her company in the neighboring suites. Inform her we will greet them tomorrow for brunch in the garden."

"Right away, sir."

Hale turned back to face us, and I looked at Callen who suddenly seemed irritated by the unexpected arrival of these guests.

"Well, I should be letting you both get some sleep," Hale said, excusing himself.

"Hale," Callen said loudly, and Hale stopped in the doorframe. "Thank you...thank you for everything."

Hale nodded and then left the room.

Chapter 21

Violet

We walked back into the Knights' suite and found the living space empty. Sean and Johanna must have turned in already... which made sense since we'd been gone for hours. The door to Charles's room was open though, so I assumed that meant Nixie wasn't sleeping well.

Creeping quietly into Callen's room, he immediately began pulling his shirt over his head, while I quietly closed the door. I could tell that he was flustered. And I knew he was confused about why I hadn't told him about the nightmare. Maybe a little hurt too, based on the vibes I was getting from him. But something about this *Tatiana* woman showin' up had him rattled even more than our talk with Hale. What kind of name was that anyway? Tatiana...I mean who did this woman think she is?

"What's going on inside that head of yours?"

Callen had appeared from the bathroom and had made his way over to his bed while I'd been lost in the jealous tantrum I was throwing in my head.

"Who is this *Tatiana* woman?" I asked, crossing the room and stepping into Callen's closet to change.

"Now, Vi," Callen began, with his macho tone. "Don't go telling me you're jealous?"

"Me?" I asked, poking my head out of the closet. "I have nothing to be jealous of."

"You're right about that," Callen chuckled.

I emerged from his closet wearing one of his shirts and walked around the bed to the side he wasn't currently occupying. I didn't know what was comin' over me. Deep down, I knew that there was nothing to be jealous of. Callen was loyal to his role as a Knight and as the prince's magical twin. That's why her sudden arrival had him so rattled. On top of battle prepping, we now had to entertain other royals. And I knew that this *Tatiana* woman was truly not a threat to me, but, sweet baby Jesus, was my blood ever boiling at the thought of her messin' with my Callen.

"Just out of curiosity," I said with the sassiest tone I could muster. "Why do I have nothing to be jealous of?"

"Violet, green is not a good color on you."

"All colors are good on me!"

"You can't seriously be this jealous. All I did was tell the guard where they should stay."

"And you've been a bundle of nerves since he said her name."

"You seriously think my nerves are a result of me having feelings for Tatiana?" he asked, choking on a laugh. "And why again do you get to be the jealous one, when you were practically drooling over Hale's magical ability to save you from a trap, I didn't even know you were in."

"I was not drooling over Hale," I defended.

"Oh please!" Callen cried, as he rolled onto his side to face me. "*Hale, please. How did you get into my head like that? How did you know? How did you know about Evey, and I before we did.*"

His voice mocking me made the magic flowing through my veins boil even hotter. But as he pretended to flip his imaginary long hair over his shoulder, I couldn't help but let out a giggle.

"I do not sound like that."

"You did though," he said, as his expression went from playful to serious. "If anyone had a right to be jealous about what just happened, it was me. I'd been trying for days to wake you up, Vi. You have no idea how hard it was for me to sit by your side and listen to Lucian say you may never wake up. To have no idea how to help you."

The anger that was fueling me suddenly evaporated in the emotion surge from Callen. I could feel my chest clenching tighter than a backyard boxer's fist.

I rolled onto my side too and stared back at him as I rested my head on my arm. He was right. One hundred percent right. He should have been the first person I confided in. But with everything going on, I had shut him out. I had done exactly what I was always cursing Evey for doing.

"I'm sorry," I said softly.

"Don't be sorry, Vi. But why didn't you just tell me about the Fear magic?"

"I didn't even know what to tell you," I explained. "I knew that I had taken Evey's magic...but that was all I had figured out. And I'm not the type of girl who goes off telling stories with little to no information. And..."

"And what?"

"And I was scared, Callen. Ugh! I can't believe I just admitted that."

"You were scared to tell me or scared of me?"

"What? Neither!"

"Violet, what are we even talking about right now?"

I flopped on my back and stared up at the ceiling. What were we arguing about? That I was jealous of someone I didn't even know? That he was jealous over my curiosity about another man's magic? I mean, *this* was ridiculous. And all because I let this damn Fear magic inside of me invade my mind.

Well shit. I was gaining an entirely newfound respect

for Evey's self-control.

"Cal, I'm sorry for not telling you about the Fear magic. Once I figured out that I had it...I was terrified. Terrified of what it might do to me. How it may change me. And also, how you would look at me. How might it change...us."

"Violet," he sighed, as he reached over and gently turned my face toward him. "I could never look at you differently. I wouldn't care if you grew a third eye."

"Oh my God!" I cried, as my eyes grew four sizes. "Fear magic doesn't do weird things like that, does it?"

"No," he laughed. "It was just a figure of speech. But clearly, I'm the one that owes you an apology."

"Why?"

"Because somehow I made you believe that your magic is what makes me love you."

"Well, isn't that how a bond works? Aren't we bound together by our magic?"

"You know, when I first met you, I would have never guessed you were as plainly logical as you are."

"I'm gonna try real hard to *not* be offended by that statement."

"You shouldn't be. I love that you are both incredibly beautiful and tremendously intelligent," he winked. "But one thing that you have to understand is that while this world makes you believe that everything in our lives is the result of our magical ancestry, it's far more than that. I'd love you if you were a non-magical, Violet. I knew I cared for you from the moment we met. And I know this is making me sound like a complete softy, but you have to understand that I never thought I would find you. Before my parents went to Estella, I was nobody. A peasant child who just happened to be the magical twin to the prince. I had never expected my life would amount to anything. Becoming a Knight was a dream come true for me. And finding you...it was like all the stars literally aligned for me."

"Callen..."

"I thought, for a brief moment, after Griffin told me how he felt about Evelyn, that what I was feeling was being manifested by his feelings for her...but even I knew that was crazy. I knew that wasn't what this was. This was real. You are my forever, Violet. And no amount of magic, or bonding laws, or prophecies, will ever change that."

As I laid there, staring at the man I knew would literally love me forever, I felt a strange twinge in my chest. This damn Fear magic was a real bitch. Even in my happiest moments, it would claw it's way in and inflict just enough doubt and pain to keep me questioning every one of the absolutely amazing words coming from his mouth.

Sure, he loved me. I loved him too. But he couldn't honestly believe that his feelings for me wouldn't change when he realized how much more powerful I was. Not just more powerful than him. More powerful than anyone. I knew that power bred envy and the envy destroyed even the purest things. I could feel this Fear inside me threatening to destroy everything I love.

"Violet?"

"What?" I asked, shaking the terrible thoughts from my head. "I'm sorry. This Fear magic was seriously messing with me.

"It's alright," he smiled and laid back down. "We will figure out how to control it. Or how to give it back."

I wanted that. I wanted to be back to my normal, happy self. And yet, there was still that little voice in the back of my head that was relishing in this newfound strength. And even I had to admit, that for once, it was nice to see the world outside of sunshine and rainbows like I normally tried to.

But who the hell was I kidding? Yeah, I knew the world had darkness, but I chose to see the good in it. That is who I am. I wanted to be the good that people saw in the world! Or, realm. Ugh, it didn't matter. I want to be good. I want to believe in the good and no matter how this Fear magic made me feel...I will not allow it to change me.

Rolling over I laid my head on Callen's chest and took in a heavy breath. His arm wrapped around me, and I heard his heart began to beat a little slower as he relaxed at my touch.

"So, tell me...who really is this Tatiana person?"

"She's the Crown Princess of Fantazi."

"I'm sorry she's the what?" I asked, turning to look up at him.

"She's the Crown Princess of Fantazi," he repeated. "Fantazi is a neighboring magical realm."

"How many realms are there exactly?"

"Nobody knows. Fantazi is by far the largest one ever discovered. Even larger than the non-magical realm you grew up in."

"So, this Tatiana, is their Crown Princess? What does that mean?"

"Her mother died about a year ago and left her next in line to be Queen. Tatiana, however, did not feel she was ready and asked for a year to prove she is worthy, rather than just assuming the throne as a birth right."

"She can do that?"

"In Fantazi, yes. In Magir, the council is a little more old school. Griffin will be King no matter what his wishes. And he knows that. But that's what he has always wanted."

"So, she is the Crown Princess and not just a Princess because she is basically a Queen? Did I follow that all the way?"

"Exactly. She is set to become Queen of Fantazi in little more than a month."

"Well then what in the blazes is she doin' here?"

"I'm sure news of Queen Ariana's death has reached all the known realms by now. If we weren't about to go to war, I'm sure we'd have more than just Fantazi on our doorsteps right now."

"But we are about to go to war," I paused. "So, why do you think she is here?"

Then a thought crossed my mind that made the hairs on the back of my neck stand up and a small twinge of anger begin to build up in my stomach.

"Wait! She's not here for Griffin, is she?"

"No."

"I mean he is about to be King and she's about to be Queen."

"No."

"It would totally make sense. She is here to take…"

"Violet!" Callen said, with a tug of my hair.

"What?"

"I can promise you that is not why she is here."

"You're absolutely sure?"

"More than you know."

"How?"

"Tatiana is beautiful and incredibly powerful. And she and Griffin have been friends since childhood, but only friends. We all only saw each other every few years. As we all got older though, it became ever clearer that they would never form an alliance like Fantazi's late queen had wanted."

"Why?"

"Griffin was…well, he was already in love with Evelyn long before he met her. And Tatiana…well, she was also in love with someone else. Plus, King Barin would never have allowed it."

"Oh, sweet Jesus. Let me guess. He didn't approve of a non-pureblood-Magirian wife for his perfect boy."

"More like he didn't approve of a non-Magirian queen *soiling* his perfect throne. Barin didn't give two shits about how it impacted Griffin."

"Meh, close enough."

"But seriously. You have nothing to worry about. Not with Griffin. And not with me."

I believed him. As much as the Fear magic in me wanted to push for more about the *Crown Princess* Tatiana, I believed him. I suddenly felt Evey with me and a warm, homey sensation relaxed the Fear magic that was simmering inside of me.

"Okay. Well, I guess we can discuss this more over brunch. I'm gonna need my beauty sleep if I'm gonna meet a Crown Princess tomorrow."

I felt his lips brush the top of my head as a small chuckle passed through them.

"She's the one meeting the real princess."

"I do have something else to discuss with you," I said, after giving him a kiss on the cheek.

"What's that?"

"I actually think it can wait until morning," I replied. "But first thing, okay?"

"It's a date."

Closing my eyes, I focused on the happy feelin's that were keeping the Fear magic at bay. Thinking of Evey, Callen, and all our friends outside the bedroom door. I smiled as the Fear magic finally conceded enough that I barely felt it.

Happiness. That was the key. Evey had always struggled with believing that she was even worthy of happiness. She wasn't able to control the Fear magic because she wasn't the master of happiness that I was.

As I smiled and let out a soft sigh, I felt myself drifting. Despite wanting to share my revelation, I really did need some sleep. Tomorrow was going to bring an entirely new start. and if it all worked out in our favor...it would bring the start to the downfall of the Fears.

*****

Cal and I woke up and had instantly gotten completely *distracted* by each other. Who could really blame me though? When waking up on the bare chest of a man like Callen Ivanti... I would have been disappointed in myself if I had even tried to resist him.

After two rounds of said *distraction*, I went to his closet and grabbed a T-shirt. I would have loved to have stayed in bed with him all day, but the fact was, we needed to have that little discussion I'd promised him last night.

"Just spit it out, Vi," Callen called from his place on the bed.

"What are you talkin' 'bout?" I asked as I pulled his shirt over my head and emerged from the closet.

"I can practically feel the wheels in your head spinning from here," he joked. "Tell me what it is you wanted to talk about this morning."

"Right. Yes," I agreed, sitting on the end of the bed. "I need to go back to WRA."

"We will after…"

"No," I interrupted. "Cal, I need to go back today."

"Vi, we'd never make it back in time," he surmised. "And I won't leave the Knights and Griffin to fight without me."

"I believe there are answers there," I pressed. "Answers that will help us win. I need to get there, and I need to get there as soon as possible."

His expression remained fairly stoic as he studied me. I could read the caring in his eyes, but they also seemed quizzical. Like he knew I was being vague, and he was clearly trying to figure out why.

"Oh, and I'd like Auntie to come with me."

"Vi…"

"She knows something about what I'm looking into," I assured him. "I need her there."

"Fine."

"Fine?"

"Vi, for you to be this passionate about something, I know it is important," he explained. "But we can't leave Magir right now."

"Then how…"

"I'll send word to Ansel," he interrupted. "I'll have him meet us at the veil with anything he thinks can help. But I need you to loop me into whatever you find."

"Done!"

I flung my arms around him, and he chuckled against

me as he returned the embrace. His faith in me had the magic inside me doin' a happy dance and I felt the room getting warmer, just as it had when we first woke up.

"Easy tiger," he smiled, as he released the embrace. "I need you to actually go get dressed and get Evelyn from across the castle."

"Wait, where is Evey?"

"Griffin's private quarters," he explained. "Take Johanna. She'll know the way. And then meet me in the courtyard of the garden."

"Why?"

"We need to attend the training session this morning," he instructed. "So, I'll go talk with Griffin and get word to Ansel. Then I'll meet you there."

"Training session?"

"Vi..."

"Okay, okay, fine!" I conceded, before placing a kiss on his cheek and heading to his door. "But don't try to tell me round three wouldn't have been way more fun."

"Woman...I fucking love you," he chuckled.

Chapter 22

Evelyn

The pounding in my head prevented me from opening my eyes. As I rolled over and reached to where Griffin was laying. I sprawled out across the bed, feeling for his chest, and found nothing but soft sheets in his space. I forced my eyes open slowly, fighting the nausea that was starting to build in my stomach. I was definitely alone in his room, but on his bed laid a folded piece of paper.

Pushing myself up, I grabbed the paper and unfolded it to reveal a handwritten note from Griffin.

Was called away and didn't want to wake you.
Meet us on the back lawn after you grab something to eat.
I love you, My Queen.

A shiver ran down my spine and I felt a burst of nausea race through me. Jumping from the bed, I ran to the bathroom before I expelled my stomach contents all over the room.

For some reason I had it in my mind that bonding would be some sort of magical experience. However, it was actually possible that this feeling was worse than the one I had at the rest stop from denying our bond even existed.

After nearly twenty minutes of vomiting, dry heaving, and hot flashes that made death sound more enticing than sex, I climbed into Griffin's shower, in hopes of getting my body to relax. Though after only a few minutes in the hot water, I knew it was a lost cause.

I fumbled out of the shower and made my way into the bedroom as I prayed there was something in his closet that I could wear to at least make it back to my suite. To my surprise, I found a section of the closet was full of women's clothes. And all clothes that I would actually wear too. Had he prepared this? Or had this been Violet's handiwork? She had been trying to get me into his bed since I'd met him.

I quickly settled on a pair of dark jeans and an olive t-shirt that, to Violet's approval, had an opening in the back. Then I slipped into a pair of tennis shoes that were at the bottom of the closet and made my way out of the room.

"Whoa!" I exclaimed as I opened the door and found myself face to face with Violet and Johanna. "What are you two doing here?"

"They sent us to come check on you," J0hanna said, studying me. "Though now it's very clear why you're so late."

"What are you talking about?" I asked.

"Oh, my Lanta!" Violet shrieked. "Evey, you dog!"

"Can we not do this in the hallway?" I groaned, as I closed the door and shifted my eyes to the guard.

"Girl, we need to get you a dolce ragus protein drink," Johanna instructed, as we began walking away.

"A what? Wait, dolce ragus is that weird sugar, right? If so, I'm already sick. I don't need it to be worse."

"Trust me. If it is that nasty drink that Callen fed me after we had sex for the first time…"

"Violet!" I whispered, nudging her. "Not so loud."

"Oh, sugar," she sighed, as she laid her hand on my shoulder. "It's adorable that you think nobody can tell."

"Yeah," Johanna laughed. "You're even paler than

normal. They are either going to think you both finally put us out of our misery and did the deed, or you're pregnant."

"Pregnant!" I screeched. "Do I actually look pregnant?"

"Who's pregnant?" Sean asked, as we made our way out of the hallway and onto the back lawn.

"I think I'm gonna be sick."

"She needs a Magirian protein drink," Johanna winked.

"I can go...oh!" Sean gasped, as he finally caught on. "I mean the timing wasn't perfect, but at least now I don't have to listen to you whine about him anymore, Red."

"I'm definitely gonna be sick."

An arm suddenly reached around me, and a drink appeared in front of me just as warm lips pressed against my cheek.

"Aren't you two adorable!" Violet gushed, as she grinned like a schoolgirl.

I took the drink from Griffin, and he shifted to my side, wrapping an arm intimately around my waist.

"Just a real Johnny and June," Sean rolled his eyes. "Now can we get started. We have brunch in a couple hours."

"Did you just make a country music reference?" I asked, as I took a sip of the drink.

"Don't sound so..."

"Oh my God!" I interrupted, as I gagged. "This is absolutely disgusting!"

The drink was more than disgusting. It was probably the nastiest thing I had ever put in my mouth. It tasted a little sweet, but even the sugar wasn't enough to mask the taste of pure dead grass.

"I promise it will make you feel better soon," Violet said. "Even though it does taste as nasty as the wrong end of a pig smells."

"Well, thanks for that," I complained, stomaching another sip. "Somehow I guess I figured the morning following the best night of my life would be a little less...nauseating."

"Damn, Red," Sean grinned. "I like this side of you."

"What side of me?" I choked out.

"I dunno," he shrugged, as he dropped the duffle bag off of his shoulder. "I guess just the happy side of you. It's nice to hear you cracking jokes and to see you smiling again."

"You're welcome," Griffin and Violet said in unison.

Silence surrounded us for a brief moment, before both Johanna and Sean burst out laughing. Violet and Griffin soon joined in, and before I could really determine if they were laughing with me or at me, I was laughing too.

"What'd I miss?" Callen questioned, appearing by Violet with a duffle bag that looked just like the one Sean had brought.

"Doesn't matter," Nicholas said behind him. "Let's get this training session going."

As Nicholas stormed past us, our laughter came to a screeching halt. The sudden mood shift made the combination of magic, and nasty juice inside me, turn to a boil deep in my chest.

"Well?" Nicholas shouted back at us.

"On our way!" Johanna informed him.

"I swear I will have him wishing he was going to Estella, if he continues to be an ass like this all day," Sean groaned, as he picked up his bag.

"Oh, be nice!" Violet commanded in a whisper. "He had a rough day yesterday."

"We all did," Griffin responded. "And he will get through it. It's just going to take time. But time isn't something he can have right now."

"All of us will get through this," I smiled, as I rubbed Griffin's arm.

"Touching," Sean joked. "Now, we should really get going before he starts having a meltdown."

"I have to go finish the preparations for brunch and finalize a couple things with the council members," Griffin said. "Sean will help you train. With the exception of myself and Callen, he is the best fighter in Magir."

"Yeah, because who wouldn't want to be taught by the third-place guy," I quipped.

"Ouch! I take it back," Sean said, as he playfully held his hand over his heart. "Your happiness is too much. I think your bond may have broken your filter. You're mean."

We chuckled as the others all walked out onto the lawn and I swallowed the last of my drink as Griffin reached out to take my empty cup.

"I'll see you at brunch," he said, before leaning in and gently kissing my cheek. "I love you."

"I love you."

He walked away and I made my way onto the lawn where the others were standing. As I walked, I realized that the pit in my stomach had faded, a lot. Clearly, despite the drink being completely disgusting, it was working just as Violet had said it would. My magic was still twisting inside me, but now I felt like I was walking on the clouds.

"Now *that* is exactly the post sex glow my bestie should have!" Violet winked, as she grabbed Callen's arms and walked away with him.

"Jesus," I sighed. "She might as well just put up a billboard!"

"Don't tempt her," Johanna laughed.

"You've never spoken truer words," I responded, as I joined in on the laughter.

"Look ladies," Sean said, coming up behind us. "As much as I love to listen to you all having your girl time...I need you both to focus up."

"First off, never...never, say *girl time* again," I snickered. "And second, what exactly are we doing here?"

"What do you mean? We're training."

Training? I looked around and realized that some type of obstacle course had been set up. There were weapons on tables all over the yard. I saw a few boxing bags on stands across one edge of the lawn, while the other was covered in targets. But what did *we* have to train for? Isn't that what our magic was for?

"Magic can't be the only weapon in your arsenal," Sean explained, as if he could suddenly read my mind. "We are going to work on a few skills and hopefully find that you have something non-magical that we can utilize."

"Yeah, I'm not sure two days is enough time to get me ready for using these," I rebutted, as I picked up a set of nun chucks from one of the tables.

"True," Sean agreed, carefully taking the nun chucks from me and placing them back on the table. "And I know how clumsy you are. Still, Griffin insists we train you on something."

His vote of confidence was overwhelming. Not. Even Sean knew this was a waste of time. And as Griffin had pointed out earlier, time was not something we had at the moment. The one thing I had going for me, was my magic. I barely had a handle on that! And now, they wanted me to focus on something else? Not to mention when it came to gym class in high school, I could barely do a pushup, let alone an entire obstacle course. I don't care what the Strength stone said...athletics, no matter how much I enjoyed watching them, just wasn't my forte.

Each skill we attempted proved just how bad of an athlete I really was. First it was a staff. Sean stood in front of me whipping it around like it was as light as a feather. And sure, when I channeled my Strength magic, I wasn't too horrible at it. But when I fumbled and conked myself in the back of the head with the damn thing, I instantly launched the stupid stick across the garden.

Next, we tried wrestling and some other hand to hand combat styles. I was surprisingly decent in one-on-one combat. But when you have Johanna as your sparring partner, I don't know how anyone could look good. Every time I thought I knew where she was going, she bobbed to the side and wacked me in the ribs. By the time that session was done I was left panting on the ground, praying that my healing magic would quickly alleviate the pain in my side.

We tried throwing knives, which was a disaster before we even really started. After picking up three knives at once, I attempted to move two into my other hand, and ended up dropping them both into the grass, narrowly missing Sean's toe. When I finally threw one, it went soaring past its target and instead almost hit Nicholas, who was too busy to even notice as he beat the hell out of a punching bag.

"Can we just face the fact that I am pointless?" I sighed, as I forcibly dropped the remaining two knives on the table. "I'm getting better with my magic. Let's just use that."

"Quit being all woe is me," Sean instructed. "I have one last idea and if you suck at this as bad as...well, everything else, I'll let you take it up with Griffin as to what your position will be when we do go to war."

"God, was I really that bad at everything?"

"Actually, you did better than most people I know," he shrugged, as he led me across the lawn. "But when you're working with people as advanced as us, you're bound to look bad."

"Not that you're conceited or anything."

"I've earned every bit of it," he winked.

We stopped when we reached the edge of the lawn that had targets lined all the way across a long formation of hedges.

"What is this?"

"Just hear me out," Sean said, as he reached over to the table, picked up a bow and handed it to me.

The cold metal touching my hands sent a tingle through my body. It was by far the most intricate bow I had ever seen. Well, most of the ones I had seen were on TV...but still. The metal looked like it had carvings all the way through it and the string...the string looked like thousands of strands of beautifully braided silks.

"You expect me to shoot this? I'm not even sure I know how to hold it."

"Well, I mean your last name is Archer."

"Very funny."

"Seriously. Maybe the answer was looking us in the face the entire time. Just try."

"Why can't you people just use guns like soldiers do in every other war?"

"Guns don't work in Magir."

Callen's voice made me jump as he appeared from out of nowhere behind me.

"And why, exactly, is that?" I asked.

"There isn't really a known reason," Callen shrugged. "But I choose to believe, it's a sense of honor."

"Honor?" Vi questioned, walking over to join us. "Y'all don't have guns 'cause of honor? What does that even mean?"

"Think about it this way," a voice I didn't recognize interjected. "Guns are too easy. For us, if you are going to take a life you had better be able to do it, not only up close and personal, but with both honor and purpose."

I studied the man for a minute. I had never seen him in the castle before and he certainly wasn't dressed like a guard. As a matter of fact, if it hadn't been for the leather armor he had on over his clothes, I would have thought that he was almost regally dressed. His eyes were a very light brown, and his blonde hair was pulled back, but looked long enough to touch his shoulders.

"I don't mean to be the cynic here," Vi began, "but my daddy sells guns and there ain't nothing about them that isn't *personal*."

"You'll come to see the beauty in our ways and gain an understanding of what's behind them," the man explained "May I stay for your lesson?"

"Of course," Callen nodded. "Always happy to have you here with us, Carney."

The man nodded stiffly and straightened his stance. Great...now I was going to have an audience to my never-ending combat failures.

Callen and Violet each grabbed a bow and a couple of

arrows.

"Now, square your stance," Callen instructed Violet, "place the arrow onto the string and pull it back. Hold it softly. You don't want a death grip on it. Eye your target, take a deep breath, and release."

The arrow left his bow and hit just off the center of the target. I was awed at his skill, but as I looked at Violet, she was grinning from ear to ear. Clearly, Callen didn't know everything about her, yet.

Vi used to hunt with her father as a child. She could shoot pretty much any weapon, and I was certain she did Callen's instructions on how to shoot a bow. Now the only question that remained...was she actually good at it?

"That was so cute," she said, placing a hand on Callen's face before flipping her hair over her shoulder and pulling back her own arrow.

I watched as she held the arrow close to her right cheek and took two deep breaths before releasing. It raced through the air and landed directly on its target. Except, unlike Callen's, it wasn't just off the center...it was a direct bullseye. Dead center. I don't think it would have been possible to get more centered than that shot was.

"Just when I thought I couldn't love you more," Callen gushed.

"Aren't you sweet?" Violet grinned, as she stood up on her tiptoes to kiss his cheek. "I still hold the title of, Youngest Archery Champion, at our local Moose Lodge. 'Aint nobody ever gonna beat my score there."

"Keep talking and our training session may need to end early," Callen winked.

"Enough of that," Sean said, with an overly exaggerated eye roll. "Red, why don't you try this one?"

He handed me a beautiful, intricately designed, arrow and I gripped it tightly in the hand that wasn't holding the bow, unsure of what to even do with it. The premise seemed simple enough — place an arrow, pull the string back, shoot —

but I knew it wasn't going to be that easy.

I was fairly certain I knew what to do, but my nerve was failing as I pondered the fact that both Vi and Callen had shot so well. Far beyond any luck I was going to have. How could I possibly be expected to follow that? I had never even held a bow prior to this moment. And at the rate today had been going, I was going to be lucky to even hit the target.

"*Don't overthink it.*" Vi's voice rang through my head. "*Just take a deep breath, and shoot!*"

Sean grabbed my shoulders and positioned me in front of the first of the three targets that were lined up in front of the hedge. He gave me a reassuring smile before stepping back to allow me room to shoot. Based on how far back he stepped, I was actually a little concerned he thought I might just spin around and shoot the wrong direction.

"*Sweet, freaking' baby Jesus! Focus!*"

Right. I could do this. Or at least...I hoped I could.

Rather than delay my inevitable miss any longer, I stepped to the side and placed the arrow onto the bow's string. Taking my first big breath, I pulled back on the string. Like Violet had done, I pulled the string close to my cheek and paused briefly to focus on the target, feeling my elbow adjust, almost instinctively, as I drew a deep breath.

When I released the arrow, it felt like only a blink of an eye before it collided with the target. I didn't realize I had closed my eyes, until I heard a gasp and felt a hand clap against my shoulder.

My eyes shot open, and as I took in the target before me, I almost couldn't believe what I was seeing. The arrow wasn't just on the target...it was dead center.

"Beginner's luck," Sean teased. "Question is...can you do it again?"

He offered me another arrow which I took, slowly contemplating my second shot. Could I do it again? I wasn't even sure how I did it the first time. Beginner's luck didn't even begin to cover what had just happened. As much as I loved sports, I was more of the admire from the sidelines type of girl. I'd never experiences beginner's luck, or any luck for that matter, at anything athletic I'd tried.

Right now, I couldn't fade into the sidelines though. I could feel Callen, Carney and Sean, all anxiously watching me. Violet was too, but she was practically glowing with excitement. It made me wonder if her Vision magic was telling her something I didn't know, yet. Not that even that notion eased the anxiety I was feeling...not even a tiny bit.

"Girl! Get out of your head and shoot the damn arrow!"

I shook my head and chuckled to myself before lining up in front of the second target. Listening to Violet's voice in my head, I raised the bow but this time I didn't have to replay the steps in my head...they just kind of...happened. I pulled the arrow back on the string and let it go before I gave myself time to overthink it.

"Wow..." Callen exclaimed. "Obviously, this is something you both excel in."

He was right. To my surprise, the arrow had, yet again, hit its target resulting in another bullseye.

"Yeah, that was impressive," Sean agreed. "But tell me what you do with the last one?"

He handed me another arrow and I moved in front of the final target. The final target still had both Callen and Violet's arrows firmly in place. Callen's just off the center and Violet's at dead center. I doubted that even the most experienced archers in the world have known where to shoot this shot.

A strange surge began to ring in my mind as I stared at the target. I could do this. I wasn't just some mousey girl...I was an Archer descendant. I was the most powerful magical to be born in all of history. And with my head held high, I raised the arrow, took a deep breath and shot.

As my fingers released the arrow, it felt as though time had slowed to a crawl while I watched the arrow soar through the air and connect with the end of Violet's arrow. I watched in amazement as my arrow moved through Violet's with ease, spilling it in two, seizing the center of the target.

"Oh my!"

I heard Violet say, as I turned around and saw that everyone on the lawn was now staring at the target with wide eyes.

"I guess being a descendant from the Archer line is more than just a name," Carney surmised.

"Told you so," Sean winked, as he nudged me and took the bow from my hand.

"Did I just do that?" I asked Violet. "Did I seriously just do that?"

"Sure did, sugar!" she giggled. "If I'm gonna be passed up, at least it's by my bestie! But seriously...I will not be taking you to my old Moose anytime soon."

I laughed a little and noticed a hint of black flicker through her eyes before they returned to normal. Having my Fear inside her was clearly something she was overcoming. Overcoming far better than I ever had.

As the thought crossed my mind, her head tilted to the side a little and her eyes narrowed a bit as she studied my face.

"Brunch is now being served!" a guard shouted from the doorway.

Violet shook her head ever so slightly, and laced her arm into Callen's with a smile before they both began to retreat back into the castle. I watched them walk for a minute, confused about why her demeanor had changed so abruptly. It wasn't until Sean and Johanna appeared at my side that I broke from my daze.

"I imagine you're probably going to want to be at brunch," Johanna smiled.

"Unless you'd rather hang out here and shoot some more," Sean suggested. "Sounds way more fun than brunch."

Johanna elbowed him in the side, and he dramatically reacted before raising his hands in surrender.

"Fine!" he conceded. "Red, what I meant to say, was how

thrilled I am to attend this brunch. So, let's get going."

I laughed as Johanna rolled her eyes, and the three of us headed inside.

As we made our way through the halls, Carney walked a few steps in front of us. Even his stride was almost regal. And it wasn't in an arrogant way either. You could just tell he was important. That somewhere, to someone, he was a leader.

"Who is he?" I asked in a very hushed tone to Johanna.

"That's Carney from Fantazi," she whispered back. "He's basically the equivalent of you to them."

"He has unique magic like me?" I asked.

"Not exactly. Let's just say he's more like you, in the romance department."

"Jo!" Sean said in a stern whisper.

"Everyone knows it!" She defended.

Before I could get any more details, we reached the dining hall and a feast beyond what I had anticipated. Griffin was already seated at the head of the table, where his father had previously sat. On his left sat Callen then Violet and to his right was an empty chair. My chair.

All of the Knights had taken their seats with the exception of Sean who was pulling out a chair for Jo beside mine and Nixie was settling quietly into her seat beside Nicholas. But it wasn't the normal attendees that caught my eye. As I proceed to my chair, I noticed, at the opposite end of the table from Griffin, sat an absolutely stunning woman I had never seen before.

Griffin rose from his chair as I reached my seat and pulled out my chair with a smile. I felt my skin start to get warm again, just from being next to him. He gave me a playful wink, which told me he was feeling the same thing. I felt my cheeks starting to get red, so I took my seat and returned my focus on the mystery guests.

"Thank you everyone for making time to gather here during this very busy time," Griffin said, as he took his seat again. "I'd like to thank Princess Tatiana and Carney for joining us in our time of need. Tatiana has offered her guidance in our tactical planning, and Carney has offered to join us on our mission. However, before we get into the logistics of what lies ahead, let us eat, converse, and enjoy each other's company. Let us feast."

Griffin sat down and everyone at the table began to fill their plates. To my surprise even Tatiana took a plateful of food. With her tiny, perfect figure, I wasn't even sure she ate.

"*Evey!*" Violet's voice rang in my head. "*Leave the sassy, judgmental comments to me!*"

"*I'm still a little unsure about this mind reading thing,*" I thought back. "*It's like I'm never alone.*"

She laughed out loud across the table and Callen just shook his head. I knew based on how the bond was working so far, that Callen and Griffin weren't able to hear the thoughts being passed between Violet and I, and they were both probably grateful for that. In the same sense, we couldn't read theirs. But since they were still mentally connected to us, I'm sure he knew that Violet's sudden laughter was at my expense.

"It sounds like training went really well," Griffin said, breaking me from Violet.

"You could say that."

"She's being modest," Johanna said, as her shoulder bumped mine.

"Well, I am not going to be a wrestling champ anytime soon," I joked. "But I'm pretty good with a bow."

"Pretty good?" Sean choked on the bite of food he'd been trying to enjoy. "You know since you were on a lawn surrounded by other Knights, he was basically there, right, Red?"

"Actually, even despite us being..." Griffin tried to say.

"Yes!" Violet and Johanna said in unison, as their forks fell onto their plates.

Man, these two were just itching for me to shout out a proclamation of what had happened last night.

"Regardless of our current situation," Griffin began,

as he smiled at Violet, "Evelyn's gift still blocks me out occasionally."

"She's probably the best archer I've ever seen," Nicholas revealed suddenly from the end of the table. "Hit all three targets dead center. Even split the arrow that was in her way clean down the middle. It was damn impressive to witness. Now can we get down to business and go after the Fears?"

Griffin's eyes were glued to him as he spoke. I had never heard Nicholas speak so sternly to any of the three Knights that were ranked higher than him. As I looked his way, I could see the regret in his eyes, but the fury growing in there was impossible to miss.

"Nicholas," Callen growled.

"It's alright," Griffin interjected, as he stood up from his chair. "I actually have something important I do need to share with you all before we move onto tactics, however."

"Yes!" Violet and Johanna said eagerly.

I shook my head and could feel my face getting hot again. These two were probably going to embarrass me to death before any Fear had the chance to actually kill me.

"The council called an emergency meeting, as you are all aware," Griffin began.

To everyone else, I'm sure he looked like a calm, noble leader, but I could see how nervous he was. Last night, he had made his declaration to me. I knew what was coming from this announcement, but the others were about to have a curve ball thrown at them that they weren't expecting yet. Not to mention that I hadn't had a chance to completely fill in Violet or Johanna about everything that happened last night.

"In this meeting they decided that Magir needs a royal on the throne. Right now, more than ever," Griffin continued. "Despite what our previous king has done, the council graciously remains faithful to me as the future ruler of Magir. And it seems that the future, is now. The council has asked that I be crowned King of Magir, and I accepted their nomination this morning, with stipulations."

"Stipulations?" Callen asked. "Are you going to remain a Knight?"

"Unfortunately, no," Griffin said, shaking his head. "I'll be stripped of my Knighthood to become king. The stipulations I've made are being discussed and if they are approved, I will be crowned King of Magir in the morning."

The table was silent for a moment. Looking around the room, everyone was just staring at Griffin. But there was something different about the way the Knights's stared. They weren't just absorbing what he was saying...they were mourning him as their leader.

"At the end of the day, I will still be your leader," Griffin assured them. "After all, the leader of the Knights does still answer to the king."

The mood instantly lightened around the table, and I watched Violet's face relax just a little. Callen was the only one whose anxiousness didn't ease. He still seemed nervous, and oddly tense. I watched as Violet reached over and grabbed the hand he had rested on the table. As he clenched her hand back, he pushed back on his chair pulling himself and Violet to their feet. Before I knew it everyone at the table, including the Princess of Fantazi, were standing staring at Griffin.

I rose from my chair just as all of the Knights put their right hand in a fist over their chest and bowed slightly. Violet and the other women followed suit with a curtsey, while Carney bowed his head.

"We stand behind you, our King," Callen proclaimed, as he straightened back up.

Cheers of agreement rang throughout the dining room, and I could see the pride emanating from Griffin's smile.

"I am honored to be the king of such amazing people," Griffin began. "But I do have one piece of news that, for me, means even more than being crowned king."

A few people around the table looked incredibly confused, while the Princess stood smiling at the other end. But it was when Griffin, reached for my hand and interlaced his fingers with mine that I knew what was about to be said.

"Evelyn," he smiled at me and then the group. "Said yes to my proposal last night and is going to be my queen."

"WHAT!" Violet and Johanna shrieked.

The Knights, with the exception of Nicholas, began clapping loudly. Violet and Johanna were making such high-pitched sounds, I was certain I might lose my hearing all together.

"We will be working on the details later," Griffin explained to the table. "We just wanted you all to know our great news and share in our excitement. I know I am Now let us sit and talk strategy."

Everyone took their seats again and I watched as the mood went from joyous to gloomy all over again.

"*Oh, don't think we aren't talking about this!*" Violet's shouted in my mind. "*We will be discussing this at length.*"

"*Discussing what exactly?*" I jokingly thought back.

"*At length, Evey!*" she reiterated. "*And don't think I didn't see what you did there.*"

I couldn't hold back the small laugh that escaped my lips and Griffin reached beneath the table and placed a hand on my knee. He had made it official to all of our friends. I was going to be his wife...the future Queen of Magir.

"Cal, when do you and Violet need to leave?" Griffin suddenly asked as we ate.

"I'd like to leave immediately following our planning session," Callen replied.

"Leave?" I questioned. "Where are you going?"

"Back to the veil to meet with Ansel," Griffin explained.

"Professor Hyperion? Why?" I questioned.

"He's bringing me some texts I need from Woodburn Rose," Violet calmly explained, without looking up from her plate. "We shouldn't be gone but a few hours."

I didn't push the matter, but I knew something was up. Violet didn't ever not look at me. Not to mention that her eyes had hardly left ever since I sat down. And if she could hear my thoughts now, she certainly wasn't responding to them. She was hiding something.

The rest of our meal was quickly eaten with minimal small talk. After what felt like only a couple more minutes, a few members of the kitchen staff came in and rapidly cleared the tables, while a small handful of the guards brought in maps and rolled them out over the table. We stood and Griffin asked for the chairs to be pulled to the sides of the room, leaving us all standing around the table to study the maps and formations in front of us.

"This map," Griffin began once everything was laid out, "shows the edge of Magir and Fantazi."

"Right here," Callen said, pointing at a spot on the map, "is where the Fears want to face off."

"Tell me about your tactical advantages," Princess Tatiana inquired from her end of the table.

"I say our best bet is to leave now and strike when they first arrive," Nicholas suggested.

"They'll be expecting that," Carney disagreed. "What you need is something that is far from your normal plan."

"If we take the Knights and a few others here," Callen began, as he pointed out another spot on one of the maps, "then we can have the majority of the royal guard hidden throughout the surrounding woods."

"No," Princess Tatiana shook her head. "They will be anticipating your every move. You can't do anything you normally would. You must do something that they would never expect."

"We do have something they don't know about," Violet began. "They don't know about my connection with Evey and the magic that gives us."

"I think Morana saw what you did when they attacked. I don't think it's a secret anymore," Sean pointed out.

"But it is," Violet argued.

"Attacking now is our only option," Nicholas reiterated.

"The princess and Carney are right," Griffin agreed.

"Attacking is too obvious."

"Do you really think that Morana knows about me and Violet?" I asked.

"No," Violet maintained. "I don't even think you and I have a full grasp on our magic."

"May I make a suggestion?" Nixie asked softly.

"Vi, I really think Sean may be right and that door may be closed," Callen negated. "She was watching you both like a hawk the entire time."

"Can I just..." Nixie tried to interject.

"There is more to our magic than she knows," Violet continued to argue.

"It's not going to work, Violet! We have to fight now!" Nicholas asserted, as his fist hit the table.

"Will all of you just listen to me!" Nixie shouted.

We all turned to her, slightly shocked by her outburst. I had heard her trying to interrupt but was so engrossed in the rest of the conversation, even I didn't pause to listen to her.

"If the door is closed, simply open it back up. That's what a door is for," Nixie said softly.

"Nixie," Nicholas sighed. "I think that door is more than closed...it's locked."

Upset by his lack of understanding, Nixie moved toward the door and then spun around to face us all.

"Then find the key. Or kick the door in," Nixie argued. "A door is never meant to close forever. Its job is to open and close. If you find it closed, fight to open it. If we can't even open a simple door, then how are we expected to win a war?"

With that she turned and walked out of the room. Nicholas hung his head for a few seconds before he moved for the door, but Griffin stopped him.

"Nick, you stay here," Griffin instructed. "Cool off. You can speak to her later, with a level head. Victor, go keep an eye on her please."

"Right away," Victor accepted.

I saw a vein in Nicholas's neck swell as Victor left the

room. He was hurting. We all were. But for him this was incredibly personal. And just when he thought it couldn't get any worse, he snaps at the one person in the realm I think he actually cared for.

While the Princess of Fantazi and Carney guided us through a couple of strategy options, I saw him glancing between the maps and the door. He wanted so badly to go after her. But Griffin's order kept him locked in the room. Knights had to obey their leader. Their magic didn't give them a choice. That was one thing about Knight magic that I fully understood.

"Wait a second," Violet suddenly interrupted. "I do have an idea."

"I think we have the same one."

Hale was now standing in the entryway looking like he was out of breath, and I just knew something was terribly wrong.

"Hale?" Griffin questioned, as he stood up straight. "What is it?"

Out of nowhere, I felt a strange surge of anger and I had to grab the table as it made me a little dizzy. Looking across the table, Violet was now leaning on Callen, and I knew she was feeling it too.

"Something is wrong, Griff," Hale said, as he began to blink extremely fast.

Another surge hit me, and all of the Knights straightened. Hale was right. Something was wrong. Very wrong.

"It's Victor," Griffin growled.

Before any of us could take in what was happening, we were rushing out of the dining hall. I wasn't sure how we even knew where to go, but something was guiding us. I wanted to believe it was something spectacular, something like destiny, but even Violet wasn't able to think that optimistically right now.

When we turned down the hallway leading to the

Knights' suite, we all froze for a moment. A guard was lying lifeless in the middle of the hall. Victor was laying on the floor with a knife in his chest. And Nixie was in front of the door... sprawled out in a puddle of blood.

"So nice of you to join us," Michael joked, as he yanked the knife from Victor's chest.

To my surprise, Victor groaned slightly as the knife was removed. He was alive. But with how fast the blood came spurting out, I was sure he would be for long.

Nicholas grabbed a dagger from his hip and launched it at Michael before any of the rest of us could figure out how to react to the nightmare playing out in front of us.

"Now, now," Michael mocked, easily dodging the blade. "I told you that you would pay, Rosey. Their deaths are on your conscience."

Hearing him call me that, made my blood boil. Glancing down at the guard, I caught sight of his sword and used my Mind, coupled with my Strength to throw it so hard that it would be fast enough to get to Michael.

And it certainly got to him. My aim wasn't great, but as it moved past his head it sliced into his face, causing him to grasp at his cheek as the sword hit the ground.

"You bitch!" Michael screamed.

The room stood still for a moment as Michael's gaze began to cut through me. My view of him was suddenly blocked by a figure I wasn't expecting, who had his arm spread wide to stop both Griffin and Nicholas from attacking Michael.

"Get out of here," Lucas demanded. "Or I will make you regret it."

"You will rue this day, Rosey," Michael snarled before turning into a puff of black smoke and disappearing.

Disappearing and leaving us with a lifeless guard and three large puddles of blood. Puddles that contained two of our closest friends. Death was surrounding us yet again. And I found myself understanding Nick's recent behavior as I realized that I wasn't filled just the sadness I would have anticipated. I was completely infuriated.

Chapter 23

Violet

Nicholas was rushing toward Nixie before the last of Michael's foul smoke had even left the air. As the other's moved, I felt the anger rising in the air and yanked Evelyn's arm so that I was right up in her face.

"Get it together!" I quietly commanded. "I know there is a lot going on around us right now, but this is not the time for you to go nuclear. I need you to keep it together for me."

"What are you talking about?" Evelyn asked, as her eyes returned to normal.

"We can discuss this later," I sighed, as I shook my head. "They need us."

I didn't have time to tell her what I was deciphering about her Fear magic. About *our* magic. I could tell she was still confused, but we proceeded toward our friends, nevertheless.

"He's alive," Callen surmised, as he leaned over Victor. "But his pulse is very faint."

I kneeled next to Nixie and Evelyn crouched down beside me. I watched as Nicholas slowly rolled her onto her back, holding her head carefully in his hands, but once she was on her back, it revealed several stab wounds to her abdomen. A rush of fury and heartbreak flooded over me, and I knew that he was already overwhelmed by the horrible truth that the rest of us had come to realize. Nixie was…she was no longer with us.

"She's gone," I said, softly as I placed my hand over Nick's.

He looked up at me and I could see the tears forming in his eyes. First Katerie…now Nixie. Poor Nicholas was breaking apart.

"Here," Evelyn began. "Let's close her eyes. She would want us to fix her to look like she's sleeping."

Nicholas nodded as Evey reached up to close Nixie's eyes. But as her hand touched Nixie's face, I watched Evelyn's body jerk forward and her eyes began to glaze over. Even Nicholas looked surprised.

"*Take my magic,*" Evelyn said in a hushed tone that sounded nothing like her.

"What?" Nicholas asked.

"*Violet, please,*" Evelyn urged. "*It's my last chance to fix something. Use my Healing to save Victor. He fought so hard to save me.*"

"Wait…Nixie?" I asked.

"*I'm barely holding on, and we're losing time,*" Evelyn said, following a sputtering cough that I didn't think was hers. "*Please, Violet.*"

Evelyn jerked again and then shook her head to turn to us.

"What just happened?" she asked.

"No time," I urged. "I need you both to scoot away from Nixie's body."

"Why?" Nicholas questioned.

"Damnit, just do what I said!"

Nicholas carefully put Nixie's head back on the ground before he and Evey both swiftly moved away. I grabbed hold of Nixie's hand and closed my eyes. Whispering as quietly as I could, I repeated a modification of the spell that I used to take

Evey's Fear.

"Gnilaeh leper. Gnilaeh leper."

I felt the surge of magic flow from Nixie to me and then I fell backward a bit. Callen's arms were around me faster than I would have thought possible, and my head started spinnin'.

"What the hell is happening?" he asked.

"I'm not sure," Evelyn answered.

"Just take me to Victor," I instructed. "Evey, I need you too."

Callen helped me off the ground and we made our way to where Victor was lying. As I knelt beside him, I looked back at Evey, who was incredibly confused.

"I need you to give me your hand," I instructed Evey. "I need you to push your Healing through me. I've never done Healing magic before, so I'll need your help."

"But Vi..."

"Will you just listen to me!"

Nobody tried to argue with me again and Evelyn grabbed my hand tightly. She closed her eyes, and I placed my hand over Victor's chest, shutting mine tightly too.

Feeling the magic flow between Evey and I was something else. With Callen, when we shared our magic, there was always a subtle, well, sometimes not so subtle, sensation of lust mixed with it. This connection was completely unlike what I had felt before and it made me feel invincible in an almost addictive way.

"Vi, I think he's too far gone," Callen said.

My eyes shot open, and I saw that his stab wound was healing, but far too slowly in comparison to the blood that was pouring out of him. Cal was right...we were too late.

"I'll help," Nicholas chimed in.

There wasn't time to get to the bottom of his magic, as he placed his hand on my shoulder, and Evelyn start muttering things I didn't understand.

When we were at Woodburn Rose, Evey had proven to be an exceptional Healing magical. Professor Calypso was incredibly impressed by her. And from what I heard other students gossiping about, Evelyn's Healing outshined anyone's that the school had ever seen. So, even though I had no idea what she was whispering, I was certain it was something that was going to get us through this. And even though I didn't need the reassurance, Nicholas picked up the mantra, repeating it along with her. Proving to me, even more, that this was what we needed. We were going to do this. Between the four people who had been providing magic for this cause...we were going to save him. We had to.

A gasp echoed throughout the room and my eyes shot open as I was pushed back. Victor had launched into a seated position and was staring at me. But before I had the chance to speak, he wrapped his arms around me and tightly pulled me in.

"You saved my life, Violet," he exclaimed.

I wasted no time worrying about the fact that he was now covering me in his blood. Instead, I lightly returned his embrace and breathed a sigh of relief that I hadn't realized I was holdin' in.

"You're family," I comforted. "But I can't take all the credit."

He pulled out of the hug as I tilted my head toward where Evelyn and Nicholas stood behind me. I watched as Victor looked at them, before his gaze moved past them to where Nixie laid.

"I'm sorry Nick," Victor groaned, as he grabbed my hands and we moved to our feet. "By the time I got to her, Michael had stabbed her already. I tried to stop him...but he was too fast."

Nicholas just stared at him for a moment. I watched as that angry vein in his neck began seething as he fought with his emotions. He took a step toward Victor and for a split second, I thought for sure he was gonna punch him into oblivion.

"Nick," Sean warned, as Nicholas moved right in front

of Victor.

But then he did one of the last things I expected. He reached out, pulled Victor close to him and I felt the anger that was tightening my insides, loosen just a little.

"I'm glad you're alright, brother," Nicholas praised, and he released the hug, holding him by the shoulders. "She knows you did what you could. Otherwise, she wouldn't have saved you."

"What?" Victor and a few of the others asked in unison.

"It's hard to explain," I intervened.

"For now," Lucas interjected. "You need to go get cleaned up. Armonee and I will take care of Nixie and Evan."

"Evan? Did you know the guard?"

"I knew him enough," Lucas said through a forced attempt at a smile.

"I'll grab you both some clothes from inside," Johanna offered.

"Sean will stay with you, Johanna," Callen explained. "From this point forward, nobody is to go anywhere on their own, I don't care who you are."

"That is my official order," Griffin seconded.

"With your permission," Nicholas interjected. "I'd like to stay with Lucas and take care of Nix."

"Of course," Griffin nodded. "Then come to the library and meet us. We can wait no longer. I am terribly sorry, Nick. I should have trusted your gut on this secondary attack."

Nicholas gave a slight nod to Griffin and our group split apart. Sean and Johanna went through the door to the Knights's hallway to get clothes for Evelyn and I, who were both covered in blood. Victor and Nicholas stayed with Lucas and Armonee. Daniel and Charles were sent to inform Princess Tatiana, Carney, and Hale of the current events and our change in plans. And Griffin, Callen, Evey and I made our way down halls toward wherever it was we were going to get cleaned up.

The four of us walked down the hallway in silence at first. I could feel the jumble of emotions running through me as each of us battled the inner turmoil brought on by the events of the last few days.

I mean, come on! How were we supposed to function like this? In the last forty-eight hours we had four people we loved killed within the palace walls. Three of which were close, personal friends. The love of my life had just lost his surrogate mother. My best friend lost her future mother-in-law. Oh, and she got engaged without even tellin' me! Magir lost its queen because its king turned out to be the evilest bastard on the planet. To say we've had a whirlwind couple of days would be a massive understatement!

We stopped abruptly and entered into a suite and Griffin explained to me that this was his room before moving into the Knights's suites. I instantly recognized it as the room where Johanna had led me to this morning when we had gone looking for Evey. He pointed out that Evelyn and I could go through his bedroom to use the ensuite to freshen up. Callen kissed my cheek before explaining that he and Griffin would be in Griffin's private study through the other archway in the room.

As we entered Griffin's room I took in a couple of things. One, the bed was a mess. Which normally would have made me grin, but considering my blood covered state, it didn't seem like the most appropriate action. Second, through the open door to the closet I saw that Griffin really must not have been living here. Most of the clothes looked far too small for his physique now. Plus, they all looked far too regal for his taste. And third, damn it must be nice to be a royal! Even I couldn't have dreamed or even afforded the bathroom he had hidden away here.

"Vi," Evelyn said, interrupting my thoughts. "Did you want to jump in the shower first?"

"You go ahead," I insisted. "I want to scrub some of this blood out from under my nails first."

She nodded and stepped into the bathroom to slip out of her clothes. I heard the water come on and then she shouted for me to come in. I entered and immediately wet a towel to start scrubbing at my hands. In my worst nightmares I had never imagined that one day I would be covered in the blood of two friends...I needed it off of me.

"How did you do that back there?" Evelyn asked from the shower.

"Do what?" I questioned, despite knowing exactly what she was getting at.

"Vi," she said, looking around the wall of the shower. "You know what I'm talking about. How did you use Healing magic? You're a Vision."

"Oh, that," I fake laughed. "Oh fine! I did it the same way I took your Fear magic. But Nixie asked me to."

"She what?" she asked, as the water turned off.

I turned around and saw Evelyn standing behind me, wrapped in a towel, looking incredibly sad.

"Vi, Nixie is dead. How could she..."

"I don't know how she did it," I explained. "One minute you were closing her eyes and the next...she was speakin' through you."

"Through me?"

"You can ask Nicholas. He heard the entire thing. You... uh...no...Nixie asked me to take her magic and use it to heal Victor. So, I did. But I didn't know how to use it. That's why I needed you."

She paused for a moment and stared at me. But the brief silence broke when Griffin knocked on the door and brought in our clothes. We thanked him and Evey went back into the bedroom to change while I got into the shower.

As the water rained down on me, I watched the reddish, pink water swirl down the drain. Scrubbing at my hair, my mind raced knowing that Evelyn was incredibly confused... but how could I explain it? I wasn't even sure I totally understood what had just happened.

The only conclusion I could come to was that somehow, when I used Evey's emerald, I took in its magic. It didn't make any logical sense. Maybe Evelyn's Fear magic was just too strong to be contained by the gem, so it latched onto me. But even that didn't make complete sense. Shouldn't some of the Fear have at least gone into the emerald? Or can magic not be split like that?

"Vi?"

The sound of Callen's voice made me jump. How long had I been in here?

"Vi, are you alright in there?"

"I'm fine," I reassured him as I rinsed off the last few bubbles and shut the water off. "Just got a little lost in thought."

I reached around the shower wall and wrapped myself in my towel before climbing out.

"Want to talk about it?" Callen offered, as he handed me my clothes.

"I'm not sure there is much to talk about," I said, shrugging off my towel and stepping into my jeans. "I don't even know what's going on anymore."

"You took in Healing magic," he surmised. "That's what's going on here."

I finished pulling on my shirt, then looked up at him with a blank stare. He hadn't been able to tell I took in Evey's Fear...how in the blazes was he able to tell this time?

"I don't really know," he answered in reply to my unspoken question. "Fear is magic we don't understand. Maybe that has something to do with it. Healing doesn't have the dark properties Fear does, so maybe it doesn't block me out like the Fear did."

I turned my eyes from him as a random light bulb flicked on in my brain. I don't know why this memory, or this specific thought surfaced when it did...maybe it was all the talk of Fear magic...but I vividly remembered Barin threatening Ariana that no prophecy was going to get in his way. And Callen...when we had gone to rescue Auntie, he had mentioned a prophecy. That had to be it. The missing piece.

"Cal, tell me about the prophecy!"

"Now?"

"Yes, now!" I demanded. "Wait, no!"

"I'm confused."

"Evey has to hear this too!"

I grabbed hold of his hand and dragged him back into the bedroom. Evey was sitting on the end of Griffin's bed, and he was standing in front of her with his hands in hers. Normally it would have made me giddy inside...but this was business...and I finally had a deal closing idea.

"What's wrong?" Evelyn asked, standing up.

"No, sit!" I instructed. "Callen and Griffin have something they need to tell us."

"We do?" Griffin asked, shooting a confused look at Callen. "Oh...that."

"What am I missing here?" Evelyn asked.

"Just sit with me."

Callen and Griffin stood in front of us for a few seconds. They just stared at us between their concerned glances at each other. I wasn't sure what the big deal was. I mean, I guess the prophecy could have predicted someone's death...but we were already down three people we love, one palace guard, and all of the innocent Magirians who had been killed in the ballroom...death seemed like the least of our worries right now.

"Oh, will you two stop with the theatrics and just tell us the damn prophecy!"

"The what?" Evelyn asked.

"Back when Griffin and I left you both at Woodburn Rose, we came here looking for answers on who was following you," Callen began.

"But you came back empty handed," Evelyn reminded them. "Why are we even talking about this?"

"Well, we came back mostly empty handed," Callen disagreed.

"I'm seriously not following you here."

"E, we did find something," Griffin explained. "We just didn't know how to interpret it. There are still missing pieces."

"Just spit the damn thing out!" I demanded.

"When balance of power shifts to dark, restoration is found through the one who was marked. Led by The Five, their magic will reign. When blood reunites, only peace will remain."

Griffin finished reciting the prophecy, and although I had some questions of my own, I knew I was right. This had to be the answer I was searching for. But how did it impact the Fears? How was it going to help us beat the Fears? And then there was the increasingly confusing question of why were these two so clearly afraid of it.

Evelyn began chatting with the guys beside me as my mind raced through the possibilities. Then I jumped off of the bed faster than greased lightenin'.

"Vi?" Evelyn asked.

"Get Ansel to meet us here," I demanded. "I need to get to the library."

"Vi, what…"

"E and I will retrieve him from the other side of the veil," Griffin interjected. "We will meet you both in the library soon after."

Griffin grabbed Evey's hand, and despite her confused look, he led her out of the room. Callen held out his hand for me and I took it, practically draggin' him behind me.

"Vi, what is going on?" Callen asked as we moved through the hall.

"I need Auntie Saraya too."

"Why?" he asked, pulling me to a stop. "Vi, what is going on? What aren't you telling me?"

"Cal, I love you," I assured him. "But this is something I have to figure out completely before I share with you. Let's just say I have a theory and I need you to trust me on it."

He stared at me for a moment and then brought my hand to his lips.

"I do trust you."

Chapter 24

Evelyn

We scurried through the halls with a haste I hadn't anticipated. My mind was racing trying to figure out why Vi was so determined to research this right in this moment. I knew it meant that she believed it was vitally important to us, but she had made the conclusion so quickly after hearing the so-called prophecy. Though even I had to admit, that alone definitely sparked my curiosity.

Griffin hadn't released my hand since we left the room. Which wouldn't have been so strange if he hadn't been practically dragging me behind him. Typically, when we walked, it was something we did side by side. His urgency wasn't helping my anxiety over everything around us.

Still without a word, we made our way to the back of the library and passed through the veil that led to the dirty garage in the non-magical realm. I took everything around me in. I could see that Vi's car and the Knight's SUV, were still parked just inside the garage door. They hadn't even been there long enough to collect a good amount of dust, yet it felt like it had been a lifetime since I'd seen them.

Suddenly Griffin spun me, causing me to collide with

his chest and he let out a heavy sigh as we embraced me.

"I'm not going anywhere."

I had no clue what made me think he needed to hear that, but I somehow just knew he did. His heart was thudding rapidly in his chest, and I just instinctively knew what was running through his mind.

He kissed me on the forehead and pulled away slightly, holding my face in his hands.

"I just can't let anything happen to you," he said softly.

"Griffin," I began as I grabbed him by the wrists and pulled his slightly trembling hands down, interlacing our fingers. "I promise you, we will make it through this. Plus, with all of the help I know we are going to have, the Fears aren't going to stand a chance."

"I certainly hope you are correct on that."

"I am," I asserted with a smile. "I never did ask you. Are those beasts going to come back to help us again? They had given me such a bad feeling when I first saw them, but Vi and Johanna both seemed certain they were on our side. Did you call them from Fantazi? Can the princess bring them again?"

"E, stop."

He let out a breathy chuckle as he ushered me back towards Violet's car. Gently, he lifted me off of the ground and settled me on the hood. I sure hoped my gift was blocking her out right now, because she would be having a fit if she saw me sitting on her baby like this.

"I have something to tell you about the beasts, but I need you to keep an open mind."

"Um...okay."

"I told you before, there are certain things about the Knights I couldn't share with you."

"Yes, I know that."

"I couldn't share them because they can't be shared outside of the Knights inner circle," he explained. "Even the King of Magir himself isn't granted the ability to know the Knight's secrets."

"But now you can tell me," I surmised. "Because we are bonded now?"

"Exactly," he nodded. "Seems antiquated but Knight magic has very specific rules."

"But what does that have to do..."

"We are the beasts, E," he interrupted.

I couldn't even speak. I was still vaguely aware that my mouth was hanging open after being cut off, but I couldn't find my words. *We are the beasts.* How was that even possible? How could I not sense him? And why did the beasts make me feel so on edge if they were really Knights?

A memory flashed in my mind of how calmly Johanna had approached the large, auburn colored beast and I began to piece together that the beast had been Sean. I wondered if he hadn't told her until that moment. Seems like a big secret to keep from her, but then again, they hadn't exactly been *together* for a very long time.

"Each time a new leader is chosen, he is given sacred knowledge of an exclusive form of magic that enables him and all of his unit to transform into something that will aid them in protecting Magir. It's magic that only Knights can perform," Griffin expounded.

"And you became that...that beast creature?" I hardly recognized my cracking voice.

"Sort of," he chuckled again, as he paced in front of me. "I asked for a creature that was more than just strong. I wanted to be wise, strong, fast, skilled at tracking, and deadly. And so, the ancestors created my beasts."

"So, you can just...transform?" I questioned, finding a bit more of my voice. "I thought you said magical creatures were in Fantazi."

"We are the only Magirian's who have such magic," he clarified. "Even now, despite us being bonded and you having access to my magic, you wouldn't be able to channel a beast. It's magic restricted to only the Knights following the chosen leader."

"But in the woods," I continued, moving to the very edge of the hood. "I felt something…dark, towards the beasts. Why would I feel that way about you? About any of the Knights?"

"My best guess is that your Fear magic brought that on," he surmised. "Which would make sense since we are granted the magic for the purpose of protecting Magir from dark magic."

While I let his words sank in, he stopped pacing and walked to stand between my legs. Placing his hands on both of my thighs, he leaned in and flashed his brilliant smile at me.

"But this has to be our secret," he explained in a soft but also authoritative tone. "Revealing a Knight secret to an outsider is forbidden and incredibly painful to the person who attempts to reveal it."

"I know," I breathed back. "I've watched you struggle when you tried to tell me things before."

"You have no idea how good it feels to share that with you."

"Show me."

The words escaped on a light whisper from my lips and before I could even allow myself to blush at my boldness, his lips were pressed passionately to mine. But it was a short-lived escape as a car approached and the crunching of the gravel had Griffin pulling back, while helping me down from where I sat.

The dark town car came to a halt just as I took my spot beside Griffin and he interlaced our hands, pulling me securely to his side. The moment the back door was kicked open, I could make out the sound of Professor Hyperion rambling. He backed out of the car, his arms full of books and watched his feet the entire time as he approached.

"Help run the school. Teach your classes. Research the Fears. Obstruction. And scurry off on missions for the crow… crown."

He stammered over his last word as he looked up and noticed Griffin and I standing before him. I couldn't hold my smile as I looked back at his bulging eyes and mortified expression.

"Your highness," he stammered. "I wasn't expecting you."

"Slight change of plans," Griffin said, using the regal tone I was getting more and more used to hearing. "Violet has asked that you join her in the royal library and asked us to come retrieve you."

"The realms have gone topsy-turvy," he chuckled. "Sending the prince on an errand. What next?"

"Desperate times," Griffin joked back. "Are you able to return to Magir with us?"

"Well, I am supposed to be running Woodburn Rose," he began, but digressed as he read the urgency in Griffin's expression. "Though I suppose Maia can handle it for a short while. Yes. Let us get going then."

I could still hear Professor Hyperion muttering to himself as we passed through the veil. Queen Ariana's death had hit us all hard, but I hadn't thought about what that would do to WRA. She had likely stepped away temporarily, leaving Professors Hyperion and Odin in charge. But it was always meant to be just that...temporary. Now they were left trying to hold up a school for magicals while the magical realm they lived in not only grieved, but also went to war.

Once we were back in the library, Violet practically shouted at us to join her. It sounded like she was calling from a corner of the library, not far from where the veil was hidden, and I quickly led Griffin in the direction of her voice.

When we found her, she was sitting on the floor crisscross applesauce in the center of a pile of books. Some were open while others had clearly been unhelpful and had been tossed to the edge of her circle. If I didn't know her so well, I would have been shocked about how quickly she had practically moved into the library. But I did know her. And the library was Vi's happy place. Not to mention, when Violet was on the hunt for information, nothing was going to get in her way.

"Vi, we brought Professor Hyperion," I began.

"Ansel, your grace."

"Ansel," I repeated with a confused expression.

Did just getting engaged to the prince come with a title?

"Of course, it does!" Vi's voice echoed in my head. *"You're a princess now, so ya better get used to it."*

I rolled my eyes at her attempt to be humorous. Vi sure knew how to lighten a mood, but the curious part was that I was looking right at her as her words flowed into my mind, and she hadn't even flinched as she continued to flip through books. Could our connection really be that strong?

At that, Violet finally looked up and gave me the *you've got to be jokin' me*, look that I was rather accustomed to at this point in our lives. Then she turned and gave a quick, warm, albeit forced, smile toward Ansel.

"Thank you for coming," she praised. "Were you able to find texts on what I asked for?"

"I was," he nodded, moving toward her with the books. "I must confess, I am rather puzzled by your urgency for needing texts such as these, however."

"As are we," Griffin agreed. "Violet, what are you looking for?"

Before she could respond, there was a faint cough behind us.

"Excuse me, your royal highness," a voice interjected.

We turned and saw a puffy faced guard standing near the edge of one of the bookshelves. I was certain he had been crying. I may not have had empathy magic like Vi, but it was painfully obvious that he was grieving. We had all admittedly been struggling with all of the death around us, but, as we all knew, when death takes one of your own, it hits you like a ton of bricks.

"I apologize for the intrusion," he said, clearing his throat again. "The council has convened to discuss your stipulations."

"Now?" Griffin questioned.

"Yes, your royal highness," he nodded. "If you'd like, I can ask them to wait."

"No, thank you," Griffin sighed, as he shook his head. "I should let them know of our change in plans. Callen and Ansel can stay here to assist Violet. Evelyn and I will go meet the council."

"We will?" I questioned.

Griffin winked at me and interlaced our fingers before we began making our way back out of the library. But he couldn't seriously be taking me to meet with the council. There was no way I was ready for that. There was no possible way *they* were ready for that.

"Oh, and send Auntie to me if you see her!" Violet yelled after us.

Griffin didn't say a word as we moved hastily out of the library, down another hallway and through a set of doors, into a room that I had yet to be in. I quickly discovered that he had been absolutely serious about taking me with him to this impromptu council meeting.

"Griffin," I whispered to him.

He didn't answer, but continued to playfully smile at me as he guided me across the room. Once we were standing in front of the group, he stopped, and I felt a pit in my stomach growing as I searched the faces of the councilmen.

I didn't know most of them. Hell, I didn't really *know* any of them. One man stood out to me with his jet-black hair and stern, yet kind, eyes. He had to be Johanna's father. Another man I remembered from the first ball Barin had thrown, but I had never learned his name. A few others I could place from the feast or Queen Ariana's funeral, but really, all of these men were strangers to me. Yet, here I stood...a Fear... hand in hand with their future king.

"You've given some thought to my proposal?" Griffin questioned.

His expression had changed in an instant. Here he was a future king and that meant he was all business. There were no pleasantries to be exchanged, just discussion of his mystery proposal.

"We have," the man from the ball said.

"What are your thoughts?"

"We think your stipulations have merit," Johanna's father grinned. "You are young, and to share the role makes logical sense to all of us."

"Though we would like for you to entertain our concerns as well," another man added.

"What concerns are those?" Griffin asked.

The room fell silent, and I knew immediately what their concern was. It was me. Him marrying me. Marrying me would make it so I was Queen of Magir. A queen who was also a Fear. None of them wanted that. Even Johanna's father seemed skeptical, as his gaze studied me. But while I didn't know him, based on how he reacted to his daughter falling in love with someone she was not betrothed to, I took him to be a good man.

"If your concern..." Griffin began.

I squeezed the hand I was holding and grabbed his arm with my free hand to silence him. Talking in front of people may not have been my strongest skill - or even in my top ten - but I knew this was one of the moments when it was absolutely necessary.

"You are all in the right to be nervous in regard to me," I began.

"Evelyn," Griffin interjected.

"Griffin, they are," I surmised. "At the end of the day, it's true...I am part Fear. And the Fears you have known are a cruel, deadly, unforgiving people. But I can assure that is not me."

I took a heavy breath and dropped Griffin's hand. Moving closer to the row of chairs the councilman sat in, I face them all, not with the nervous jitters I usually had, but rather, I was filled with of burst of confidence and conviction in the words I needed to say. I hadn't even spoken them yet, but I knew I needed to say them and that they needed to be heard by

230

this audience.

"I am a Fear. There is no denying that," I paused. "But that is surely not all you see me for. I am also Healing, Strength, Vision, and Mind. I am the granddaughter of a man that was not only a councilman, just as you all are, but a man whom others describe as truly inspirational. The daughter of two incredibly powerful, albeit vastly different, magicals. I am a descendant of all five families. But magic isn't all that I am. Deep down...I don't fully know who I am. A few months ago, I was a nobody. Someone that wouldn't have stood out in a crowd of only five people. And yet, I stand before you right now asking you all to give me a chance to prove that I am much more than just a woman chosen by the Fear stone.

"For I am also a woman that your beloved Queen Ariana had faith in," I continued. "Someone that your future king believes in. And someone who is willing to risk everything for the sake of protecting her newfound home and family. I am not asking that you accept me as a wife to your king. I am not even asking that you accept me as a Fear. I am simply asking that you accept me for me. And that you afford me an opportunity to show you that being a Fear does not make me evil. That it makes me rounded. That it makes me...well me."

The room was still quiet when I stopped talking. Even Griffin, who was behind me just enough that I couldn't see him, didn't say a word. Maybe I had done it wrong. Maybe I really wasn't made for this grand speech thing.

As I attempted to release a deep sigh, it quickly hitched in my chest as Griffin was suddenly beside me lacing our fingers together again. However, it was when Johanna's father stood from his chair, that I truly felt like I may either faint or get sick.

"Young lady, in all my years I have never seen anyone, king, queen or other Magirian stand before this council and speak to us in such a way," he scolded.

Great...I had blown my one chance at being Griffin's supportive, yet strong other half. They were never going to accept me as his wife, nonetheless, their queen. Before we even had a chance to prove ourselves, I had opened my big mouth and ruined it.

"It was incredibly...refreshing."

"I'm sorry?" I asked, shocked by the words that had come from his mouth.

"My dear," another councilman began. "We are advisors to the royal family. While we may have quite a bit of influence, it is ultimately those who wear the crown whom decide how to govern the realm."

"And if you run it the same way you just stood up to us," Johanna's father continued, "then I am confident that Magir will prosper under your reign."

"With our honored prince by your side," another man chimed in, a smile on his face.

I wasn't even sure how to respond to them now. I had hoped they would say that they would consider me. After all, Fears didn't even live within the confines of Magir. But they weren't just considering...they had accepted me. They stood up and blatantly said I was the queen they wanted. Me...with all of my magic and all of my flaws. Me.

"Thank you," I finally choked out. "I can only hope I live up to your expectations."

"You'll exceed them," Griffin smiled. "There isn't a doubt in my mind."

I smiled at him and felt the magic heating between us before I turned back and saw even the councilmen smiling knowingly at us.

"So, it's settled," Griffin said, as he returned to the business side of the conversation. "You approve of my giving up a single role, for a shared royalty?"

"We do," the older man from the ball said.

"With two final stipulations on our end," Johanna's father interjected.

"Let's have them."

"One, your heir is still next in line," he instructed. "We

approve of you sharing your throne with the expectation that your family line will still be the ones to continue ruling for centuries to come."

"I'm sure my other party will have no objection with that, so long as their children are treated as royals too," Griffin agreed. "And your second?"

"That you remain the High King," another gentleman added. "You can split duties, share responsibility and power with whom we discussed, but you will still be the overall High King of Magir, and your vote will outweigh any other."

I wasn't even sure what we were talking about. Griffin was asking to split the duties of being king? It clearly wasn't me he was referring to if he was talking about someone else's children. But who else could he be referring to?

"I accept these terms as requested," Griffin answered suddenly. "I shall speak with the other parties to confirm, but I believe we have a solidified plan for the succession of the Magirian throne."

There was smiling and quite a bit of clasping each other on the shoulder, as the room rejoiced at the crowning of a new king. Or was it kings? I wasn't even sure what it was Griffin had just agreed to, but this wasn't the time for me to ask.

"I do have another subject of business to discuss with you all," Griffin announced, interrupting the merriment. "The Fear, Michael, attacked us again a few short hours ago."

Whispers began to fill the room and I felt my body tense automatically in response to the sound of his name. It disgusted me that Michael still held that much power over me. But my muscles slowly began to relax as Griffin tightened his grip on my hand and pushed himself closer to me, instinctively providing me some much needed comfort.

"He killed a guard and our friend Nixie. Had it not been for Violet, Evelyn and Nicholas, he also would have successfully killed Victor," Griffin explained. "As a result of this second attack, I feel we can wait no longer. We are moving up our timeline. We will depart before sunrise and proceed with our plan to meet the Fears at the Fantazi border for war."

The room remained silent while the men studied our faces and each other's. Rightfully so...this was a lot to take in. And it certainly was not a decision to be taken lightly. Yet, as they all began to nod, returning their confident looks to Griffin, I knew they had come to the same conclusion. War was inevitable at this point...and it was our turn to strike.

"Princess Tatiana and her best soldier have arrived and offered their assistance," Griffin continued. "With their experience, the Knights, and the royal guard at our disposal, I believe that we will emerge victorious from this battle. And as your future king, I am not seeking permission for this war. I did however, out of courtesy, want to inform you of our plan. It is my expectation that upon our victorious return, we will then crown the new royalty of Magir."

Griffin stood tall beside me while we awaited their response. His words sinking in, as the council continued to stare at us.

When they all began to rise, that pit in my stomach started to form again. It was almost like we were back in school being judged by our peers. But when they began to bow their heads, the pit receded, and I looked over just enough to see Giffin return their nods with a smile.

"Your mission shall be successful," Johanna's father concurred, standing back up. "You have trained your Knights well, and we know you will put the wellbeing of the realm first when in battle."

"I appreciate your well wishes," Griffin said, reaching out a hand.

The men shook hands and then the council began to dismiss themselves. When it was just Griffin and I in the room, I turned to him with a look that practically screamed how confused I was about every aspect of what had just happened.

"You're sharing the throne?" I asked bluntly. "With who?"

"Well, hopefully with you," he winked. "We should get

back to the library."

"That was not a conversation about having equal power with your wife," I corrected. "Who are you planning to share your throne with?"

"Wife?"

Lucas had entered the room without my knowing and was standing just inside the doorframe.

"I apologize, Lucas," Griffin said, moving towards him. "This is not how I had intended for you to find out. But yes. Evelyn has agreed to be Queen of Magir."

Lucas's gaze moved between Griffin and me. I wasn't sure what to do...and the emotions I was feeling were completely foreign to me. Auntie Saraya was protective, but having your father face down with your boyfriend, or in this case, fiancé, was something I never imagined I'd experience one day.

Just when I thought the situation couldn't have gotten any more awkward, a wheelchair began to roll through the door and Auntie Saraya came into view.

"I can understand *him*," she said, pointing at Lucas. "But not telling me! I have half a mind to drag you to whatever room you're staying in and ground you for the rest of your life."

"Auntie!"

I rushed over and hugged her. After all of the loss we'd suffered in the past twenty-four hours, I needed to feel her embrace. Until I was wrapped tightly in her arms, I didn't even realize how much I'd needed this.

"I am so sorry," I said, not wanting to break our embrace. "I should have told Griffin to ask you first. Vi, would never get engaged without her father's blessing."

"Oh please," Auntie Saraya sassed as she pulled away from me. "We all know magic sort of *engages* people the moment they make certain choices."

She winked at me, and I suddenly felt my cheeks getting pink, not wanting my father or fiancé to be around while Auntie showed her true boldness.

"I heard from outside," she began again, "that you two have a mission to take off for, but your father and I are hoping to have a word with you first."

"Of course," Griffin agreed. "I'll give you three some privacy."

He kissed me on the cheek and then made his way out of the room without another word. The two guards at the door were instantly at his side and were followed down the hall. I smiled, as I felt a rush of gratefulness at the sight of him being protected by his people. Oh, if only they knew what he could really do.

"It's sweet," Auntie Saraya began. "It's sweet how much you both care about each other."

"Though any decent man would have asked her father first," Lucas quipped.

"Any decent father wouldn't have been MIA for twenty years," Auntie Saraya snapped back.

"Touche," Lucas laughed. "I truly have missed you, Sar."

"Meh...what's not to miss."

She winked at me and then rolled herself over beside one of the chairs.

"Come sit with me," she instructed me.

Oddly hesitant, I stepped forward and took the chair in front of her. Lucas then shifted to stand behind her, placing a hand on her shoulder.

"Why does it feel like I'm finally going to get that *birds and the bees* speech?" I joked.

"Do we still need to have that talk?" Lucas asked, shifting his stance in discomfort.

"No," Auntie Saraya and I said in unison.

I narrowed my eyes at her. We talked about everything...well almost everything...never my sex life. That was something that I only ever talked about with Vi. And even then, it was generally something I preferred to keep to myself. But with how Auntie was looking at me now, I was certain I had a tattoo on my forehead that read *no longer a virgin*.

"You can't seriously think I didn't know?" Auntie questioned. "Did you think I actually believed that you were just out dancing, after we moved? There were a few nights even Violet returned home before you."

"And now I am uncomfortable," Lucas muttered.

"Sex is a natural part of life," Auntie Saraya smirked at her brother. "Or do I need to explain to you how your *daughter* is sitting before us."

"Let's not," I quickly rebutted.

Lucas almost blushed as he spun around to remove himself from the conversation.

"As much as I am *not* enjoying this conversation," Lucas began, as he turned back to us. "I think we should cut to the important topics of this conversation. I believe the Knights are hoping to leave soon."

"Fine. But if you think your twenty-year-old daughter isn't sleeping with that godlike man, you are incredibly naive," Auntie Saraya laughed.

"And she went there," I groaned, burying my face in my hands.

"In all seriousness though," Auntie Saraya said, tapping my leg. "Your father has a few things he would like to explain to you."

I looked up at both of them and could sense that the energy in the room had changed. It had gone from humorous embarrassment to a serious reality check that I was pretty sure I didn't want to be part of right now. I had enough going on with my friends dying all around me...throwing in family issues was only going to make matters worse.

"I'm not going to take much of your time," Lucas explained. "I know you have far more important things. But there are a few things that I need you to know before taking on the Fears."

I still wasn't sure that I even wanted to hear what he had to say. He had left me for the majority of my life. Actually about 95% of my life...but who's counting, right? But even I couldn't deny that what he had to say may prove to be useful. Maybe he knew some secret that would allow us to defeat Morana. So, despite how badly part of me wanted to dismiss him, I nodded for him to continue, as I crossed my arms over my chest in a small gesture of defiance.

"I'm not even sure where to begin," Lucas exclaimed with a heavy breath.

"How about when you left me?" I suggested.

Auntie Saraya cleared her throat loudly and I knew I had given a childish response. Hence the child-like punishment I received in the burning glare she fired at me.

"That's a fair start," Lucas nodded. "But I think I should actually start before that. You see, when your mother left me, she was still pregnant with you. I knew she planned to return to Sephtis, but nobody knew where that was. No non-Fear anyway."

"That's when you found Armonee?" I asked.

"Sort of. Armonee found me," Lucas corrected. "She was sent to kill me after Morana left. But she couldn't. She is a strong and loyal ally, but she is not what Magirian's would define as a *Fear*."

"What do you mean?"

A guard returned to the door, and we all looked in his direction. I knew that his return meant that Griffin was back with Violet and Callen, and that I needed to hustle this up and get back to the others sooner rather than later.

"We can discuss Armonee later," Lucas said, returning to his confession. "My point is, I think I know how you and Violet became Shadow Twins."

"What?" I questioned, giving him my full attention now.

"Your mother left, and I tried my damnedest to track her, but she kept evading me. When she made it to Georgia, I lost her trail for a brief period."

"Georgia..." I repeated quietly, knowing full well what that meant.

"Yes," he confirmed. "I knew there must have been some hidden veil there and with Armonee's help, I was able to locate it and walked directly into Sephtis."

"So, you kidnapped me from my mother," I surmised. "Who had kidnapped me from you?"

"In a sense you could say that," he shrugged. "My point is that just as we emerged back into the non-magical realm, it felt like an earthquake hit. I believe most Magirians just refer to it as *The Quake*."

"I don't understand," I admitted.

"I believe we emerged on the day that Violet was born."

"I think the magical universe decided that you two were meant to be connected," Auntie Saraya clarified. "When your father got you away from the Fears in the same place your cousin was being born, it magically tied the two of you together. It was almost like you were reborn."

"But that doesn't make sense...can magic just do that?" I asked. "I know I'm new, but it doesn't seem fair, that magic can just dictate a person's life like that."

Auntie Saraya and Lucas exchanged glances for a few seconds before looking back at me. There was confusion and sadness in their eyes that I didn't know how to interpret. It was moments like this when I usually would have relied on Vi's empathy to guide me.

"I can't say for sure," Auntie Saraya began. "But according to my research, Violet's parents were living in Georgia at the same time that your father left Sephtis. Since you and Vi weren't born at the same time, this is what makes the most sense. Magically, you were reborn and tied to Violet on that day."

"But you seriously had no idea who Vi was before now?" I questioned. "I mean, we only met Vi in Harbor. Why wouldn't you have magically sensed her or something?"

"A person would have to be blind to not see your connect to her, but I never thought it was because she was my niece. I honestly had no idea who she was, Evelyn. I didn't even know I had another brother, nonetheless a niece. But the moment she told me about her grandmother, I knew it was something I had to look into. I promise...I didn't know before you left for Woodburn Rose. And I wasn't able to confirm my suspicions until she used the emerald against Morana."

"So, what you're telling me is that Hale was right?" I questioned. "Violet and I aren't just cousins, but we're Shadow Twins?"

"It would seem so," Auntie Saraya responded.

I took a deep breath and then stood up. Now it was my turn to pace around the room with my hands on my head. Despite how much sense it made...and man, it put a lot of pieces together...it was still hard for me to hear. It would have been a lot to take in for anyone on a normal day...nonetheless on a day like I was having.

"I understand what you may be feeling," Lucas began.

"All due respect," I snapped. "You have known me for less than a week! You have no idea what I'm feeling."

"Actually, I've known you all your life," he said as he walked over to one of the chairs and held tightly onto its back. "I told you before, I never truly left you."

"How is that possible?" Auntie Saraya asked. "I kept us hidden. How would you have been able to find us."

"I'm just that good, Sar," he winked.

"Armonee told me. But why didn't we recognize you?" I interjected.

"Magic," he explained. "Fear magic can make a person see whatever the Fear wishes. I had Armonee shield my true identity. EvelynRose, I..."

"Stop!"

He took one step toward me, and I brought him to a halt. I hadn't intended to be so harsh, but my mind was racing, and my chest was starting to tighten. Emotions...especially expressing them...is not something I do. I don't share my feelings. I don't wear my heart on my sleeve like Vi. And now, with everything happening at once, I felt like I was drowning in emotions that I had zero time to deal with...not that I would have known how to deal with them if I had all the time in the world.

"I just...I just need a few minutes."

With a quick turn, I walked past them to the door. The lump in my throat was making it hard to even speak. I stopped just before I reached the guard and as he began to open it for me, I remembered Vi's request.

"Auntie," I choked out. "Vi needs you in the library right away."

Before she could reply, I walked out of the room and quickly made my way down the hall. I could hear the footsteps of a guard behind me, but that didn't slow me down. I wasn't even sure where I was going. I just knew I needed to be anywhere but in that room. I needed space to breathe. Space to think about everything happening around me.

Three women I respected and cared for had been killed in the last two days. My best friend turned out to be my cousin and Shadow Twin...whatever that meant. The man I was in love with had proposed to me, and together we were chosen to be the next rulers of Magir. Oh, and of course through all of this, woman who raised me was still rolling around in a wheelchair because of me!

Before I let myself acknowledge where my feet were taking me, I was outside the castle, crossing the grass and grabbing one of the bows, along with a few arrows.

Placing the first one on the string and pulling back, I took a quick breath before releasing it and burying the arrowhead into the edge of the target's inner circle.

"You've got to have a clearer head if you want that bullseye."

I glanced at the woman behind me and picked up another arrow. I had barely placed it on the string when she continued to approach.

"Do you want to talk about it?"

"No," I groaned, as I released the arrow and once again

missed just shy of the center.

I rolled my eyes and moved in front of the third target. Raising my bow again, I felt the anger rising inside me, when I suddenly heard snickering behind me.

Before I could stop myself, or even think about what I was about to do, I spun around, and the arrow left the bow. It seemed to move in slow motion as it narrowly missed Armonee's head and her eyes narrowed at me. A puff black smoke appeared and before I could take in that she had vanished, she reappeared in front of me.

Yanking the bow out of my hand, she stared at me intensely. The guard at the nearest door flinched slightly, unsure if I needed help, and I raised my hand to dismiss him. The anger continued to boil inside me, but it wasn't the same feeling as I normally had with my Fear magic. Though even I had to admit, this was the angriest I had allowed myself to get since Violet took my magic.

"If you continue to deny your emotions," she lectured, "then you risk being more of a liability than an asset."

"You don't know what you are talking about."

"I know more than anyone else here. I know what it feels like to have your magic amplify every angry thought you've ever had. If you continue to let it get the better of you, then, like I said, the benefit of having you around isn't worth the risk."

My face contorted as her words fueled my growing rage. I didn't know what to say and I didn't want to take part in this discussion any further. So, I turned and moved back to the table to grab another bow.

Smoke filled the air as I spun, and before I could even get close to the table, Armonee was again in front of me.

"Move."

"Or what?" she asked. "Are you not even going to try to control your magic?"

Unable to stop myself I shoved her forward using my Strength and to my surprise...she barely moved.

"Is that all you've got?" she taunted. "Come one, kid. Let me have it."

I couldn't stop myself at that point. I was so angry at everything around me that I launched at her with everything I had. Using Strength and Mind, I struck her repeatedly as I anticipated each of her moves. But this woman was not backing down, and she certainly wasn't going easy on me. Instead, she was throwing magic and hitting me back with equal force. Making sure that each hit hurt just enough to stun me for a moment but not cause any physical injuries.

"Come on! Get those feelings out," she shouted at me. "Tell me why it is that you're so damn angry!"

"You...want to...know...why I'm...angry?" I questioned, as I landed a few strikes.

"Well, you could just go off and cry in a corner if that makes you feel better," Armonee mocked. "Or you could hit me and let it out!"

She hit back, this time landing a blow to the side of my ribs, and I buckled a bit. As I leaned over only for a moment, I realized how right she was. It did feel good to let off this steam. With all of the events from today...I had more anger to let out than I think I had even realized. And as bad as I knew it was to vent by physically assaulting someone else...man, did it feel good.

"I want the death to stop," I emphasized, as I swung for her and missed.

"Well, that's obvious," she rolled her eyes. "Give me the good stuff."

"I am tired of people treating me like I'm weak or naive."

"Now we're getting there. What else?"

We'd battled our way across the lawn and were now over where I'd had been attempting to throw knives earlier in the day. I reached for Armonee just as she leapt backward flipping over a table and landing flat on her feet.

"I'm fucking tired!" I screamed, as I tossed the table to get to her. "Tired of my magic failing me! Of being unable to control it! I'm tired of everyone risking their lives for me! I'm furious that my father thinks he can just walk back into my life after letting me believe he was dead! I'm sick of not being able to understand emotions like Violet. And..."

I spun around quickly, and my foot connected clean with Armonee's chin, sending her tumbling to the ground.

"And I'm tired of being so angry *all* the damn time," I cried, looking down at her. "I'm just...tired."

For a moment we just stared at one another. Armonee on the ground and me standing over her. Both of us breathing as if we had run several marathons.

"Now that," she began, as she lifted her hand and I instinctively helped her up, "is much better. Now, care to share a little more?"

She moved back towards the archery station, and I followed her, slightly confused, and yet, quite thankful for her tactics.

"How do you do it?"

"Do what?" she asked back.

"How do you control your Fear magic with such ease?" I inquired. "If someone had attacked me the way I just attacked you, I wouldn't have been able to control myself. Shoot, I almost killed Johanna once because I couldn't control myself. How...how do you make it look so easy?"

She put down the bow she was preparing for herself and turned to face me again. Her expression did not appear very happy...but it wasn't angry either. From the look of her eyes, she almost appeared...sad.

"Easy?" she questioned. "You think this is *easy*? EvelynRose, I fight with myself all the time. Having Fear magic emphasizes every dark feeling we've ever had. Even in moments where it makes no sense at all."

"Yes, but you don't go nuclear like I do," I reminded her. "You aren't causing storms that tear apart parks. You aren't stabbing your aunt through the chest with a spear. How do you stop yourself?"

"I accept my fears, EvelynRose. I accept all the evil things I have done, and I don't punish myself for them any further. I do not dwell on the cruelties of my past. That is how I control it."

"So, as long as I accept my fears...I can control my Fear magic that feeds off of them?"

"So long as you accept yourself," she corrected. "Look, you're never going to change the core of who you are. For Estella's sake, your friend literally stripped you of your Fear and yet I can still feel it rebuilding inside you."

"You can?"

"EvelynRose," she sighed and shook her head. "Stopped fighting who you are. You are an Archer descendant. Lucas and Morana are your parents. You will likely be Queen of Magir one day. And you will always...*always* be a Fear. Once you've accepted that, you will learn to control the magic within you. And once you do that...well, then you will truly be the descendent of The Five that the prophecy speaks of."

The prophecy! She was right. Griffin had said that *led by The Five their powers will reign*. It didn't say led by five...it said *The* Five...it was me. The prophecy was about me. If I led them into battle, we would come forth victorious. I was the only descendant of all five families. I was the one who was predicted to overthrow the Fears. Me...a Fear myself.

"Thank you, but I have to go," I exclaimed, as I rushed back toward the door.

"EvelynRose," Armonee called after me.

I paused and turned to her just as she shot an arrow, but rather than watch it sink into the target, I watched it soar across the lawn and land in the combat dummy.

"Fear carries a darkness with it that is impossible to deny," she reminded me. "But we must also realize that fear is a necessary part of survival. Without it, we shall all surely perish."

Nodding at her, I turned back and headed into the palace. With a guard still on my tail, I did feel safe, but I was

245

far too distracted by my thoughts to even care about my own safety right now.

Armonee had given me more in our few minutes together, than I had managed to dig up in all of my months as a magical. Fear wasn't just about darkness. There was far more to it than that. And with a clear head, I think I finally understood why.

I understood why my father had to leave me, and why Auntie Saraya kept so many secrets. I understood why I guarded myself and shut people out of my life. I think I even understood why, in her final moments, Queen Ariana chose to give Griffin her blessing for our relationship. But I had to tell the others. And I had to tell them before we left for the Fantazi border.

As I hustled my way through the corridors with my mind creating all kinds of strategies, I knew this was the answer. The missing piece that we needed. This was what was going to make us victorious against the Fears.

As I turned down the hall that led to the library, an unanswered question hit me. Griffin had said the prophecy mentioned restoration through *the one who was marked*. But we were all marked. As magical twins and Shadow Twins, all four of us possessed birthmarks that linked us. So, *who* was going to bring this restoration? With four possible candidates...which one of us was it?

Or was the wording slightly deceptive in the same way that *The Five* was. Maybe it wasn't an actual mark. But how can someone be *marked* without actually *being* marked. Or was it possible that the mark wasn't something the person was born with. I still leaned toward my initial theory but with magic, it was hard to say, and the numerous possibilities made my head spin.

Violet. She would have the answer. She always had my answers. I just needed to talk to Vi.

Chapter 25

Violet

I was throwing books around the library like a tornado ripping through a town. Books were flying everywhere, and I could hear the confusion of Callen and Griffin behind me. But I couldn't care about that right now.

I had left Ansel with Auntie Saraya and Lucas to investigate their assigned project. Magical creatures. Lucas had thought I was crazy when I told them I needed their opinion on something, but the look on Auntie's face said she believed that I was heading in the right direction. It was like she knew something even her brother didn't...and that something was about our family.

For me, I knew that I just needed to find anything and everything I could on empathy. And not as an emotion, but as a magical gift. I had to know what sort of abilities it gave me. I had a feelin' that there was something extra special about my form of empathy...but who could really say without all of the facts. I certainly wasn't goin' to.

From the corner of my eye, a book with a leather spine etched in gold caught my attention and I leaned on the ladder to reach for it. My fingertips pressed against the bottom of the book, but just when I thought it was coming loose, I slipped off the step and crashed into Callen's arms.

"Vi!"

"Good catch, handsome," I gasped, patting his chest and climbing out of his arms.

"Which one?" Griffin asked.

I pointed at the book and Griffin waved his hand through the air. The book came floating off the shelf and landed in my hands.

"Aren't you Strength?" I questioned. "How in the hell do you do that?"

"I'm a Mind too," he answered.

"Oh, sweet baby Jesus," I exclaimed, as I plopped into a chair. "Just when I started to think that I had some of the pieces to this puzzle, I turn out to be wrong and more get tossed onto the table. We better hope this book has the answers I'm thinking it does."

"And what's that?"

"I need to know about empathy."

"Vi," Callen began in a confused tone. "You have empathy...what more do you need to know?"

"Can you just..."

Evelyn came bursting into the library talkin' a million miles a minute and everyone turned to her. I couldn't keep up and something inside me was screaming that I didn't have time to. So, I focused on the book and tried to find anything about empathy. But page after page...there was nothing. A heaping pile of absolutely nothing.

I put my hands in my face as, yet another page revealed no information. And it was in that second that I finally listened to what Evey was going on about.

"I'm the Five!" Evelyn exclaimed.

"Wait!" I shouted as I jumped up from my chair. "Say that again!"

"Which part?" Evelyn asked.

"The prophecy! Griffin, tell me the prophecy again," I

instructed.

"When balance of power shifts to dark, restoration is found through the one who was marked. Led by the Five, their magic will reign. When blood reunites, only peace will remain," Griffin repeated.

"Blood! That's it!"

They all looked at me like I had completely lost my mind. But, in their defense, I was jumping up and down clapping my hands while I chanted about blood.

"Vi?" Evelyn questioned.

"Blood had to reunite in order for the prophecy to come true," I cried. "It's you and I, Evey!"

"Oh..." Callen and Griffin collectively sighed in agreement.

"That...that actually makes a little sense..." Evelyn said slowly.

"But what about the rest?" I questioned, as I turned back to the book, I'd throw on my chair.

"And what about the mysterious reason that you dragged us all in here?" Griffin asked.

The doors flew open again and Nicholas, Victor, Lucas, and Armonee came bursting through the library. I couldn't help but notice that Victor looked oddly rejuvenated for someone who was nearly dead just an hour ago.

"I think we should get moving," Nicholas urged.

"I second that," Victor agreed. "I can't explain it, but it feels like something isn't right here anymore."

I stared at him for a moment and realized that he looked more than rejuvenated. His muscles had returned from their weakened state to looking like he had just left the gym. The sandy color of his hair had lightened into a bright dirty blonde. And as I shifted my gaze back to his eyes, I realized their usual hazel color was now almost golden brown.

There was more than a chance that between my silence and hard-core staring, everyone had noticed that I was having a revelation. But was it possible? Was what I was thinking had happened truly possible? If it was...it would certainly answer the question of what my gift could do.

"Violet," Callen whispered. "You're glaring."

I knew it. I mean I could feel the mean mug I was giving him. But I didn't care. The more I stared at him, or glared, as Callen said...the more I knew that I was right. He had not only been brought back to life...he was different.

"What did ya mean by that?" I finally asked Victor.

"Violet."

"Callen, I need to know!" I snapped. "Victor, why did you say something is wrong?"

"I...I don't know. I can just feel that something isn't right here anymore," he stammered.

"Have you ever felt something like this before?"

"Everyone has gut feelings, Vi," Evelyn interjected.

"This isn't a damn gut feeling," I quipped. "Victor?"

He stared at me before he glanced at the others.

"I...I guess not," he answered. "I mean, I have good instincts, but you are right...this feels different."

"Holy sweet baby, mother freakin', Jesus!" I exclaimed, as I literally shook with excitement and gripped tightly onto the closest thing I could find — which luckily for me was Callen's muscular biceps.

"What is it, Vi?" Callen asked.

"It's Nixie!"

"Excuse me?" Nicholas questioned. "What the hell do you mean, *it's Nixie?*"

It was making sense now. Empathy had allowed me to take in what others were feeling. In the same way that the absorbing emerald could absorb the magic of any magical with the right spell. I was like a living version of the gem. Finally, it made complete sense!

"Violet!" Evey shouted, bringing me back to reality. "I realize sometimes your brain needs time to sort out the details, but right now we are sort of in a hurry."

Just then, something else hit me. We needed something

to shock the Fears with. We need an angle that they couldn't see coming, which was proving to be very difficult since they seemed to have predicted every move, we've made...they seemed to have a way of knowing everything. Maybe...just maybe...this was what we needed. *This* was how we stole back the advantage.

"Never mind!" I shook my head. "We can discuss this later. Let's get moving."

"What about the library search?" Griffin questioned.

"I have what I came for," I shrugged. "Let's grab the others and get to the battlefield."

"But..."

Evey tried to protest but I shot her a look and mentally pleaded for her not to press the issue. I watched as she gave a quick nod and her jaw visibly tensed. She was confused and worried, but she would have answers soon. Hopefully, we both would.

"Well, you heard the lady," Nicholas asserted, as he narrowed his eyes a little at me. "Let's go kill us some Fears."

We all shuffled out of the library and as we walked toward the front castle steps, I felt Callen pull on my arm. We paused for a brief moment while the others continued and slowed our pace to keep ourselves out of earshot.

"What was that about?" Callen asked. "What are you planning?"

"What makes you think I'm plannin' somethin'?"

He didn't even speak...just raised an eyebrow, which told me everything I needed to know.

"I'm formulatin' a theory," I compromised.

"A theory?"

"You're going to have to trust that I know what I'm doin' here."

The sound of rapidly spinning wheels began to echo in the hall, and I turned to find Auntie Saraya racing toward us.

"Vi," she said on an exhausted breath as she brought her wheelchair to a stop. "I think you're right. About our family."

"You do?"

"Yes," she confirmed. "I will project to you once I have confirmation, but to do this, I need to tell Ansel everything."

"Do it."

"You're a genius, angel girl."

She grabbed my hand, gave it a tight squeeze and then quickly rolled herself back toward the library.

Turning back to Callen, his expression filled with curiosity, but his lips curled into a smile as he let out a chuckle before leaning down, softly kissing my cheek.

"I trust that miraculous mind of yours," he whispered against my cheek. "I'm here, whenever you're ready to loop me in."

He stepped back, grabbing my hand, and began practically dragging me down the hall until we caught up with the others. Our group had grown while we'd stopped to talk. Princess Tatiana, Carney, Charles, Sean and Johanna were all marching down the halls with us.

When we made it down the front steps, I noticed that Evelyn was looking around with a puzzled look on her face. But before I could ask, all of our heads whipped towards a side entrance, where Hale was waiting.

"Hale..." Evelyn said softly.

I watched as Griffin's eyes bounced between the two of them, before ultimately settling on Hale.

"Are you heading to Magir's edge?" he asked.

"We are," Callen responded.

It wasn't as cold as their normal communication, but there was still a lingering distrust there. The tension emanating from the other Knights was making my hands sweaty...and if I was being one hundred percent honest...other places too. I couldn't fathom why all of them still felt the way they did about him even after he helped us when King Barin went bat shit crazy. Not to mention he'd saved my life. In my eyes, he had more than redeemed himself.

"Well, part of the royal guard is set to stay here to

protect the Magirian's, should they need to," he informed us before turning back to the door.

For a brief, and I mean very brief, second, I thought they were actually going to let him walk away. They'd have to dumb as a box of rocks not to realize what an asset he would be to our team.

"Reignn!" Griffin shouted suddenly, as all of our party, and Hale, turned to face him. "Fight with us."

With a quick nod, and momentary flash of that arrogant glint that Hale usually had in his eyes, he moved toward us, ready to face the Fears in battle.

"Wait," Evelyn interjected. "How are we getting there?"

"You'll need to prepare yourself for this next part, E."

All of the Knights then moved away from us, and I knew exactly what was about to happen. However, based on the faces of everyone but Johanna and I...nobody else did.

Watching Callen transform into a beast had been the most unbelievable experience of my life. And that was coming from someone who could now perform magic just by doing some deep breathing. But as I watched all of the Knights begin their transformations all at once, the beauty and power of it was incomprehensible.

As we observed the change process, I felt the pain they were all in. Watching them go from looking like ridiculously buff, pro athletes to those massive, fur covered beasts that now towered over us, was somethin' I would never be able to fully appreciate...nor understand.

Forcing myself to look away from the Knights, I glanced over at Lucas and Armonee who were both glued to the scene before them with a look of sheer amazement on their faces. Clearly, I was not the only one who was dumbfounded by this experience. But it was when I looked at Evey and Hale that I felt a pit grow in my stomach.

They both watched with wide eyed stares as the transformation continued. But their amazement was coupled with something I hadn't expected...rage. They hated the beasts appearing before them and as I looked at Evey, whose green irises were now surrounded by a black circle, I felt the same unexpected and purely instinctive anger beginning to boil inside of me too.

When the transformations were complete and the Knights...well beasts, all stood in front of us, I moved closer to Evey and leaned toward the beast that was now where Griffin once stood.

"Vi..." Evey sputtered out through her trembling voice.

"Just listen to him," I encouraged.

"*If she has any of Fear still, it will block him if she doesn't control it,*" Callen's voice echoed in my mind.

"Evey," I said, grabbing her shoulders and forcing her to look at me. "You are stronger than your Fear. You are the kitten who sees the lion, not the lion who sees the kitten."

"He told me..." she trailed off.

"He did?"

"Yeah, but I didn't expect...that."

She continued to look at me and then turned to look at Griffin. Moving slowly, she approached him, and he held his giant hand...paw...out for her to touch.

It took her a moment to reach out, but once she did, I watched her incredibly tense body relax a bit. Although I couldn't see her face, I knew she was smiling at him. But it was when she turned to me, with that excited glint in her now fully green eyes, that I knew she could hear him.

"Amazing," Lucas breathed beside me.

"It's incredible," Armonee added.

"It's Fantazi magic," Hale questioned. "How is this possible?"

I heard Callen in my head for a moment and listened carefully to the message he wanted me to convey. When he'd finished, I turned to Hale.

"It's a secret of the Knights," I began. "A magic only those who are chosen can possess. One that nobody can know about. You are now part of a very small, entrusted circle.

They suffered a great amount of pain to show you their secret without you bonding with one of them. Don't take that trust they placed in your for granted."

"They have my silence," Hale said, still ogling over the beasts.

"Good," I added, as I moved toward Callen and his voice rang through my head again. "Because if you do tell anyone, Callen will order Sean to tear you apart."

A rascal's smile spread across Hale's lips. It seemed as if the moment of understanding and forgiveness had finally come.

"Griffin put faith in him," Callen's voice said in my head, as he bent down, and I climbed onto his back. *"I am indebted to him saving you. Though, I'm still not entirely certain I can trust him."*

"Don't be a grump!" I sassed back. *"We need him, and you know it."*

I felt him growl beneath me and I was certain he was rolling his eyes at me in his own, beastly way. As I gave him a playful tap, I heard Griffin growl from beside us.

"Nick will take Hale. Charles will take Armonee. And Daniel will take Lucas. Ask Princess Tatiana and Carney to stay behind. We need them to protect Magir if we fail."

Before I could verbalize his orders for the others to hear, Evey did it for me. I could still see that she was battling with herself to a degree, but there was also a childlike excitement in her eyes, as if magic had finally given her somethin' to appreciate.

Once we were all mounted on our assigned beast, they broke into a sprint out the front gate toward the edge of the town. Which made sense. Couldn't just go galivanting through town on magical creatures that shouldn't even exist in this realm.

Stealing a quick glance at the castle behind us, I saw more soldiers than I even realized Magir had, swiftly assembled outside. I wanted to ask about them. For starters, where had they all come from? But as we raced through the dark side streets and into the trees, I knew this wasn't the moment for it.

After all...Magir was beautiful. Like, truly the most spectacular place I had ever seen...and that meant a lot considering how many places I'd lived in and traveled to. I decided, in that moment, the right thing to do was to let go of the chaos for a moment and take in the beauty around me. Breathe in the sweet, smelling air. After tomorrow...I wasn't sure the air would smell this sweet. Then again...I wasn't sure if I'd be alive to smell it at all.

Chapter 26

Griffin

I didn't want this moment to end. Running in my beast form had always been where I felt most at peace, but having E perched on my back while I was in my beast form was exhilarating. No, it was absolutely addictive. I knew the pain that came with keeping the secret from her would dissipate after our bonding and my finally being able to reveal this part of me...but this was not what I had expected at all.

I loved how our magic moved together, even despite my transformative state. But my favorite part had to be how, in this form, I could hear all of her thoughts racing through my mind. She was rambling on and on about how unbelievable this all was. How'd she read countless fantasy novels and never once thought something like this could be real.

"*We've never let anyone in the non-magical realm see us,*" I said, biting back my urge to laugh, which would have come out as a low growl. "*Mythology and folklore come from creatures exposing themselves. Intentional or not. Part of the Knights's code is to never be seen. We made an exception in Sephtis, and it was excruciating for us. But like I said earlier, now that you and I are bonded, we can share this secret.*"

"But you showed the others too?" she thought back.

"Showing the others was not an easy order to give. It was painful. But we all agreed long ago, when the inevitable time came, we would share our secret with those we trusted. Magical connection or not," I explained. *"All of the Knights were willing to take the pain."*

Before she could ask the rest of the questions, I knew she had, Sean, who was carrying Johanna, slid to a stop and brought an immediate halt to everyone in our group.

Evelyn's confusion rushed through me. I could understand her reaction. We were still inside the woods. Through the edge of the tree line, we could see the open fields in front of us, but here we were hidden just enough to provide some protection. We had said over and over that the battle would take place at the edge of Magir. And, as Evelyn now knew from having seen the actual edge on our date, this was not that place.

I gave a mental order to the Knights to have their passengers dismount. Once they were all on the ground, we sprinted back, deep into the trees, leaving Evelyn, Violet, Hale, Lucas, and Armonee alone in the clearing.

The transformation back into our normal selves was far less excruciating than it had been in the past and took a surprising short period of time.

"What exactly are we doing here?" Armonee questioned. "This is not Morana's requested battlefield."

"We will walk to our base camp location from here," Sean explained, as we quickly emerged from the trees.

"Base?" Violet questioned.

"Yes," Callen confirmed. "We will establish a base camp where we can sleep before the battle begins tomorrow. That is, of course, assuming our earlier arrival doesn't provoke an early attack. This will also give us a place to rest and refuel on the off chance there are any ceasefires during the battle."

"Do you think it could actually take that long?" Johanna questioned.

All of the Knights and I exchanged glances. In moments like this we needed to remember that although we had all been in battles before, only us Knights had been to war.

"Unfortunately, yes," Lucas intervened, before I could speak. "Historically, Fear battles tend to last a few days."

"Days..." Violet groaned. "I knew I should have taken that palace worker up on her coffee offer this mornin'."

We all fell silent as everyone tried to process the fact that Vi's biggest concern was her missed cup of coffee, but the silence broke when Evelyn couldn't hold back her laughter any longer. But even as we all began to join in, there was a somberness that even the laughter couldn't diminish. As much as we all appreciated Violet's ability to lighten the mood, no matter the circumstances around her, but as we pressed on into the woods, the gravity of the situation was weighing on our spirits, making a simple smile a grueling task to achieve.

As we approached the camp, I felt Evelyn tense beside me. Taking in her expression, I could tell she was shocked by what she was seeing. Before us Magirian guards and staff were bustling around carrying various boxes and a couple were even wearing aprons. There were a few large tents, surrounded by several smaller ones. I'd seen war camps assembled more times than I could count. I knew as soon as we put the plan in motion, the Mind magical guards and a handful of supporters were sent to set everything up. The idea being that the Mind magicals could block our foes from knowing our location, or the fact that we were even there.

It was second nature to me. So, I couldn't help but smile a little as I heard Evelyn's thoughts, comparing what she was seeing to movies she'd seen in the non-magical realm. And I relished in the fact that our still forming bond was enhancing my ability to hear her, despite her magical gifts. But then I felt her heart start to race as she made a strong revelation...*we are really going to war.* Her thoughts weighed heavily on me. Was I right to bring her here? Should the Knights have handled this alone?

I moved my hand, entangling my fingers with hers and felt her body reactively relax. I still hadn't gotten used to the way our bodies now responded to even the smallest touch. Before, just being close to her sent me into a magical heat wave that was suffocating. Now, there was a peaceful sensation that rushed through me just by being in her space. And there was a strength it gave me that made it feel like we were the most powerful magicals in the realm.

"Everyone will find their names on their assigned tents," Nicholas explained, clearly growing impatient with Evelyn mentally distracting me. "Lucas, will you and Armonee, please join me in the command tent? I'd like to go over our positions before we move out. Armonee, can you assist with knowledge of their movements?"

"Of course," Lucas and Armonee said in unison.

Everyone dispersed and we each walked to our separate tents. I couldn't help but follow Evelyn's gaze as I led her toward our tent. She was watching Violet as she walked with Callen, and even I could recognize the worry on Violet's face. I didn't know her very well, but she didn't strike me as the type of person to get worried the way she seemed to be now. She was genuinely scared. And I wondered if it had to do with whatever our library trip had been about. There was something she knew. Something she knew, but we didn't.

Once we made it to our tent, I held open the flap of the tent as Evelyn shifted her gaze away from Violet's tent to ours. Walking inside, I heard her release a small gasp as she took in the space.

It wasn't what one might expect after experiencing other magical spaces. Sure, the tent was far larger than it appeared from outside. Yes, there was a king size bed in the middle, nestled between a large lamp and an armchair, but there was no ensuite or any other extra rooms attached. Considering the other magical places, she had been in the last couple months, I'm sure she was expecting more.

"It's a war base," I grinned, enjoying watching her eyes

relax as she took in the simplicity of our space. "The Knight's and I don't typically require the fancy stuff."

"It's actually kind of perfect," she replied. "The simplicity is a welcome change of pace with everything going on."

Her response caught me off guard and I shot her a concerned look, feeling my brows even wrinkle a bit. I knew I was overthinking her response, but when I was with her... it was as if my sole purpose was to make certain that she was happy beyond belief.

"Not that all of it has been bad," she retracted. "It's just...it's been a lot."

"I know," I sighed, as I hung my head slightly and sat heavily on the edge of bed. "I hope you are feeling..."

"But," she interjected, as she sat down beside me and rested her hand on my knee, "if there is one thing I've learned here, it's to tackle one thing at a time. We will get through this. Just as long as we're a team. There is, however, one thing in particular that I have to ask you about."

I turned to look at her and a jolt of magic surged through my body as her eyes connected with mine. Based on the pink tint that raced up her neck, she was feeling the same thing.

"Can you explain to me how I just watched my future husband turn into some sort of beast! And yes, I know we discussed this beforehand but did not discuss *that*."

As she spoke, she waved her hands around as if she was outlining a massive creature in front of her. She was so damned adorable, trying to explain the magic she had witnessed, that it took everything in my power not to interrupt her questioning with a kiss. But before I had the chance, she planted her hands on her hips and continued with her interrogation.

"Exactly how do you guys do that, again?"

"That's Knight magic," I chuckled, as I lifted her hand to my lips and placed the kiss I had been dying to give her. "We are somehow able to channel the magic and literally transform our physical forms."

"Somehow?"

"Nobody has been able to figure out exactly how it works. Like I said before, we can't disclose the details of our magical gifts to just anyone. So, it hasn't really been studied. We just know that when a new leader is appointed, he is given the ability to choose what this unique magic can do, and it becomes so."

"And your magic is transforming?"

"Transforming into the beast," I corrected. "We can't transform into anything else, E. But I can't imagine why we'd ever need to. The beast form gives us magic and power that is beyond anything I had ever felt before."

"What do you mean?"

"When I'm the beast, there's a different feeling behind our magic," he explained. "It's like we're indestructible. We have strength, agility, hell, we've even got night vision! If you can think of a combat skill, the beast likely has it."

"So, you feel your strongest as the beast?"

"In a way."

She gave me an annoyed look. We were engaged now. Bonded to each other for eternity. I knew that we were way beyond the half-assed answers, I was providing, but I also loved watching her react to my teasing.

"Before I met you, I would have answered that with a resounding yes. But being around you gives me an even stronger sense of invincibility. One that I don't need to be transformed for."

"Isn't that what bonding is supposed to do?"

"It's not just that," I continued. "Before we even sealed this bond between us, I could feel it. There were times that Callen had to help me sit down after I was around you, because leaving you left me so drained."

"You've never told me that."

"Don't take this as boastful, but I am strong magical,

E. For you just walking away from me to drain my magic like that...it meant our connection was a force. And if I'm being completely honest, I was afraid the pull behind our magical connection may scare you away," I confessed. "And that wasn't a risk I was willing to take."

Her cheeks began to turn a deep shade of red and she instinctively looked down at her toes in an attempt to hide her blush from me. I wanted so badly to pull her to me and kiss her until that blush became a flushed desire, but I needed her to understand what this bond meant.

"Bonding with someone is an experience that has been explained to me so many times throughout my life that I was certain I knew exactly what it would feel like," I continued. "But you took me completely by surprise. You and I don't just share magic in the way the books, or professors who studied bonds have even been able to explain. Whatever this magical connection is that you and I have, it's far deeper than that. I can feel your magic blending with mine, but it's still more. It's as if I can feel your heart beating in tune with mine. And, yes, I know that all sounds like a cheesy pick-up line, but it's the truth."

"So, together, we are stronger than the beast?" she inquired, still trying to hide how badly she was blushing by avoiding my gaze.

"Without a doubt. The beast is always inside me. And I'd be lying if I didn't think that magic added to our strength," I explained. "However, I do genuinely believe that you and I are going to be a story that is told for centuries to come."

She finally looked back up at me and I felt my pulse quicken. This woman was going to be the death of me.

"So," she finally sighed, "let's get through this war so we can get started on the next adventure in our story."

"Which is?"

"Surprise me," she winked.

I couldn't hold myself back any longer. Before she could let out another breath, my lips crashed passionately with hers.

And I noticeably groaned against her lips, because damn if there wasn't still one last thing I had to do before our kiss could continue. I forced myself to pull away, then pushed myself off the bed and closed my eyes as I stood. As soon as my message went to Cal, I opened them and smiled at her with an outstretched hand.

"There is one other thing I really need to talk with you about," I said, as she accepted my extended hand. "Cal and Violet are waiting for us to come to their tent to discuss it."

"Why?"

"Because E...it involves all of us."

****

The three of them sat quietly as I continued to lay out my plans when Sean came bursting into the tent directing all of us to join the others in the command tent. Something had gone wrong. Even though Sean hadn't outright said why we were needed, it was painfully obvious that we had a problem.

When we arrived in the command tent, I knew my assumption had been correct by the tension that was filling the room. Our entire party was crowded inside around a large table. On the walls hung a bunch of maps of the woods and the clearing. A low, warm light shined from the corner of the room, as the mystical border between Magir and Fantazi glowed brightly on our 3D planning model. Yet, it was the orb, floating just above the center of the table, that had captured everyone's attention.

"What in the blazes is that?" Violet quipped.

"It's a messaging orb," Callen answered, while I tried to control the unexpected surge of rage that had suddenly flooded through me.

"A what?" Evelyn questioned.

"It's a ball of energy that is used to transport a message. Sort of like the magical equivalent of a really important voicemail message," Nicholas explained quickly. "But this one wouldn't release its message until you were here."

"Me?" Evelyn questioned.

"That's all it said," Sean explained further. "We tried to open it, but it would only whisper, *EveylnRose*."

"So, it's from the Fears?" I surmised, as I tightened my grip on Evelyn's hand.

"Yes."

Everyone turned to look at Hale who was standing at the corner of the table. I owed him a lot for what he had done for Violet and Evelyn as of late, but there was still a voice in the back of my head that had its doubts.

"How do you know for sure?" I questioned.

"I know that it is from the Fears. This is their magic," he clarified. "I can feel it."

"What do I do?" Evelyn asked.

"Announce your name. Let it know you are here. But be wary," Hale instructed.

"Why?" Violet challenged. "If it's just a glowing answering machine it's not like it can actually harm her... right?"

"Fear magic is never what it seems," Armonee asserted. "*Always* expect the unexpected."

Evelyn nodded as she dropped my hand and approached the table. I could feel the tension flowing through her as she tried to maintain her composure, just as I was fighting to keep mine with this unexpected rage still churning inside me. She glanced over her shoulder at me and then shifted her gaze over to Hale's quizzical expression before moving again to look at Lucas, who gave his nod of approval.

"EvelynRose Archer."

Nothing happened for a second. I knew better than to hope we were wrong, but as the seconds continued to pass, I was genuinely becoming hopeful that this was nothing more than a shiny ball sent to distract us. Just as I was about to take my place at E's side, the orb began to glow brightly before us, and the room began to fill with a hazy smoke. Before I could get a grasp on what was happening, I felt a sudden twinge in my back, and I darted forward to Evelyn, getting to her just in time to catch her as she collapsed.

Chapter 27

Evelyn

Darkness. That was all I could see…that was all I could feel.

I tried to keep myself as calm as possible. Granted, I had just been standing in a room surrounded by allies and now I was pretty certain that I was trapped inside of some wicked Fear trick…but I could still hear Griffin in the back of my mind, calling my name, telling me it was going to be okay. I just needed to stay calm and figure this out.

Even as I tried to stay focused on Griffin's calming, reassuring voice, but I knew it wasn't working. And truth be told, as I felt the Fear magic beginning to boil inside of me, I wasn't entirely sure I wanted to stay calm anymore. Armonee had been right about my magic restoring itself. I'd tried to deny it, but I could feel the Fear getting stronger inside of me, and being surrounded by so much Fear magic seemed to be rapidly restoring my own.

Feeling like I was beginning to lose control of my magic again, I closed my eyes and began to take a few deep breaths. I murmured quietly to myself a mantra of peace that Violet had once told me.

"I am at peace. Let peace surround me. I am peace."

From behind my closed eyes, I suddenly saw a bright light. Slowly opening them back up, I realized that the dark fog I was trapped in was beginning to dissipate. But the scene that was revealed was something I had not expected.

I had anticipating finding myself in some sort of Fear dungeon...or maybe in a field with Michael preparing to attack me...but this was neither of those. Instead, I found myself standing inside some sort of castle. However, this castle wasn't anything like I'd experienced in Magir. Griffin's castle was welcoming and seemed to ooze the history that was held in its walls. This place, however, was cold. There were no colors to brighten the rooms, just plain shades of gray and very little in terms of decoration.

More than its appearance, the gut feeling I had just being inside this place was beyond ominous. My regenerating Fear magic racing inside me, couldn't stop me from shivering in the chilled air that felt like I had just stepped into a freezer. And as I wandered down the hallway the trap had dumped me in, I felt a tightening in my stomach that told me I was not safe here.

This had to be the Fears's castle. My mother's castle. There was no other explanation.

"Of course, it is."

The voice made me spin around so fast I was surprised that I was still standing when my eyes finally landed on her.

She was incredibly pale, almost sickly looking. Her blood red hair was long and perfectly curled in waves surrounding her face. Every feature, from her hips to her cheekbones, appeared dangerously sharp. I thought if I touched her, she'd either shatter right in front of me or slice through me like a knife. But it was her eyes...her jet-black eyes, that commanded my attention and made the magic inside me simmer in a way I had never felt. In front of me wasn't just one of the most striking women I had ever seen...it was my mother. Despite seeing her at the feast, I hadn't had the chance to fully take in her enthralling appearance until now. And the longer I stared, the more terrified I became.

"Didn't think Minds were the only magicals capable of reading thoughts, did you?" she smirked. "May want to practice keeping those to yourself."

"How am I here?" I questioned, avoiding her taunt and trying with everything I had to sound authoritative and unphased by my situation.

"Who says you are?"

Her shoulders rose in a questioning shrug as an evil grin spread across her lips. Clearly, she was beyond impressed by whatever *this* was. And based on the uneasy feeling it gave me, she probably had every right to be.

"You know," she began, "this was never how I imagined meeting with you again."

"You wanted to meet me?"

"Oh, I've met you," she corrected. "You were just too young to remember. You were barely one when Lucas snatched you away from me. Had he not taken you away from here, none of this would even be happening. There would be no pending war. We would have conquered Magir long ago. You were always meant to be here, EvelynRose."

"No, I wasn't," I argued.

I let my mind slip to the prophecy. Even magicals who lived long before us had known that I wasn't meant to be here.

"You think that because some prophecy says a descendant of The Five will save the day, you're going to be some kind of *hero*. Who even says that it's about you?" she laughed. "Don't give yourself so much credit."

She spun on her heels and began to practically float down the hall. I just stood there for a moment, completely unsure of what to do. I didn't even know how I was here...or if I even really was *here*, after her comment. Deep down, I knew it wasn't safe to follow her. And yet, there was this tiny part of me that felt a pull toward her. Like something inside of me was yanking me in her direction. So, against my better judgment... I followed.

At least ten minutes of silence had passed before she spoke again. And when she did, it wasn't the continuation of degrading comments I'd prepared myself for. Instead, she started giving me the lowdown on Sephtis. She pointed at things outside of the windows, creepy sculptures in the halls as we passed them, and an occasional picture of the wall. I felt like a tourist...actually more like a long-lost puppy following their master home.

When she stopped outside of a dusty, old door, for a moment I thought I caught a glimpse of softness cross her face. Like something about that door brought forward an emotion that she was trying hard to keep hidden or had locked away long ago. But as she opened the door and stepped inside, her face quickly returned to the stone-cold expression I was growing used to. The moment was gone just as quickly as it had come.

"What is this?" I asked.

As I scanned the room, I couldn't comprehend the scene around me. Unlike the rest of this dark and gloomy castle, this room was actually welcoming. A warm yellow color was painted on the walls, with little clouds and suns splattered throughout the room. In one corner of the room was a white rocking chair, and in the other a white bassinet with a yellow blanket draped over it.

It was a child's room. A baby's room, to be precise. The room was warm, inviting...and so out of place. Everything I'd learned about Fears had told me they weren't capable of the happiness this room brought me to feel. But then again, I could feel happiness...and so could Armonee. Had all of Magir been wrong about the Fears?

"It was your room," she stated plainly, her face still unchanged.

"Mine? Are you saying you...did all of this?" I questioned. "You made this...for me?"

"No," she replied frigidly. "You made this for you."

"I don't understand..." I shook my head. "What is this?

Why am I even here? Is this some sick attempt to try and bond with me so that I'll join your side? What the hell is the point of this?"

There was a twinge of pain in my chest as she so easily dismissed the idea of doing anything kind for me. I didn't know what she meant by *you made this for you*, but she'd just clarified that she never really cared for me. And as much as the idea of getting her to see that Fears can be good had originally appealed to me, I knew she would never be the mother Ariana thought I needed.

"You're here because you need to understand who you're up against," she growled, as she moved a step closer to me. "This is not some fairytale where I am going to come back into your life and let you whisk me away into your world of sunshine and rainbows. There will be no happily ever after for us."

"Then what is this?" I asked again, as I flailed my arms around me.

"This is who I became when you were inside of me," she groaned, grabbing the blanket and tossing it onto the floor. "A weak, pathetic fool who actually thought the realms might one day accept the Fears."

She spun back around and stormed toward the far wall before flipping back around to glare at me.

"My assignment had been simple. Trick the strongest magical I could find into loving me. And it was so easy for me to do...your father was weak and believed that all magicals, especially the *outcasts*, had a bigger purpose."

"That doesn't make him weak," I snapped.

"But it does!" she bellowed, making the walls shake around us. "His deplorably naïve vision of everyone in all the realms singing around a fire hand in hand, was sickening! Pathetic, beyond reason! But you...you changed everything."

I straightened up, instinctively mirroring her own posture adjustment. My gut was telling me, whatever this vision thing was, I couldn't actually be hurt while I was here.

But as she narrowed her eyes at me, I felt a twinge of fear run down my spine.

"From the moment I realized I was pregnant with you, everything about me changed. I couldn't control my magic anymore. One minute I was happy and the next, Fear magic was oozing out of me so fast, even your pitifully optimistic father was hiding in the corner from me. When I couldn't take anymore, I returned to Sephtis as an unrecognizable shell of my former self. I was so far gone that despite being back in the sea of Fear magic, I was still somehow compelled to create *this*! A bright yellow, happy space just for you...my baby girl," she snarled.

"Yellow is a neutral baby color," I sassed.

Her eyes narrowed again, and her lips pressed tightly together in an irritated grin.

"Yellow isn't Fear," she hissed back. "After I finally managed to expel you from my body, I slowly returned to normal and quickly realized the plan that had been put into place so many years ago was becoming a success."

"Wait," I interrupted. "You said you were assigned to fall in love...by who?"

"Don't be naive," she said, continuing to scowl at me. "I haven't been queen forever."

She straightened her back and slid out the door, leaving me, yet again, unsure if I was supposed to be following her. But really...what else was I going to do? Sit in what may have been my nursery and pout about how my conception was an order rather than the result of two people who cared for each other? Pouting had never been my style and I wasn't about to start now. Not to mention I still didn't know exactly what was going on...I still wasn't sure that any of this was even really happening. For all I knew, I was going to wake up in a few minutes and find this had all been just a weird...albeit incredibly vivid...dream.

As I followed her through the halls, I realized again how miserable this place seemed. It wasn't just that it was dark and gloomy, either. There was next to no color in these corridors. There were no plants or signs of other life. And while I didn't see any dust, it just gave off an aura of not being cared for whatsoever.

A large set of doors opened as we approached them, and Morana moved through them without so much as a glance back at me. Again, I felt that pit in my stomach telling me not to follow her in, but I still didn't heed its warning as I continued through the doors.

The room we entered was long and unlike any other room in the palace I had seen thus far. There was a bright red carpet that ran down the middle, providing some much-needed color, but still making it feel incredibly sinister. Along the walls were small tables, each with plants or statues of some kind, and large portraits of people wearing extravagant crowns lined each wall.

"Are these all..."

"Past Fear leaders," Morana announced, as she stood at the head of the room, in front of the largest picture of all.

I stared at every inch of that painting, absorbing every detail of the silent story it told. Morana was straight faced in the portrait. There was no sign of happiness, no sadness, no emotion whatsoever to the untrained eye. But I knew better. I knew because I'd seen that look many times. The wicked, sinister expression in her eyes told me everything I needed to know about her. She was ruthless and cruel...but it was still more than even that. She was completely unrelenting. She was never going to give up being the leader. Not to me, and most certainly, not to Griffin.

"You could have easily been up on this wall one day," Morana gloated. "Long after I was dead of course."

"And you would have allowed that?" I questioned.

"Well," she began, as a corrupt smile spread across her face. "Like I said before, only after I was long dead."

"If you didn't want to give up your throne, then why have a child in the first place? I have a hard time believing it was just because you were ordered to."

Her eyes narrowed and I felt the room growing colder by the second as she became more and more enraged at my responses. If I hadn't been successfully antagonizing her before...I certainly was accomplishing it now.

"You think you're so clever don't you," she hissed. "You have no idea the plans I had for you. The plans I still have for you."

Chapter 28

Violet

"Sweet baby freakin' Jesus! Wake her up!"

I'd lost track of how many times I had paced around the tent at this point. Though I wasn't entirely sure *tent* was the appropriate term for the magical structure we were in. But it had tent walls and looked like one from the outside...so I suppose it was still appropriate.

"Vi, try to relax," Callen pleaded for the millionth time.

"Relax?" I scoffed, utterly exasperated. "How in the hell do you expect me to relax? I mean, did your best friend, slash, magical twin, slash, cousin just collapse to the ground in the middle of a big-ass cloud of creepy, black smoke? I don't fuckin' think so!"

The room fell silent as I ranted at Callen...well really, I was ranting at the entire room. Swear words weren't a usual part of my go-to vocabulary but I couldn't stop myself. I was so flustered, I couldn't focus. I couldn't feel her. I couldn't hear her. It was like our bond was suddenly broken somehow. Just the idea of that had my heart racin' so fast I couldn't keep my thoughts straight.

"Go for a walk, Violet," Griffin sternly suggested. "You

don't need to be feeling all of this."

"Stop worrying about me!" I demanded. "Y'all need to figure out whatever Fear hell she is in and get her the hell out. None of you have any idea what that torture is like. Wake her the hell up!"

"Violet!" Hale shouted at me, as he stood from where he'd been kneeled down beside Evey. "If you want me to be able to wake her up, then I need you to get out. Your energy is distracting, and your empathy is taking on too much of the emotions around you. Go for a walk!"

I huffed and made a slightly over dramatic turn, then stomped my way out of the tent. Callen's intense desire to follow me flooded through me as I made my exit, but something held him back.

Alone, I trudged through the woods. I'd never felt more useless than I did in this moment. Not only did I have no clue how to help her...but now I had literally been kicked out of the tent. It just wasn't like me to be useless in a situation like this. I was the one who'd studied hard to have the answers. I was the one who took the time to really read people and made certain I always knew how to help them. This sidelined position where I warmed the bench for the "A" team...this just wasn't how I rolled.

"They'll figure it out," a voice behind me said confidently.

I whipped around to see Johanna and Armonee standing beside a couple of trees. Johanna offered a welcoming smile that took away a bit of the edge off my frazzled nerves, but it was the emotion coming from Armonee that actually made me feel like I could breathe again.

She wasn't smiling, but she wasn't upset either. There was no worry or fear swimming inside her. Despite everything going on around us, she was cool as a cucumber. It was as if she was at peace here. At peace...in a war zone...what was wrong with her?

"Mind if we stay out here with you?" Johanna asked.

"I don't need babysitters," I sassed. "You'll be more help in there."

"Who said we came to babysit?" Johanna questioned, tossing me far more attitude than I'd anticipated.

"Do I look like I should be babysitting anyone?" Armonee joked.

"I'm sure Callen didn't want me out here alone."

"With over half of the Magirian guard out here, did you really think for two seconds that someone didn't have eyes on you at all times?" Johanna corrected. "We are out here because we want to be. We were worried about you."

"Well, that and I couldn't take the bickering in there...or all of that Fear magic," Armonee added.

I turned to Armonee and just stared at her for a moment. I hadn't yet gotten the chance to really speak to her before. There was something about her that both set my teeth on edge and made me feel practically bullet proof at the same time. Even though that internal struggle made my stomach twist, I also knew that she and Evey had some sort of connection. And it was more than their links to Lucas. But the moment she spoke of Fear magic...it clicked!

"Jo!"

Sean's voice bellowed toward us, and we all looked in his direction.

"We need you back in here!" Sean instructed. "Just Jo."

Johanna turned back to me, placed her hand on my arm for a moment then walked back to the tent to rejoin the others. I knew they needed her gift. Whatever Evey was trapped in, the others were surely going to need Johanna's magical boost to get her out of it.

"Her gift really is quite impressive," Armonee agreed. "I'm sure you're correct, and they are calling just her to utilize the magic she can harness."

"What?"

"Magical gifts may seem rare, but those of us that have them, tend to hang in the same circles. You know, the whole idea that power attracts power...it's pretty accurate."

"I'm not followin'."

"I can read thoughts," Armonee informed me. "Though I must say, yours are particularly hard to get to with everyone else's emotions and EvelynRose's Fear magic running through you."

I was quite certain my brain exploded as she spoke. Very few people knew of that secret. And something told me that Lucas and Armonee hadn't quite made the cut for family secrets just yet.

"It's alright," she assured me with a smile. "You can't really hide it from me. Even if I hadn't been able to read your mind, I'd have known."

"So, I'm right then," I surmised. "That's how you can move in the black smoke."

Armonee nodded and stared out into the trees. It was hard to tell how old she was, but she had to be somewhere between my age and Lucas's...and granted that was a gap...she was just so beautiful and youthful, it was impossible to tell. Even now, knowing she was a Fear, there was something about her gold eyes that made it hard to see her as one of them.

"You're right again," she chuckled. "I'm between your ages, but that's not important. What I want to know is how you are handling magic that isn't yours with such ease?"

Now it was my turn to laugh. *With such ease,* was not how I would have described my current situation.

"I feel like a tickin' time bomb sometimes," I joked. "But I guess...I just choose to live in the light. Always have. I want to live a happy life, so I force myself to do so. Sometimes to the point where I very much annoy those around me...but what can ya do? It's who I am, and I have zero intention of lettin' this darkness change me."

"Then why hold onto it?" Armonee inquired with genuine curiosity. "Why not give it back to her?"

"She wasn't ready. I'm still not certain she is," I sighed. "But soon, I'm afraid I won't have a choice. She's going to need it when we fight them."

"Them?"

"I'm sorry. That was insensitive. I didn't…"

"You did," Armonee winked at me. "But it's alright. That's how it has always been. Fear's versus all the other families. Being chosen by the Fear stone shouldn't come with a label of evil. But I suppose there always has to be an enemy right?"

Taking in what she said, I realized I had become something I had read about in history over and over again. I had taken an entire group of magicals and lumped them all together…I'd labeled them all based on the poor choices a few of them had made. Sure, having their magic inside of me made me understand what drives some of them to do bad things, but how can there be light if there isn't dark? The answer was quite simple. There can't be.

"You're a smart woman," Armonee laughed again, as she continued to read my thoughts. "Can you answer one more question for me?"

I nodded.

"Why is what is happening now bothering you so damn much?" she asked. "I've seen what you've all gone through, and I have seen you lose your cool. Why is *this* so horrible to you?"

I sighed heavily as I thought about how to answer that. Armonee had been honest with me…so I guess I owed her the same. Not to mention, out of everyone here, she was probably the most likely person to understand.

"I've been through what she's going through."

"I heard you say that inside. What did you mean though?"

"In the Dark Woods…after I stripped all of Evey's Fear magic…I was trapped in the same thing I think Evey is in now."

"But how could you know what she's going through? Even Griffin said he can't feel her."

"Our connection is just…special," I shrugged. "For weeks after I took in her Fear magic, I was trapped in my own head. In a nightmare that was my own creation but induced by Fear magic."

Armonee stared at me. Not asking for clarification. Not pushing for more. Just waiting for me to continue at my own pace.

"I was in a forest," I continued. "Not just any forest. It seemed endless when you looked around, but it was really a box with invisible walls. Time was funny there. There was no normalcy to the days. If I was angry, it only got darker. If I was calm, the sun would start to come up. There was no way to know how long I'd stuck there...stuck there alone. I tried to use magic to talk to Callen, or to Evey, but neither of them realized it was actually me speaking to them. They thought I was just a voice in their heads that they were imagining. By the time Hale got through to me..."

"Hale?" she interjected, seeming very surprised. "I'm sorry, continue."

"When Hale finally got through to me, I thought I was genuinely going mad. My magic was all over the place, the woods had started to change. It was...it was the worst, most terrifying experience of my life."

"Who pulled you out?"

"All three of them. Callen, Evey, and Hale. But why does Hale's role in this surprise you so much? I can feel how much it surprises you, remember? Not to mention your poker face isn't the best."

She swallowed a lump in her throat, and even though it was quick, I was sure this was a rare moment of weakness or worry for her.

"I don't know much about Hale, himself," Armonee began. "But I know of his family. The family most other magicals may not know. Only even a handful of Fears know who he truly is."

Listening to her, I felt both confused and highly intrigued. Hale had been a mystery to me from the moment we met him. When he was dancing with Evey at the WRA

Welcome Ball, I thought he had been a student. Then he turned out to be a teacher…and a wicked one at that. After he betrayed Evey, I wanted to harm him. Harm him in ways, I didn't think I would ever want to harm anyone. But now…ever since he had helped me escape from my nightmare…I trusted him. Even though I knew there was something I still didn't like about him…I trusted him.

"Hale's mother was believed to be an only child by all of the outside families. When she abandoned her birth family, that was how she wanted it. And she had good intentions, because her family was…well they were Fears."

"Hale is a Fear? Like an actual Fear?"

"No," Armonee corrected. "That stone never chose him. That much I do know."

"But his mother was?"

"Actually, no."

"Ya lost me."

"His mother came from a Fear family. Their reputation for cruelty was well known. They were basically equal to what the Archer line represented for the other magical families, but for us Fears."

"So, council members?"

"More like, nobility but without the crown. Hale's mother was different from the rest of her family though. From the stories I've heard, when she wasn't chosen by the Fear stone…well her family was basically disavowed by the other Fears," she explained. "But as you know very well, most Fears don't take rejection well."

"Yeah," I scoffed. "You could say that."

"Well, the family refused to be shunned, and made Hale's mother their slave. She was no longer considered a member of their family and they tortured her in unimaginable ways. One day, after taking a beating from her parents, she ran for it. She made it out of the Dark Woods and into Magir, where it was said that she changed her name and completely put that life behind her."

"What happened to her family?"

"Her parents were murdered. Rumor has it, that was the only way for the last member of the family to get back in good standing with the reigning queen."

"So, all of Hale's Fear family is dead?"

"Not exactly," she sighed. "The last member of the family...the one who was willing to kill Hale's grandparents, was their oldest daughter."

"So, Hale has a Fear aunt. Does he know?"

She shrugged her shoulders that she didn't know. Now my mind was really spinning. It made so much more sense — why Hale had wanted so badly to learn Fear magic. After his father died, it hadn't just been about impressing Barin...it had been about discovering where he came from. What child wouldn't go looking for that answer? Shoot, I felt like that's all I'd done since I found out about my magic. Well, that and fight against the Fears.

"Do you know who his aunt is?"

"She married another Fear shortly after she murdered her parents. The man was from another noble Fear family."

"What's their name?" I asked, as a painful lump grew in my throat.

"She married into the Kane family," Armonee said. "When I left Sephtis, their son had just turned two, I believe."

"Oh my," I breathed.

"Everything okay?" Armonee asked, her eyes narrowing on me.

"It's just...oh my..."

"Violet, are you—"

"I have to get to Evey!"

I couldn't let her finish and I couldn't keep my thoughts straight. My hands were now profusely sweating, and I could feel Evey's Fear magic going insane in my veins. How had I not seen it before? They may not have looked exactly alike...but there was that grin. Oh my gosh, the damn grin! That wicked smirk that made my stomach turn. And that look in their eyes when they watched Evey. Granted there was something definitely different in Hale's...but still...

And sweet baby freakin' Jesus! Why was this always coming back to him? Out of every magical or non-magical in the realms, it just had to be him. We couldn't shake him. He was impossible for Evey to escape. Damn you, Michael Kane.

Chapter 29

Evelyn

"Enlighten me then. What were...are your plans for me?"

Morana continued to grin at me, and I felt my resolve slowly starting to melt away. Even though I still strongly believed this was some sort of dream, I knew deep down how evil this woman was...and it frightened me. I'd have been naive if it didn't.

Without answering me, she glided back across the room and straight out the door. I followed her, knowing I had no other real choice, and she began to lead me through her castle again. As I walked behind her, she explained certain paintings on the walls. She showed me various rooms and explained what they were used for. She led me to a walkway that overlooked the town square, where the boxing ring Violet had once described was sitting vacant in the center.

This went on for what seemed like hours. The two of us just walking through the Fear castle. Morana explained all of the history within the castle and along with it, some of the history of the previous Fear leaders. None of which were as great as she was, of course.

As she led me into another room that reminded me of a

stuffy art exhibit, she began telling the story of another long dead family member. One who had apparently slaughtered an entire Fear family line to ensure none of her descendants would end up with them. Even as she told the story, I could see her almost smiling. What kind of person actually grins at the memory of an entire family being killed?

In all the time she'd led me around, she never let me get a word in. Each time I'd attempted to say anything, she just cut me off and kept going. So, I'd just stopped trying to speak at all. She never even asked if I was still listening, or if I was following her tales of horror. Obviously, it was just something she expected to be occurring. People didn't ignore her when she spoke. They listened. Took in every word. While I wasn't sure what the point to all of this was, I, too, was unintentionally following her unspoken commands. And that level of mind control absolutely terrified me.

"Why are you telling me all of this?" I finally interrupted.

"I don't need a reason to talk with my own daughter," Morana snapped.

"Since when do you care about me as your daughter?"

"I don't."

She looked me straight in the eye when those words passed her lips. I knew she meant it. Shit, the entire realm of Magir knew she meant it. I was never born to be an heir to her throne or even to make her a mother. There was something else. Something bigger.

"When I was assigned to get the strongest magical outside of the Fear line to love me, the task made me sick," she said, a cringe crinkling her hard features. "Why would I waste my bond magic on someone whose magic would never match my own? But the more I thought about it, the more I saw the opportunity it would provide me."

"Yeah, so, you've already said," I quipped. "And what opportunity?"

"To create the most powerful magical weapon alive,"

she sneered. "My magic mixing with the most powerful magical of another line...the child would be unstoppable."

"But I thought magic didn't work like that," I argued. "Can't magicals have non-magical children?"

"Rarely," she chuckled. "And this is my magic we are discussing. Do you truly think that someone as powerful as myself could produce anything short of another champion magical? I don't think so. Now, as I was saying, the goal was simple. Create a magical child so strong that I would have the most impressive magical weapon the realms had ever seen at my disposal. And as I told you earlier, I knew there was something powerful about you even during pregnancy. But I never got the chance to see what you could be."

"Because Lucas took me back."

"Because your blasted father stole you!" She corrected me. "And then the coward hid you with that pathetic magical of a sister."

"Watch it."

"Your loyalty to her, despite all the lies she's told you, is yet another reason why you won't win this war," she snickered. "After Lucas took you away it took me years to track even a scent of you. But when some of my scouts reported a magical surge in Harbor, I knew it was you."

She walked over to a portrait of a family that looked almost as angry and arrogant as the ones in the room with the red carpet. She stood there for a moment and then began to move toward the end of the room.

"Once I'd finally found you, I had to convince you to join us. Join us or die. Your choice. But I wanted you. I needed your magic to overthrow the pompous, pathetic excuse for a king and his mousey, spineless queen. I knew Saraya would poison your mind against me, so I thought I'd get to you through a non-traditional, non-Fear way. Through your heart."

"You mean through Michael?"

"Michael's job was simple. Get you to bond with him."

"You literally assigned someone to sleep with me? You

do realize that you basically pimped out your own daughter, right?"

"I told you already. This wasn't personal. You are a weapon to me. Nothing more. I could care less about who crawled into bed with you. It just had to be a Fear."

Lovely. My mother really was a straight up bitch. I was suddenly so thankful that I had gotten this creepy chance at mother-daughter bonding time. All it was doing was reinforcing that I never needed her in the first place.

"But you denied him," she continued. "Time after time, you denied him. So, I went to extreme measures and made a deal with Barin. He'd let me use Hale against you while he was teaching at WRA."

"And in exchange?"

"Do not interrupt me again," she snapped. "And in return, Barin would rule by my side in the new era of Magir."

"What about Ariana?"

"What about her? Between her love for your father and her compassion for the rest of the peasants, she was useless to my plans. Killing her had always been part of my plan."

I felt my hands begin to clench in fists as my heart began to pump louder in my chest.

"Oh, calm down. You'll burst a blood vessel or something," she laughed. "But even as good of a soldier as Hale was. He failed me. Which was entirely your fault."

"My fault? Hale left me to die. He managed to break down the WRA border and let Michael in. How was it my fault that he, too, failed you?"

"You truly are naive, aren't you?"

She tilted her head to the side slightly and studied me before she grinned.

"I thought after your physical attraction to Michael, Hale was the obvious choice. But I never imagined that his own feelings would get in..."

Before she could finish, I felt the magic around us phase, and the room tore apart for a moment before settling back.

When the fuzziness in my vision cleared, Morana was standing right in front of me.

"I'll give you one last chance to save yourself," Morana hissed. "Be the weapon I made you to be. Do that and I won't make them all suffer when they die."

"You won't lay a hand on them," I growled.

"Then I'll start with him," she sneered, as she began to fade away again. "Your precious Griffin will be the first to die."

*****

When the gray smoke cleared, I expected to find myself back in the tent with the others, but I wasn't there. I blinked several times to make sure I wasn't imagining things. But the clearer the air around me became, the more I realized I was standing on what appeared to be some sort of cloud. Actually, come to think of it, it sort of reminded me of what it was like to be inside Griffin's head. When Hale had assigned me to see Griffin's fears.

"I needed to explain myself before you went back."

His voice startled me, but part of me had almost expected to hear it. He was, after all, the only person other than myself and Armonee that could have created this vision.

"There is nothing to explain, Hale. I know Morana was trying to bait me. I know why you did what you did for her."

"You don't," he sighed, as shook his head and took a few steps closer to me. "You don't understand."

"Uh…okay," I stammered. "What don't I understand?"

He let out a heavy breath once he was directly in front of me. I had never seen him flustered like this.

"My job wasn't just to make you weak that day."

"I know. You had to let Michael into…"

"No," he interrupted me. "My job was to get you to fall for me in the same way you did Michael."

"Yeah, she mentioned you being the obvious choice after my feelings for Michael. I don't know why she would…"

"He's my cousin."

I felt like my eyes were bulging from their sockets and like every bit of food I had eaten of the past few days was going to reappear. Before I could stop myself, I instinctively took a step backward. Michael and Hale…Hale and Michael…

"I'm not like him. I'm not a Fear, like he is. My mother escaped Sephtis. I just…I didn't realize the truth about my family until after Morana agreed to let me learn Fear magic. Barin had thought it was his idea, but it was always hers."

I turned away from him and began to pace back and forth. It felt like my lungs were closing and I could hardly catch my breath. Placing my hands on my head, I tried to focus on getting my breathing back to normal.

"It was never my intention…"

"Why couldn't you do it?" I blurted out, interrupting his apology.

"Do what?"

"Why couldn't you go through with it?" I repeated, as I dropped my hands and turned back to face him. "We had a connection when we first met. Even I couldn't deny that. Why didn't you push it? Why couldn't you follow her order?"

The expression on his face betrayed his usual hard to read demeanor. My question had rattled him. And not in the ways I was used to, where he seemed almost angry or enjoying himself, either. He actually seemed scared…no, more like terrified, of the answer he was about to give me. My eyes bounced around his facial features, and I watched as his face scrunched slightly before he looked away from me at his own feet.

"I…I cared too much about you," he finally said.

"All the more reason," I pressed. "I need to know why, Hale."

"It wouldn't have been fair to you," he insisted with a heavy sigh. "Your connection with Griffin was stronger than any bond magic I had ever been around. When you two were around each other, I felt like I was going to suffocate in your magic. And when he left you at WRA...I watched you fall apart. It wouldn't have been right for me to take away your chance with him. At the risk of this sounding incredibly cheesy...I knew he was your soulmate. And I was just...well I was just the traitor who betrayed a trust he hadn't even earned yet."

"So, you didn't follow her order...because you didn't think you were good enough for me?"

"No," he said, his eyes almost going cold. "I don't know if anyone will ever be good enough for you, EvelynRose. I just know I wasn't going to stop you from achieving true happiness with the one person who may come the closest to good enough. No order, no matter who it was from, was going to make me hurt you like that. You didn't deserve it. And like I said...I just care about you too much."

Nothing could have prepared me for this moment. Hale's emotions were always so heavily guarded and unreadable...yet, here we stood with him pouring his heart out. My head was spinning with so much information that I felt like I was going to get sick. How did I not recognize that he was related to Michael? Moreso, how was it possible that I hadn't put his feelings for me together? Was I that self-absorbed? Was I so stuck in my own world that I couldn't see what was going on with the people right in front of me?

"We should...we should be getting back," he insisted. "Griffin will be able to feel your magic soon."

"Hale, wait a second."

He lifted his eyes and stared at me.

"Thank you."

I don't know what I was really thanking him for. Maybe it was for letting me fall in love. Or for helping me figure out my magic - even if his methods weren't always the greatest. Saving Violet. Or the countless other things he had done since I met him. Regardless of the exact reason behind my statement, the simple thank you seemed to cover it all, as he accepted my thanks with a bashful smile before he nodded, closed his eyes again, and the cloud around us began to fade into oblivion.

When my eyes opened this time, I was back in the tent. Griffin quickly wrapped his arms around me, and I looked to the side just as Hale released his grip on my hand, before standing up.

"Thank you," Griffin exhaled. "Hale, thank you."

Hale nodded and moved to stand closer to Lucas, whose eyes seemed to be glistening as he held back tears of relief.

Before I could take in any of the others, Griffin's hands were on face, and he pressed his lips to mine. Our magic surged inside me for the briefest second, and then he pulled away, leaving his forehead pinned against mine.

"I thought I was going to lose you there for a moment," he whispered.

"You won't get rid of me that easily," I whispered back.

We laughed quietly together, then he helped me to my feet just as Violet came bursting into the room with Armonee on her heels.

As she barreled in, I couldn't help but notice the glare she gave Hale. Her urgency, coupled with her optical daggers at Hale, told me that she must have figured something out, but she didn't say anything. Instead, she ran straight for me and wrapped me tightly in her arms.

"Will you stop droppin' dead on me!" she cried. "It's puttin' a lot of strain on my perky nature."

"Next time I get tricked into a Fear mind trap, I'll be sure to let you know first," I joked.

"So, it was a Fear trap," Violet gasped, as she held me at arm's length.

"Sort of," I countered.

I looked around the room as everyone anxiously watched me, just waiting to hear what I had to say. Violet had moved back a few steps, and Callen draped his arm over her shoulder, as they all continued to stare. But I wasn't even sure where to begin.

"Who was behind the trap?" Sean asked, breaking the silence and clearly seeing how lost I was.

"Right," I nodded. "Um…it was Morana. My mother set the trap."

"What did she want?" Lucas asked.

"Honestly, in her own strange way, I think she just wanted to talk."

"Morana doesn't *just* talk," Armonee interjected. "She always has a motive."

"Oh, she did," I concurred. "She still wants me to join her. If I do, she says that she won't torture you all to death. She still has every intention of killing you all, just without the torture."

"Comforting," Sean quipped.

"She said she had zero intentions of being my mother. That she didn't care for me one way or the other. That I… that I was just a weapon she wanted on her side. Her ultimate weapon."

I heard a low growl from where Lucas stood behind me. I quickly looked over just in time to catch the scowl on his face, before he could force his smile to return…though now I knew it was obviously a facade. It had to hurt to hear how the woman you thought you loved, never loved the one piece that remained of the relationship.

"Where did she take you?" Violet asked.

"Her castle."

"You saw the inside of the Sephtis castle?" Armonee practically shouted. "Only her most trusted soldiers are allowed in."

"Well, that makes sense. She was showing me around like I was in the secret wing of the freaking White House."

"She pulled you into that trap for a tour of her home?" Johanna questioned.

"Why would she waste time doing that?" Nicholas added.

"Not just that. She was telling me about Fear history, and…other things."

I was unable to stop my gaze from shifting to Hale, who

smiled slightly. Griffin had to have noticed, because I felt him move just a little bit closer to my side.

"Regardless, I still don't know what the point of it all was. She could have just asked. My answer would have been the same."

"So, you told her no?" Armonee questioned.

"Of course, I told her no," I concurred. "Yes, was never even an option in my mind."

A collective sigh filled the room. Had they all really thought I was going to join her? The confidence our team had just displayed was less than inspiring.

"Don't take it personally," Griffin said, softly beside me. "They are just scared. We all believe in you."

"Was there anything you saw that stood out to you?" Nicholas asked. "Anything that could help us?"

"Not really," I shrugged. "Honestly, I only ever saw Morana. She walked me around and ta…"

"Wait!" Armonee interrupted. "You didn't see anyone else? No palace workers? No one in the square? No one was in the ring?"

"Huh uh."— I shook my head. — "Not a soul."

Armonee and Nicholas exchanged glances and I knew what that meant.

"They're *all* coming…aren't they?" I asked. "She's bringing every Fear to fight this war."

"We need a new strategy," Nicholas surmised. "And quick."

*****

With the plans set in motion, we all went back to our own tents. As I entered mine, with Griffin close behind me, I felt my stomach starting to churn. But it was surprisingly not in the nervous way I was expecting. It was more…anxious, excitement. Which was not something I was used to feeling.

"Are you feeling alright?" Griffin asked, as I plopped

down on the edge of the bed.

"Surprisingly," I said through a sigh. "Yes. I mean…I can't believe I'm saying that just before we are about to go fight in an actual war, but I feel…ready. Even after everything that just happened. I feel ready. Does that make sense?"

"To me," he chuckled, "it makes complete sense. When I went into my first major battle, shortly after being appointed leader of the Knights, I expected myself to be nervous beyond belief. Yet, from the moment we left, all I felt was confidence. Even knowing that failing may bring peril to all of Magir or the death of a fellow Knight, I was completely confident that I was ready. I didn't worry about the outcome because failure was never an option."

I knew his speech was intended to reinforce my own confidence, but as the words *peril* and *death* left his lips, I felt a shiver run down my spine. Linking my arm in his and resting my head on his shoulder, I felt our magic surge through my veins as I pondered the event that would begin in mere hours.

The odds of all of us surviving were slim, at best. I knew that. But it wasn't something I wanted to truly think about. It was something my heart was ready to accept. There wasn't a single person here I would be okay with losing. And my track record for going a little crazy when people got hurt…well, it wasn't great. Not to mention that Michael would definitely be there, and he knew how to get under my skin quicker than anyone.

"I don't mean to barge in," said Violet softly, as she stood at our tent's entrance. "But may I have a minute with Evey?"

"Of course," Griffin nodded, as he stood and kissed my forehead before leaving the tent.

Violet stepped into the tent and paced around slowly in front of me for a moment, then suddenly froze, staring at me with a piercing glare in her eyes.

"You already know?" she challenged.

"Already know what?"

"Why didn't you say anythin'?"

"Vi, you're going to have to be more specific," I pleaded in complete confusion.

"Hale!"

"Oh...wait, how do you know about that?" I asked, jumping off the bed.

"How do *you* know?" she countered.

We stared at each other for a moment. As if somehow just by looking at each other our minds would open, and all the truths of the world were going to magically reveal themselves.

"Armonee!"

"Hale!"

We both gave the other person's answer in unison.

"So, I guess this twin mind connection really does work," I surmised.

"Of course, it does!" Violet cried. "When, in all of this, did Hale have the chance to tell you?"

"When he pulled me back from Morana's mind trap."

"Then why doesn't Griffin seem to know?"

"Well, he sort of told me while I was still inside the mind trap. Just without Morana there. I think he was able to keep it between us in the same way Morana was able to block all of you out while I was in Sephtis with her."

Violet stared at me like she was waiting for me to elaborate, but then she turned away, and sat on the bed, as she stared at the wall of the tent.

"Vi?"

She didn't say anything as she sat there, facing the wall with a blank expression. I stepped directly in front of her, unsure of what had just happened and with no clue what to do. As I leaned closer to her face I watched as her eyes glazed over and slowly began to shut.

Chapter 30

Violet

When the vision started, I didn't know what was happening. It wasn't like any vision I had ever had before. Though that seemed to be occurring far more often than the normal than the visions WRA had taught me about.

I was still staring at Evey when I suddenly saw Michael in the corner of the tent, and then Hale materialized beside Evey. But they weren't real people...they were like shadows. As the vision started to become clearer, I felt like even the ground beneath my feet was spinning, so I moved to the bed and sat down.

I don't remember watching Evey fully fade away, but before I knew it, I was in a field full of people fighting. Not just fighting though...they were out for blood. I watched as a couple of men dressed in the Magirian guard leather armor moved around a group of people that I didn't know, as if they were wisps in the wind. As I continued to stare at them, I witnessed the random people suddenly wince, as if pain had been inflicted on them...but I hadn't seen anyone lay a finger on them.

A spear suddenly came flying in from behind me. I

heard the whistle it sent through the air and then turned around just as it pierced through the back of someone, I did know...Sean. He went crashing to the ground and I spotted Johanna through the maze. She abruptly came to a halt in her own battle before letting out a cry that would have pierced anyone's ears.

As I followed her moving through the crowd, I finally saw Callen, in hand-to-hand combat beside Armonee. Lucas wasn't far from them, blood trickling down his arms, but he didn't seem to notice. And then there was Hale...he was walking through the crowd like nobody there. I tried to look ahead and couldn't tell who he was going after with such force...but man...he was on a mission to get to them.

The vision started to go fuzzy, just as I saw his target coming into view. Sean let out a scream and I whipped my head back for just a moment. Then he screamed again, this time yelling *Red*, as loudly as he could. I flipped back to Hale's target and saw her hair...he was going for Evey.

*****

I opened my eyes and quickly blinked several times. Finally moving my gaze from my fixated spot on the tent, I found Evey staring at me with wide eyes.

"What the hell just happened, Vi?"

"I had some sort of vision," I groaned, as I stood up. "I think we need to tell Sean about Hale."

"Why? What is that going to accomplish exactly? If he knows then they all..."

"Evey, for once, will you just trust what I'm sayin'!"

I hadn't meant to snap at her in that way. It had definitely come out as more of a yelled command, than a friendly request.

"I'm sorry..." I sighed. "But good gracious! I'm so tired of everyone treatin' me like I don't know what I'm doin' out here."

"Vi, we don't," Evey argued. "When have either of us

ever been in the middle of a war zone? And don't throw out the Dark Woods, because that happened so quickly, I don't feel like that counts. I mean, just a few months ago we didn't know about any of this."

"You think I don't know that! Ugh!" I growled, as I moved around the room. "Evey, do you even know who you are talking to right now? You think I don't know about war? I may have grown up a princess, but I'm not naive."

"Vi..."

"No, just listen to what I'm tellin' ya. What I just saw in that vision wasn't something I want comin' true. And you can sit there and pretend like you're protecting me, or whatever this is, but you need to understand that just because I wasn't chosen by all five families doesn't mean I'm not just as strong as you."

She just stared at me. I hadn't even realized how badly I needed to say that, until I took a deep breath and felt weight literally lift from my shoulders. But there was something about this Fear magic coursing in my veins that made it impossible for me not to spill these feelings.

"Listen..." I began.

"I've never thought that," she interrupted.

"What?"

"I have never thought that!" she yelled back at me. "Never once have I thought I was stronger than you. You gave up your entire life for me, Vi. You've stood by me no matter what life threw at us. You left everything you knew, accepted this magical world with ease, and you are literally walking into a war without a single reservation. Never...not even once have I thought you were weak, Violet...not once."

The emotions flowing through the both of us was causing my heart to beat at a rapid rate. The Fear magic I had absorbed was making me say these things...I knew it was. But as they poured out, I saw a bright side to Fear magic. There was something about not caring about the consequences and allowing myself to fully embrace what I was feeling. It was empowering.

Evey let out a heavy sigh and before she could say anything else, I grabbed her by the shoulder and hugged her tightly. Magic surged inside me, but it wasn't the sickening overload I was used to getting. Instead, it was soothing.

"I'm sorry I made you feel that way," Evey apologized. "I wouldn't be able to do any of this without you by my side. You're literally the sister I never had."

As the words left her lips, I practically shoved her out of the hug, holding her shoulders at arm's length as I stared at her.

"That's it!"

"Vi?"

"No, Evey, that's it!" I repeated, excitedly. "We may not be real sisters, but we are bonded like we are. You and I are blood relatives!"

"I get that."

"Don't you see!" I exclaimed. "I know how we can win this war. But it has to be between you and me."

"What about..."

"You and me, Evey. It has to be our secret."

Her eyes bounced around my face like she was trying to decide if I was brilliant or on drugs. But she gave a slight nod, and I gave her shoulders a quick squeeze of understanding before dropping my arms to place my hands on my hips.

"Now," I began, "like I said before, we need to go talk to Sean."

This time, I pulled her out of the tent before she could protest. Luckily, Griffin wasn't waiting outside for her, so we didn't have to explain anything to him. However, I could sense Callen trying to connect with me, and being blocked by Evey's gift. Which was perfect because I was a woman on a mission. A mission that couldn't be stopped...not even by his gorgeous face.

When we went bursting into their tent though, I was instantly distracted from the goal at hand. Sean was standing just inside with all of his rippling abdominal muscles on display. Granted, yes...I was a very taken woman...but man...a girl could ogle at that all day.

"Violet," Johanna coughed.

"Girl, you are lucky I am spoken for," I joked. "Sean, that is one hell of a body you've got."

"Oh, good Lord, Vi," Evey groaned beside me.

"What?" I shrugged. "I can appreciate a good, tone, and attractive body. And that is most definitely..."

"We get it!" Johanna and Evelyn said in unison.

Sean chuckled to himself, then turned around to grab a shirt. That was when I noticed the scar that ran along Sean's left shoulder blade. I mean, how would I have noticed before... not like I'd seen Sean without a shirt on before...but it seemed weird I knew nothing about it.

"Sean!" Evelyn gasped, as she read my mind and moved across the tent toward him. "Where did that come from?"

"Oh, this?" Sean asked, just before pulling his shirt over his head. "I've had that most of my life."

"What happened to you?" I asked.

Johanna's nose scrunched up a little as she rearranged her clothes and then stood up from her place on the side of their bed, moving toward Sean's side. Damn...I hadn't realized we were interrupting something.

"I was in an accident as a kid," Sean explained.

"The one you told me about?" Evelyn questioned.

"Very same. Considering what happened to my friend, I got lucky."

"You know," I grinned. "It kind of looks like an olive branch."

"Yeah, the stitches didn't heal correctly at first," Sean shrugged. "And when my magic really kicked in, my muscles grew so quickly, they just stretched out. So instead of little dots, I had those little ovals next to the scar line."

"Scar or no scar," I concurred. "Your body is still fantastic, handsome!"

Evelyn groaned and rolled her eyes at me. Granted, nothing beat what Callen looked like without clothes. I mean if I could have asked someone to sculpt the perfect body…it was his. But I could always appreciate a good set of abs.

"Well, now that we have that out of the way," Sean began. "Care to tell us why you just busted into our tent?"

"Yeah," Johanna agreed, crossing her arms. "I'm assuming you have something important to tell us."

"You better believe we do!" I answered.

I dove into the tale of Hale and Michael. Explaining everything that I knew, and Evelyn shyly explained the pieces that she knew. As she explained I felt like she was being vague. Like there were details that she was leaving out. I just couldn't fathom why she would protect him still. After everything that Michael had done to her. But the more I thought about that, the more I questioned if it was really Michael she was protecting. I had managed to trust Hale, yet even I was questioning my judgment on that. And now, it seemed like Evey had really grown a soft spot for him.

Don't get me wrong, the guy had done some good. And he had come through for us a few times when we desperately needed him. Like rescuing me from my nightmare. And while I had learned to trust him before…knowing what I know now… I don't think I would have trusted him to babysit my enemy's dog.

"And that's what I know," Evelyn finished.

"So, now you understand why we had to come *bursting in*," I added, snapping out of my daze. "I'm worried that when the time comes, Hale won't turn out to be…well whatever we think he is."

Johanna's eyes were huge. It was clear that she was just as shocked about this as Evey, and I had been. Sean on the other hand just stared at us. There was no shocked expression on his face. No eyes narrowing in anger. Actually, there was nothing at all. He just stared back at us like he was waiting for us to say something else. Even his emotions weren't giving me anything to go on. He was like a statue in front of us. But before I could even ask him what he was thinking, he blinked several times and cleared his throat.

"We need to get ready to go," he said sternly.

"Did you hear a word that we just said?" I asked, frustrated.

"Yes," he nodded. "And as valuable as the information may be on the battlefield, we have a mission at hand. We must defeat the Fears."

"But what if Hale turns out to be one of them?" I asked.

"He isn't," Evey defended.

"And if he is?" Johanna reiterated for me.

"If he is," Sean began, "then I will kill him myself before he has the chance to harm any of us. Especially you three."

Evelyn looked down at her feet and I felt worry suddenly clenching at my chest. Johanna moved a few steps closer to Sean and grabbed hold of his hand.

"Now, we need to get ready to go," Sean repeated. "Nick says a guard spotted what looks like Fears nearing the clearing already."

Evelyn's eyes shot back up and Johanna's jaw clenched tightly. But I hadn't told Evey the plan yet! I needed her to know the truth about who we were before we left, but I was out of time.

This was it...we were going to war.

Chapter 31

Evelyn

This war was nothing like what you saw in the movies. There were no army uniforms worn by anyone. In Magir, there were no guns or cannons. No tanks or really weapons of any kind. We had some spears, knives and arrows, but that was really it. Though, I suppose when you've got magic behind you, you really don't need heavy weaponry.

When Sean handed me the bow and no arrows, I was confused at first. How was I supposed to use it without arrows? Clearly the name Archer had given me some genetic disposition for archery, but still...I couldn't make arrows appear out of thin air.

"With Mind magic you can."

Griffin's voice rang through my mind, and it made complete sense. Now I just had to get past the fact that I normally needed to focus really hard in order to use my Mind magic. Something was telling me that in the middle of a war was probably not going to be the best place to pause and focus my Mind.

By the time we made it to the clearing, I knew that would be the case. As the Fears began to show themselves from the other side, I was immediately aware that there would be little time to focus here. It would have to come from instinct, something I wasn't confident that I had mastered yet.

Looking out at the Fears, and at all of the Magirians fighting with us, just solidified for me that this was no movie. There was no awkward stare down between the leader of each side. There was no monologue of how the fight would go, or who would win. There wasn't even the slow-motion clash between the two sides.

It was just...a giant fight. Like something you would expect to have seen when two rival gangs met up in the 1960's. Neither side waited for the other to attack. Instead, the minute eye contact was made in that clearing, bodies were flying.

Griffin pulled me close to him, leaning his forehead against mine for just a second. I knew what it meant, but neither of us said anything. Stay close, stay safe, I love you. That's what it was. A brief moment to try to say so much, without saying a word. But there was no passionate kiss, no long embrace. Just that brief moment of being together.

And then it was gone. As quickly as everything was happening around me, I shouldn't have been surprised by how fast our moment passed. Griffin moved quickly and transformed into the beast that only the Knights could become. I couldn't help but wonder how he was suddenly able to do it with such ease in front of everyone. Was it because he had done it in front of so many of us before? Or were the Knights suddenly drawing magic from something else? There was no time to unpack the details as I saw a few other beasts start to pounce across the battlefield. Some of the Knights, like Nick, were still in their normal forms and I wondered too, if that was part of their strategy. Maybe they were trying to make it look as if only some of them had the ability to transform?

Yet, there was an intensity as I watched Nick fight. It was as if he was so angry at the world right now that he didn't want to give his beast the satisfaction of doing the attacking. If he was going to avenge Nixie's death...it was going to be with his own two hands.

Spears were flying all around me. A couple knives and an arrow flew dangerously close to my head. Yet, despite my surroundings, weapons flying, people shouting, some screaming, and blood starting to show on almost everyone I could see, my body wouldn't move. I just wasn't sure what to do...so I found myself doing nothing at all.

Somehow, not a single Fear had gotten to me yet — and for that I was grateful. For as much as we had talked about this war, and despite my academic knowledge of what a war *should* be like, I wasn't ready. No matter the confidence I had shown back at camp...I definitely was not ready for this. I wasn't sure I would ever be ready at this point. Fighting may have been something that was in the genes of the Fears, but I wasn't a Fear anymore. Violet had that magic now. Even though I knew it was replenishing somehow inside me, it wasn't the same. And without it...I felt helpless.

"For Heaven's sake, what are you doin'?"

I hadn't seen Violet come over to me until she was gripping both of my shoulders and shaking me back to reality. Just as I was about to respond to her...I saw him. Grinning with that smirk that made my stomach turn as he pulled a spear from the chest of a fallen Magirian soldier. Blood splattered across his face, and I watched as he licked the blood away from his lips.

Rage rippled through my body, and I tried to push past Violet, but she was planted to the ground so hard, it felt like I had walked right into a 100-year-old tree. Callen's Strength had to be surging through her right now. Or was it mine?

"Remember the plan," Violet urged. "Do not let him get to you."

"Vi, he's right..."

"No!" Violet demanded. "If you let all of this magic take control of you, then we are fighting for nothing!"

"What magic?"

"Evey, we don't have time for this!"

She spun around quickly, throwing a knife with such force that it buried itself in the skull of a Fear, directly between the eyes. I watched as blood began to trickle from the wound, and he collapsed to the ground almost in slow motion. Vi turned back to me, looking unphased by the fact that she had just killed someone.

"Who are you?" I asked.

"Channel Griffin. His experience will help you," she explained. "But stick to the plan. And remember, keep it to yourself."

I nodded and she was quickly gone, making her way back into the fight. My sweet, kindhearted, sometimes frightening, best friend, was turning out to be one of the greatest warriors history would ever know. Not to mention her ability to form a battle strategy...which brought my mind back to the plan.

As we had made our way away from the camp, Vi had mentally begged me to channel my magical gift so she could silently pass me her secret plan. There were parts of it that didn't make sense to me, but I wasn't about to question her here. If there was one thing I had learned about Vi since we discovered we were magicals, it was that her magic had only made her more determined and even more intelligent.

Glancing back at the spot I had seen Michael in and finding he was already gone, I took a deep breath, and focused on Griffin's fighting instinct coupled with my own magic abilities. Once I felt myself harnessing both, I finally took a step and headed into the fight.

Sean had been right about my Mind magic. I pulled up the bow and reached for my back as if I would find an arrow there. Sure enough, one collided with my hand before I could even really think to call for it. And before I could second guess whether I had dreamt the arrow up or not, I placed it in my bow and shot, piercing completely through one Fear's shoulder and landing in the chest of the Fear behind her.

"Nice shot, Red!" Sean exclaimed.

I gave him a quick grin and continued to move though the war zone. It went surprisingly smooth at first. I had to call a few arrows, and throw a couple of punches, but that was it for the first forty yards or so of my venture. Even I knew my progress was too good to be true though. War was never this simple.

Sure enough, just moments later, I was face to face with two Fear men. Both of whom had that same wicked grin I had seen so many times on Michael. And on Morana for that matter. It was clear that they wanted blood. And spilling mine was going to be their crowning achievement. Too bad they hadn't realized that I had no intention of bleeding for anyone.

They exchanged a quick glance then charged at me together in one fluid motion. I felt that twinge of anger pulse through me when the first one landed a punch to my ribs. My other forms of magic had depended on my Fear to amplify them. Yet, even without my Fear fully restored, I could still feel my magic bubbling up inside me.

When the second blow came, it landed on my side, but I met it back with even more force. I watched as the Fear, who I had landed the hit on, launched across the battlefield, right into the mouth of the sandy colored beast that I assumed was Daniel.

The other Fear became even more angry, and before I could take in what he was pulling out of his pockets, a sharp pain coursed through my arm. I watched as blood began to pour out of the deep gash.

Thinking I was distracted, I heard the Fear spin and come back toward me for another hit. But boy was he mistaken. I turned around just as he got close to me and punched so hard that I heard bones breaking in his body. He, too, flew through the air, landing limp on the ground almost a football field away from me.

The arm I had hit him with, was unfortunately the one he sliced...almost to the bone. It began to ache instantly, and I knew it was going to prevent me from getting where I needed to be. Closing my eyes for a second, I placed my opposite hand over the gash. Feeling the skin beginning to reconnect, I opened my eyes just in time to see the gash begin to heal before I had to reach back to call an arrow and shoot it at the next Fear that was racing toward me.

When Griffin appeared at my side, in his full beast form, I smiled a little. Channeling him was one thing. Having him standing beside me, literally giving me strength, gave me the surge of confidence I needed to push forward.

Griffin gave a low growl next to me and I climbed onto his back. I knew Violet wanted the plan between us, and I understood why completely...but this war zone was massive. Far bigger than it had looked mere hours ago. It would have taken me a lifetime to get where I needed to be at the rate I had been going on my own.

So, without telling him where I needed to go, I let Griffin push on through the Fears as I shot arrow after arrow and searched for my target. Not to my surprise, the more I searched, the more discouraged I became, and the more worried I became about those fighting for Magir.

I watched as Magirian soldiers fell. I saw Sean and Johanna standing beside each other, fighting a large group of Fears, and while they were holding their own, the Fears never stopped coming. I saw Callen next, he had blood pouring down one of his arms and not far from him was Violet. A couple cuts across her face, but otherwise visibly unharmed.

Suddenly, Griffin made a hard turn and I had to grip his fur tightly to avoid sliding off his back. As I steadied myself, I shifted my gaze to find what had caught his attention. I instantly felt my heart start thumping rapidly as I realized who he was racing toward. Hale was on the far edge of the field. He appeared to be fighting his way through Fears, also on his way to someone specific. And a few yards away from Hale I could see who both men were targeting.

I may not have found my own mark, but Griffin and Hale had both found theirs. And since mine was missing in action, I opted to settle for this one, for now. For as badly as I knew Griffin and Hale both wanted him, I had a score to settle still. Violet could yell at me for going off script later. Right now, our sights were set on Michael.

Chapter 32

Violet

I almost couldn't believe my eyes as I looked up from the Fear I was pulling my blade from to see Evey riding a beast toward Michael. Damn him and his power over her. Even if she did truly hate him now, he still had this strange pull over her. I should have known she wouldn't have been able to resist going after him. I would be the first to admit that Michael deserved what was coming to him...but not from her and not right now.

The minute I saw her, I knew I had to make my way over to her. But it was when I saw Hale that I knew that I had to stop her. That I had to get to her before he could. After saving me, I wanted to believe that Hale had changed, but I had seen this before. I knew that he wouldn't be able to abandon his love of family for the love I knew he felt for Evey. He didn't care for her nearly as much as I did. That Griffin did. Or even Sean did.

Sean! As soon as his name crossed my mind, I remembered him falling to the ground, with a spear through his back. I remembered him using his last breath to shout his nickname for Evey, as blood poured from his mouth. And Johanna's scream...I doubted I would ever get that out of mind...it was going to haunt me forever.

I glanced over and saw Callen, just as he had been in my vision, fighting beside Armonee, and I knew immediately this was about more than getting to Evey. I had a vision of the future for a purpose. And dang-nab-it, I was going to put that vision to good use and change it.

"Callen!"

Screaming as loudly as I could, I shouted his name. I knew our bond would have drawn him to me if I had used it, but this seemed like the best way for me to show my urgency. It also may have been the fact that I had a flare for being slightly dramatic. Either way, he sent a Fear falling to the group and began instantly moving towards me.

Time wasn't on my side though, and I had far too many lives to save in this particular moment. Knowing that he was far faster than I was, I took off running toward Michael in hopes of heading off Evey.

When Callen reached my side, I saw the Magirian soldiers moving with the air and the Fears all winced in pain as their invisible enemy got the upper hand on them. Knowing what was coming next, I froze and looked past them at Sean. He wasn't far from me, but I knew I wouldn't have made it in time to warn him.

"Sean!"

I yelled for him, just as the spear whistled past my ear. The sound drew my attention and forced me to watch as Sean turned toward me just as the spear went straight through the upper part of his abdomen. He fell to his knees just as Johanna's screams filled the field.

"Help him, Cal," I instructed quickly. "I can't explain, but I have to get to Evey now."

He didn't even ask a single question. Instead, he nodded and raced toward where Sean had fallen. Embracing his trust and faith in me, I felt like someone had lit a literal fire under my ass. I took off and ran faster than I had ever run in my life. I knew I had to get to Evey before she got to Michael, or Hale, got to her.

A few Fears tried to come at me as I raced toward Evey, but I was in no mood to be messed with right now. The first one took my small blade to the throat. The second took a leaping kick to his groin — which, had I had more time to think, I would have gone crazy tryin' to figure out how I could suddenly do something like that — and then a knife to the stomach. Yet, despite havin' to take both of them out in gruesome ways, I didn't stop. Shit, I hardly slowed.

Just ahead of me, I saw Evey leap from Griffin's back and he raced off into the clearing just as she began to move toward Michael. Before she could move more than a few long strides, I practically plowed into her and spun her around to face me.

"Evey!"

"Vi, let me go!"

"Evey! Just listen to me!" I begged. "I've seen this. I know what will happen to you if you go after him."

Her eyes narrowed at me for a moment and then shifted back to look at where Michael was standing. Quickly I grabbed her face in my hands and forced her to focus back on me.

"Hale will come for you if you kill Michael, Evey! I saw him going after you in a vision."

"You saw wrong, Vi. He was probably coming to help me."

"Is that really a risk you want to take?"

"Yes!" she shouted, as she pushed my hands down. "Violet, I appreciate you looking out for me, but I have to do this! Before she gets here, and I can't spare my focus. I *have* to do this. I thought you, of all people, would understand."

"I do, but..."

"Then let me go," she interrupted.

Staring at her I could see the small flecks of black that told me how angry she was becoming, but I could also feel her desire...her *need* to end him once and for all.

"Fine," I succumbed. "But I'm coming with you."

"Vi..."

"We don't have time for this," I argued and pointed at

the trees that Griffin was emerging from in the form of a man. "It's now or never!"

She gave me a slight nod in agreement and then took off in one direction while I went in the other. We both knew the best way to get to Michael was to come at him from all angles. He would be expecting Evey and Griffin. Maybe even Callen, if I hadn't sent him to help Sean. But me...Michael thought I was weak. He had made it clear to me from the moment I arrived in Harbor that I was nothing more than a pretty face...that I was good for one thing and one thing only. And as I ran around the Fears coming up on his left side, I couldn't help but smile at the idea of knocking out a few of his teeth.

"Well, well. If it isn't my least favorite Southern Belle," Michael mocked.

A Magirian soldier came up behind me and launched right at Michael, so I used the slight distraction to make my first move. As he pushed off the soldier, with unsettling ease, I managed to pull from Callen's Strength and landed a hard blow on Michael's ribs. Or, at least, I thought it was hard. But I knew Michael wasn't going to be that easy to defeat. And when his eyes barely winced at my hit, I was quickly reminded of that.

"Lucky shot," he scorned. "Your little boy toy teach you that worthless move? Hopefully, he showed you a little more than that if you plan to even put up a fight against us."

I couldn't even dignify his criticism of Callen with a response. I pulled one of my smaller blades from the leather belt I had on, and watched as Michael gave a wicked, arrogant grin.

"So, knives are your thing?" he quipped, as he pulled a much larger blade off the body of the soldier at his feet. "That's cute."

Evey's Fear magic surged inside me, and I couldn't take listenin' to another word that came out of his mouth. I lunged at him, and he unsurprisingly dodged my advance, almost sending me stumbling to the ground. But just as he let out a chuckle of amusement, an arrow pierced through his shoulder from the back and he spun around, revealing Evey standing just behind him.

"The shoulder? Really?" I thought to Evey.

"Didn't want to risk hitting you," she thought back.

A smirk formed on my lips as I returned my focus to my opponent. I expected him to show at least some form of pain from that, but when he turned away from Evey to face me again, I saw the grin on his face go from wicked to downright evil. He grabbed the front of the arrow and pulled it all the way through his body, before snapping the arrow in half and tossing it onto the ground. The only sign of pain he showed was a slight scrunch of his nose.

"I should have known you wouldn't have been far away," he growled. "You two never could do a damn thing without each other."

Steadying myself, I looked at Evey for guidance on our next action. Michael's eyes bounced between the two of us, and when Evey shot a wink my way, it was time to attack.

We launched at Michael at the same time. Each of us landing a few blows and taking a few too. After he shoved Evey off, he turned for me. I pulled up my knife, but before I could get to him, he grabbed me by the throat, lifting me off of my feet.

"Violet!"

Evey screamed my name and tried to come to my rescue. But Michael used his free hand to hit her so hard that she launched away from us, landing hard against a rock.

"You know," he began, as he turned back to me, unphased by leaving Evey motionless on the ground. "There is something different about you. Something...not so...ray of sunshine."

"Death will do that to a person," I choked out.

"No," he disagreed, as he tightened his grip. "It's something else."

Suddenly Michael released his grip, sending me crashing to the ground and he strategically rolled away from me. Coughing and blinking a few times, I saw that Griffin had finally made it through the battle to our aid. He had a sword in his hand and as I looked back at Michael, he was crouched on the ground, pulling another sword off of the body of a different soldier.

"About time you got here," Michael laughed. "I can't wait to show Rosey who the better man really is."

Griffin let out a primal growl and launched at him. I watched only for a moment, as their swords clashed with each other. Then, through all of the noise around me, I heard Evey groan, and pushed myself to my feet. As I made my way over to her, my leg ached so badly that walking was almost unbearable. But no broken bone was gonna stop me from gettin' to her right now.

"Sugar, are you alright?"

"Where's Michael?"

I forced myself onto the ground and couldn't hide my painful squint.

"Vi? What happened?"

"I'm fine."

"Violet."

"Fine...I think my leg may be broken. But we have..."

"Jesus Christ, Vi."

She grabbed my hand in hers and then placed her other hand over my leg. She closed her eyes only for a moment before I felt a snap and couldn't hold back my scream.

"Good gravy!" I shouted. "Give a girl a damn warnin'!"

"Didn't have time for that. Where's Michael?"

I nodded my head in the direction of where Michael was still sword fighting Griffin. But this wasn't like any sword fight I had ever seen. One minute their metal blades were crashing together and the next they were using magic to attack each other. Griffin was using Mind to throw anything he could at Michael. And Michael was somehow pulling things from the ground to almost tie Griffin down so that he could attack him.

"I have to help him, Vi," she pleaded, as lifted me from

the ground.

"Evey, you can't."

"I have to! And I have a plan."

Staring at her I saw that small fleck of black coming into view.

"Wait," I exclaimed, as I grabbed her hands. "I need everything you have if we are going to make this work."

"Vi, trust me, it's barely there."

"Just trust me!"

She nodded and I said the incantation once. Afraid to say it twice, I felt the surge and then dropped her hands. As I opened my eyes, I saw her racing back toward Griffin and Michael. I knew she needed this. It was the final piece of closure she really and truly required to move past her history with him. But damn it was hard to watch her run back toward him. And as I saw Hale approaching the three of them, I felt a pit in my stomach. But I couldn't interfere. I had asked Evey to trust me with our strategy to win this, and she did. Now I had to trust that she was right about Hale. That he would back her...not his cousin.

A few Fears and a Magirian soldier headed towards me, and I knew that I wasn't going to be able to watch out for her like I wanted to. Our connection would have to be enough for me to know that she was safe. So, I took a deep breath and pulled the last knife from my belt, before aiding the soldier and getting back into the battle.

Chapter 33

Evelyn

I wasn't entirely sure what I was hoping to do when I got back to Griffin and Michael, but I knew it wasn't going to be in Michael's favor. In true Violet fashion though, after a brief moment with her, I felt immensely better about the fight I was heading into. And as much as I wanted revenge on Michael for everything he put me through, now it felt more like I just wanted to make sure he could never do it to someone else.

Griffin saw me coming up behind Michael and swung his sword to keep Michael's attention away from me. That slight second distraction allowed me to call an arrow and shoot it straight at him. My heart almost stopped entirely when Michael spun quickly around...catching the arrow in his hand.

"Nice try, Rosey."

Hearing that name sent me over the edge. Pulling on all of the Healing magic I could, I remembered the lesson that Hale had first taught me about the boundaries of magic. Nothing was as simple as it seemed. So, I pressed my palms hard on the ground, healing anything that once had life beneath it.

As the ground shook, Michael and Griffin both froze with confused expressions, but I remained focused on my Healing. Moments later, trees began to rise from the ground. The grass began to get a little taller, and to my surprise, the best thing that came up were the massive rose bushes that began to rise and wrap around Michael. Watching him struggle against the spiked stems brought a smile to face. He would be brought down with something as beautiful and prickly as a rose.

I stood back up, but the trees and bushes continued to rise. Taking advantage of the few seconds of magic that was still lingering in the ground, Griffin and I both moved in on Michael. But just as we got close, the bushes surrounded him, making it almost impossible to even see him, nonetheless, attack him.

Michael remained hidden for a few seconds and then his head shot out of the bushes. Before we could react, he pulled out one of his arms and pushed magic that I had never seen before towards Griffin. Red sparks literally launched from Michael's hand and hit Griffin directly in the chest. I could do nothing but watch as he spun through the air landing several feet away from Michael and I.

In the mere millisecond that I had glanced at Griffin, Michael had managed to break free from the roses, and was slowly walking towards me.

"This is between you and me, Rosey," he barked.

"Couldn't agree more."

We advanced on each other without an ounce of hesitation. Michael dropped his sword and I, my bow. There was no need for weapons between us. We were the only weapons we needed to inflict pain on one another. And that is exactly what we did.

Going blow for blow, we fought against each other. Neither of us really trying to win, but both of us trying to inflict as much pain as possible. I didn't want it to end swiftly.

Michael deserved to suffer for everything he did to me...and everything he had done to my new family. And I wasn't going to let him have the satisfaction of beating me...never again. But I should have known he wasn't going to play fair. When something appeared behind me, causing me to fall off of my feet, I felt a twinge of fear as he stood menacingly, over me.

"You chose the wrong side, Rosey," he emphasized as he picked his sword back up. "I told you I would never let anyone else have you."

Just over of his shoulder, I saw my opportunity approaching. I could hear Violet in the back of my mind, but I had to go with my gut...we only had one shot at this.

"And I told you," I asserted, as I pushed up onto my elbows. "I would never let you hurt me again."

Just as the final word left my lips I called upon a sword, but instead of it having it land in my hands, it flew past Michael into the hand of Hale. Then it was as if everything moved in slow motion.

Hale caught the sword while leaping through the air. Michael's eyes followed the blade, and he began to slowly spin, turning his own sword in Hale's direction. But Michael couldn't get his sword in position in time. So, while Michael's sword stabbed through Hale's shoulder, Hale's pierced directly through the center of Michael's chest.

My eyes almost didn't believe what I was seeing, as I watched Michael's lifeless body fall to the ground. It was over. The man who had tormented me both mentally and physically for years was gone. Michael was dead.

"Nice toss," Nick praised, as he appeared beside me and helped me off of the ground. "Two more seconds and I would have done it myself. But Nix would have been glad it was you."

I shot him a smile, and to my surprise, he actually smiled back. I guess I wasn't the only one who needed some closure when it came to Michael. And as I looked back toward Michael's body, I saw something I never thought I'd see. Griffin kneeling over Hale, pulling the sword from his shoulder, and then using his Healing to help him.

Before I could really react to the moment they were sharing, thunder cracked through the sky causing all of us, Magirians and Fears alike, to look towards the small hill in the center of the clearing.

When I saw them both standing there, Michael's death no longer mattered. We had two more major targets. Morana and Barin both stood on the hill, and even at a considerable distance away, I could see their smug expressions. They were next.

After the very brief acknowledgement of their arrival, the fight was back on. Griffin moved quickly to my side and Hale wasn't far behind him, stretching out his newly healed shoulder.

"Nick, you and I will head for Barin," Griffin instructed. "E..."

"Hale can get me to her. Can't you?"

"Happily."

Griffin kissed my cheek and then rushed back into the fight with Nicholas tight to his side. Nick was bleeding from a few different spots on his arms and Griffin was too. Though both of them were so focused on the next target, that neither of them cared in the slightest.

I'm sure I was a sight for sore eyes myself. Between taking the blows from Michael and tumbling around on the ground, I'm sure my skin was turning bluish black, and my hair was filled with leaves. But as I moved towards Morana, everyone seemingly paving my path to her, none of it mattered. Now it was time for the real plan. And even though, at the moment I wasn't even sure where Violet was, I knew that this was going to work. It had to.

We had to stop our progress towards the hill when two Fears challenged us. Hale and I made quick work of them, but it gave me a quick second to look towards Griffin and see that he had already made his way to Barin and with Nick to support him, they were already in combat. Barin had to have advanced on them too, in order for them to be fighting at the base of the hill already. And the idea that a father would willingly move to attack his own son made my chest hurt.

With that thought already haunting my mind, I couldn't help but think about what that would do to Griffin... having to kill his own father. Though I guess it was going to feel similar to what I was heading to do. After all, I was going to have to kill my own mother if we wanted this war to end.

There were four Fears waiting for us at the bottom of the hill, as we made our approach.

"I can handle them," Hale informed me. "Just win this."

"All four of them?"

"Don't you know who I am?" he jokingly questioned, as he stepped a few paces in front of me and then headed for all of them.

I shook my head and smiled at his ability to make this humorous, and then knelt down on one knee. Harnessing my Strength, I pushed myself off the ground and launched over the top of the Fears, landing just a few feet away from Morana.

"Was that supposed to impress me?"

"I'm not here to impress you," I rebutted.

"So, you came to die then?"

"Wrong again."

She snapped her fingers before I could attack, and Griffin appeared from a cloud of smoke. His body was floating beside her, his head tilted up as if someone was holding him there by the throat.

"You truly believe that your magic can compare to mine? You may be the descendant of The Five, but you are untrained, and pathetically easy to defeat."

I studied the Griffin floating beside her as she spoke. Part of me wanted to look off to the side and see if he was still battling Barin, but I didn't want her to know that I was on to her. So, instead I hoped that my gift would block her from my bond with him and tried to push my thoughts to him.

"It's not me."

It was hard not to let my expression give me away, and when she began laughing before me, I knew I had her right where I wanted her.

"Fine!" I falsely conceded. "Kill me. But leave him out of this."

"That's not the way of the Fear," she countered harshly. "Had you chosen the right side, you would have seen that!"

She snapped her fingers again and the neck of the Griffin beside her turned sharply before the false body fell to the ground. Even though I knew it was fake, watching Griffin fall to the ground was gut wrenching. Which was probably a good thing because I needed my reaction to sell my belief. But I was sure that image would haunt me for lifetimes to come.

"No!"

The scream echoed around us, before I could even muster up my own. I knew that voice better than anyone, but as Morana and I turned, I saw what had caused it.

Griffin was standing beside Nick, while Lucas pulled back on a sword that he must have just used to stab Barin.

"He was mine!" Griffin shouted angrily, as he shoved Lucas backward.

I whipped my head back to Morana just as she started laughing again.

"It was worth a try."

"You tried to trick me!" I exclaimed, pretending to be upset by her deceit.

"Don't be so melodramatic," Morana instructed, as she rolled her eyes. "At least Lucas was good for something. Now I don't have to be the one to kill that arrogant, disgusting excuse of a man."

"You planned to kill Barin?" I asked, genuinely shocked. "He was your partner!"

"I will share the crown with no one. Now, enough of this."

She snapped her fingers again, but it wasn't Griffin who appeared at her side this time. It was Lucas. Even though he was my father, there was no bond between us to tell me it wasn't him. My chest immediately tightened when I turned to look where he had just been standing and saw he was gone.

"No more games!" Morana shouted at me. "*This* is the product of *your* own choices!"

"EvelynRose," Lucas said softly. "He couldn't live with killing his own father. And I couldn't let Barin torture him anymore."

"I should have known the feeble Archer line was the wrong choice," Morana groaned. "You all think you are so noble and kindhearted. It's disgusting."

She spun her hand around and Lucas suddenly lifted his arm holding the sword before plunging it through his own stomach. That caring smile on his face didn't fade for a moment, but as she relinquished her grip on him and he collapsed to his knees I watched his face wince in pain, as blood trickled slowly from his mouth.

"Dad..."

The word left my lips as such a light whisper that I wasn't even sure I had said it. He slumped over, but before I could move to help him, Morana closed the distance between us and magically lifted me from the ground. My airway immediately constricted as her fingers magically wrapped tightly around my throat from her place on the ground.

"To think they thought you would defeat me," she smirked. "The last hope of Magir dies tonight."

"Does it though?" I choked out, trying to remember my role in all of this. "What if I'm not the only descendent of The Five?"

"Don't delay the inevitable," she argued. "I created you, remember. I know what you are."

"Look inside," I coughed. "Look inside me then."

She paused for a moment and that was all I needed. Her eyes traveled up and she lost the control she had on me. Landing on the ground, I stumbled back to my feet clearing my throat.

"How?"

As Morana questioned what she was seeing, I turned and saw Violet rising into the air, similar to how I had seen myself in the visions of Rosebud. But unlike how I was floating in the sky, Violet was not merely floating. Instead, she had two breathtaking, lacelike, white wings spanning far beyond her body. As she rose higher in the middle of the field, everyone had their eyes on her. Her long blonde hair whipped in the wind as she held her arms out to the sides, eyes fixated on our target.

As she glided through the air towards us, I noticed that her eyes were not the same as mine had been in the memory I was shown of Rosebud. There was no deep sea of black. Instead, her eyes showed a black center, surrounded by rings of red, orange and purple. Violet had figured out how to control the Fear and use it to her advantage. But it was more than that...there was something behind her transformation that had my own magic bubbling again.

"How did she take your magic?" Morana screamed at me. "Never mind! It changes nothing. You were a mistake, and you are still going to die here."

Morana tried to raise her hands, but Violet was there, lifting her off the ground, and magically pinning Morana's arms to her sides, before she had the chance to come for me.

"Don't threaten the life of my cousin unless you are prepared to pay with your own."

Violet's voice sounded coarser than normal, but not nearly as demonic as mine had when my Fear had taken over me.

"Cousin?" Morana questioned. "That...that's not possible!"

"See," Violet smirked. "You don't have all the cards. You may have brought the straight flush...but you'll lose to the royal every time."

Her jest ended and the sudden sound of a bow string snapping caused my head to spin. I barely caught sight of the arrow before it impaled Morana, right through her cold, empty heart.

Violet's eyes went back to their normal bright blue as she released her magical hold on Morana, who fell to the ground with a loud thud. I saw everyone whipping their heads around to see who had fired the shot, but I knew immediately. When I looked toward him and saw him gripping the bow to his side I knew for sure.

Without hesitation, the remaining Fears began disintegrating into the ground just as they had in Rosebud. And when the last one was gone, a few of the Magirian soldiers let out a victorious cry.

The celebration began but I felt my chest getting tighter, as I turned around and rushed to where Lucas had fallen. I could see the sword had not made it completely through his body, so I rolled him from his side, onto his back and saw he was barely breathing. The sword would have to come out in order to start healing him. But he had lost so much blood already...I knew pulling it would kill him instantly. I was frozen.

"Evelyn!"

Violet's voice rang through the field, and I turned to see that she was now with the others, all of whom were surrounding someone that was lying on the ground.

"Evelyn, we need you!"

Something grabbed my hand, and I realized Lucas had opened his eyes and was now holding onto me.

"I've lived a...full life," he rasped. "Help him...I'm proud...of you...I...love you...Evelyn...Rose."

The grip he had on my hand loosened, and he let out a final breath that made tears race down my cheeks.

"I love you too, dad."

I brought his hand up to my lips and kissed it softly. Not being close to him...losing him once...getting him back... and losing him again...our journey made this so much worse. I didn't want to leave, but Griffin was suddenly by my side with a hand on my shoulder.

"E, it's Sean."

I looked up at Griffin and he looked terrified. I didn't think he had lost a Knight before...and Sean was more than just a Knight, he was one of my best friends. He was his brother.

Getting up as fast as I could, Griffin grabbed my hand, and we raced toward where the others were standing over Sean. But when I got there, I wished my eyes weren't seeing what was before me.

Just like Lucas, Sean was lying with a sword in his stomach and a puddle of blood beneath him. Johanna was next to him, tear lines streaking down her face, and her own breath sounding wheezy. I remembered Professor Hyperion's lesson on bonds right away. *It is said that magicals who are fated cannot live without the other. Even without sealing the bond, they are connected from the moment they meet. And if the bond is sealed, death to one, usually means death to the other.*

His words echoed in mind as if it had been yesterday. Those who were bonded by fate tended to die together. I didn't care how rare they said fated bond magic was, I'd witnessed the love they had for one another, and I immediately knew there was a high chance that we weren't just losing Sean, but Johanna too.

"Evelyn, can you help him?" Victor asked.

Letting go of Griffin's hand, I crouched down by Violet, near Sean's head. Placing a hand on his forehead, I could feel how cold he was getting. Glancing at the wound and the puddle, it didn't appear that more blood was coming out which could be a good sign that clotting had begun...or it could mean his heart was barely pumping anymore.

I looked at Johanna, but her eyes never left Sean's face. I could see how pale she was getting as the life began to slowly fade from her eyes. I wasn't just losing one best friend...I was losing two. After everything we'd been through, I couldn't stand by and let that happen.

"I need everyone except for Violet, Amonee and Johanna to leave," I sharply instructed. "Now!"

"What?" Griffin asked, clearly confused.

"Evey...are you sure?" Violet asked me.

"I'm sure. And we don't have a lot of time. I need you all to get as far away from here as fast as possible."

No one moved. They just stared at me as if I'd lost my mind completely. Like they weren't sure I had really thought through what I was saying.

"Go!"

"Okay...back to camp..." Griffin instructed, with an uncertain tone.

Once the others had cleared away, I turned to Johanna and took her face in my hands. Making her look away from Sean and forcing her eyes to meet mine, which may have been a poor choice on my part. I had never seen her so defeated...so completely broken. But I needed her to hear what I was about to say.

"If you want me to save him, I need you to pull everything you have left. I don't have another Healing magical with the strength to help me. I'm going to need the strongest boost you can give me. Can you manage that?"

She didn't say anything. Just moved her eyes back to Sean and I quickly pulled on her head, not allowing her focus to leave me.

"Johanna, focus! He will die without this. I need everything you have."

Clearing her throat, she nodded slowly and sat up a little straighter. I knew she wasn't going to have much, but even a little boost from her would increase our odds.

"Alright, here is the plan. Vi, I need you to give me back my Fear."

"Are you..."

"I'm sure, Vi. I can handle it. That magic makes me stronger and without it I can't give my Healing the boost it needs right now."

Violet nodded, though I knew she was hesitant.

"Armonee, as soon as I have my Fear back, I need you to pull that sword out in one motion, as fast as you can. Then check on Violet. Once she gives back my Fear..."

"I got it," Armonee agreed without question.

"Now, Johanna," I said, pulling her attention back to the mission at hand. "As soon as that sword is out, I'll put one hand on his wound and one on his heart. The second my hands are in place, hit me with everything you have. Got it?"

"Yes," she sighed.

"Then, let's do this!" I said, turning to Violet. "You're first. Ready?"

"If you are," she said, grabbing my hands, as we closed our eyes. "Erotser Raef! Eroster Raef!"

Magic coursed so quickly between our hands that my heart started racing and I was breathing so heavily that I thought I might have been having a heart attack. I could feel the magic rapidly dancing in my veins, feeding my anger at the thought that Sean had only been here because of me. That he was dying because of me. Then my eyes shot open, just as Violet fell backward. But I knew I didn't have time to check on her.

Spinning towards Sean's body, Armonee yanked the sword out and blood began to pour from his wound again. I threw my hands over his heart and his wound, before I looked to Johanna, waiting for her boost. She was frozen in fear at the sight of all the blood oozing from his chest and I knew time was running out.

"Johanna, now!"

My command broke her out of her daze, and she placed her hand on my chest, screaming so loudly, if I hadn't been so focused on my Healing, I was certain my eardrums would have burst.

The magical boost she'd given me was so much more than I'd ever felt before. The power jolted through every fiber of my body like I'd been struck by lightning. My heart pounded rapidly in my chest as my body fought to process the magical overload it was now carrying.

As I harnessed the magic, I stared down at my hands and watched as a bright light began to illuminate from each of them. I had never seen this happen before. The light got brighter and brighter, until I couldn't see anything around me.

Using that much magic was making me dizzy and nauseous, but I couldn't see if he was healed enough, so I couldn't let it go yet. When that nausea turned from tolerable to excruciating, I let out a scream that even I didn't recognize.

This was an entirely new level of mental and physical pain. I felt so much pressure to heal Sean in that moment. To save not just his life, but potentially Johanna's too. Then there was the grief. Good God, the grief. Grief from losing Ariana, Katerie, Nixie, and now my father. And atop the grief, my anger boiled. None of this would have happened if I hadn't been born. This all came back to me. All of this death was my fault. Just as I thought I might drown in this pit of despair...there was a spark of happiness. No...not just happiness...of pure joy. We had won. At the end of the day, we had defeated Morana. Barin was dead. Michael was dead. We had won the war.

As my brain — or perhaps my heart — grappled with the emotions I was feeling, I let out another painful scream as I forced out one final burst of magic and collapsed over Sean's body.

*****

"EvelynRose!" Armonee exclaimed, as she grasped my shoulders. "Evelyn, are you alright?"

I lifted myself up a little and looked at the bodies around me. Johanna had fainted next to Sean but was stirring back awake. Violet was laying back against her elbows, though she seemed unscathed by it all. But it was Sean's smile that actually brought me back to reality.

"Red," he coughed. "I think you're breaking my ribs."

"Sean!"

Without a thought about how he was probably still sore and recovering internally from being stabbed, I hugged him as tightly as I possibly could. As he began to push up off of the ground, I finally released him. Just as I let him go, Johanna let out a heavy sigh of relief and kissed him with such sweet desperation, even with my Fear magic back inside of me, I felt the tears of joy and relief welling up in my eyes.

Giving them their moment, I turned back to Violet, who was smiling at me, and Armonee, who looked oddly like a proud older sibling with visible tear tracks down her cheeks.

"You okay?" I asked Violet.

"Girl, did you see the magic you just performed?" she jokingly asked. "I don't think anyone within fifty miles is feeling even a headache right now. You Healed all of Magir!"

"She's right," Armonee said. "I'm not entirely sure how you just did what you did, but I've never seen anyone use Fear to amplify other forms of magic like that. You impressed the shit out of me."

"And me," Sean groaned, as he moved to stand. "You saved my life, Red."

"From how it felt to watch you die," Johanna lamented. "I'm pretty sure she saved us both."

*****

When we arrived back at camp, everyone cheered and rushed for Sean. Griffin embraced him, then quickly moved to me. He wrapped his arms tightly around my waist and twirled me through the air. When we stopped spinning, he placed me, dizzily, on the ground before kissing me so passionately, I thought the magic between us was going to melt away my clothes.

"You're amazing," he said softly, but with a reverence I had never heard before. "You saved us all, E. You, Violet, and your secret plan, saved us all."

More cheers erupted and Griffin moved to my side so I could see that everyone was looking at us with expressions of admiration and gratitude. Violet was pressed tightly to Callen's side, and I could see that her warmhearted nature had completely returned with the departure of my Fear magic.

"Now, I think we should probably change before we head back to the palace," Nicholas prompted.

It was then that I looked around and noticed Charles was missing. Griffin's grip tightened on my hand, and I knew that meant that he was gone. And no matter how strong my magic had been on that field, I knew if he was gone...there was no bringing him back.

The others began to laugh about our blood-stained clothes and which of our wounds would leave scars, when I saw Johanna helping Sean pull his torn and blood-soaked shirt carefully over his head. As she lifted it over his back, I saw the scar again. The olive branch scar that he had gotten as a result of the worst day of his life...and then it hit me.

"Oh my God!" I exclaimed, causing everyone to turn in my direction. "Sean, it's you!"

"Yeah...it's me, Red. Were you expecting Johanna to be undressing someone else?"

She playfully hit his arm and I rolled my eyes at his uncanny ability to find humor in everything someone said.

"You're the one in the prophecy!"

"Evelyn, are you okay?" Hale asked. "Because we all know that prophecy was about you."

"Part of it, yes! And then part of it was about me and Vi. But that last piece was..."

"Oh!" Violet exclaimed.

"You're following this?" Callen questioned.

She nodded slowly, as I moved toward Sean and turned him around so that I could see the detailed scar on his back.

"I thought it was Hale," I explained. "But it's you. Sean, you're *the one who was marked*."

"Me?" He questioned, looking over his shoulder at me.

"Yes! I can't believe I missed this before!" I cried, as I began to move towards Hale. "I just assumed it was you. You had literally been marked by the leader of the Fears. And you were one of our biggest assets when it came to defeating them. But while your help was invaluable, you didn't bring the *restoration* that the prophecy claimed the marked one would. Even if it was you who landed the fatal shot on Morana."

"And thank you for that," Griffin interjected.

"I second that," Callen added.

"To Hale!" Nicholas shouted, as he triumphantly raised his fist in the air.

The group rejoiced in cheers of appreciation for what Hale had done for all of us by taking that shot. He made it so that Violet didn't have to take yet another life. And I...well, I didn't have to live with knowing I had killed my own biological mother. Regardless of who she had turned out to be.

"Not to interrupt," I announced through the celebration. "But back to Sean."

Violet was smiling as she put together all the pieces my brain had been laying out, and I was suddenly so happy I could no longer contain the tears of joy that now filled my eyes.

"What we needed to restore Magir was right in front of us all along!" I declared. "Sean, it's you! You're the missing piece to the prophecy!"

Chapter 34

Violet

Two days had passed since the war had ended. To most of Magir, they were wondrous days. I mean, if I thought people partied hard outside of the magical realms, well I was sorely mistaken because these people knew how to party! I thought alcohol made people crazy...but when Magirians celebrate with substantial amounts of their magical sugar...sweet baby Jesus, it was a celebration!

While I was always down for a good party, I had spent most of the last two days helping Evelyn prepare her big speech. Which was also the reason that we were currently standing in the woods just outside of where we had attempted to enter the Dark Woods a month ago.

I had been adamant that I was not returning to this place after what had happened the last time. And when I made up my mind about something...it was a permanent choice. Yet, as I stood beside my friend, surrounded by the people who I cared about more than anything, I couldn't help but smile. Even with all of the dark emotions looming around us, I couldn't help but feel proud of my best friend and all that she had accomplished.

When we returned to the camp after saving Sean and Evey had put together the last pieces of the prophecy, I couldn't believe I had missed it. Seriously, it was right in front of our faces. A scar like an olive branch. Talk about hittin' the nail on the head.

"It's sunset," Victor surmised. "They should be here."

"They'll come," Callen nodded.

"And if they don't?" Daniel asked.

"They will," Griffin assured.

Together we all stood in the clearing waiting...and waiting...and waiting some more. But not a single living thing emerged from beyond the trees. No cute little bunnies hopped out of a nearby bush. No birds were soaring in the sky. And there were most definitely not any Fears emerging for our scheduled meeting.

At first, waiting was fine. We were all still so full of anticipation that we were almost bouncing in our places...but after over an hour of standing in the middle of the creepy woods, I could feel everyone's resolve was starting to fade.

"How much longer are we going to give them exactly?" Johanna groaned.

"They're coming," Eveyln assured us with a heavy breath.

After a few collective groans, a few of us gave up and found places to sit. Callen yanked me over to a stump where he sat and pulled me into his lap. Johanna and Sean chose a piece of the ground next to us and I watched as Sean struggled down to his seat.

"You alright?" Johanna asked him.

"Woman, you have got to stop coddling me," Sean urged, as he leaned back on his elbows, before giving Johanna a nudge with his shoulder.

"Can you blame her?" I asked. "You did basically die, just two days ago."

"But I'm alive now," Sean reminded us. "And I don't plan to leave this one again."

He grabbed Johanna's hand and she smiled before she leaned over, kissing his cheek. I thought for sure my heart was going to leap from my chest, but then I looked up at Nick, who still had that lost puppy expression on his face. I watched his face cringe away from Sean and Johanna's happiness. I couldn't imagine how much pain these events had caused him...and I could legitimately feel how bad he was hurting. Watching Michael die had provided some momentary relief, but his mourning was far from over.

"So," Victor said slowly, as he clearly sensed the same discomfort I was. "I saw Charlie's parents leaving yesterday. How did that go?"

Evey's special gift truly had its perks, but blocking the Knights from reading one another, was not one I was very fond of. No part of me wanted to relive that moment. I had seen death. Even been there during a notification...but being the one to give that notification. The one to hold the hand of a crying mother who was wailing in your ear. Then sitting in your tear-stained shirt long after they left, knowing that you are wearing another persons' sadness.

"They are devastated," I choked out.

"But his father was proud," Callen added, as he squeezed my shoulder and forced a smile. "He said Charles had always dreamed of being a Knight and of keeping Magir safe. That Charlie would have said dying in battle, for the safety of Magir, was the ultimate honor."

Everything Callen said was true. And a hush fell over our entire group while we tried to embrace Charles's philosophy. It was especially hard for me though, because I didn't really even know Charles. Of all of the Knights I had spent the least amount of time with him. Yet, I was the one who was hugging his grieving mother. There was just something disheartening about that. Something that made me feel like a fraud.

"Don't you dare call yourself a fraud."

Callen's voice rang through my head, and I turned to

him and attempted to smile. I wanted to believe him...but the pain in my stomach at the thought of that woman crying... well, it made that belief smaller than that damn needle hiding in the haystack.

"Look!"

Nick's voice was so soft, I almost missed his decree. For a brief second, I thought I had actually made the whole thing up in my head. But when everyone started moving, I realized I hadn't and looked in the direction Nick had nodded his head in.

Eveyln and Griffin had been optimistic...and rightfully so. The Fears may have been late, but they were finally arriving! At first, only one or two of them emerged from the trees at a time. But then, a sea of people started pouring out into the forest. Before I knew it, not only were we surrounded by Fears — not to mention, incredibly outnumbered — but there were so many of them that my mind could barely process what I was seeing. I mean, for a hidden realm within a realm...that Sephtis place had to be huge!

We were all standing back up now, and we had moved closer to where Evelyn and Griffin stood watching with eager anticipation across their faces. And even though Evey had her Fear back now, I could feel the excited and nervous energy she was emulating. She really was getting the hang of this.

"We are here," a Fear man suddenly announced, as he stepped in front of his family. "We sent word of our surrender. You will not be bothered by us anymore. What is it you want of us?"

Evey took a deep breath and straightened her stance.

"We want to offer you a fresh start," Evelyn began.

"A fresh start?" the man questioned, as he let out a chuckle. "Since when does Magir care about us?"

"Let me rephrase then," Evelyn clarified. "We want us *all* to have a fresh start."

The man's eyes narrowed, and I could tell, that although he was extremely guarded and apprehensive, he was now genuinely interested in what Evey had to say. Behind him I watched as the other Fears moved in a bit closer to hear what it was that she was offering them.

"I'm sure by now, you all know that I am the daughter of Morana," Evey explained. "But I'm sure I speak for many of us, when I also say that it was very clear she was not exactly the mothering type."

The slight sound of a chuckle filled the woods, and I knew Evey had drawn them in. Looking at Evey, the smile on her face told me that she knew it too.

"There was a reason that Morana wanted to have me," Evey continued, "and it wasn't because of an inner desire to be a mother. No, Morana decided to take matters into her own hands and had me in an attempt to control a long-foretold prophecy."

"The prophecy stated, *when the balance of power shifts to dark, restoration is found through the one who was marked. Led by The Five, their magic will reign. When blood reunites, only peace will remain,*" Griffin recited.

"Now, being the new Magirian that I am," Eveyln joked, "I wasn't sure what any of that meant at first. But when the answers finally began to reveal themselves, I thought for sure I knew how to get through the war."

"And you did," the man interrupted. "You've won the war."

"We won a battle," Evelyn corrected. "You see, we thought we had the answers to what the prophecy was trying to tell us. Morana thought she knew too. But we had all misinterpreted the most important part.

"The prophecy stated that restoration would be found through the one who was marked. At the same moment when I learned about the prophecy, Hale had begun helping us."

Hale stepped forward and the Fears eyed him warily. Clearly the mark across his face really was something the other Fears were truly fearful of. That, or the fact that he had been the one to actually kill Morana...something about him genuinely had them even more on edge, but who could really say what their reasoning was.

"It made perfect sense at the time," Evey continued. "Hale had been marked by the very same Fear we were going up against. Restoration coming from him made sense...but it was too easy. And while Hale was invaluable in battle, he didn't bring restoration to Magir. No, the one who brought restoration was my good friend, Sean."

Evelyn turned, motioning toward Sean who stood as tall as he could — considering his insides were still sore — and gave a half smile as the Fears stared at him.

"To all of you, Sean is a Knight, and likely has been an enemy to you since becoming one. But what you may not know, is that Sean, who is not a Fear, knows firsthand what it is like to have your magic do a terrible thing. He lost control of his magic before he knew how to use it. Even when he was trying to do something noble, protect himself and a friend, his uncontrolled Strength brought down a group of massive, hundred-year-old trees. As a result, his childhood friend suffered a traumatic head injury and was ultimately left unable to hear, and Sean was gifted a scar along his back."

The crowd returned their stare back to her. I was pretty certain they weren't followin' her logic whatsoever. To them it was a tale of woe, not the answer to the prophecy.

"Don't you see," Evelyn pleaded. "Sean's magic is Strength. A magical family that has long been revered as protectors. Yet, when Sean lost control of it, he almost killed himself and his best friend."

I watched as the eyes of the crowd began to widen. She was getting through to them. If I hadn't been there to see it, I may not have believed it...but she was actually getting through to them!

"Magic is not black and white," Evelyn encouraged. "There is no form of magic that is all good or all bad. It all—"

"Fear is different," the man interjected. "No good comes from Fear magic."

"That's where you're wrong," I stepped in. "I am not a

Fear, but I have held Fear magic inside me. While yes, there is a darkness surrounding it, if you look deep down inside yourselves, you will see that there is light there too. And there is such vigor behind the magic that it can allow you to do just about anything."

"Like what?" a Fear woman sneered from behind the man.

"Like save a life," Johanna answered.

They all looked back at Johanna in disbelief. After being conditioned for so long to think that their magic was solely for dark, truly evil things, they were all beside themselves as they grappled with the concept that Fear magic could help anyone, nonetheless save a life.

"It's true," Sean seconded. "I was seconds from death just two days ago. Laying in the middle of the battlefield with a sword through my stomach. If Evelyn hadn't pulled all of her Fear to strengthen her Healing, I probably wouldn't be standing in front of you. Actually, I know I wouldn't be."

A few gasps and many whispers moved with the breeze that had started to blow through the trees.

"There is no clear definition of good and evil in this realm, or any of them," Evelyn expounded. "Regardless of which magical family you hail from, it cannot define whether you will be good or evil. I refuse to believe that we don't have a choice when it comes to the person we grow to be. Look at me...I'm all five families balled up into one and until the last few weeks, I couldn't manage any of them."

"That may be true," the man argued. "But it wasn't your other forms of magic that tore up your local park in a hurricane, now, was it?"

A week ago, I would have expected that statement to make Evey stir. I would have expected to feel her heart start racing, as nerves fired rapidly throughout her body. But now, she was different. She was calm and collected. I even watched her smile a little as she looked out at the Fears.

When she took a few steps toward the man, I watched

Griffin step as if he was going to move with her and then he stopped. I wasn't sure what she was going for, or really what the hell she was thinking, but she didn't stop walking until she was face to face with the man who now appeared to be leading the Fears.

"Was it?" she asked him, so softly I barely heard it. "Was it truly my Fear magic that caused that hurricane? Or could it have been my Mind throwing those trees? Could it not have been my Strength making the ground move in waves? Was it not my Vision that was telling me exactly where to throw those trees? Could it have possibly been my Healing that was truly pushing my friends from the park? What if it never was caused by Fear? What if my Fear just makes me stronger?"

The man standing before her, as well as all of the other Fears, studied her silently. Shoot, we were all studying her! I had been in complete agreement with her when she came to the conclusion of what the prophecy meant. I knew good and evil weren't actual constructs one could easily define. But to hear her explain what happened in Rosebud like that...

I mean...I was there! I had been standing in that park when she called upon that hurricane. I had watched in awe — and somewhat in fear — as she tore the park apart. Never did I think for a second that it was anything other than her Fear magic that was behind it. But now that she said it...it all made sense...it made so much sense.

"Think about all of the ways that an actual fear can give you strength. A mother protecting a child. That rush of adrenaline that allows a man to save a person by lifting a car off of them. Fear isn't just darkness. It's so much more than that. Light and dark aren't meant to be defined in one way. Magic is no exception to this," Evelyn urged.

I watched as she grabbed the Fear man's hand and he flinched at her touch but did not pull away from her.

"People," she continued, "aren't meant to be defined in one way. Our magic makes us special. And no matter what form of magic we have, we should never be punished for it.

Both good and bad things can come from any form of magic. It all depends on the choices of the person who wields it."

The man gave a slight nod, and Evelyn tightened her grip on his hand as they turned to face the rest of the Fears behind him.

"Magir was formed centuries ago by all five families because, at the time, they saw that there was value in each form of magic," Evelyn articulated. "And they were right. Every family has something to offer. No one form of magic is more dangerous than the other, and it is time for Magir to embrace that knowledge again. It is time for Magir to accept all of us are equal.

"Now, I won't lie to you and say this will be easy. The road to equality is never paved smoothly. But I can promise you that it will be far better than living in the Dark Woods just to avoid potentially being banished to the non-magical realm. And while I acknowledge that your home may be lovely, and where you wish to remain, what I mean is that you don't have to hide there. You would be welcome in all of Magir, not just the Dark Woods."

Pausing only for a moment, Evelyn took in a deep breath, before warmly smiling at the Fears before her.

"Together," she continued, "all of us can bring Magir back to its former glory. We can show all the realms that Magir is not a place where we are afraid of our own kind, but where we are one family. One family of united magic that will carry Magir into a new age. No more misconceptions. No more prejudices from your fellow Magirians. And vice versa. If we work together, I know we can build a realm that is truly spectacular. I only ask that you give us the chance to earn your trust, just as we promise to give you the chance to earn ours."

As she finished speaking, everyone stood silently contemplating her words. The Fears exchanged glances, then the man beside Evey turned to her and bowed, as he brought her hand to his forehead. He released her hand and walked back toward his family, as all of the Fears began to disappear back into the woods.

I was about to protest their sudden departure, when Evey turned back to us with a smile and shook her head at me. She walked slowly back toward us and interlocked her hand with Griffin's, her smile still plastered on her face.

"Well?" I finally asked. "Where exactly did they just disappear to?"

"They are returning to Sephtis," Evey replied, still smiling.

"Wait, for real?" I pushed. "Did they not just hear everything you said? I mean...you had me eating out of your hand and I already knew your message!"

"Violet!" Johanna groaned, as she nudged me.

"What? That was a genuine question."

"They need time to process all of this as a family," Evelyn explained. "They appreciated what we had to say but wanted to discuss it further amongst themselves."

"I can respect that," Callen said behind me.

"You can?" Daniel questioned.

"Well, yeah," he confirmed. "This would be a major lifestyle change for them. I would want to discuss any major changes with my family."

We stood there as we all took in the historicness of this moment. Even if the Fears said no, what Evey just did was going to open the gateway for a herd of change in Magir. With her and Griffin leading Magir together, there was no doubt that they would be going down in history. More like, that we would all be going down in history, that is.

"We should get back," Griffin instructed. "We have a lot to do over the next few days."

"I'm not sure Magir is ready for so much change happening at once," Sean joked.

"Well, they better get ready," I winked. "Because this change is comin' in faster than a bull out the gate."

All of them, even Nick, stared at me with narrowed eyes and smirks as they took in, yet another, one of my idioms.

Eventually they were going to have to get used to them. I highly doubted livin' in Magir was going to change that, no matter how long I stayed here. And based on our plans for the coming days, I wasn't gonna be leavin' any time soon.

Chapter 35

Evelyn

The next day was a whirlwind of appointments and meetings with people I didn't even know. When we returned from the Dark Woods initially, it was almost like I was riding on some sort of high. Saying I was going to be Griffin's wife and become a queen was one thing. Actually, standing in front of a group of people and leading them was an entirely different feeling altogether.

Standing in front of the Fears, promising better tomorrows, not just for them, but for all of us was exhilarating. And as we all left the woods this time I felt, for the first time, like I could actually do this. Like I would be able to lead Magir into the future it deserved. Into a future that all of those who had fallen during this war would be proud of.

After we finished breakfast, a few guards came in asking Griffin and Callen to join the council in their meeting chambers. They followed them out of the dining hall and our group dispersed as Violet and I made our way into the garden.

"It's beautiful out here," Vi gushed through a smile. "I can't believe we get to live here now."

"Seems like a lifetime ago that I was living in that tiny

house with Auntie Saraya," I added.

"Shack," Vi corrected with a wink. "That *place* was a shack."

"Vi, there is still something I wanted to talk to you about."

"You want to know how I grew wings."

She guessed my question without me even needing to ask. We hadn't had a moment for just the two of us to discuss what had happened. Not even Griffin or Callen had asked how she had called upon such magic.

"You can do it too," she claimed. "At least, I think you can."

"But how?"

"Do you remember Thomas?"

"Of course," I smiled. "Our great-grandfather who was reborn as phoenix and came to us in our moment of need."

"That's just it," Vi shook her head. "In my research, I discovered that Johanna was right. A phoenix is a rare creature in all realms, and it isn't just something a magical *comes back as*."

"So, what does that mean?"

"Evey, I think our family has phoenix blood inside us," she confirmed. "I think that's part of the reason our magic manifests so strongly and you have so much Healing power. Yes, part of it is you, but I think part of it is who we are. I don't know exactly how to channel it, but at that moment, I knew I could pull from its power. Ansel is still researching for me."

I stopped in my tracks and just stared at her for a moment. After everything we'd been through since discovering magic, I couldn't even confidently question her assessment. It seemed impossible, and yet it made all the sense in the world.

"After all that we've been through, Evey," she continued, "I just think this is something you and I are going to have to figure out as we go. Together. When the prophecy spoke of blood reuniting, I don't even think they anticipated us finding each other the way we did. The bond we would form. How that ties into us also having magic a Magirian should not possess...I just think this is going to have to be something you and I figure out with time...but figure out together."

I watched as her face scrunched up a bit. Vi despised not having answers, and watching her in that moment, I could tell she was confident in her discovery but dying to know more. It was quite clear how she felt about everything we had been through. This was something we needed to do together, but we also deserved to bask in our current happiness for now. So, even though I wanted to ask a million questions about how she came to that conclusion or what other magic she thought we may be able to perform, instead I laced my arm through hers and continued into the garden.

"Well, if we truly are part phoenix, then can you teach me how to sprout wings too?"

"Yes, Grasshopper," she joked. "Teach you, I can."

"Those are two completely different references!"

"Yet both so incredibly appropriate."

We laughed together as we approached the gazebo where, to our surprise, Hale was leaning up against the side rails.

"You two should talk," Vi whispered to me.

She must have sensed something that I didn't, because before I could even respond, she had unlinked our arms and disappeared back into the castle.

"I didn't mean to disrupt your walk," Hale said, continuing to stare out into the garden.

"You didn't," I answered and moved to lean on the rail beside him. "Is everything okay?"

"Big day today," he responded, still not looking at me.

Now that I knew about his feelings toward me, I could only imagine what he was going through. Maybe that was what Vi had sensed and why she wanted us to talk alone.

"I'm happy for you," he assured me as he bumped my shoulder with his.

"Thank you," I smiled, even though I knew he was holding back how he felt about it. "I never really did thank you for everything you did out there."

"Don't thank me."

"I can't *not* thank you," I argued. "You took out the two worst people in my life."

"Don't…"

"You made it so that I didn't have to kill my own mother and—"

"Eveyln don't!" he snapped at me.

He moved away from me to another spot in the gazebo. My Fear bubbled a little bit and part of me wanted to shout back at him, but there was a little voice in the back of my head that told me he wasn't really trying to be cruel. There was something else going on here.

"Why?" I asked, moving back beside him.

"Because I don't deserve your praise," he replied. "I don't deserve any of you treating me like I was an ally in this."

"Hale, you—"

"I spoke to Michael," he interjected.

"What do you mean?"

"Before the Fears attacked the feast," he answered. "I met with Michael in Sephtis."

"You've been in Sephtis?"

"That's what you took from that?" he asked, half smiling. "Yes. I've been in Sephtis a few times."

"Why did you meet with him?" I asked.

"It was the first chance I had to find out how he did it. How he was able to get into Katerie's head."

"What are you talking about?"

"Evelyn, I did plant a trap in Katerie's mind before you left for Magir," he explained. "But when you told me she had fainted, I knew something had gone wrong. And my magic doesn't go wrong."

I stared at him as he continued his confession. Magic was simmering inside of me, so I just stood beside him, silently listening in an attempt to keep myself as calm as possible.

"I convinced Lucian that Barin had asked me to evaluate her and discovered there were traces of Fear magic inside of her. I knew immediately it was Michael. He was constantly trying to sabotage my helping Morana."

"Some sort of cousin rivalry?" I asked, sassier than I intended.

"You could say that. But it was all from him. I could have cared less that he was my cousin. He is...was a vial person and while I had already believed that to be true, it was only confirmed when I met you."

"Why?"

"You know why," he said softly.

I could hear the hint of pain in his voice. The idea that his own cousin...his own family...had harmed me in the ways that Michael had hurt me, really hit a nerve with him. But it was something I knew he wasn't going to admit, or even want to talk about, so I left it alone.

"So, what did he tell you when you met with him?"

"Nothing," he shrugged. "Nothing of substance anyway. It was all meaningless bragging about how much better his magic was than mine. How you would never stand a chance against him. I should have known that they would attack. And after the feast...when he attacked Nixie and Victor..."

"Yeah, how did you know that something was wrong?"

"I could sense it. I can't really explain why, but I just knew he wouldn't be able to resist after failing to really hurt you at the feast. Morana and Barin killed Ariana. He would be looking for that same satisfaction."

"I see."

"I swear to you, the same I did to Violet and Callen," he insisted. "I knew nothing of Barin's true intentions in allying himself with Morana. If I could have seen Ariana's death... maybe I..."

"I still don't understand. Why exactly are you blaming yourself?"

He turned to me, finally meeting my eyes and I could see the seriousness in his expression. It wasn't just the feast, Ariana's death and what happened with Katerie that he was feeling guilty for...it was everything.

"I should have known," he confessed, as he hung his head. "I should have known that Michael would attack you again. Known that Barin was plotting against all of you. I'm a Mind. I should have known everything. And I should have been able to prevent it."

"Hale, stop."

I grabbed his face in my hands and forced him to look directly at me.

"You've made some poor choices. You put your faith in the wrong people. But nobody here blames you," I assured him. "You went searching for the family you were longing to have. Just because it took you to some horrible people, doesn't make it your fault."

He grabbed my wrists, pulling my hands from his face and turned back to look at the garden.

"Look," I began, as I moved back beside him. "You can sit here and pout about everything, or you can move forward."

"You think I'm pouting?" he asked, with an arrogant smile on his face.

"Yes," I sassed back. "I do."

He let out a laugh that shocked me so much, I had to fight the urge to jump when I heard it. In all the time I had spent with Hale, I couldn't think of a time when he actually had laughed...like really laughed. I couldn't contain my smile as I stood beside him. But as his laughter stopped, I heard him let out a heavy sigh.

"We all have demons, Hale," I reminded him. "I'm learning that those demons are actually a strength, not a weakness."

"It was an amazing opportunity that you offered the Fears," he said, taking the focus off himself.

"It's not just for them. It's for all of us. I don't care about what or who you were before this war. I appreciate who you are now. I *trust* who you are now. Magir is stronger because of people like you. You just need to believe it."

He looked back at me and gave me his thin pressed smile, that a few weeks ago made me more nervous than actually facing the Fears. But now it almost settled the discomfort I had been feeling. Because now I knew that was just Hale, being Hale. He may not have been the nicest person in the room...he was more likely to be the most arrogant...but that was him. And as much as he didn't think he was worthy... he was one of us.

"You really will make a great queen," he concluded, still smiling at me.

"I know I will," I joked.

"There's that arrogant side of you I saw in class," he winked at me.

"Don't go thinking I've forgotten about that lesson with Johanna that you put me through," I reminded him with a light shove. "And don't think for a second I'm not still formulating a plan to get you back for that."

"I'd expect nothing less."

We laughed together for a few more minutes before Hale offered to walk me back to the Knights' guest suite. I couldn't be certain if my gift was blocking Violet, and if it wasn't she was going to be sending the entire Magirian guard if I didn't return soon.

As we made it to the door, he grabbed me softly on my arm, and I turned back to look at him. Saying nothing for a moment, he just studied my expression before smiling and letting out a heavy sigh. And his smile wasn't the normal one I was used to. This was almost bashful, and I couldn't help but give him a questioning look, causing him to laugh.

"I'll see you in there," he said, letting go of my arm. "You're going to be beautiful."

He turned to leave but I grabbed his arm before he had the chance. When his eyes met mine, I knew what to do. I wasn't sure why I hadn't thought of it before, since it was a perfect solution. It was a place he felt so comfortable, and after being his student, I was certain it was where he belonged.

"I have a proposition for you," I blurted out. "I'd have to talk it over with the others first, but I think I may have a way to repay you for both helping us and for putting me through that awful Fear lesson."

A gleam appeared in his eyes as the corner of his lips curled up on one side.

"I'm listening."

Chapter 36

Evelyn

Violet had a million questions when I returned to the suite. Apparently, my obstruction really had blocked her from parts of our conversation but not for all of them. Luckily, she never asked about what Hale meant when he had said, you know why. Then again, Violet was more in tune with emotions than anyone, not to mention the connection we shared, so it made sense that she already knew what he'd meant. She had probably picked up on it far before I had even considered the truth.

Listening to everything I shared with wide eyes, Vi sat with Johanna at the bar in our kitchen. I answered all of her questions the best that I could and surprisingly neither of them pressed when the details I gave were slightly vague.

"I love it!" Violet exclaimed, after I explained the proposition I'd given to Hale.

"Agreed. He was always a great, albeit tough, teacher," Johanna added. "But he will need a Vision to assist him with placements."

"I was leaning toward Auntie Saraya," I suggested.

"She'd be great!" Violet concurred. "Plus, maybe she

could whip his attitude into shape a little."

None of us could hold back a laugh as we thought about Auntie Saraya reading Hale the riot act from her wheelchair, all the while still looking just as frightening as she did standing — maybe even more so from her chair.

"Excuse me, ladies," a guard said, after a soft knock on the doorframe of our open suite. "Your hairdressers have arrived."

"Thank you, Marcus," Johanna smiled.

"Yes, let them in!" Violet clapped.

The three of us moved to the vanities that had been placed where our couch once was, and sat patiently while Marcus held his arm out to invite the others in. Our suite seemed a little less cheerful without Nixie and Katerie here with us, but today...today we were determined that nothing was going to dull our moods. As the six women and three men entered the room, even I couldn't hold back my smile. Which despite having my Fear back, seemed to be my new normal. Hard not to smile, I guess, when my life was going the way that it was.

The man who came up behind me was by far the most exotic person I had ever met. He had his makeup done even more eccentrically than Violet used to do hers, and his long hair hung down in perfect ringlet curls that sat just above his shoulders.

"Now this," he grinned, as he pulled his hair back into a ponytail as if preparing himself to play a sport and then ran his fingers through mine. "This is my dream canvas!"

He spun the chair I was sitting in and studied my face for a second, before smiling even brighter than he was before.

"This is Danelle and Roman," he explained, as he pointed at the man and woman beside him. "And I am Relic. Together the three of us are going to transform you. Now tell me...what is your vision? Any childhood dreams coming true today? Well of course there are...I mean anyone lucky enough to snag Griffin. Can you say mmm!"

He spoke so fast, I didn't even have time to respond. Before I would have even had the chance, he spun my chair around again and I watched as the three of them went to work. Danelle was brushing, Roman was spraying my hair with God knows what, and Relic was flipping my hair into various positions as he continued to ask me questions and drool over every detail of Griffin.

"Relic, let the girl breathe!" The man doing Violet's hair urged, as he rolled his eyes. "I swear, you get so wrapped up in your own blabbing, that you don't even realize that you are the only one actually speaking!"

"Oh hush, Cyrus. Don't you listen to a thing he says," Relic instructed me. "He's just jealous because I won at cards last night, so I get to pick out our new bedspread."

"You two can never get along on a job," the woman leading Johanna's team said. "I'm not sure why I even drag you along."

"You drag us along," Cyrus informed her, "because we are the best hairdressers in all of Magir. Not to mention I'm the only brother you have."

"You're all related?" Violet asked.

"Unfortunately," the woman joked. "My name is Sienna and Cyrus is my baby brother. We started our salon almost twenty years ago and when Cyrus married Relic, he joined the family business."

"You two are married?" I questioned.

"Magir may be a bit old fashioned," Johanna grinned, "but we aren't completely out of touch."

The group laughed and we all fell into small talk with ease. Violet had Cyrus practically falling over in laughter with her phrases, as his assistants, Mia and Daisy, tried to mimic Vi's accent with a horrible likeness.

Johanna must have already known them because she was chatting with Sienna like they had known each other for years. Sienna's assistants, Bailey and Millie, both seemed close to our age and Johanna must have known them too because she was asking about their families and laughing about shared memories.

"So, what's the dream hairdo girl?" Relic asked me.

"Um...I guess I haven't really thought about it."

"Haven't..." he began, before pausing for dramatic effect. "Every girl has a vision of their wedding day, gorgeous."

"Yeah...not this girl."

"She likes simple," Violet interjected. "I'd go with some curls. Maybe pull a little bit back from her face. Ooo and maybe do some sort of floral headdress."

I watched as Relic practically drooled over Violet, and Cyrus grinned as he continued to work on her hair.

"Brilliant!" Relic clapped, as he blew a chef's kiss into the air and went back to work on my hair. "I couldn't have dreamt up a more perfect hairstyle for this magnificent head of hair."

We spent hours being primped and primed for the big event this afternoon. It seemed like between all nine hairdressers, that they had to have used at least one full warehouse of salon products on the three of us.

It was amazing to watch a magical do a job that I had seen done by so many non-magicals before coming to Magir. Sure, the general concept was the same, but how they did it... wow. Bottles were literally flying around the room as they used Mind to call for them. I was pretty certain that Danelle was a Vision, because on more than one occasion I saw something almost fall to the ground, but before anyone could react, she was there, catching it and getting back to work like nothing had even happened. Either she was a Vision, or she had the best reflexes I had ever seen.

To my surprise they had all come to do more than style our hair. Turns out their business was an all around beauty salon. After assisting Relic for a little while, Danelle put herself right in front of me, brushes floating around her head and began patting my face with creams and powders. I followed the instructions of closing my eyes, turning slightly — which was usually followed by a Relic protest — and even puckering my lips. I had never imagined that a makeover could be so much fun until these nine people came bursting into our suite.

Even while I made sure to admire the beauty of the magic around me, the company was impossible to ignore. Cyrus and Sienna were definitely siblings. One minute they were bickering about whose style was turning out better, and the next they were giving each other advice on which products to use where. Throw in Relic and it was like the three of them were a comedy crew on tour. Then once you added in the extra crew members, it became like watching a family sitcom on TV.

"C'est manifique!" Relic cried suddenly.

"Mmm...mmm!" moaned Cyrus.

"Couldn't have said it better myself," Sienna sighed.

They spun all three of our chairs away from our mirrors so we could look at each other and I was in awe. Each of us were beautiful in our way before — I was even willing to admit that about myself now — but wow. I was stunned by the two women sitting before me.

Violet stood slowly from her chair and spun as Cyrus handed her a mirror to look at the back of her hair. Her long blonde locks were curled perfectly down her back. A small amount had been pulled back and it looked like a tiny, messy bun had been tied into the back. Though, truly it didn't look messy at all. And to top off the beauty of her flawless hair, Cyrus had added in little pieces of baby's-breath and pearl beaded flowers. Top it off with her elegant, yet bold, make-up and I don't think even Violet could have imagined herself looking the way she did right now.

As she spun around, I turned my focus to Johanna. Her makeup was simple for the most part, but around her dark colored eyes was a shimmering eye shadow that made her skin shine and her eyes pop. Johanna's hair had always been so traditionally done, that I was shocked at how thick her hair actually was.

Sienna had pulled her jet-black hair into the most gorgeous low ponytail I had ever seen. She had curled it into a perfect bunch down Johanna's back. But the most amazing part was the Dutch-style braid that crowned her head. It was made from the strands of white hair that I had accidentally given her, and the end of the braid was being used as the tie that held the ponytail together. It was breathtaking, and as Johanna ran her hand along the white pieces of hair, I finally saw the beauty behind them that everyone was trying to convince me was there.

"Well?" Relic urged. "Are you going to turn around and have a look?"

I'd been so distracted by my beautiful friends, that I had yet to even sneak a peek at myself. I smiled at him, but before I could turn around, Violet threw her arms up.

"Wait!"

Relic grabbed me by the shoulder, not allowing me to turn back to my own mirror or to even glance over my shoulder. We both watched anxiously as Violet began digging — and by digging, I mean she was literally throwing things — around in Cyrus's bag.

"Yes!" she cried, as she pulled a headpiece out of the bag.

She quickly moved Relic out of her way and before I could even get a good look at it, she placed her finishing touch on my head. Relic let out a gasp and Cyrus clapped, while Sienna smiled at Violet.

"You're a goddess!" Relic told Violet. "I didn't think she could be more perfect!"

Violet passed me a handheld mirror rather than turning me around and I lifted an eyebrow to her before I looked at the mirror behind me. The moment I saw my reflection, everyone in the room let out a breath as my face fell in pure shock.

My hair had always been stringy, frizzy, and frankly incredibly hard to tame. But Relic was definitely a wizard. He hadn't just managed to tame my crazy hair, but he made it look shiny and sleek. I couldn't have dreamt up a more perfect style for myself as I admired the loose curls that fell from my head. I had to turn around to fully embrace the entirety of the style and as I did, what I was seeing nearly brought me to tears.

There was nothing extravagant about it, and yet, I had never felt more beautiful. The front two bunches of my hair had been loosely pulled back to frame my face. But rather than pinning them on top of my hair, they were hidden inside, much like how I tended to tuck my hair behind my ears when I got nervous. As beautiful as Relic's design was, it was the piece that Violet had added that made tears actually well in my eyes.

It wasn't the typical crown of silver jewels often worn on a wedding day. This was almost a rose gold and looked like tree branches intertwined with one another. There were no flowers, only white and silver beads that almost looked like tiny pieces of cotton. It was simple. It was elegant. It was me.

"Don't ruin the makeup," Danelle said, through a quick sniffle. "It's waterproof but let's not test that out before the ceremony."

Oh...my makeup. For as many brushes as she had touched me with, I couldn't believe how much I still looked like...well me! The colors were natural and blended well with my eyes. But it was the way that she managed to highlight the green in my eyes that made me feel like I truly was a princess.

"You are magicians!" I sighed excitedly.

"Well...magicals, but who needs to clarify," Sienna joked, with the wave of her hand.

"Plus," Relic added, as he leaned against my shoulder, "when we are given canvases as exquisite as you three, our job is easy."

There were a few moments of laughter, countless thank yous, then Sienna stood up straight and clapped her hands loudly.

"We must be off," she instructed.

"Yes!" Cyrus confirmed. "This wedding is the social event of the season."

"More like the century," Relic corrected.

"Exactly, and I shall not be showing up in this garb," Cyrus complained, as he waved his hands down his body. "I'll need at least an hour to prep."

"That man just can't see how delicious he already is," Relic fawned.

We said our goodbyes and they were gone as quickly as they had come. A group of guards came into the suite and began rearranging at lightspeed. Vanities and stools practically vanished into thin air, as large pieces of wood and tall mirrors took their place. And this time it wasn't just Violet and I that were watching in amazement, even Johanna seemed enthralled by what was happening around us.

When the guards had finished assembling what appeared to be a stage surrounded by mirrors, they politely dismissed themselves and left the three of us alone in the suite just staring at the monstrous mirrors in front of us.

"I had heard that they rolled out the red carpet for royal weddings," Johanna began, as she sat herself onto the oversized, plush stool in front of the stage. "But this...whoa."

"Right!" Violet said, as she jumped up onto the stage and spun herself around. "I mean, it is like the dress shop from town just appeared right smack in the middle of our suite!"

"I think it has," I laughed, as I sat beside Johanna.

Just as I sat down, the door flew open, and guards began rolling in racks filled with dresses. I had lost count after the first five or so racks that came in, but when they eventually slowed, we all stood and smiled as Calista made her way into the room.

"I'll tell you three something," she grinned. "You definitely know how to throw a wrench into a woman's schedule!"

"We are so excited you can be here to help us," Johanna said, as she quickly went to hug her.

"It's my honor," Callista said proudly.

"Look at all of these options!"

Violet practically threw herself off of the stage and began running her fingers through the racks.

362

"Well, I did foresee at least one set of upcoming nuptials," Callista said, eyeing Violet and then turning back to Johanna and I. "But three! You're just damn lucky I work fast."

"If it makes you feel any better, we were all just as shocked. When Sean proposed, my jaw almost hit the ground so hard that Evelyn here nearly got stuck having to heal me again," Johanna joked.

"You'll have to tell me all about it," Callista said. "But we must talk while we work. Now, who's first?"

"Me!"

Violet's arm was in the air so fast that even if Johanna or I had wanted the chance, we would have lost by minutes. Callista smiled at her, while Johanna and I sat back down on the large stool.

"Prepare the royal wedding gowns," Callista mumbled to herself, as she looked over Violet and then moved amongst the racks. "A triple wedding...what will these kids think of next?"

Chapter 37

Violet

Callista was a freakin' genius! The fact that she had made all of these dresses was unbelievable. And the fact that she knew exactly what each of us wanted before we even knew...I mean, I had been to some of the most prolific stores in the country and never had anyone been able to style me in the way she was right now. And Callista was going to make certain each of our dreams came true.

Every girl dreams about the day that she gets to pick out her wedding dress. What Evey told Relic about not thinking of her wedding was an absolute crock of shit. *Every* girl dreams of the day that she can try on dress after dress and feel more beautiful than she has ever felt before.

As she studied me, I had an instant fear that she was going to think I wanted some type of mermaid gown that hugged me in places that I did not need all of Magir to see. But she didn't pull a single tight-fitting gown from the rack. By now I should have known not to worry about her choices. This woman had a way of knowing our every heart's desire when it came to fashion and she sure as heck hadn't failed us yet!

Instead, the first dress she pulled was a strapless,

Cinderella ball gown that would have almost put a quinceañera dress to shame. It fit amazingly...but just didn't give me that *beautiful bride* feeling. The next one was still a ball gown, but it was fitted all the way down the bodice and while it too was princess worthy, it wasn't worthy of this princess.

"Try this one," Callista instructed, as I stepped out of dress number two.

She placed dress number three on the rack beside where we had been instructed to change and I immediately cringed as I saw something I knew I did not want.

"I don't want sleeves, Callista," I informed her.

"Trust me on this one," she winked at me, before she went back around the curtain.

I wanted nothing more than to protest her decision, but as I moved closer to the dress and got a full view of it, my mouth almost hit the floor. Unzipping the clear garment bag, I couldn't step into the dress fast enough.

Callista must have been a seasoned Vision because the second I pulled the dress over my shoulders, she was behind me, assisting with the corset ties. I couldn't even see myself yet, but I knew. I'd always taken pride in my beauty and knowing exactly what would make that beauty stand out. But this...never in a million moons would I have picked this dress out for myself.

She placed a gorgeous pair of silver heels on the floor, and I stepped into each one without question. Not speaking a word, she drew back the curtain and I couldn't hold back my grin as I stepped onto the stage, watching Evey and Johanna's eyes bulge.

"Oh, Vi," Evelyn sighed.

"It's perfect," Johanna agreed.

Turning to the mirrors, I couldn't have found any better words to describe how I looked in this dress. It was a full ball gown, but instead of the large *poof* at the bottom, there was a mass amount of tool that began to fray just at my hips. But it was the top of the dress that made it so unique. The lace covered bodice was form fitting with a heart shaped neckline, that plunged just enough to be both sexy and elegant. The small straps continued the same lace pattern and the intricate design inside appeared to almost be shaped like the leaves of a fern. It was sophisticated, attractive, and just downright the most perfect, envy winning dress I could have imagined.

Callista added a few accessories before I wiggled out of the dress and was placed into a slip to wait until it was closer to go time. As I sat myself onto the cushy stool, I could hardly believe what was happening. I was about to marry the man of my dreams. And while smiling was my normal expression, I knew it was going to be extra bold today.

Johanna was slipping behind the curtain with Callista, when a loud knock rang through the suite and Marcus, the guard, peered his head through the door.

"Apologies for the intrusion," he began. "Lady Violet, your presence has been requested."

"Me?" I questioned.

Marcus nodded and Callista came storming out from behind the curtain. She rushed over to the rack of short dresses and threw one at me.

"I'll give you about ten minutes before I send out the search party," Callista instructed, as she went back behind the curtain cursing and muttering to herself. "Who calls upon a bride on their wedding day?"

I quickly put the plain champagne colored dress on and headed out of the suite. Marcus nodded in the direction of a door at the end of the hallway, and I quickly made my way there. I had expected that behind the door, I would find Callen tryin' to sneak a peek at me, but instead I saw the backside of a man with sandy-brown hair staring out a window.

"Nick?"

"Violet," he acknowledged, as he turned to face me. "I apologize for taking you away from your preparations."

"It's no problem," I assured him. "Is everything alright?"

"Of course," he answered, though the look on his face

told another story.

"How 'bout a walk?" I suggested, sensing his discomfort.

He gave me a brief nod and together we walked down the hall toward the garden. His nervousness could have choked a horse, and as it flowed into me, I felt my hands start to sweat. When we made it outside, I began wiping the sweat onto my dress and took a heavy breath to calm myself.

"Want to talk about it?" I asked him.

"About what?"

"Whatever in the blazes has you jittery enough to cause even my hands to be sweatin' like a stuck pig."

"Oh…that…" he conceded.

"You can talk to me," I promised. "About anything you'd like."

"How did you do it?" he asked without hesitation. "How did you give up your entire life to move away with Evelyn?"

"How did you…" I tried to ask.

"Knights are mentally connected," he reminded me. "I know more about you than you think."

"Right. Well…I guess it really wasn't much of a decision. My friend was in trouble, and I was going to do anything to protect her. Even if that meant giving up my own life."

"So, you did it for Evelyn?"

Disappointment rushed through me. But it wasn't my disappointment I was feeling. I wasn't giving him the answer he was hoping to hear.

"Well, I suppose it was a little for me too," I added, as he began to appear more intrigued than sad. "I knew I wasn't exactly happy in my life. I didn't fit into my family the way they wanted. I love them all dearly, but I just never belonged there, you know? My parents haven't even called me in over a year. My dad occasionally sends me an email with job openings at his company…but that's it. And even though he rarely attempts to contact me, I'm quite certain if I don't respond soon, he will probably start sending armies to find me. Life if never as simple as we want it to be."

"I see."

"We all go on our own journey, Nick. Mine led to Evey, away from my old life, and then to Magir. Where is yours leadin' you?"

"That's just it," he sighed. "I'm not really sure."

"My grammy used to say that if you aren't sure where you need to be, then you aren't there yet," I said, as I grabbed his hand. "You are an amazing Knight, Nick. But if you feel like leavin' here is what may be next on your journey...then maybe that's what you need to do."

"One just can't give up being a Knight."

"I never said you had to give it up," I reminded him. "I'm merely suggesting that you maybe go on sabbatical for a bit. It's not like we couldn't call you if we really needed you."

"Magirian Knights don't go on sabbaticals," he insisted.

"Yeah, and there hasn't been a Magirian descendant of The Five in centuries. A Magirian royal has never been a Knight. Oh, and my personal favorite...Magir has always had only one king."

His eyes narrowed as he studied me and took in everything I was tryin' to say.

"Nicholas Kirchik, listen to what I'm tellin' you," I insisted, as I moved my grip from his hand to his shoulders. "The future is being written every day. If you only follow the patterns of the past, you're gonna be stuck there. You'll complete miss everything the future is trying to bring you if you live in the past. Bein' a Knight will always be a part of who you are. But if you need to leave here to figure out the rest of who you are...then go. Who knows, your journey may even lead you back here faster than you think."

He just stared at me. No words. No change in facial expression. I couldn't even sense the emotion that he was feeling. Then out of nowhere, he pushes my hands off his shoulders, wraps me tightly in a hug, and an immediate sense of relief flooded my veins.

"Don't mess up the hair!" I choked out through his grip.

"I apologize," he said, pulling away from me.

"You don't have to be so formal with me," I informed him. "Regardless of what is about to happen today, you and I are friends. Never feel like you have to talk to me like you are anything less than a friend to me. Be honest, blunt even. I'm tough enough to take it. In this case, a simple, I'm sorry, would suffice."

"You people from the non-magical world really are odd," he grinned.

"See," I winked. "Speaking freely already."

"We should get you back."

We walked back smiling, but in silence. Nick had been through a lot in the last several days. I knew his heart was hurting, but the relief that was pouring from him to me in that moment was enough to assure me that he was going to be alright. Even if bein' alright meant bein' away from here.

"Can I ask you one more thing?" Nick asked, breaking our silence.

"Fire away!"

"What did you mean about Victor and Nixie that night in the library?"

I stopped in the middle of the hall and stared at him. In all of the excitement of us going to war, I had completely forgotten to explain it to all of them. I guess I assumed Callen would know and therefore all of the other Knights would too. But as I looked at Nick now, I knew that wasn't the case. And I knew deep down, that as soon as I told him, all of the Knights, including Victor, would know the truth.

"Violet?"

"Will Victor know what I tell you?"

"Probably. Knights don't really have secrets."

"Okay," I sighed. "I just hope this doesn't totally weird him out."

"You're definitely *weirding* me out," Nick half smiled.

"Here goes," I began. "When Nixie let me take her magic

to save Victor...I believe I actually transferred her magic into him."

"How would you have done that?"

"When I took Evey's Fear magic in the woods that night, it was supposed to go into her necklace," I explained. "But instead, her magic went into me and so did the magic of the necklace. I physically became the absorbing emerald. That's how I was able to take Nixie's magic when she asked me to. Though I still haven't figured out how she knew I could do it, when I still hadn't put all the pieces together myself. Must have been her tinker gift."

He stood there blankly staring at me as he processed what I had just told him. I could feel his emotions doing somersaults as he grappled with all of the information.

"So, then Nixie is..."

"No," I interrupted, placing my hand on his shoulder. "Just her magic is inside Victor."

"Makes sense," he said, as a genuine smile began to form on his face. "She would have been eager to share her magic if it meant saving him. One last thing for her to fix. And she'd have wanted her gift to live on."

"I couldn't agree more!"

Chuckling to himself, he turned to walk back toward the suite, and I linked my arm into his with a smile. When we approached the door to the Knight's guest suite, he hugged me again, and when we pulled away, revealing his still elated expression, I had one of my fantastic ideas.

"Nick!"

"Violet?"

"Do you mind if I ask a favor of you?"

"Anything."

*****

"Everything okay?" Evey questioned, as I sat back beside her on the large stool. "Callista was seriously about to send a search party."

"Dandy!"

"Dandy, huh? Well, who was it?"

"It was...oh my."

Johanna emerged from behind the curtain in the most exquisite, yet simple dress I had ever seen. It wasn't white, but instead was a color somewhere between cream and ivory. The a-line, v-neck coupled with the lace bodice and two-inch straps, framed her face in a way that had her shining. Finished off with a subtle chiffon skirt...the dress couldn't have screamed Johanna any louder.

"Damnnnn girl!" I cried.

"Do you think it's too simple?" Johanna questioned. "You think Sean will expect more?"

"He expects you," Evelyn assured her. "If he had his way, you probably wouldn't be wearing anything."

Johanna laughed and turned back to the mirrors, examining every inch of the dress.

"The most important thing is, do you love it?" I asked.

She paused for a moment and continued to study her reflection. Evey's hands moved quickly into her lap as Johanna ran her fingers along the white braid that crowned her head, and then began to smooth out the chiffon with a smile.

"It's perfect!" Johanna beamed.

"Of course, it is!" Callista confirmed. "I did make it after all. Now, let's get you a necklace and you can sit. I've got one more of you to dress and only one hour left to do it!"

"An hour," Evey whispered under her breath.

"You did say yes, before either of us did," I reminded her with a nudge.

"Oh, I'm fine marrying Griffin," Evelyn defended. "It's marrying him in front of all of Magir that has me sweating."

"No need to sweat," Johanna chimed in. "It's not like you'll be up there alone."

"Not to mention sweatin' will definitely ruin your makeup," I added. "And you don't want Relic and Danelle catching you ruining their work."

"Come with me, dear," Callista instructed Evey. "I have a few choices I want you to look at."

Evelyn took a deep breath and moved towards the dresses. I knew from experience that dressing Evey up was no easy task. She had always had this image in her head that because she wasn't a double zero and her hair was kinda crazy, that she was never pretty enough. Damn society and their ridiculous concepts of what a *perfect woman* should look like. But Evey was different now though. She was really coming into her own here in Magir. I just hoped it would translate to making Callista's job easier. After all, she was able to find Evey several perfect gowns before. And while this dress was the most important dress of Evey's life...if it wasn't me pickin' it out, I would want it to be Callista.

In a few moments, they disappeared behind the curtain with a couple of options. I used that moment to slip out of my temporary dress and back into my wedding dress. Johanna helped me with the small corset tie in the back and held my arm as I stepped into my shoes. As I fussed with the tulle at the bottom, Johanna let out a gasp causing me to quickly spin and look back toward the stage.

Evey was breathtaking. I mean...I was at a loss for words...and that was saying a lot. The dress was just barely off white, with an a-line, scoop neck and gorgeous cap straps, made of lace and a thin layer of tulle, so she was proudly showing a lot of her skin. The lace bodice accented each of her curves in the most regal way I could have imagined, and the lace continued into the ruffles of the tulle at the bottom. Just as I thought that nothing could make Evey's appearance more stunning, I noticed the delicate silver, beaded belt that framed the bottom of the bodice. It so perfectly complimented the crown I'd picked for her that I would have sworn I must have seen them together in a vision in order to have picked it randomly from Cyrus's bag. It was simple. It was elegant. It was regal. It was Evey.

"Is it possible that the first dress is *the* dress?" Evey asked, as she stared at herself in the mirror with wide eyes.

"When you look like that," Johanna began, "absolutely!"

"Oh, sugar!" I finally gasped. "You're as pretty as a peach!"

"A peach? Really?" Johanna joked.

"Sorry...you're right," I shook my head. "Granted, that is a high compliment where I was born, but it still doesn't come close to doing justice to how spectacular you look, Evey."

"You think so?"

"EvelynRose!" I cried, as I stomped my heel. "Don't give me that self-conscious side of you right now! How do *you* feel about it?"

She paused for a moment just like Johanna had, but she smiled much faster and spun around to face us. Nearly trembling with joy, she nodded yes and after a brief moment of the three of us squealing, Callista placed Evey's necklace back around her neck and helped her into a pair of silver — incredibly low — heels.

Once we were all dressed, accessorized and ready to go, Callista stood us just behind the door and studied her work. She smiled brightly as her eyes moved over each one of us, slowly making certain every detail was perfect. I stood to the right, Evey in the middle, and then Johanna to her left. Each of us was ready...no, excited for what was about to happen. How our lives were about to forever change.

"I've got to say," Callista finally began, "I don't think I've ever dressed more perfect canvases. You three truly will lead Magir into a new age. I'm honored that I get to be part of the history you will make."

"You'll be front and center," Johanna insisted.

"I reckon she sure will be!" I agreed. "There will be many more events in the future and one can never wear the same dress twice. Plus, even I can admit, that we would never have looked this jaw droppin' without you."

"She is definitely right about that," Evelyn added. "Let's

be honest, nobody else is going to be able to get me into the dresses that you have."

We all laughed for a moment, before Callista moved in for a group hug. It lasted only for a moment though because Marcus suddenly poked his head through the door again.

"My apologies again, my ladies," he began. "But it is time."

Once Callista had said a quick goodbye and rushed out the door, the three of us just stood together for a moment as we exchanged quick glances. I had expected at least one of them to have an anxious or nervous expression...and maybe a little bit on my own face...but all I saw was pure joy. We were all beyond ready for this moment. More than ready...we were excited and eager for our next chapter.

We stepped out of the suite and stood in the hallway as Marcus quickly hustled down the hall in front of us and opened the door that led back into the castle halls.

"Well," Johanna breathed. "I guess that means it's time."

"Yep," Evelyn confirmed. "I suppose if anyone wants to back out...now is your last chance."

Again, we all laughed loudly, and even Marcus couldn't help but crack a smile. Nobody was backing out...we all knew that.

"You know what that means then don't you?" I asked.

"Do we want to?" Evey joked back.

"It's triple wedding time, bitches!"

Chapter 38

Evelyn

It wasn't that I was nervous about marrying Griffin. It wasn't about sharing my wedding ceremony with two other couples. No, I was certain that my hands were sweating simply because this was my wedding day...something only a few months ago, I wasn't sure I would ever have...or that, prior to meeting Griffin, I was even sure I wanted.

I knew how people outside of Magir would view our whirlwind romance being topped off with a wedding. They would all be thinking I was pregnant. Probably that all three of us were. Hurry up and get married because heaven forbid you have a baby out of wedlock...all that stuff. In Magir, however, there was excitement all around us. And it wasn't just for Griffin and I.

The concept of three couples getting married in one ceremony was mind-blowing for the Magirians. Double weddings weren't unheard of in the non-magical realm, but even I had to admit, that a triple was a lot. The most surprising piece for me what that, as much as I was certain both Violet and Johanna had very different dreams for their weddings before this, we were all ecstatic about getting to share this day with each other.

Over the last couple of months, we had become closer than friends...we were family. Getting to share this moment had become a different sort of dream come true. Plus, as someone who hated to be the center of attention, I was more than happy to share the spotlight. Not to mention that all of Magir was beyond thrilled to get to throw the party of the century. And they deserved to have something to celebrate in light of all the dark events they had been through recently.

As we approached the doors to the grand ballroom, I felt the lump in my stomach rise into my throat and Violet tightly grabbed my hand. Waiting at the door was Auntie Saraya, Johanna's father, and Nicholas.

Auntie Saraya quickly spun her wheelchair to look at us and her hands went to her face. Johanna's father looked so proud as tears began to slowly well in his eyes. And Nicholas was wearing the first genuine smile I'd seen on his face in quite a while. as he stood tall in his very Knightly stance.

"You three look stunning," Auntie Saraya said through her hands.

"As radiant as queens," Johanna's father beamed.

"Three of the luckiest guys in the realms are waiting through those doors," Nicholas added.

I knelt down slightly and hugged Auntie Saraya. When I asked her to be the one to walk me down the aisle, she had cried tears of joy. I knew some of those tears were probably from sadness...she wished Lucas had returned with us and was here to give me away. Part of me had hoped one day he and I would have had that relationship...but life doesn't always work the way we had planned. Auntie Saraya had always been my parent...my rock...one of very few people in any of the realms I had always known that I could count on. She had more than earned the honor of giving me away.

Johanna's father walking her down the aisle, made perfect sense. Though I half expected him to show some degree of disappointment. Afterall, his daughter was supposed to be the Queen of Magir one day. Johanna had explained to us what had happened when she told him about Sean, but he was still a councilman. Violet's father was also a politician — in his own way — and nothing was more important to him than being at the top of the ladder of success...even if that meant sacrificing his family. But Johanna's father was different. He was embracing his daughter and practically glowing with excitement.

I was still a bit confused as to why Nicholas was waiting here with them. Obviously, Violet's father wasn't going to be here, but I had just assumed Auntie Saraya would walk us both down the aisle together. Yet, as Violet moved over to Nicholas, he hugged her and admired her like an older brother would.

"Thank you," I heard Nicholas say to Violet, as we lined up in front of the door. "I'm honored to be escorting you."

"We're family," she smiled, "and the honor is mine. Thank you."

Music began to play on the other side of the doors and the guards on our side nodded their heads toward us. It was time. First in line was Johanna and her father. They would enter, followed a few seconds later by Violet and Nicholas. Leaving myself and Auntie Saraya to enter last.

"Nervous?" Auntie Saraya inquired through a whisper.

"A little."

"I'd be worried if you weren't," she smiled. "I know it seems fast. But you're more ready than you know. And Griffin is a wonderful man."

"I know he is."

When the doors opened, I felt like I was going to throw up. Johanna walked in with unwavering grace. A few moments passed, then Violet stepped forward with Nicholas and made her way through the door. She held her head high, with a huge smile across her face. When the music gave us our cue, I took a deep breath and Auntie Saraya gripped my hand tightly as I used Mind to move her down the aisle.

The first thing I noticed was all of the people. The grand

ballroom was huge, but I hadn't anticipated all of Magir being able to fit in here! Perhaps it wasn't all of Magir...but damn in that moment...with everyone's eyes on me...it sure felt like it was. But that lump — which had moved well into my throat now — vanished the moment I laid eyes on him.

At the end of the aisle stood my best friends in any realm. Violet and Johanna looked gorgeous, of course. Callen looked very dapper in his light gray pants and jacket, which was of course unbuttoned, revealing his dark gray suit vest and dark purple tie. Sean was on the other side. He had tamed his red hair for the first time since I'd known him and was also wearing a light gray pants. Unlike Callen though, Sean did not have a vest, but instead wore a simple white shirt with a pale-yellow bow tie.

Neither of them even looked in my direction as they were completely enthralled by the sight of their own brides. Which was totally fine with me...the less attention the better, considering it felt like everyone's eyes were all transfixed on me. But all of their gazes fell to the back of my mind as I quickly fixated on Griffin who was standing between them. The anxiety I was feeling vanished as his eyes met mine and magic suddenly surged in my veins.

He was exceptionally handsome in his navy suit, with a bright white shirt and dark colored shoes. His dark brown hair had been slicked to one side and he had a dark green tie that was tucked neatly into his jacket. But the most mesmerizing thing about him, in that moment, was the way his silver eyes embraced mine. Those silver eyes that had drawn me in from the first moment I saw him. The eyes that, if I continued to take steps closer, I would get to look into for the rest of my life.

Once we were directly in front of Griffin, we came to a stop and the audience took their seats. I was certain Callen and Sean were both smiling from ear to ear, but all I could focus on was Griffin. I didn't think I had ever seen him happier.

"Who comes forth as witnesses to bless these Magirian bonds of marriage?" the councilman at the front of the room asked.

"I stand as witness, and father of Lady Everton," Johanna's father said, as he smiled and gave Johanna's hand to Sean while placing a pat on his shoulder.

"I stand as witness, and friend of Lady Rae," Nicholas said, as he placed a soft kiss on Violet's hand before placing it in Callen's.

"I stand as witness and aunt..."

"Mother," I interjected as I turned to look at my aunt. "You're my mother. Regardless of genetics."

"I stand as witness and...mother of Lady Archer."

Auntie Saraya reached for me, and I knelt down to hug her tightly, before she placed my hand into Griffin's. Our three escorts then moved back and joined the audience as we all turned our attention to the councilman at the front of the room.

"To marry in Magir is not to take a partner only in this realm, but across all realms. Here you make a promise, before Estella, that even in death, this person shall be your partner and your souls shall forever be together, written in our stars."

He gestured his arms toward the ceiling, and I watched as it faded away, revealing the night sky. I glanced to my side at the other windows, knowing it was still mid-day, and saw the sunshine pouring through. Somehow, they were using magic to create the illusion of it being night for the ceremony...and it was amazing.

"Lady Everton and Sir O'Connor," the man began, and we all turned our heads to Sean and Johanna. "Your star shall be known as the Destiny Star. As your lives together have bloomed, you have chosen to trust the paths you were both put on. Those paths that have continuously led you back to one another. May the Destiny Star be a reminder of your love for each other, and an inspiration to all of Magir."

Sean and Johanna then slipped rings onto each other's fingers with a smile and stared back at the councilman.

"Lady Rae and Sir Ivanti," he began again, as we turned

to Vi and Callen. "Your star shall be forever known as the Serenity Star. For you two not only will forever find peace and happiness in each other, but you shall also bring it back to all Magirian families."

Violet's eyes began to tear up as she slipped the ring on Callen's finger, and he placed one gently onto hers before they both turned back to face the front.

"And last, but most certainly, not least," the man sighed, as he turned to us and my cheeks instantly flushed. "Lady Archer and Prince Ranieri, your star will be the most unique star we ever named. For your star will shine, not only with your love for each other, but also with your love for all of Magir. Your star shall henceforth be known as, The Star of the Devoted. For not only have you stood by each other's side since the moment you met, risked your lives for each other time and time again, and shown all of Magir the Fated Bond is real, but you have become devout leaders to Magir and its people."

I felt my hands trembling as I placed the ring on Griffin's hand, but they settled slightly as he held me softly and pushed the ring, covered in multicolored stones, onto my finger.

The councilman then moved his arms through the air, silently instructing each of us to look at our partner. Grabbing my other hand as we turned, Griffin held them both like he was never going to let them go. The happiness and excitement enveloping his entire expression was enough to make a girl weak in her knees. I could only imagine and hope that Vi and Jo were experiencing the same thing.

"Do you each take the other to love and cherish under the guidance of your star?" he asked.

"I do," we all said in unison.

"Then by the power vested in me by the Magirian Council, and under the watchful eye of Estella with all of Magir as a witness, I seal these bonds of marriage. We truly wish each of you, all the happiness in the realms," he smiled.

That must have been the Magirian way of saying *you may kiss the bride* because Griffin dropped my hands and quickly cupped both sides of my face, pulling me in for a sweet, passionate kiss that had magic coursing through me with such a vigor and intensity, I was shocked I didn't pass out right there.

When we finally separated, a small ball of light formed between us and slowly began to rise toward the night sky illusion above us. I watched in awe as it floated higher, and I noticed two other balls of light rising as well. Just as I thought they were going to travel forever, each ball burst open in a thunderous pop and showered the sky in fireworks. The trails of light poured through the night sky and once they began to stop, in the place where the ball had been, a beautiful, shining star sparkled brightly.

"It is my honor to formally introduce, Mr. and Mrs. O'Connor!" the councilman shouted to the crowd.

A thunderous cheer began to erupt in the room. Sean even let out his own cheer of joy as he raised their interlaced hands and began to guide his new bride out of the ballroom.

"Mr. and Mrs. Ivanti!"

More cheers rang through the crowd as Callen scooped Violet up off her feet and carried her through the guests.

"And, Mr. and Mrs. Ranieri!"

Griffin kissed me again before grabbing my hand tightly and walking down the aisle, pressed closely to my side. I could see his regal side as he waved to a few audience members and then turned his smile back to me. He wanted to make it clear that the waves were a necessity, but this moment was purely about me...about us.

As soon as we were out of the ballroom, the doors closed behind us. Violet and Johanna hugged me tightly and I could see all of the guys shaking hands. We were all officially married couples now. We did it!

"I can't believe none of you ran for it," Sean joked.

"Well, if anyone should have been running, it should have been Johanna," I fired back. "Girl, take it from me, you do not want red headed kids."

"Ouch, Red!" Sean said, as he feigned being stabbed. "Griffin, you may have to rein in your wife in public places."

"Well, I may be a magical, but I don't think even magic could rein her in," Griffin replied, giving me a wink and pulling me back toward him. "However, I will enjoy calling her my wife, very much."

His lips met mine again and this time there was a lot less gentle passion behind them. The kiss was fierce with desire, and warmed every part of my body, as Violet let out an *ooo* that made us pull apart.

"No kidding," Johanna added to Violet's taunt. "Save some for the honeymoon, won't you."

"Oh! Magirian's actually do honeymoons?" Violet asked excitedly.

"Not really," Callen replied. "But we've done everything else different up to this point, so why break our streak now."

"Not to mention after the last few weeks," Griffin began.

"And literally dying," Sean interjected.

"We all agreed that you ladies...well all of us really," Griffin continued, "deserved some time to ourselves."

"Oh, I'm seeing warm beaches and drinks on the sand in our very near future!" Violet said excitedly.

The guard at the door walked over to us and patted Griffin on the shoulder. Griffin turned to face him for a moment, nodded, then turned back to all of us.

"They are ready for us again," he informed us.

"One last thing before we get to actually celebrate," Sean added.

"I think I'm more nervous for this part than the wedding part," Violet sighed.

"You have nothing to be nervous about," Griffin assured her, while leaving his eyes focused on me. "You ladies are going to make Magir very proud."

"We all are," I corrected, with a warm smile.

The guard pulled the door open, and we all stood up a little bit straighter.

"Let's make history," Callen said proudly.

Chapter 39

Evelyn

Entering the ballroom again, you would have never thought a wedding had just taken place. Well, technically it had been three weddings...but that was beside the point. All of the flowers had vanished, the giant altar was gone, and rather than the one councilman standing at the front, the entire council now stood in long robes on a small stage.

When you marry a prince, you know what will naturally come next...someday you will become a queen. But to do both in one day! I felt like I was going to start sweating from every possible pore as we approached the steps of the stage.

We had gone over the ceremony and how it would work, several times...but in my nervousness, I almost stepped up onto the first step of the stage, but thankfully, Griffin gently pulled me back.

"Today will be a historic day for all of Magir," Johanna's father began. "Our history has been..."

He stopped mid-sentence as his gaze suddenly became fixated on the back of the room. I began to feel the Fear magic inside of me boil and whipped around to look back toward the doors. As I spun, I heard some gasps and whispers, which I immediately knew the cause of, when I saw the group of people standing before me.

They had come. The Fears had chosen to leave Sephtis and join the rest of the families in Magir. I stepped forward and so did the leader that had spoken for them in the Dark Woods.

"We would like to talk more about your offer," he said.

"I'm honored," I responded. "You will be our first meeting following the ceremony. You all are welcome to have a seat and join us."

"The honor would be ours."

He bowed slightly and the Fears that were with him filed into open seats, where they were welcomed with a heartwarming amount of grace and kindness from the other Magirians in attendance. I turned back around and returned to my place by Griffin's side. He quickly grabbed my hand and gave me a quick wink before we returned our attention to the council before us.

"Our history," Johanna's father continued, "has been full of traditional royal bloodlines and leaders that have led us through both bright and dark times. In recent weeks, however, our crown has betrayed the foundational morals that Magir was built upon."

I felt Griffin's hand tighten against mine, and I ran my thumb over his until he let out a small breath.

"However," Johanna's father began again, "in the darkest of times, in our worst heartbreaks, and in moments of sheer disaster, Magir has prevailed. New leaders have risen to bring our realm into the future. And this moment shall mark the most historic rise, Magir and its leaders have ever made."

With the wave of his hand, Johanna's father directed Griffin and I to step up onto the stage, directly in front of him.

"Griffin may be the son of our former king, but more importantly, he is the son of our former queen," he informed the audience. "As your prince it has been well known that, when his predecessor was no more, Griffin would become King of Magir. But, as a true tribute to his mother, who always did what was best for Magir, when we as a council approved Griffin to become king, he declined."

Whispers filled the crowd again. I hadn't realized just how different this was going to be for Magir. And while we knew the changes were necessary for the future of Magir, I just hoped that the citizens of Magir would all be as understanding as the council had been.

"He declined because he felt he wasn't the only person meant to rule Magir."

Johanna's father waved his hand again and before we knew it, Callen and Violet were standing beside us again. Whispers again erupted throughout the room.

"As all of Magir is aware, our prince was born a magical twin to Callen Ivanti. The son of a palace staff member, who lost both of his parents when he was very young. Callen was welcomed by our late queen into the royal family, and she loved him as if he was her own child. It is Griffin's wish that he not be crowned the only king, as he would not truly be the only one wearing the crown or harboring the burdens that come with the role, because as we know, magical twins are immensely intertwined.

"Instead, he has requested to share the duties, and thus the crown that was his birthright. So, for the first time in our history, Magir shall have two kings and beside them, two queens. Two members of the same noble Magirian family, EvelynRose and Violet, are descendants of the powerful Archer family line. Each of them bringing magical gifts, the likes of which Magir has never before seen, and also providing a wealth of knowledge from their lives in the non-magical realm.

"So, it is with the blessing of the council and in the presence of the citizens of Magir, that I ask you this." As the last word left his lips, I watched our friends move to their knees. "Callen and Violet, do you vow to honor Magir and lead our wondrous realm into the future with both resilience and compassion as Magir's King and Queen?"

"We do," they said in unison.

Two other council members stepped forward with beautifully jeweled crowns in their hands. Callen and Violet both bowed their heads slightly and the council members held the crowns just barely off of their heads.

"Then on behalf of the Magirian Council and Magir's people, we crown you, King and Queen of Magir."

The crowns were laid on their heads and cheers filled the room. I felt my chest get lighter as the Magirians that were present not only accepted Griffin's decision to share the throne, but also clearly approved of his choice.

"And now," Johanna's father began again, as Griffin and I crouched to our knees. "Griffin and EvelynRose, do you vow to honor Magir and lead our wondrous realm into the future with both resilience and compassion as Magir's High King and High Queen?"

"We do."

Our voices blended seamlessly, and I couldn't help but tip my head slightly, so that I could see the large, sparkling crowns that they were bringing towards us.

"On behalf of the Magirian Council and Magir's people, we crown you, High King and High Queen of Magir."

The crown nested perfectly into my hair, though its weight was more than I had anticipated. Griffin began to rise next to me, and I followed his lead.

"Magir, I present you with your new royals!"

The crowd erupted as the four of us turned to face them. I stole a look at Violet just as she looked at me, and her eyebrows shot up in excitement.

After several minutes of cheering, Griffin smiled, then gestured to the audience to be seated again.

"I realize that coronation day is traditionally to honor Magir's new leaders," Griffin explained. "But based on my first royal act being to split the crown between four leaders, I think it is clear that I am not always one for following tradition."

The crowd laughed and I smiled beside him as I watched him lead his people.

"For the last year, I have had the honor of leading our Knights with Callen at my side. As we have both now been crowned your kings, we cannot hold that honor any longer and must relinquish our Knighthood," he explained, as he gestured toward Sean, who rose from his seat and moved to the bottom of the steps.

"Sean O'Connor has more than proven himself, not only also as Knight, but as a loyal Magirian and a close personal friend. He has vigorous strength, and a heart that I know will allow him to not only lead the Knights with valor, but to protect Magir no matter the cost."

Griffin took a step down and held his hand out to Sean, who clasped it tightly.

"So, it is with these traits in mind, that I, Griffin Ranieri, Leader of the Knights, do hereby, relinquish my leadership of the Knights of Magir to you, Sean O'Connor."

Both of their bodies jolted, and the crowd let out a gasp. I hadn't realized how much it meant for Griffin to give up being a Knight. But as their bodies jolted again, the transfer of power even resonated in my own magic.

"You will be a phenomenal leader," Griffin assured Sean, as Griffin regained his composure after the transfer of magic was complete.

"It will be my honor to follow in your footsteps," Sean bowed.

Sean moved to stand off to the side of the stage and Griffin returned to my side.

Once he returned to his place, I stepped forward and so did Violet. When we had talked about this during the ceremony planning, we knew that we wanted our first declarations as queens, to be ones we made together.

"As two Magirians who are…well…new to Magir," Violet began with a smile.

"And also, as descendants of the Archer line," I added.

"We wanted to be the first to welcome your two newest members of the Magirian council."

"Johanna Everton," Violet announced.

Johanna's jaw practically fell to the floor, as she slowly rose from her chair.

"Johanna," Vi began. "As a trusted Magirian and one of the strongest gals I have ever met, our council will only be wiser with you as a member. As a descendant of the Everton line, you shall be the first family to hold two seats within the council. Do you accept this position and the duty to always put the wellbeing of Magir, and its people, above all else? Do you henceforth swear to use the power bestowed upon you with honor and integrity that will bring prosperity and happiness to all of Magir?"

"It will be my honor," Johanna sighed.

Violet hugged Johanna then directed her up the step to stand beside Sean.

"And Saraya Archer," I announced.

Auntie Saraya was sitting in her wheelchair in the very front row. When her name left my lips, at first, I thought she was upset. The emotion completely left her face and she just stared at me. I willed her chair towards the stage with my Mind, and I saw the tears beginning to form in her eyes the closer she got.

"Saraya Archer is not only the only living magical child of Thomas Archer, but she is by far the most resilient person I know. She risked herself time and time again to keep me safe. But it wasn't just about keeping me safe. It was about keeping all of Magir safe. She fought to give Magir its best possible future. Even losing her ability to walk in the process," I explained to the crowd. "Saraya is strong, resilient, and above all, an amazing mother figure. Saraya will fill the long vacant council position of the Archer family line. Do you accept this position and the duty to always put the wellbeing of Magir, and its people, above all else? Do you henceforth swear to use the power bestowed upon you with honor and integrity that will bring prosperity and happiness to all of Magir?"

"I will, with pride," Auntie Saraya replied.

I reached down and hugged her before making sure to spin her around to face her people.

"And with these appointments by your queens, history is made again," Callen said, as Violet and I returned to our spots on the stage. "Join us in welcoming our first female council members in Magirian history."

Cheers erupted in the crowd again and before we knew it everyone was on their feet. There was clapping, shouting, and even some tears. In the back of the room, I could see that even a few of the Fears, had joined in on the celebration.

We didn't even have to announce our departure. Griffin grabbed my hand and began to lead me out of the room. Callen and Violet weren't far behind us, followed by Sean and Johanna, Nicholas and the other Knights, and finally rounding out our group with Auntie Saraya and the rest of the council. When we made it out of the room, I expected us to stop walking, but Griffin continued to guide us through the corridors.

"Time for the reception," Griffin said quietly beside me.

"Just remember I am a terrible dancer," I joked.

"Not with me you're not."

When we made it out to the garden, I was taken back by the beauty of everything that had been set up. There was a large, dance floor made from panels of wood that rested on the grass in the center and cocktail tables had been scattered along its edges. There were a few drink stations off to the left and a couple of large speakers beside them. A buffet table sat not far from the drink stations, overflowing with mouthwatering treats. Lights were hung over the dance floor, though they appeared to be floating, because they weren't actually attached to anything. All of which were adorned with elegant, but subtle flowers that compliments the area rather than overpowering the scene like I had seen in weddings before.

Before we knew it, people were pouring in behind us to join the celebration. Soon we were surrounded by people dancing, eating, and smiling as they shared stories of Magirian history and their excitement for what the future may hold. Sean and Johanna spun around the dance floor while Callen and Vi stood just off to the side shaking hands with their new subjects. Griffin had finally managed to pull us away from the council members and was leading me towards the dance floor when the Fear leader stepped toward us.

"Your majesties," he bowed.

"That's not necessary," I insisted. "Griffin and Evelyn shall do just fine."

"It is my understanding that in Magir a title is used as a term of endearment," he argued.

"That it is," Griffin responded. "However, we are in a casual setting. No need for titles or formalities here."

The man nodded and I took a moment to study him. I could see a few long healed scars on his jaw line and a scar in his eyebrow that made it impossible for hair to regrow. I could only imagine what he had endured living under Morana's cruel reign.

"I never did properly introduce myself," he continued. "My name is Novak. And it is with a mixture of pride and great shame that I disclose to you that I was, and am still, a high-ranking leader in the Fear army."

"Nonsense," Griffin said before I could. "A leader should never feel shame for defending their people. Whether you believed in your previous queen is irrelevant now. You've defended your people, your family, and I will never fault any man or woman for that."

He studied us for a moment and then nodded with a smile.

"You truly are the strangest royals I have ever lived under," he chuckled.

"Not under," I corrected. "Nobody in Magir is placed beneath another. Royals and the council exist to help matters of state and keeping everyone safe, but in Magir everyone is equal. That includes you."

I didn't even need to look at Griffin to tell he was smiling brightly at me.

"If I may," Novak began. "I do have a question for you."

"What's that?" I asked.

"How did you do it? How did you manage to turn the darkness of Fear, into a boost of power?"

Griffin turned to me like he had been wondering the same thing. I knew he could feel and sense changes in my magic, but with my obstruction, even he wasn't privy to everything that happened inside my mind.

"I actually didn't figure it out," I smiled and pointed toward the dancefloor. "It was her."

"Queen Violet is not a Fear though?" Novak questioned.

"I'm going to let you in on a secret. Violet is an empath, and a powerful one at that," I explained. "In a moment of desperation, she used an absorbing emerald to take away my Fear magic when I couldn't control it. But rather than absorb the magic into the emerald, she pulled the magic of the emerald into herself."

"So...she holds the magic of the emerald now?"

"She does."

"That's remarkable!"

"She is," I smiled. "While she had my Fear magic inside of her, I noticed that she was still able to be her same bubbly, eccentric self, most of the time. When the Fear magic had been inside me, I was angry all the time...but not Violet. And that was when I knew. Violet never let the dark side of life get to her. She uses every dark experience in life to create something bright and to come out stronger on the other side. Violet taught me that Fear, in terms of magic or emotion, doesn't have to be something bad. On the contrary, it is a necessity for a person to embrace in order to conjure the strength to move forward in life."

"I see."

"It seems sort of crazy," I continued. "To think that something so simple could eliminate all of those dark feelings we have inside of us...but the truth is, it's not simple at all. I still have my moments of anger. I have felt my eyes go black, as that anger takes its hold. But that doesn't make the magic we have bad. It makes it something real. Something that is tied to us in more than just a magical way. It's part of who we are."

Novak just stared at me for a moment. His eyes narrowed as they moved over me a few times and then flipped back to Violet, before returning to me with a smile.

"We shall be honored to learn from the two of you," he avowed. "From all of Magir."

"You will all be welcomed with open arms," I said, sticking my hand out. "The barrier that only allows Fears into Sephtis should be brought down. Let all of Magir see what you have created and allow yourselves to come and go as you please."

"I shall discuss that with those who chose to remain in Sephtis," he agreed. "I look forward to our next encounter, my Queen."

He turned to walk away, and I knew immediately what had to be done. I was going to need Griffin, and all of Magir, to trust my instincts on this one, but I had to do what I believed was right for all of our people, including the Fears.

"We believe in you."

Griffin's words echoed in my head, and I walked quickly after Novak.

"Novak, wait!"

He spun around and gave me a confused expression.

"I have a proposition for you," I informed him.

"A proposition?"

"Yes. And you may feel free to decline if you wish."

"I'm listening."

"I'd like your permission to move forward with a requested seat on the Magirian Council," I explained.

"A seat for whom?"

"You," I bluntly answered. "No person on our council has the experience that you have. Besides Violet and I, there is not a person in this castle that has felt what it is like to hold Fear magic within themselves. Having a Fear on the council will help us bridge the gap that has been separating Sephtis from Magir for centuries."

"You want a Fear to join the council?" he reiterated.

"Not just any Fear," I rebutted. "I would like you to be the first Fear to have a seat."

"Why me?"

"Only once have I met another individual that was magically chosen by Fear who has been willing to come forth in the way that you have," I illuminated. "You have put yourself out in front of all Magir, to give your people a better life. You understand what it means to be cast out and forced to play a role you wanted no part in. Our council will be stronger with you on it."

Novak studied me again. It was almost as if he couldn't believe what I was saying. As if he lived through so many broken promises, that it was nearly impossible for him to embrace the opportunity that was being presented to him now.

"You don't have to give me your final decision now," I added. "Either way I am going to the council in the morning to initiate the addition of a seat dedicated to our Fear family. Our people have been exiled long enough. It's time everyone had a seat at the table. Don't you agree?"

He gave me a nod, but still did not speak.

"Before tomorrow night, I would like to meet with you regarding the council's decision," I informed him. "Enjoy the rest of your evening."

I turned back to Griffin and gave him a nervous smile, as I walked back toward him. He returned it with a bright smile of his own, just before bobbing his head, telling me to look back.

"Evelyn."

Turning around I saw Novak walking quickly back

towards me, with a slightly befuddled, but joyous expression on his face.

"I accept your nomination," he said. "And I am honored that you have put such trust in me when you barely know who I am."

"Our pasts made us who we are today, but it is who we choose to be now that will forever be imprinted on our future."

"I am honored to call you, my queen."

He bowed to me, then turned to rejoin his fellow Fears near the buffet table. Griffin's arms quickly wrapped around me, and he spun me back to face him. He moved a strand of hair from my face, and his fingertips gently caressed my skin.

"Let's dance."

Without giving me a chance to protest, he spun me around again, until we were suddenly moving flawlessly together on the dance floor.

"You know," he began. "Novak was right."

"About?"

"You are going to make an amazing high queen."

"I don't know about that."

"I do," he defended. "After seeing what you just did for our people, there is no doubt in my mind."

"The Fears deserve a seat just as much as any of the other four families."

"True," Griffin agreed. "Did I ever tell you what Thomas told me before I went into Rosebud Park?"

"Thomas?" I questioned.

"Yes. Did I ever tell you what he said to me?"

"No. No, you didn't."

"He told me that I had been entrusted with the heart of a phoenix," Griffin explained. "A heart that is beautiful and kind, but also fierce and unyielding. He said that this heart was not my own, but that of the woman I loved, and the woman who loved me. He said that only when the heart was embraced for what it was, would the heart truly ignite."

"My grandfather told you that?"

"At the time he had said it, my only thought was trying to figure out how he could possibly know the woman who loved me," Griffin smiled. "Which immediately told me, that woman was you."

"Griffin, there is no doubt that I love you...but I'm confused."

"I was too. Until I saw you talking to the Fears a few days ago. Welcoming them into our world without hesitation. And just now, offering Novak something that no Magirian would have ever even considered offering to a Fear."

"So, Vi was right..."

"What?" he questioned.

"The phoenix really does exist?"

"They do," he answered. "They haven't been seen in Magir for centuries because no magical before you has been able to call to one. I think that is because you are a descendant. E, I think the heart Thomas said I was entrusted with, is yours."

"Mine?"

"You are a descendant of the Archer line, and I think that means you have phoenix blood coursing through you."

"Violet came to the same conclusion," I admitted. "But how is that possible?"

"Trust me, I know it sounds crazy," he said, as he spun me out and back to continue our dance. "In order for your heart to ignite you had to accept being an Archer and having the magic of The Five. It would also explain how Violet was able to suddenly sprout wings in the middle of the battlefield. But if I'm correct, then what we've always been told about magic will, once again, be proven wrong."

"Why's that?"

"Magicals from Magir and magicals from Fantazi would have to have formed a bond in order for a child to be born with both forms of magic. We've always been told such bonds couldn't be completed. That magicals from separate realms couldn't have children."

Spinning around the dance floor for a few more seconds, I pondered what he had said. It made sense...in some crazy way. Thomas knew so much about what I was going through and he never questioned me. It was like he had been watching over me for years. But the idea of having phoenix blood coursing through my veins...despite Violet already offering up this scenario...it just seemed surreal.

"I should have told you before," Griffin whispered as he pulled me closer to him.

"You should have," I agreed. "But you've got many years of marriage to make up for it."

He laughed in response, then pulled me in for a kiss.

"Plus," I added, as we separated our lips. "The idea that magic can be shared across magical species will give Violet an entirely new area of study. She is going to be thrilled."

Griffin and I laughed together and continued to dance for hours after that.

A lot had happened since the first moment I met him. I learned magic was real. Had nearly gotten my aunt killed... twice. Discovered I was a missing piece to a prophecy far older than I was. Then there was learning that Violet and I were both Shadow Twins and cousins. Connected by magic, blood, and friendship. I'd gotten revenge on my abuser. Reconnected with my father and mother, just to have them both die in front of me. Made amazing new friends, for whom I would lay down my life. I'd lost more people who were important to me than I cared to think about, but most importantly, I had found myself.

Gone was the girl who had been left defeated and bruised in Rosebud Park over two years ago. Gone was the person who had zero self-confidence and wanted nothing more than to blend into the back of the crowd. I had emerged victorious in the face of challenges that were beyond the imagination of most people.

Magic wasn't only real, it was part of who I am. I

had found a family I didn't even know I needed. And a love that would be forever engraved in the stars. I was more than EvelynRose Archer. I was the only living descendant of The Five, the magical shadow twin of my best friend, the fated partner of my true love, and now I was the High Queen of Magir.

My path may not have been paved in smooth asphalt, and instead was more like a winding gravel road...but it brought me here, to this dance floor, with Griffin at my side. It brought me to Violet, Callen, Sean, Johanna, Nicholas, and all the other people of Magir. And it was here, that I knew I belonged. It was here that I knew my destiny was only beginning.

For I am the daughter of Lucas Archer, former Councilman of Magir, and Morana, Queen of Sephtis. I hold within me the magic of Healing, Strength, Fear, Vision and Mind. I may actually be part phoenix, and who knows what else the future may bring.

I am EvelynRose Ranieri, High Queen of Magir, Descendent of The Five. And nothing can ever take that away from me.

Epilogue

Violet

"Excuse me, sweet cheeks!" I called. "Would you be a dear and get me a refill on this, please?"

"Right away, ma'am."

"Oh, please." I waved my hand. "Just call me Vi."

I shot him a wink and then he vanished with my empty glass. I wiggled back into my beach chair and adjusted my sunglasses, as I stared back up at the sky.

"Good lord, Vi," Evey laughed beside me. "You know you're on your honeymoon, right?"

"Yeah," Johanna agreed, sipping down the last of her own drink. "With your new husband."

They both made sure to emphasize the words *honeymoon* and *husband,* as if I wasn't fully aware that I was married now and here to celebrate said marriage.

"Being married doesn't mean I can't use my charms to get a drink now and again."

"Vi...sweetie," Evey began, as she took a drink from the waiter beside her. "That is exactly what it means."

"You two are no fun! Remind me when we get home to seek out new friends."

"Good luck with that."

We laughed together before the on-beach waiter returned with my drink order.

"So, how's Hale holding up in his new role?" Johanna asked, taking the one he had brought for her, without her needing to order.

"So far, so good," Evey answered. "He left for Woodburn Rose right after the reception and has been sending consistent communications regarding the changes he wants to make to the curriculum. He's already appointed Armonee to teach all of the new classes relating to Fear. And Ansel is so excited to be working with Armonee, he's beside himself. I think that man truly enjoys having another subject to study."

"We may have been a little crazy to make Hale headmaster," I joked. "I have a feeling those change requests are going to get more frequent than less."

"Yeah...and those poor kids. At least Auntie Saraya is there to help him out a bit."

Hale had turned out to be of one of the goods guys after all, but there was no denying he was definitely the hardest professor WRA had ever seen. And what do Evey and Griffin go off and do...make him the damn headmaster. There was no doubt in my mind that he would succeed, but in his own words, only after he made some extensive changes he wanted to see at the school. Though admittedly, most of his suggestions were needed changes from the updates we were receiving from him. But just the thought of what Auntie Saraya was going to be putting up with when it came to helping him made us all laugh again. After all they were both so headstrong...I wasn't entirely sure they would ever completely see eye to eye.

"You three seem to be having far too much fun without us," Sean said, as he appeared with Cal and Griffin.

I sat up in my chair, allowing Callen to slide in behind me and I laid back against his chest. Griffin had settled in beside Eveyln and Sean was leaning against the back of

Johanna's chair.

"When I told you to take us to a beach," I began. "I hadn't expected you to rent an entire island."

"So, we wanted a little privacy," Sean defended, as he rubbed Johanna's shoulders. "Can you blame us?"

"It would just be nice if we could go on an adventure or somethin'," I added. "I love a good tan as much as the next girl. But some mental stimulation would be a welcome change to baking in this sun."

"Stimulation? Callen isn't enough for you?" Sean joked.

"Watch it," Callen quipped, as he reached back and smacked at Sean.

"She's right through," Johanna added.

"Yeah, it would be nice to leave the beach for a day," Evey seconded.

We all sat there thinking for a minute. This island they had found was in the middle of nowhere, and while it was beautiful...there was nothing to do. I wasn't even certain the island had a name...that's how small it was.

"You could explore the underwater caves."

Spinning around to see where the suggestion had come from, we all excitedly left our seats and all of us girls embraced our visitor tightly.

"Princess Tatiana!" I exclaimed.

"To what do we owe the honor?" Griffin asked, in his very kingly tone.

"Actually, I was about to ask you," Tatiana smiled. "Carney and I are here on Fantazi business. We were surprised to see all six of you lying out on the beach."

"Fantazi business?" Callen questioned. "Is everything alright?"

"All is fine for the moment," Tatiana replied.

There was a strange emotion that moved through Carney who was still tightly at Tatiana's side. I felt his nervousness, but there was also an underlying twinge of anger. I wasn't sure what was goin' on here, but everything was certainly not fine.

"So!" I said, possibly too eager. "How about you take us to explore the caves? I just need to change out of this swimsuit first."

"We'd be honored," Tatiana smiled.

As we walked back toward our little bungalows, we exchanged a few pleasantries and small talk, but I was trying hard to focus on understanding Carney's emotions. He still hadn't said a word since running into us. And while he hadn't spoken much when I'd met him before, it just seemed a little off. Not to mention they had both abruptly left following our wedding rehearsal with the same excuse...Fantazi business.

After quickly changing our clothes, we all emerged from our bungalows and followed Tatiana and Carney toward the underwater caves. Talking was still pretty minimal, as we made our way to the entrance of these mysterious, hidden caves. I tried to walk closer to Carney to pull from his emotions more, but I was quite certain he was catching on to me when he picked up his pace before I could get anything.

The entrance to the caves was beautiful, though it was mostly concealed from passersby in the side of a pile of rocks on the shoreline. As we entered, it almost looked like blue crystals were hanging from the ceiling. The crystalized rocks behaved almost like lanterns as the light from outside bounced off each of them, illuminating the pathway through the cave.

"What's going on with you?" Evey whispered in my ear. "You've been impossible to reach since they showed up."

"I'm not sure," I answered through a whisper. "There is something weird going on."

"Why do you say that?"

"Just trust me. Their running into us wasn't an accident. I don't know exactly what's going on, but that much I'm sure of."

Callen and Griffin moved back to join us, and I wondered if Evey's gift was keeping my suspicions a secret from them. I knew Cal was feeling my discomfort because he interlaced our fingers and squeezed my hand tightly. I returned it with a smile, in an attempt to assure him I was fine...but darn that man for reading me like a book...he just shook his head and moved us closer to Carney.

We walked for what seemed like an hour before we came to the center of the first of the caves. Despite being focused on my detective work, I couldn't help but admire the beauty nature had created here. The rocks shined as the small, crystalized pieces glowed brightly around us. In the center, was a small pool of water that created a reflection of the gems above, that made them look like stars.

The others began to move forward through the cave, when I noticed Tatiana was admiring one of the gems in the wall, rather than continuing with the others. Even Carney was leaving without her...and that never happened.

"Vi?"

Evey's voice echoed in my head, but I ignored it, and instead continued toward Tatiana.

"Beautiful, aren't they?" Tatiana asked me, without actually turning to face me.

"Breathtakin'," I replied. "Why are you really here?"

"For Fantazi," she answered, as she turned in my direction.

"And out of all of the places in the non-magical realm, your mission for Fantazi brought you to the small remote island we were honeymoonin' on? I don't think so."

"You really are observant," Tatiana smiled at me.

"Everything okay over here?"

I hadn't even heard Evey come up behind me, but there she was.

"She was about to tell me why she and Carney are actually here," I answered Evey.

"The truth is," Tatiana began. "I need your help."

She suddenly placed a hand on each of our shoulders. I felt my body jolt upward, as the cave began to spin around me, and the ceiling of gems quickly blurred in a haze of smoke.

Looking to my left I saw Evey was still with me. She had managed to travel into the forming vision with me just like she had when I looked into her past back at Woodburn Rose. But this vision wasn't taking form like mine normally did. Instead, the walls continued to spin, and in the smoke, images began to form.

"What's going on?" Evey asked. "This looks like my Fear magic. When I am able to see someone's darkest fears. How is this happening?"

"I'm not sure," I replied with heavy breaths. "But try to focus on every detail. It must be important."

The images slowly became clear, and we could see what appeared to be people fighting. Wait, no, not people. I saw creatures with wings, giant wolf-like animals, and various characters that looked almost human except for their blood red eyes.

"Is this a war?" Evey asked.

I ignored her. The vision was exhausting, and I felt myself getting lightheaded as it continued on. The next image that appeared was of Carney, standing in front of Tatiana fighting off someone who was coming for her and...was that Nick with them?

A blinding light suddenly separated the smoke for a moment, and I had to blink several times to keep my eyesight from blurring any more than it already was. When the light began to fade, I saw a woman in the fight. She was all gray, just like the smoke, but her hair was long and crazy dark. It must have been jet black...just like Johanna's. But when she turned to face me, I saw that her eyes were that same evil red, with just a hint of bright gray around the edge. It eerily reminded me of how Evey's eyes would change when her Fear took control.

She continued to fight until she was face to face with a large man whose face I couldn't see. She held a blade tightly in her hand, and a moment later, I noticed it slowly beginning to slip from her grasp. As soon as it landed on the ground the man grabbed hold of her and quickly snapped her neck.

I heard Evey scream beside me, but I couldn't react myself. My chest tightened and I had to fight to breathe as the smoke quickly shifted again and the woman was once again facing off with the man. This time with the blade remained in the tight grip of her hand. But, as she moved to plunge it into his chest, another woman, with much lighter hair, practically leapt over her and shoved a stake through the man's heart.

****

When I opened my eyes, I was back in my bed inside the bungalow Callen and I were staying in, surrounded by my husband and our four friends.

"What happened?"

"You tell us," Callen encouraged, with a hint of worry in his voice. "One minute you were talking to Tatiana and the next you collapsed."

"Where is Tatiana? And Carney? I need to speak with them, now."

"They left," Johanna explained. "With quite haste, actually."

"Evey, are you okay?" I asked, as I sat up, my brain still fighting to put the pieces of the vision together.

"I'm fine, Vi. I can't remember a thing after I came back for you two," she answered.

"Wait, what? But you were there. You were in the vision with me."

"What vision, Vi?" Callen asked.

"It wasn't like anything I had seen before. Everything was choppy. It didn't flow together the way a vision should. And everything around me was smoke. Even the images I did see were formed from the smoke."

They all stared at me like I'd lost my marbles. But even if Evey couldn't remember what we saw, I knew it had happened. And the worried expression on her face told me she understood the type of vision I had just come out of.

"Go on," Griffin prompted, softly.

"I saw a bunch of people...things...beings of some kind...fighting. It was like I was back at war. But it wasn't our war. There were creatures there I can't explain. Creatures that I thought...well, weren't real."

"Did you recognize anyone?" Sean questioned, clearly intrigued.

"Yes!" I exclaimed. "I saw Tatiana, Carney and I think Nick."

"That would make sense," Sean concurred. "Nick asked my permission to travel to Fantazi with Tatiana when we returned. I gave him my blessing with the caveat that he be available if, and when, the Knights need him."

Griffin nodded at Sean, then turned back to me. Cal, on the other hand, hadn't taken his eyes off of me.

"But there was a woman. Two of them actually. In the first sequence, I saw only the dark haired one and she dropped her weapon just before being killed. But in the next, I saw them both, in the same situation, and when the dark-haired girl attacked, her friend came in from behind and killed the man instead."

"Is that everything?" Griffin asked. "Do you remember anything else?"

"I think that's it," I groaned, as I finished sitting up and squeezed my eyes closed for a moment, as I tried to get my bearings.

Griffin and Callen exchanged a quick glance, and I knew they had drawn a conclusion they hadn't shared with me.

"What? What do you two know?"

"Vi," Callen said, leaning on the bed next to me. "That doesn't sound like you had a vision. I think you produced a prophecy."

"A what?"

"A prophecy. Visions are the only ones who can have them. And with how powerful we already know your magic to be, it makes sense you would have that gift too," Callen explained.

"And it makes sense why Eveyln can't remember," Griffin added. "She may have been there with you, but she doesn't have your magic, so she wouldn't be able to retain what the prophecy told her. Despite your bond, the prophecy was meant for you to see, which means you alone could retain its message."

"That's why she came here!"

"What are you talking about?" Johanna asked me.

"When I stayed back to talk to Tatiana, I was questioning her true reason for coming to this particular island. It makes sense! She knew I could give her the information they needed. She practically forced the prophecy on me. Once she knew about the women I saw, she had what she needed and left. Question is, why did she need it? Is Fantazi going to war? Are they in trouble? Wait! How would Tatiana be able to remember the details of the prophecy if Evey can't? She isn't a Vision either."

"No, she isn't. But Tatiana *is* a fairy," Griffin concluded. "Her magic would enable her to see that you were the one destined to have the prophecy she needed. However, there is no guarantee that she would remember what she saw. And if E can't remember it, I have my doubts."

"She's a fairy?" I questioned, ignoring his skepticism that she saw the prophecy.

My mind immediately trailed back to the people with the red eyes in the vision...or prophecy, as I was being told. If a fairy was real in Fantazi...what else could be?

They asked me a few more questions, then our friends left our bungalow, leaving Callen and I alone. I could tell Evey was hesitant to leave me, and clearly Griffin had picked up on it too. He had gently ushered her out, with the promise of returning soon, but only after he had consulted someone back in Magir about the state of Fantazi. Once it was just Callen and I left in the room, he grabbed me a bottle of water and laid beside me on the bed.

"You feeling okay?" he asked. "I imagine that prophecy drained you. Magically and physically."

"I'm alright," I assured him, as I took a large gulp of the water. "I mean don't get me wrong, I'm exhausted, but just bein' near you is like having my own magical battery pack."

I playfully nudged him with my shoulder and a genuine smile spread across his face.

"Magic is funny that way," he laughed.

"Cal..."

"What is it?"

"There is one thing I saw that has me curious."

"What's that?"

"What kind of creatures exist in Fantazi?"

"All sorts of magical creatures. Did you see something specific?"

"I think so...but it might be crazy."

"Violet, what did you see?"

"You're going to think I'm insane."

"Just tell me. I already think you're a little crazy. So, there's nothing to worry about," he said with a wink.

"You're hilarious," I replied, rolling my eyes. "But seriously...I saw...vampires. But they can't be real...can they?"

His face fell and I knew I was right. While I was growing up in the non-magical realm, vampires were a popular part of pop culture. I had read the books and seen the movies. It didn't matter how many times the depiction of them changed, there was always certain aspects that remained consistent. I knew what red eyes meant...and although it was entirely illogical... vampires were my only conclusion.

"What makes you think you saw one of them?"

"So, I'm right?" I questioned, with far too much excitement. "They really exist?"

"How did you come that conclusion, Violet?"

Callen still wasn't answering my questions. He just continued to pry for more information. And there was something very stern and protective in his voice. Something I had only heard a couple of times before and that made all of the hairs on my arms suddenly rise with unease.

"Red eyes. Everything I could see was in various shades of gray, except for a bunch of red eyes," I explained. "And I've read my fair share of fantasy stories, Cal. And in all of them, the bad vampire always has blood red eyes."

"Well, actually they all do, not just the bad ones. And to be completely honest, there are few good ones from what I know."

"How are they even real? And how did I not know this? Do they live in Fantazi?"

"Fantazi accepts all kinds of magical creatures. However, the vampires come from the realm known as Hadeon. We refer to it as the Shadow Realm because all creatures that thrive in the dark hail from Hadeon," Callen confirmed. "The few who have left Hadeon, tend to try to escape to the non-magical realm, but they are always... handled. I wasn't aware there were any of them residing in Fantazi anymore."

He paused for a moment, contemplating the idea that the vampires had relocated.

"I've never met one in person," he continued. "But I've heard the stories, Vi, and they are far worse than any fictional adaptation you read growing up. Vampires can be vicious and brutal. There is a reason they are bound to the Shadow Realm and only a select few have been allowed in Fantazi. Are you positive that's what you saw?"

"I know what I saw, and I'm tellin' you I saw vampires. And I think the dark-haired girl...I think she may be one of them."

"The one who died and was then saved?" he questioned. "Her eyes were red too?"

"Sort of," I shrugged. "It was like watching Evey with her Fear magic. But instead of black and green, this girl had red eyes with a ring of silver."

"That's not possible. I may not know much about them,

but their eyes are always solid red."

"Well maybe she's partially something else, like me," I countered. "I mean, my magical blood is distant. I'm more non-magical than magical really. She could be something else."

"You are far more magical," he smiled. "But I'm telling you that isn't possible, Vi. You can't have vampire with mixed blood. They are neither alive or dead, so they can only reproduce with their own kind. It simply isn't possible to have a hybrid vampire."

"Well, we know better than most that magical rules aren't exactly set in stone," I reminded him.

"That's true," he agreed. "But I don't know any magical being that would reproduce with a vampire."

"I'm just tellin' you what I saw. She had red eyes surrounded by a ring of silver," I defended. "Just like Evey gets. Black with a green outline. It's impossible to mistake, Cal."

He stared at me for another moment before kissing my forehead then laid back beside me on the bed. I curled up beside him, pulling myself onto his chest.

"Cal, if what I saw was an actual prophecy, like you and Griffin think it was," I began, as his fingers ran through my hair. "Then these girls may be the ones who decide the fate of Fantazi. If Fantazi is in trouble...I think they may be the key to its survival. And I'm telling you...one of them...she *is* part vampire."

Books In This Series

The Archer Chronicles

Magic Of Fear

Bonds Of Power

Rise Of Magir

About The Author

Shantel Norton

 Shantel Norton is an author, a human resources analyst in local government, and a proud mom. She was born and raised in the small town of Rainier, Washington, where she currently resides with her husband, two daughters, and their black Labrador, Scout. Shantel earned her bachelor's degree from Saint Martin's University in psychology and criminal justice, which she uses to enhance her writing skills and character development. Having loved reading from a very young age, Shantel took up writing when she was just seven years old. The passion she felt for writing continued to grow as she got older, and she had drafted several novels before she finished high school.

Shantel's story lines create engaging, compelling tales filled with unexpected surprises that keep the reader at the edge of their seat with the turn of each page. The characters she brings to life are unique, dynamic, relatable, and fun. Her stories enchant the reader from the first page to the last and leave you craving more.

Made in United States
Troutdale, OR
11/24/2023